A WORK of ART

MELODY TYDEN

~**Nadiya**~

Laying back on the pillow with my eyes closed, my mind was entirely focused on work.

For months, my current project had occupied most of my waking thoughts. Everyone had said it couldn't be done, that I could never convince a bunch of proud, stubborn Texans with property in the centre of Houston to sell to me. Against the odds, I had done just that by charming, cajoling and coaxing each one until they signed on the dotted line. The price I paid was more than fair for the rather faded and run-down buildings. The property going up in their place would be infinitely better, and most of the owners agreed with that once they saw the size of the cheque I offered.

Everything was in place and we were ready to break ground as soon as the following week, except for one small problem: one lone hold-out who refused to sell or even to meet with me.

Dexter Callahan.

My lips pulled downwards into a grimace as soon as he crossed my mind. Although we'd never met in person, the emails I'd received from him were memorable enough to let me form a pretty good mental image of him, and I disliked him more than I'd ever disliked anyone. From the way he quoted city regulations to me, and the name Dexter for that matter, I had him pegged as a fastidious, neurotic man, tall and skinny, who probably wore glasses and either had a comb-over or wore a cowboy hat to cover up his bald spot. He had to be the type of man who got a kick out of sending letters to local politicians complaining about parking or people watering their lawns on the wrong day.

He told me – over email, naturally, since he refused to speak to me even on the phone – that the little workshop and gallery which sat right in the middle of my proposed development were part of his 'family legacy', whatever that meant, and he wouldn't sell them no matter the price.

In my reply, I tried to point out - very politely, I might add - that with the money I offered, he could easily set up a brand-new shop somewhere else, somewhere bigger and brighter and altogether more suited to whatever trinkets he sold. I didn't phrase it quite like that, since I didn't actually have any idea what he sold in his gallery, and I didn't particularly care. It only mattered that his building was in my way, but he was being completely intransigent, refusing to even consider the possibility of making a deal.

All of which left me with no other choice: first thing the next morning, I would have to cancel all my meetings, go down there myself, and talk to him face-to-face. He might have avoided coming to my office every time I invited him, but he couldn't ignore me when I turned up at his door.

And who could say: maybe I would even be his type. A little harmless flirting to help ease things along never hurt. After all, I had to deal with all the prejudice that came from men in the city who thought talking business with a woman was beneath them, or that I was just there to make the coffee rather than make the deal. I might as well enjoy the advantages that my sex gave me too.

I'd have him begging me to buy him out before the morning was over.

"Nadiya?" The deep voice from between my legs startled me out of my thoughts. "Am I wasting my time down here?"

Oh, shoot. I'd been so caught up in visions of my imminent triumph that I completely forgot why I was lying on the bed in the first place.

I opened my eyes to see my boyfriend of three years looking up at me in annoyance, so I let out a low moan, hoping it sounded convincing. "Of course not. That feels so good."

To my ears, the lie sounded pretty good, but he didn't buy it. "For fuck's sake, Nadiya." He scowled as he pushed himself up from the bed and got to his feet. "I can't do this anymore."

Well, that came as a relief. Obviously, an orgasm wasn't anywhere on my radar, so if he called it quits, it would be one less I'd have to fake. "I'm sorry, Greg," I apologized, closing my legs and pulling my nightie down before rolling over onto my side to give him my sweetest smile, the one he'd told me made me look a little less serious than usual. The one he'd never been able to resist before. "I'm just a little distracted. It's got nothing to do with you."

"That's the first truthful thing you've said all night," he muttered as he started rooting around in my closet. "It's got *nothing* to do with me. The problem is definitely you."

My smile faded away at his angry tone. Greg had never spoken to me like that before and that level of frustration over a little bit of distraction seemed like an overreaction. "What does that mean?"

He grabbed a few hangers from the closet with some of his suits on them, the ones that he kept at my place for when he stayed over, like he was meant to be doing that night. My friends thought it odd that we still didn't live together after three years, but I liked my space. Sometimes, it came as a relief to not have to worry about anyone else besides yourself.

"It means we're finished, Nadiya. You want to spend every waking moment obsessing about work? Fine. It's your life, go right ahead, but you don't need me here for that, and I'm sure I can find someone who appreciates me more than you do."

I sat up in surprise as he continued to grab clothes out of the closet. He actually sounded serious.

"You want to break up with me because I was a little preoccupied tonight?" I asked in disbelief.

"Tonight?" he repeated just as incredulously. "Do you really think it's just this one time? How many times have we been in bed and you've been thinking about work instead of me?"

The question made me wince. He had a point: it happened a lot. In my defense, my work was important, and nothing that happened between us in bed was all that stimulating. The sex was fine, but I wouldn't go farther than that. It hadn't excited me in a long time. Sometimes, I wondered if it ever had at all.

But that happened after being with someone for a while, didn't it? Nobody was going to still be just as passionate after three years together. We had sex twice a week, whenever I let him stay over. What more did he want?

Besides, we couldn't break up. Everyone expected us to be getting engaged any day. My father had expected it a while ago, actually, and he kept asking me when it was going to happen.

Our business ventures aligned perfectly. I was about to take over the largest real estate development corporation in the state, and Greg's family owned a chain of construction supply stores. We were a match made in bookkeeping heaven.

The wedding had already been planned for the following summer. He just didn't know that yet.

"I just need to finish this deal," I reminded him as I got up and walked over to him, letting the straps of my nightie fall down over my shoulders. He glanced over at me, and I saw the flash of desire in his eyes, a brief glimpse of the Greg who had fallen for me in the first place, but he pushed it down and turned back to what he was doing.

When he refused to turn around, I wrapped my arms around his waist, pressing my body against his back.

"As soon as Callahan sells, I'll have a lot more time for us," I promised. "It's literally one more day. You're not going to give up everything we've built over one day, are you?"

I slid my hands lower over his stomach and down towards the waist of his pants, but he grabbed my wrists before I reached my destination.

"And after this deal, there will be another one," he replied, his voice no longer hot with anger, but cold and detached, and somehow the cold burned more than the heat had. "I've been on this ride before, Nadiya, too many times. This time, I'm getting off."

He put my hands down firmly and picked up his pile of clothing, heading for the door.

"But... we just opened that investment fund together," I reminded him as I trailed after him, still not believing he actually meant it. How could he? It made no sense to be so upset over something so minor. "We've already started merging our assets."

"Varma Corporation has a lot of accountants and lawyers," he shot back with more than a little bitterness. "You can pay them to sort it all out."

As I watched, he moved around the living room, picking up a few of his other things. There weren't many, I had to admit. I liked my house arranged a certain way, which didn't leave a lot of room for anything that belonged to him.

"What about your parents?" I tried, though even I could hear how desperate that sounded. "They'll be devastated."

As desperate as it might have been, it was true. When Greg's parents found out their son was dating the daughter of one of the richest men in the city, they'd been nearly beside themselves with joy. Greg's family were upper middle class, but his mother in particular had always felt she was meant for greater things. She hoped that through me, she would finally get them.

Greg turned to face me, shaking his head with just a touch of sadness. "It's never been about my parents, or the money, or whatever other reasons you think I was with you. You don't get it, Nadiya. If you'd just said 'don't leave because I love you', I might have thought about staying."

He brushed past me on his way to the door, but that time, I didn't move to follow him. My feet were frozen to the spot as the door to the house opened and closed, not with a slam but with a quiet click that was somehow worse than if he'd pulled the door off its hinges.

The silence left behind quickly engulfed me as Greg's words ran through my mind, over and over.

If you'd just said don't leave because I love you...

It wasn't the fact that I hadn't said it that bothered me.

It was the fact that it hadn't even crossed my mind.

~Dex~

My knee bounced anxiously as I sat behind the counter, trying to look busy. Sitting still could be hard for me at the best of times, and that day, things could certainly be going better.

My arms, head and torso - every part of me visible above the counter - were perfectly calm and controlled, but behind the counter where no one could see, my nerves made themselves known in the rhythmic vibration of my leg.

The well-dressed couple looking around the gallery were the first customers I'd had all day. Although I desperately needed a sale, I couldn't let them know that. I had to pretend to be completely uninterested as they pointed at different pieces and murmured to each other.

One sale. Just one of my sculptures leaving with that couple would be enough for me to get the mortgage payment in that night, like I'd promised to do when the bank gave me the extension. The third extension, if I remembered correctly, though I was trying not to keep count.

The couple had already been in the gallery for at least fifteen minutes, which I took as a good sign. There were people who wandered in and did a circuit of the floor in hardly more than a minute before heading back out the door, quickly deciding that the work wasn't for them. If people lingered as long as these two had, they were usually pretty interested. I could also guess from the way they were dressed that affording the pieces wasn't going to be an issue; it would just come down to whether they liked any of them enough to see it in their home.

To me, art was about the most personal thing you could ever buy. The kind of art a person had in their home sent a message to everyone who saw it about what they found beautiful or intriguing or challenging. Impersonal art, like the kind found in hotels, was worse than blank walls. At least with a blank wall, you could fill it in with your imagination. Bland art simply sucked the life out of a room.

No one could say any of my pieces were bland, but were they to this particular couple's taste? I could only hope.

"Excuse me?" The woman called out to me and I jumped up in what I hoped was a friendly but not too eager way.

"Yes, ma'am?" I asked, walking over to them with a smile. "Did y'all find something you like?"

"We did," she confirmed, and it took all my self-control to keep my smile steady and not whoop in delight.

Thank the Lord. That was just what I needed to hear.

"But there's no price on it," she continued.

My smile faltered just a little. All my pieces were clearly priced, but maybe something had fallen off and I hadn't noticed. "Which one were you looking at?"

When she pointed to the sculpture in the window, my heart sank. "That one's beautiful," she said with genuine admiration in her voice, the kind that did an artist's heart good to hear it.

I had to agree with her about its beauty, but I also couldn't part with it. That was the reason it sat in the window, unpriced.

"I'm afraid that one's not for sale, ma'am. But that's the only one, everything else in the store is ready to go today."

I gestured to all the other pieces around us, hoping to redirect her attention, but her gaze remained focused on the window.

"Has someone already reserved it?" she asked. "We can outbid them."

That confirmed what I'd already guessed about their means, but it didn't change the fact that I still couldn't sell it. I kept my reply as honest and straightforward as I could. "No, ma'am. That one's just a bit sentimental for me. I can't part with it."

Her lips pursed in disapproval. "Well, it's the one we want."

From her tone and the way she crossed her arms, I could see the way the interaction would end already, but I forced myself to go through the motions anyway. "I've got a few back here that have the same kind of lines and feel..."

I took a step towards the back of the gallery, but she made no move to follow me.

"If we can't have that one, then we're not interested." She planted her feet firmly, like a child prepping for a tantrum.

"Maybe if you explain to me the space that you're looking to fill, I can show you a few things that might work," I suggested as politely as possible.

"*That one* will work," she repeated stubbornly, pointing to the front window again.

I thought as much, and her answer confirmed there was no need to draw things out any further. "Well, I'm sorry to hear that, ma'am. I hope y'all have a nice day."

Her mouth fell open just a little at my dismissal before she turned on her heel and left the store without another word, her partner trailing behind her after shooting me an apologetic look.

When the door had closed behind them, I closed my eyes and let out a frustrated breath. *3...2...1...* and breathe in... *3...2...1.*

That was an old anger management technique I'd learned a few years ago, back when I struggled to control my anger over the hand life had dealt me, and I still used it whenever I needed to take a step back.

When I felt calmer, my eyes opened and immediately flew up to the clock on the wall. Five o'clock would be there soon, and I couldn't put it off any longer. I'd have to call the bank and see if there was any way they'd give me another extension. Anxiety pooled in the pit of my stomach as I picked my phone up off the counter, and while I punched in the number, I glanced over at the statue in the window.

"I might not be able to keep the gallery," I said in apology. "But at least

I'll still have you."

Squaring my shoulders, I hit the call button on the phone, hoping for the best.

"Mr Callahan." The agent who took my call, the one who had been handling my case for the last few months, sounded less than pleased when she answered. "I hope you're calling to tell me the payment has been made."

"Not exactly," I admitted before doing my best to offer some reassurance. "I've got this month's amount, but I'm afraid I still can't quite manage the backlog. I've got a couple of real good prospects for next month though."

She let out a long sigh. "That's what you said last month."

She was right: I *had* said that, almost word-for-word. "It's just taking a little longer for some of those prospects to pan out than I expected, but I'm fixin' to have it all for you at the end of next month."

"I'm sorry, Mr Callahan, but my manager was quite clear last month that this would be

the last extension we could give you. If you haven't paid the overdue amount in full by the close of business today, we'll have to begin foreclosure proceedings."

Although I had half expected it, the idea of losing the space around me still made me feel like a part of me was being ripped out.

"Please," I pleaded as my eyes scanned the gallery that had been my lifeline for the last six years. "There must be something else we can do."

"I'm afraid there isn't. I wish I could help, but those are the terms that you agreed to."

Once again, she was right. I had to accept that there was nothing unreasonable or unfair about it.

"I understand." The words were bitter in my mouth, but what else could I say? She was just doing her job. "Thanks for your time."

I hung up the phone and tossed it onto the counter before letting out a deep growl of frustration.

Just as quickly as it came on, my anger quickly faded into sadness. The blame lay at my feet and no one else's. I failed. I'd failed the business, I'd failed myself, and most importantly and worst of all, I'd failed Shawna.

"I'm so sorry, baby," I whispered to the air above me. "I know you'd've never let this happen."

Shawna had been the brains of the whole operation. In a way, it was a miracle I'd managed to hold out as long as I did without her. I'd let the last member of staff go six months earlier and since then, I'd been trying to run the gallery and work on my art at the same time, and it didn't work very well at all. Something had to give, and knowing that I wouldn't have to try anymore almost came as a relief until I remembered everything I'd be losing.

I could still see the place the first day Shawna and I had walked into it. An abandoned, dusty old ghost of a building, it probably would have sent most people running but Shawna could see its potential. She was sure the area would be the next big hot-spot in the city and that we could get in and establish ourselves here before it started heating up.

And in a way, she'd been right. Once Varma Corporation put up their new complex on the very spot I stood, it would be the success Shawna always thought it would be. I just wouldn't be there to see it.

But then, neither would she.

At least with the bank foreclosing, I wouldn't have to deal with Nadiya Varma's emails anymore. She'd probably have the mortgage bought out from under me in a matter of days. That was her reputation: ruthless and cold. I'd never met her, and now it looked like I would never need to.

That was the one silver lining in the whole goddamn mess.

~Nadiya~

The next morning, I got ready for work like I was preparing for battle. I may have been dumped the night before but no one would know it by looking at me. My long dark hair had been pulled back into a professional twist and my makeup was done to perfection, with a hint of black eyeliner highlighting and drawing attention to my eyes. My eyes were my most important feature. People needed to look me in the eye for me to win them over.

I chose one of my most flattering and expensive white suits, an Alexander McQueen design, professional yet feminine, and paired it with gold jewellery. It contrasted nicely with my brown skin, making the colours pop.

Anyone who looked at me would see a woman on top of her game, not one whose personal life had completely imploded less than twelve hours earlier. Other women might sit at home and mope with wine or ice cream, but not me. I had a company to run and, now more than ever, I was grateful for the distraction.

I would be better off on my own, I'd already convinced myself. Greg had taken up too much of my time anyway. Without him, I could devote myself fully to my work, which would be crucial in the coming months as I stepped up into the new role I'd been preparing for all my life.

My driver arrived precisely at 7:30, getting me to my office by 8:00. I was always one of the first ones in, partly because I liked to get a jump on the day, and partly because when people knew the boss got there first, it made them more diligent about showing up on time too.

Normally, I used the time to catch up on emails or review my calendar, but that morning, I wandered over to the floor-to-ceiling window behind my desk, looking out over the city. Varma Corp's head office was located in the city's iconic Williams Tower, away from the downtown core, but I considered that an advantage. From my office, I could look out over the whole heart of the city. From sixty stories up, Houston looked just like one of the architectural models our team built to plan new projects. It almost felt like I could reach out and pick one building up and replace it with another, reshaping the city just as I wanted it.

I had long ago pinpointed the exact block where my new development was going, and my eyes zeroed in on it again that morning. "You picked the wrong morning to get on my bad side, Dexter Callahan," I whispered to him across the miles. After the events of the previous evening, I needed a win more than ever.

His gallery opened at ten o'clock, according to my assistant, and I planned to be there at 10:01.

"Good, Nadiya, you're here." My father's voice pulled me out of my daydreaming and I spun around guiltily, as if I'd been doing something wrong even though the working day hadn't strictly begun yet. My father had always made me feel that way. No matter how hard I tried, I could always do slightly better.

"Good morning, Daddy," I said politely, as I had been trained to do since I was a little girl. "What are you doing here?"

My father had semi-retired from his position as CEO months earlier, not that it made much difference. As Chief Operating Officer, I had been running the business for all intents and purposes for the last three years anyway. We were only waiting for my 30th birthday, in just a couple of weeks, for the board to approve promoting me to CEO and then I would be the head of the business in name as well as in fact.

"I came to see you."

He stepped into my office and closed the door behind him, which only made me more curious. What did he have to speak to me about privately so early in the morning?

"I had supper last night with Mr Tucker and Mr Cruz," he began, taking a seat on the sleek, modern chairs I'd chosen for my office. The whole office was decorated in monochromes: mostly black and white, with the odd touch of grey. Squares of black and white hung on the walls. Nothing about the decoration could be considered superfluous. Everything was designed to convey strength and power with no distractions. "They wanted to speak about the handover."

He had my full attention. Tucker and Cruz were two of the most influential members of our board, and if they backed my approval for CEO, there was no question that it would go through. There shouldn't be any question anyway, based on how the company had performed under my leadership, but boards could be fickle, especially one made up of rich Texans who were more than a little skittish about letting a woman take over their favourite cash cow. I always kept that in mind.

"What did they say?" I asked, trying to sound uninterested though he knew as well as I did how much I wanted to know.

"They're impressed with the company's performance," he started, and I tried not to smile. Of course they were. They'd be crazy not to be. "But they're a little concerned about your image."

The smile quickly left my face. "My image?" I repeated curiously. What was wrong with my image?

"People see you as tough," he continued, and the frown on my face deepened. "Very focused on the business."

Neither of those sounded like bad things to me. "Those are good qualities in a CEO," I pointed out.

My father eyed me shrewdly. "Yes, but these days, everyone wants to work with a company that cares, not just one that wins. They want a CEO that people can relate to."

It sounded like he was speaking a foreign language. "But... they make more money if I'm focused."

"It's not just about the money, Nadiya."

His words shocked me, partly because I had never heard my father say anything remotely close to that before, and partly because it so closely echoed what Greg had said to me the night before. Had the whole world suddenly gone crazy?

"What is it about?" I asked, trying to understand where this was going.

"They want Varma Corp to have more of a family-friendly image, and they want it to start at the top."

Family-friendly? I couldn't help thinking back to my own childhood and how rarely I saw my father who was always at the office or on business trips.

As if he could read my thoughts, he gave me a rather sheepish smile. "Perhaps I didn't give the best example either, but at least I had you and your mother to attend events with me."

Visions of getting dressed up and paraded in front of businessmen flashed before my mind. I hated it at the time, but those events were where I learned how to keep people's attention, how to read a room, and how to make small talk. They had all helped to shape me into the businesswoman I'd become.

"And they want the same from you," he continued. "They want to see you with a husband and a child. It will be good for business."

Perhaps I should have expected that conclusion after he had started down that road, but I didn't. His words took me completely by surprise. "They want to force me to get married?"

What century were we living in?

He chuckled at my outrage. "No one is forcing you, Nadiya. They just think a married CEO would be better for the company's public image, and it's long past time that Greg asked you anyway. All you need is a picture of the two of you and a ring and that will appease them in time for the vote."

Me and Greg and a ring? My stomach sank down to the floor as everything Greg had said to me the night before flashed across my memory. "Daddy, that's not going to happen."

He laughed again before getting to his feet. "Of course it is, beta," he said, using his old pet name for me. "I know you. You can close any deal if you put your mind to it. That's all this is: one more agreement to strike."

"What if it doesn't happen?" I called out as he headed towards the door. Our relationship always worked that way. He said what he needed to say and the conversation was over. It never mattered if I had more things I wanted to discuss.

"Then they'll consider all their options," he replied, a little ominously. "Brad Sherwood has a beautiful wife and two kids. They would look great in the papers or at the company barbeque."

My mouth fell open in disbelief. He couldn't be serious. Brad was one of the directors beneath me and I knew that many of the board preferred dealing with him to me. He was 'friendly' and 'fun', wasting time on small talk when we could be discussing business.

And apparently, he had a family. I had never paid attention to his personal life before.

"I know you'll take care of it, Nadiya," my father told me, giving me an appraising look as he opened the door. "The sooner, the better."

Out he went, closing the door behind him and leaving me in stunned silence as my mind raced with everything he'd just said.

How on earth was I supposed to get engaged within the month when I didn't even have a boyfriend anymore? This was a complete disaster.

Though the day had just begun, I couldn't see how it could get any worse.

Chapter Two

~Nadiya~

Two hours later, sitting in the car heading downtown, I had completely refocused on the task at hand. If I could get Dexter Callahan to agree to sell and finally get my project started, the board would have to be impressed with me, married or not. I would focus on work, just like always. It had never let me down before, so by the time I got out of the car in front of the little gallery, marriage was the last thing on my mind.

Although I had seen pictures of the building before, that was the first time I'd been there in person, and it looked more appealing than I had expected. The storefront stood out from the other recently-abandoned buildings on the block with its slate blue exterior, highlighted by splashes of colour. The gallery name, A Work of Art, was written in colourful, elegant script above the door.

Bright and full of contrasts, it contrasted strongly with my office or my home, or even the way I dressed. If I were being honest, all the colours made me a little uncomfortable. It felt unpredictable, and therefore dangerous; I was used to far more order in my life.

As my eyes drifted down from the sign above the door, they were drawn instead to a sculpture in the window of a young woman bound in chains. Her body looked frail but her face tilted up proudly, with an almost radiant expression. It gave the impression that something inside her couldn't be restrained, no matter the weight of the chains.

Unable to look away, I took a step closer. What did the chains represent? Were they a literal restraint, or perhaps simply the weight of expectations? For just a moment, I could see myself in that woman, bound by what everyone else wanted of me. Did I have that same light inside me that shone out of this woman despite her chains? When people looked at me, what did they see?

"Ms Varma?" The driver's voice shook me out of my thoughts. "Is this the right place?"

He must have been wondering why I was just standing there and not going in, and honestly, I couldn't explain it. Art had never interested me before, but something in that sculpture spoke to me in a completely unexpected way. I felt connected to that woman somehow, as though she and I had something important in common. For a moment, I even considered buying it for my own home, but almost as soon as the thought crossed my mind, I had to laugh at myself. I came there to buy the gallery, not its contents.

With a deep breath to refocus my mind, I pushed the door open and stepped inside.

The interior of the gallery was just as appealing as the outside. More sculptures were displayed around the room along with charcoal sketches and a few paintings on the walls. Full of character, it was also much more refined than I had anticipated. Several of the pieces wouldn't be out of place in any of the city's major museums or galleries, at least from what I had seen when I attended business functions at them. I'd never paid a great deal of attention, and when I stopped to think about it, I couldn't be sure if I had ever been to an art gallery simply to look at the art.

If all the pieces on display were his work, then I had to admit that Dexter Callahan had talent, and I was surprised I'd never heard of him in that context before. Many of my friends were art collectors. Well, they were more like business acquaintances than friends, to be truthful. I didn't have a lot of friends. Regardless, they would love this kind of thing. They especially loved to brag about having discovered the next up-and-coming artist, yet I had never heard any of them mention Callahan. Maybe he needed a better manager or a proper marketing plan.

Once again, I had to shake myself out of my wandering thoughts. What was wrong with me? I wasn't there to improve his business but to get the building from him. However, I faced an immediate obstacle in that, although the door had been unlocked, the gallery was completely empty. Where *was* everyone?

A noise from an open door in the back of the room got my attention, so I made my way over to it. It seemed to lead to some kind of workshop, far more chaotic than the gallery space. Half-finished works were scattered around the room as well as different materials and tools.

At first glance, the only sign of life I could see was the backside of a man. Literally, only his backside as he bent over, rooting around in a crate that sat on the floor.

I took a few steps closer without thinking about it. He wore jeans and, from what I could see from that angle, a tight t-shirt, showing off an impressively muscled physique, and it took a few seconds before I realized I was staring.

Get a hold of yourself, Nadiya. I hadn't even been single for a full day yet. Surely, I wasn't so desperate that I needed to ogle a complete stranger, no matter how splendid the view.

He must be an employee, I guessed from the way he was dressed, but at least he should be able to point me to Callahan.

"Excuse me?"

I spoke loudly and firmly, to be sure he heard me, and he jumped in surprise, spinning around to face me.

For a split second, I took in his ruggedly handsome face and the surprisingly sexy tattoos on his arms, but it didn't really have a chance to register, not when the paint he'd been holding splashed out of the cans and directly onto my perfectly-pressed white designer suit.

~Dex~

The woman's face froze in disbelief as the paint in my hands went flying, spattering all over her pretty white clothes.

"Oh, fu... I mean, shoot. I'm so sorry, ma'am," I stumbled through my response, looking down at her suit in dismay. "I didn't know you were there."

Where did she come from? And why had she snuck up right behind me like that?

I had opened the gallery as usual, even though I wasn't expecting any customers, then I went back into the workshop to start packing. It would take a few days for the foreclosure proceedings to get going, but I might as well accept the inevitable. Not ready to share the news with my family yet, I'd drowned my sorrows the night before in a few beers with my good friend, Sawyer, and my head was a little worse for wear that morning. Was that why I hadn't heard her come in? Or maybe I'd just been too focused on what I needed to do.

I had no idea who she was, but I couldn't seem to stop staring at her tailored suit, covered with drops of red and yellow paint. I kind of thought it looked better with a bit of colour, but from the look on her face, I was pretty sure she didn't agree. The colour only gave me an excuse to keep looking, though; what really caught my attention was the way the suit fit her, perfectly highlighting every curve and dip and swell of her form. It was a work of art in its own right.

It had been a long, long time since I'd noticed any woman in that way.

Swallowing, I brought my eyes up to her face, but that didn't help much either. Her copper-coloured skin and the fullness of her lips only enhanced the effect of the suit. She was truly stunning.

And stunningly upset, by the look of things.

"Look what you've done!" she exclaimed in a slightly unusual accent that partly distracted me from the anger in her tone. "I don't suppose those are washable paints?"

I gave her my most apologetic look as I shook my head. "I'm afraid not."

Her eyes closed in frustration. "Just what I needed," she muttered under her breath, making me feel even worse. It sounded like we were both having a bad day.

"I'm sorry, ma'am, but the workshop is a messy place. That's why we've got the sign on the door."

"What sign?" she snapped, so I pointed to it and she turned to take a look at the door where it clearly said: *Artist at work: knock before entering.*

"I really am sorry," I apologized again as I placed the paint cans I still held into the crate I'd been packing and wiped my hands on the rag hanging from the belt loop of my jeans. "I can replace it for you." Although I didn't think the situation was entirely my fault, it seemed the right thing to do.

"You're going to replace a $2000 designer suit?" she asked, her eyebrows raising in a bit of amusement at the idea, and my stomach sank.

Fuck. I certainly couldn't afford that.

My dismay must have shown in my face because she sighed and shook her head. "Never mind. It was an accident."

I appreciated that she could see that, and I seized on the slight softening in her tone to satisfy my curiosity about her accent. "Where are you from?"

As quickly as it had disappeared, the hardness in her face returned. "I was born right here in Houston," she replied defensively. "I'm just as American as you are."

Shit, I hadn't meant that how it sounded. She must have dealt with that question from a thousand rednecks before, and I quickly tried to explain myself. "I meant your accent. It's not really Texan."

Once again, my reply relaxed her a little, though some wariness remained in her eyes. "I studied at Cambridge in England. I picked up a bit of the accent while I was there."

That explained it. The tone had just a touch more refinement than I was used to. Although I would have liked to know more about how she ended up there and why, I decided not to attempt any more small talk, at least until I could stop shoving my foot in mouth. "So, what can I help you with?"

She gave the room another glance before looking back at me. "Can you tell me where I can find Dexter Callahan?"

The leaden feeling in my stomach returned as I realized she must be with the bank, or perhaps a law firm based on the way she was dressed. She obviously hadn't come there just to chat.

Still, whoever she was, I couldn't hide from it, so I spread my arms invitingly and offered her my best smile. "You've found him."

Her eyes widened as she looked me up and down, and I couldn't help feeling just a little satisfied. She was checking me out just as much as I'd done to her. Maybe she felt some kind of attraction too?

However, her next words quickly dashed any budding ideas I might have had about a personal connection.

"Mr Callahan, it's a pleasure to finally meet you. I'm Nadiya Varma."

~Nadiya~

Nothing was going the way I expected it to.

Aside from the fact that I stood there with multi-coloured paint soaking into the fibres of my now-ruined suit, the rather charming man I'd been speaking to just revealed that he was none other than the very man I had come to see, the one who had been a thorn in my side for months.

How could *he* be Dexter Callahan? He was nothing like I'd imagined. Where was the skinny, middle-aged man with glasses I had pictured sitting behind his computer, sending me pedantic emails? That was the Dexter I wanted to deal with, not the distractingly handsome man in front of me.

His dark hair was cut short, his eyes a piercing shade of blue and he had just the right amount of stubble on his strong, defined jawline. His hard, muscled body, wrapped in his tight t-shirt and jeans, made him look much more like a cowboy who spent his days in physical labour rather than someone who sat around in front of an easel all day.

I hate this man, I reminded myself, even as I put on my best professional smile. He was my adversary in the deal I'd gone there to close, and I was pretty certain from the emails he'd sent me that he hated me too.

Sure enough, as soon as I introduced myself, the friendly, open look on his face disappeared, replaced by distrust and, surprisingly, perhaps even a bit of disappointment.

Almost as if he had wanted me to be someone else too.

"You really couldn't wait to come down and rub my nose in it?" he demanded, crossing his arms across his chest. I tried not to notice how the muscles in his arms flexed as he did it, keeping my eyes on his face instead. "Do you have spies at the bank or something?"

Spies? What was he talking about? "Mr Callahan, I don't know what you mean, I just came to introduce myself and..."

"And do a victory dance on the ruins of my life's work," he scowled, his mood growing darker by the second. "Well, you can turn around and come back another day, because no eviction papers have been served yet, and according to state law, I have..."

There was the Dexter Callahan I knew, the one who loved to quote legislation at me. My familiar irritation with him began to rise again, but I ignored it to focus on something else he'd just said. "Eviction papers?" I repeated curiously, cutting him off. "Have you defaulted on your mortgage?"

His scowl grew deeper. "As if you didn't know. This innocent act ain't foolin' me, darlin'. Why else would you be at my door this very morning like some kind of vulture?"

Both his tone and his words made me bristle. He had no right to speak to me like that. "First of all, I'm not your 'darling'. And second, I honestly had no idea about your mortgage. If you were in that much trouble, why didn't you contact me? The amount I've offered you is more than fair..."

He cut me off again. Neither of us seemed willing to let the other one get a full sentence out. "I didn't call you 'darling'." He mimicked my accent, like a child would, even though he had seemed to rather like it before he found out who I was. "I said darlin', and trust me, it ain't a term of endearment. And as for your offer, you can take it and shove it..."

"Mr Callahan." This was getting out of hand. We were both adults, surely we could act like it. "I didn't come here to fight with you."

He raised his dark, handsome eyebrows at me. "Really? What were you expecting then? A tea party?"

For a second, I let my eyes close in frustration. This man was just as impossible in person as over email. At least that helped to quell any attraction I might have been feeling, since that wouldn't have helped matters anyway. *Focus on the job, Nadiya. Just like always.*

"Listen to me for a minute. If you've defaulted and the bank fore-closes, you'll lose everything, but you don't have to. I'll still honour the previous offer I made you. The gallery is going either way, you must know that, but at least if you accept my offer, you'll have something to show for your loss."

It went against every cut-throat instinct my father had ever tried to instill in me, but heaven help me, I felt a bit bad for the man. I didn't want him to lose his 'life's work', as he'd called it.

Apparently, my sympathy wasn't welcome. "I don't need your pity, Ms Varma." He leaned into my name, mocking me once again by using my full name as I'd been using his. "The bank technically owns the gallery now. If you want it, go talk to them."

Why was he being so stubborn? It didn't make any sense. "If you just defaulted, they won't have done anything yet. I can have whatever amount is outstanding transferred to your account today so you can stop the foreclosure, and then you'll be free to sell to me."

It should be a simple enough concept for anyone to grasp, even someone with no business sense as he was clearly demonstrating himself to be.

But for some ridiculous reason, he still disagreed. "I'm not selling it," he told me firmly. "If it's taken from me, then fine. There's nothing I can do about that, but I ain't putting my name on anything that says I chose to give it up."

There must be some way to get through that thick skull of his. "What about your family?" I asked, trying a new angle. "You must have a wife, maybe children? How are you going to support them?"

Although I found him incredibly frustrating, I couldn't deny he was a very attractive man. There must be some woman out there who could put up with his bullheadedness.

However, his face hardened further at the question. "Not that it's any of your business, but no, I don't have a family. It's just me, and I can take care of myself."

"But you'll lose almost a hundred thousand dollars..." I tried to explain, but he cut me off yet again.

"Some things aren't about the money, Ms Varma."

The frown on my face deepened. Why did people keep saying that to me?

His words brought Greg's similar words, and my father's, rushing back to me, as well as the whole ridiculous situation with the board. Nothing about this interaction was going to help me with my image. Instead of being the conquering hero that convinced Callahan to sell, I was going to be the vulture, as he had just termed it, who swooped in to snatch the gallery from the bank. It made a far less appealing story.

My father said the board already saw me as cold. This would just be one more example of that, and the fact that I was newly single would be the final nail in the coffin of my CEO dreams. I could see everything I'd worked for going up in smoke.

And truth be told, even aside from what it meant for my career, I didn't want this annoying, stubborn, talented man to lose his gallery completely. He could still sell his art, just not right on this spot. If he took my offer, he'd have more than enough money to relocate somewhere else. Why couldn't he see that? What was it about this particular location that was so important to him?

Although, now that I'd seen his work for myself, I had to admit that his gallery would actually fit in well with the development I had planned. The type of people who would move into the luxury condominiums which would rise where we were standing would love to buy the kinds of things he sold. The building had to go, there was no question of that, but maybe we could find another solution.

He'd just told me he was unattached, and my eyes scanned him once again with new interest. He was a very attractive man. Charming, even, if he chose to be. A proper Texan man, the kind that all the 'good old boys' on the Varma Corporation board would admire.

Maybe there was a way we could compromise.

Maybe there was a way for both of us to get what we wanted.

"You've gone quiet," he pointed out sarcastically as I reviewed everything in my head, looking for any flaws in my plan. "Should I be worried about that?"

I gave him my steeliest look, the one that had won me more deals that I could count. "It just means I'm thinking, and lucky for you, I think I've come up with a deal that just might fix everything."

Chapter Three

The woman was really unbelievable. I didn't know how I could possibly make it any clearer that I wasn't going to take her money. It wouldn't matter if it meant I could open a gallery somewhere else. It didn't matter if it meant the difference between me starving or not. Losing the gallery to the bank, I could deal with; I knew that I'd done my very best to save it, but to willingly hand it over to someone who only wanted to destroy it? I simply couldn't do that, no matter how tempting the offer.

Nadiya Varma didn't understand that at all. She'd never even tried. Not once did she ask me *why* I was so dead-set on not selling. Not that I would have shared all my reasons with her, since they were personal, but at least it would have shown that she cared about something other than herself. As it was, I got the picture of what kind of woman she was in all the things she did and didn't say.

Since she looked mighty pleased with herself at the moment, I let her speak. Whatever offer she planned to make me, I would refuse, and then I could kick her out of my gallery. For the time being, the building still belonged to me, so if I told her to go, she had to go.

She began by looking around, as if really seeing the space around us for the first time. "Is your attachment to this gallery because of the physical building or because of the location?"

The question caught me off guard. I'd just been thinking about how she never cared to ask me about my reasons, and straight afterwards, she did. She couldn't somehow read my thoughts, could she?

Not only that, she phrased the question in quite an astute way. The truth was: the building had a lot of problems. It had been built a few decades earlier and I'd been putting off a lot of maintenance work since funds weren't available. Every dollar I made had gone into simply trying to keep the business afloat. When Shawna and I first bought it, she actually wanted to tear it down and build something brighter and better in its place. She had so many big dreams. 'As soon as you're a success...' she would say before launching into one of her crazy blue-sky ideas. However, that success had never come and so the building had never changed.

Nadiya Varma didn't need to know any of that, so I stuck to the basics.

"I don't see how it makes a difference," I pointed out. "It's the location you want."

She had no interest in the building either, I knew that. Her interest started and stopped at the ground beneath it, the ground where she wanted to build her new gentrified condos.

She didn't deny it, at least. "It's the location I need, but when the development that's going up here is complete, there will be some retail space available within it. If being in this spot is important to you, per-haps we could negotiate a lease for your gallery within the new building."

That idea had never been mentioned before, and I knew straight away that Shawna would have loved it. It was just the kind of thing she would have jumped on, so I couldn't deny that it interested me, but I remained skeptical. What would the benefit be to the woman in front of me? She could buy the gallery out from under me by walking into the bank that day. She didn't need to make me any kind of offer at all, and I couldn't imagine she did it simply out of the kindness of her heart. From what I'd heard, kindness was not a quality anyone would associate with Nadiya Varma, so what was her game?

I decided to ask her straight out: "What's in it for you?"

She looked away from me, with something that almost looked like embarrassment. "This is going to sound a little crazy."

That piqued my interest even further. For the first time, she actually sounded like a real person. "I can handle a little crazy," I assured her. "It's kind of in my wheelhouse."

That made her smile, and for just a second, I almost forgot who she was.

She should smile more. It looked good on her.

Almost immediately, she composed herself, putting her business face back on, and the brief moment of connection vanished. "It will take a while before the new building is ready to move into, so even if we can reach a deal on a lease, it will be some time before you can be back in business."

Sure, I understood that. I wasn't a complete idiot, despite what she seemed to think.

"So you'll need something to tide you over in the meantime," she continued. "Money-wise."

We were back to money again. I should have guessed, but her next words took me genuinely by surprise. "There's a specific role I'm looking to fill, on a temporary basis. It would pay very well and leave you plenty of free time to continue working on your art while the building work gets underway."

She wanted to offer me a job? I certainly hadn't expected that, and I didn't really understand it. What kind of job paid very well but didn't take up much time? There had to be some kind of catch.

Unless working with her was the catch, since I couldn't imagine she'd be much fun as a boss.

Since I couldn't imagine what she might have in mind, I had to ask. "What's the role? I'm not much good with numbers or anything like that. I've always been better with my hands."

As her eyes dropped to my hands, I could have sworn I saw a slight pink tint creep up her cheeks, though her expression never altered.

"This wouldn't involve any number crunching," she promised. "It's more of a... public relations role."

"Spit it out, Ms Varma," I instructed. The beating around the bush was getting tiring. "What would you want me to do?"

Her face twisted in discomfort for just a second, but then she nodded, almost like she was encouraging herself to continue, and she looked me straight in the eye once more.

"I need a fiancé, Mr Callahan, and I think you just might fit the bill."

~**Nadiya**~

Dexter stared at me as if I'd just suggested he get into a rodeo ring with a bunch of enraged bulls or step out in the middle of rush hour traffic on the I-10.

"You want me to *marry* you?" he asked, his voice dripping with disbelief.

Well, he didn't have to say it quite like that. He made it sound like a fate worse than death.

Besides, I wasn't suggesting that anyway. "Nobody's getting married," I quickly assured him. "I simply need a fiancé for a few months, someone to stand next to me while I'm wearing a ring and say all the right things. It would only be for show."

He squeezed his eyes tightly shut as if it might help the idea make sense in his brain.

"I'm not even going to pretend that's not the craziest thing anyone's ever said to me, darlin'," he said when he opened them again, his blue eyes filled with amusement. "And I grew up in a small town where half the folks were all hat, no cattle."

Since I had freely admitted I knew how it would sound, I didn't take offense to him calling me crazy. Already, I was learning more about him, like the fact that he came from a small town. That was the kind of thing his fiancée should know.

It made sense that he didn't grow up in Houston. His Texan drawl was more pronounced than most people I did business with in the city, not to mention his irritating habit of calling me darlin', which needed to stop. That would be one of the first ground rules I set if he accepted my proposal. *When* he accepted it, I quickly corrected myself. I went into every deal expecting to come out on top; that was the only way to win.

"I know it sounds a little insane," I conceded. "But hear me out: we're both in a bit of a tight spot here. You're going to lose your gallery, I might lose my promotion. I'm willing to help you out if you help me out. It's a business deal, nothing more."

He gave me a curious look. "What kind of promotion? I thought you already ran this damn town."

Though he clearly didn't mean it as a compliment, I took some pride in the observation anyway.

"I'm the obvious choice to be the next CEO of Varma Corporation," I explained as succinctly as I could. "However, I've been told the board would prefer if I was married, or at least on my way to it."

"Well, that's some Grade-A bullshit," he replied bluntly, and I couldn't stop the corners of my mouth from twitching upward at his directness. "Being married or not's got nothing to do with how well you do a job."

Compared to the men back in the office, his rather refreshing point of view came as a relief. "I agree, but I'm afraid you've got more sense than my board does. Apparently, it could be the difference in me getting the position or not."

"And there ain't no one else you could ask?" His eyes travelled down my body, down my ruined suit all the way to my toes before returning back to my face. I almost felt flattered at the implied compliment until he spoke again, making it clear he'd been looking at my suit and not my body. "You're clearly not hurting for means. I'm sure there are plenty of other men who would take your money."

Annoyance shot through me again. Did he actually mean to imply that the only reason anyone would want to be with me was for the money? Wasn't that sweet of him? And did he think he was such a catch? I hadn't sought him out for this specifically.

"Don't flatter yourself. You're simply in the right place at the right time. My boyfriend and I broke up last night and you're the first man I've seen since then. There's nothing more to it than that."

I expected him to be offended by that, since I meant it to be offensive, but instead, something close to sympathy flashed through his eyes. "I'm sorry to hear that. Breakups can be rough."

The last thing I needed was him feeling sorry for me. Feelings in general were best kept out of this. "It's fine. It doesn't bother me, it's just bad timing."

He raised his eyebrows in a way that made it clear he didn't believe me. "If you say so, darlin'."

Okay, maybe it bothered me a little, but I had no intention of discussing my personal life with him. "Look, the clock is ticking here, Mr Callahan. The bank's going to start moving on your foreclosure soon. Do you really want to throw away everything you've built here?"

I spread my arms to include his workshop and the gallery through the open doorway as well. Creating a sense of urgency always worked well as a negotiating tactic. Make them think they have to close the deal immediately or they'll lose the opportunity forever, my father used to say.

But to my frustration, he just smiled in amusement, as if he saw straight through me. "The way I see it, Ms Varma, you need this more than I do. I've got other options. I can just move all this stuff to my garage and start selling online if I want to, but you must be pretty desperate to be making this offer to someone you don't even know."

I swallowed the lump in my throat as discreetly as I could. He had a point, but he was bluffing a little bit too. If he was so fine with just working from home, he wouldn't have fought me on the sale for so long. He wanted the gallery space I'd offered him, he just wanted to pretend he didn't. I hadn't missed the flash of interest in his eyes when I mentioned it.

"I can agree that we're both a bit desperate," I offered as a compromise, and he gave a small smile of acknowledgement. "That's why my solution makes so much sense. We both get what we want and there's no harm done."

"No harm done," he repeated quietly, looking away from me as he weighed things over. "And you really expect me to just agree to this right now? It's kind of a big decision. You're not exactly an under-the-radar kind of woman. My friends and family would all hear about it. I'd have a lot of explaining to do."

Once again, I bristled at the implication. He made it sound like no one would approve of him being with me, which was ridiculous. I was a prize, in more ways than one.

"As I said, the clock is ticking," I repeated. "For me as well as you. As you already pointed out, there are other men who would probably jump at the opportunity. If you're not interested, I'll have to go find someone else who is, and you can deal with the foreclosure all on your own."

His nostrils flared in frustration, which I took as his acknowledgement that he knew there *would* be plenty of men willing to take my money. But even more true was the fact that I wouldn't have the first idea where to find anyone else I could make the offer to. I couldn't let just anyone into my life and trust them to keep my secret.

So why did I feel comfortable asking Dexter Callahan, a man who I'd privately cursed for months? I couldn't say for certain, but it must have had something to do with how he stuck to his guns over the gallery for so long. He clearly wasn't after money, and he had principles that he stood by, even if they didn't make sense to me.

I trusted that if he gave me his word, he would keep it. It really came down to that.

But did he feel the same? Would he trust me?

I couldn't be certain, but when he finally looked back at me, his jaw clenched with a rather grim determination.

"Tell me exactly what you would expect me to do."

~Dex~

Nadiya looked surprised when I asked her to tell me what being engaged to her would entail. Maybe she thought I would refuse outright, like I probably should have, or maybe she thought I'd hold out longer, just like I had with the gallery. I wasn't agreeing yet, not exactly. I definitely wanted more details first to make sure my understanding of her offer matched with what she envisioned. Even so, I had to admit I was at least thinking about it.

I couldn't even really explain why. The idea was absolutely ridiculous, completely crazy as I'd said to her straight out when she first mentioned it. And yet, as we argued, somehow it became a little less insane. I began to see how it could benefit both of us, just like she'd said, and when she assured me that there would be no harm done, I had to agree. What was the worst that could happen? We weren't actually going to fall in love or anything.

The benefits to me were obvious: I would get the money from selling the gallery to her, money that would help to pay off some of my debt and allow me to keep working on my art while I waited for the new gallery space to be ready. I would also *get* that new gallery space, right in the spot where Shawna and I had always dreamed I'd make it big. There were less obvious benefits too. People close to me had given me some leeway for a few years after my loss, but after six years, they were beginning to lose patience. Friends and family were trying to set me up left, right and centre, even though I told them over and over again I wasn't interested.

My heart belonged to one woman and one woman only. I'd had a love that most people only dreamed about, and I knew that lightning didn't strike twice. It didn't seem right to me to lead anyone on. Every woman out there deserved to be loved the way I had loved Shawna, and since

I couldn't give that to them, they deserved to find someone else who could.

But no matter how often or in how many ways I tried to explain that to my well-meaning sisters, they wouldn't accept it. If I suddenly told everyone in my life that I'd gotten engaged, they'd be shocked, but it would also get them off my back about finding someone else.

It would be a welcome reprieve.

Lastly, I had to consider the woman in front of me. I still thought of her as a pain in the ass with her priorities in all the wrong places, but there had been just enough of a glimpse of vulnerability to let me know a real person lay behind the designer suit. She'd just broken up with someone, and from the way she said it, I was pretty certain it hadn't been her decision. That had to hurt, no matter what she said, and people were trying to force her to get married just to keep her job? It didn't sit right with me, and I couldn't see someone in need of help and not lend a hand, especially when it seemed as harmless as her plan did.

Those considerations all led to me asking for more information, and as soon as Nadiya's initial surprise at my reply passed, she jumped right in as if she had the script already prepared. "We'd need to make some kind of formal announcement about the engagement. As you already said, it will be public, so it will probably appear in the papers. I'll have to introduce you to my father and the rest of the board, and there will be some public events to attend. Outside of that, we wouldn't have to spend any time together. You'd be free to do whatever you like. In a few months' time, when I'm firmly established in my role, we can quietly break it off."

My eyebrows rose higher and higher as she spoke, sounding much more naïve than I would have expected. Did she really think it would be that simple? "And you think people will buy it if we're never seen together outside of a few public events?"

"Why wouldn't they?"

"Well, call me crazy, darlin', but I think two people who are planning to marry each other might want to spend a bit of time together. How are you going to get to know anything about me so you can answer questions when people ask? What if we go to a supper where they're serving something with nuts and you don't know that I'm deathly allergic?"

Nadiya's eyes widened in concern. "You are?"

I couldn't help smirking just a little. "No, but you didn't know that, did ya?"

Her look of concern turned to a scowl, making it clear she didn't appreciate my joke. "We can do some preparation first. I'll draft a list of things you should know about me, and you can do the same."

"Or we could just have a conversation," I pointed out, my amusement growing even stronger. "Get to know each other like normal people do."

"I'm sure you're very busy," she demurred, and that time, I laughed out loud. It couldn't be any more obvious that she didn't want to talk to me, and that was going to come across to everyone else as clearly as it did to me. If she really wanted this to work, she'd need to loosen up. Maybe I could teach her a thing or two.

For the time being, I limited myself to responding to her excuse. "You're about to put me out of business, I think I can spare an hour to have a chat."

She pursed her lips, seeming to debate whether arguing the point with me would be worthwhile, but ultimately, she shook her head. "Fine. We'll work something out."

"And what about public displays of affection?" She'd already made it more than clear she wasn't expecting anything in private, but people would expect an engaged couple to look like they could actually tolerate each other.

"What do you mean?" she asked in such dismay that I had to smile again.

"If you stand next to me with your arms crossed like that, people are going to think you don't like me or something," I teased her, enjoying the way she immediately dropped her arms, then tried to pretend like she hadn't. "How are we behaving at these events? Are we kissing? Hugging? Holding hands?"

Her scandalized look was almost more than I could take. She was going to be fun to tease, I could see that already from the way she took herself far too seriously. "I'm a professional businesswoman, and I behave like one. I will take your arm if the occasion calls for it, but that's all."

I was starting to get some idea about why her boyfriend might have upped sticks and left. "You *have* kissed a man before, haven't you?" Suddenly, I couldn't be entirely sure.

Her withering look made me smile yet again. "Not that it's any of your business," she said, repeating my earlier words back to me. "But yes, Mr Callahan, shockingly enough, I have."

Good. I would have felt bad for her otherwise, but her response brought up another point I wanted to make. "You might want to call me something other than Mr Callahan if you want people to think we're sleeping together."

As I expected by that point, her cheeks went red. Lord, she was easy to rile up. "No one has to think we're sleeping together."

"That's usually a part of being engaged, especially at our age."

She took a deep breath as if trying to keep calm. "Fine. I'll call you Dexter."

My name sounded stilted and awkward in her mouth. No one would believe she liked me if she said it like that.

"Dex," I corrected her. "Everyone calls me Dex."

"Dex," she repeated cautiously. A bit better, but not much. "You can work on that. What do I call you?"

"Just Nadiya is fine. Look, Mr Call... Dex. I have to get back to the office, but since you're arguing semantics with me, it sounds like we're in agreement on the basic principle. Are you saying yes?"

Was I? I'd been having so much fun playing with her that I hadn't even really thought about the big picture, but in the end, why the hell not? Financially, it was a no-brainer, and it could be good for a laugh. Lord knows my life had been short enough on those lately, not to mention I really couldn't wait to see the look on my sisters' faces when I told them

I was engaged.

And to whom.

"You've got yourself a deal, Nadiya."

Her cheeks coloured again, almost imperceptibly, as I said her name. "Fine. I'll be in touch with more details soon. I already have your email address."

Of course she did. Her emails had been the bane of my existence for the past few months, and I never could have imagined I'd be making that kind of agreement with the woman behind them.

Life really was full of surprises, I thought, as Nadiya Varma walked out of my gallery in her paint-splattered suit. Mine had just got a whole lot more interesting.

Chapter Four

~**Nadiya**~

My driver gave me a curious look as I got back in the car in my ruined suit, but he didn't say anything and I didn't offer any explanation. Instead, I pulled out my phone and got my assistant, Luisa, on the other end.

"I need my grey Armani suit waiting for me when I get back." I always kept a few backup suits at the office, just in case a button popped or a hem frayed. I'd never anticipated having paint splashed all over me, but at least I was prepared anyway. "Find out which bank has the mortgage on Dexter Callahan's gallery, and set up a supper reservation with my father, for three, for the end of the week."

I would have to introduce Dexter – or Dex, I reminded myself, since I had to get used to thinking of him that way – to my father first if we had any chance of pulling this off. He was the one most invested in my future with Greg and the one who would be most suspicious of the sudden change in my relationship status. If we could fool him, we could fool anyone, and a few days should give us a chance to prepare.

Greg and I had met at one of my father's business events. I wouldn't say we were set up, exactly, but my father certainly gave me a firm nudge in his direction. In some ways, Greg was a mirror image of my mother: pleasant in public, undemanding in private. Someone bland enough to be inoffensive, who could deal with playing second fiddle to the demands of the job.

Or at least, we had both *thought* Greg could handle that, but apparently, in the end, he couldn't.

When it came to Dex, on the other hand, I wouldn't use any of those words to describe him. Pleasant? Undemanding? Bland? None of them seemed to apply.

What would my father think of him? I didn't know, but for some reason it gave me a little thrill of excitement to think about it. I had always done exactly what my father asked of me, but as I approached thirty, maybe it wouldn't hurt to do something different for a change.

Half an hour later, I sat at my desk in my office, wearing my grey suit, on the phone with the bank explaining that I would like to pay off Dex's mortgage. I could have had someone from the finance team take care of it, but in order to follow proper Varma Corp procedures, they would want to see the sale contract signed by Callahan, and we hadn't signed any contract yet. In moving forward without one, I'd broken one of our rules, not just the company's but one of my personal rules too: get everything in writing.

But again, for reasons I couldn't quite explain, I knew I didn't need to worry. His word was as strong as his signature; I knew that instinctively. He wouldn't back out of the deal we'd agreed to any more than I would.

The rest of the day sped by with my usual mix of meetings and work. There was hardly a spare moment for Dex to cross my mind again, and the day ended with my regular operations meeting with all my directors, including Brad Sherwood, the man my father had suggested the board might choose over me for the CEO position. He looked particularly smug that day, though I had to admit I might be projecting. Maybe I just thought he looked that way because I would feel the same in his position.

However, as the meeting ended and the others filed out, Brad lingered behind, pretending to be occupied with something on his phone until only the two of us remained in the conference room.

"I just want to tell you how much I admire you, Nadiya," he said as he casually got to his feet, acting as if he hadn't been waiting for a chance to speak. "It's tough to keep things together after you've just been through something like that."

What the hell was he talking about? "Something like what?" I asked testily. I hated not understanding the subtext of a conversation, and this one had me thrown right from the beginning.

"A breakup," he replied in faux sympathy. "I ran into Greg at the gym this morning and he told me you guys have ended things."

He did *what*? What exactly was Greg telling people? And why didn't I know that Brad and Greg went to the same gym?

Despite my surprise, I refused to let myself appear flustered. In fact, he'd just given me a perfect opportunity to lay a little groundwork for my upcoming announcement. "It's for the best. We were both looking for new things."

Brad's eyebrows raised in surprise. "Really? That's not what he said."

Had Greg really said he dumped me, or was Brad just trying to get a rise out of me? Either way, I wasn't going to fall for it.

"Things aren't always as they seem," I replied, trying to sound mysterious as I gave him a smile. "But I really think it's best for both of us."

"I hope so," he said, returning my smile just as insincerely. "I know some of the members of the board will be disappointed to hear it."

That little snake. He knew exactly what was going on with the board, but *how* did he know? I only found out through my father, so Brad must have had his own sources. And now he thought he had the advantage because I wouldn't be getting engaged after all.

We would see about that.

"I don't think they have anything to worry about," I replied as politely as I could. "If you'll excuse me."

Picking up my files, I walked out the door without giving him a chance to respond, my mind whirling the whole time. Who did Brad have on his side on the board? Obviously, I hadn't been paying enough attention to internal politics. My father might know, but I hated the idea of admitting to him that Brad had done a better job of ingratiating himself with the board than I had. It would be better to handle this on my own.

I was so caught up in my thoughts that I didn't notice the man standing in my office until I nearly ran straight into him.

"Whoa there, darlin'." Dex sounded amused as I stopped abruptly to avoid a collision, and he reached out a hand to steady me. "You're lucky I didn't have any paint with me this time or you'd have another suit ruined."

As I looked up into his blue eyes, my heart beat a little faster than usual. He was so *close,* his face just inches from mine and his hand still on my arm. His sudden appearance had surprised me, I told myself. That explained my racing pulse, and nothing else.

Taking a step back, I cleared my throat. "What are you doing here?"

"It's nice to see you too, *honey*," he teased me, gesturing with his head to my still-open office door where anyone walking by could hear us.

He had a point. We had a charade to maintain, so although I didn't reply to his comment, I did go and close the door so that we would have some privacy before questioning him again. "How did you get in here?"

"Your assistant let me in when I told her we needed to continue our discussion from earlier. This is some office."

He looked around the room and I followed his gaze, taking in the modern furniture and the floor-to-ceiling window with its bird's-eye view of the city, trying to see it from his perspective. "Thank you."

His eyebrows raised as he looked back at me with a slight smirk. "I didn't say it was a compliment. What is the point of those?"

Dex pointed at the black and white squares on my wall, and I frowned. Surely, he would know the answer to that better than anyone. "They're art."

"Darlin', that ain't art. Those are paint samples. Would a little colour kill you?"

"It's distracting," I pointed out, walking away from him to put my files down on my desk. "I need to concentrate when I'm in here. And please don't call me 'honey' or 'darlin' or anything other than my name."

"Sorry," he apologized, actually sounding sincere. "I meant nothing by it. It's just a habit, but I'll try to stop."

"Thank you." Inhaling deeply, I tried to put on my game face. I hadn't been prepared to see him again already and the day had been a crazy one, but since he'd made the effort to come and see me, the least I could do was find out why. "What can I do for you?"

He dropped into the seat across from my desk without an invitation, so I sat down too. "I got a call from the bank, telling me everything had been paid off. You move fast."

"There was no need to wait. We agreed on the deal. The cost of the mortgage will be deducted from the overall sale price for the gallery. You'll just need to give my assistant your bank details and she'll have the remainder wired to you."

His lips pursed in confusion. "But I didn't sign anything yet."

My accountants would say the exact same thing, but I played it off as if it didn't really matter. "No, but you agreed. You can sign now, if you like. Luisa can bring the paperwork in."

As I reached out for the phone on my desk, Dex leaned forward too, placing his hand on mine to stop me. "I'll sign it, of course I will. I gave you my word. But first, if you don't mind, there's something else I'd like to talk to you about, something I probably should have told you before."

~Dex~

Nadiya's expression immediately turned wary when I said I had something to tell her. I could see her mind getting to work right away, trying to figure out what it might be, and before long, a look of dismay crossed her face.

"Don't tell me you're gay," she groaned. "Brad would definitely find out, and he would have a field day with that."

Brad? Was that her ex? She'd lost me.

"No, that's not it, it's just..."

I trailed off as what she'd just said fully sunk in.

"Wait, why is that the first thing you thought of?"

She shrugged as she settled back in her chair. "Past experience, I suppose. The last few men I've met who looked like you already had a husband."

"Looked like me how?" I couldn't help glancing down at the way I was dressed. I really didn't know what she was getting at and whether I should be insulted or not.

Nadiya squirmed in her seat, clearly not wanting to answer. "Just... men who were as attractive as you, alright?" she said through gritted teeth.

A grin spread across my face as I leaned back too, enjoying her discomfort at the admission. "You think I'm that good-looking, huh?"

She rolled her eyes at my teasing, but it seemed to help her to regain full control over her reactions. When she spoke again, her confidence was back. "There's no need for false modesty, Dex. You know you are, and I know that I am too. I ought to be for how much work I put into it. We'll look good together."

Well, I certainly couldn't say she had any self-esteem issues. I'd never had a woman straight out tell me she thought she was pretty before.

She was right, but that was beside the point.

"So what is it, then?" she asked, looking me over curiously. "Do you have a criminal record I should be aware of?"

The conversation was giving me an interesting insight into how her brain worked, and for a moment, I was tempted to let her keep guessing to see what other things she thought would be most damaging to my reputation as her fiancé, but I had a feeling that could take a while and I did have other plans for the evening.

"It would be easier if I just told you," I pointed out, and she nodded.

"I'm sorry, you're right. Go ahead."

It had occurred to me shortly after Nadiya walked out of the gallery this morning that she should probably know about Shawna. If we were going to be subject to any kind of public scrutiny, it wouldn't take long for anyone with the time or inclination to dig up all kinds of happy photos of me and my wife. I certainly wasn't ashamed of – quite the contrary, in fact – but she should be aware of it all the same. I didn't want her to be surprised or taken off guard if anyone asked her about it.

"I've been married before."

I kept my explanation as strictly to the point as possible. Though she should be aware of it, she didn't necessarily need or want to know all the details.

A flicker of surprise registered in her eyes, but she quickly covered it up. "I suppose I should have expected that. You must be the same age as me, more or less, and most of my social group are married or have been. How old are you?"

"Thirty-two."

She nodded again, obviously making a mental note of it. "And how long were you married for?"

"Three years."

"How long ago?"

"I was twenty-three when we got married." I stuck to answering only the questions she was asking. If she wanted to know more about Shawna, I would tell her, but I wasn't going to simply start gushing about my wife if Nadiya didn't show any interest.

For now, she quickly did the calculations in her head. "So, your marriage ended six years ago."

"That's right."

"Any children?"

"No."

She seemed to breathe a sigh of relief at that response, and I suddenly had an image of her standing in a classroom full of children running around, like my sister, Billie, who was a teacher, trying to keep them from getting her expensive suit dirty. She didn't really come across as a natural caregiver.

"Is your ex-wife still involved in your life?" Nadiya asked next. "Will she be upset about your new engagement?"

I should have seen it coming that she'd be more concerned about how it would affect her and her plan than she was about how my marriage ending might have affected me. Also unsurprisingly, she had completely grasped the wrong end of the stick.

"We didn't get divorced," I replied bluntly. If I were talking to anyone else, I would have just told them what happened, but with Nadiya, I was curious to see how long it would take for her to figure it out.

Sure enough, a look of confusion and dismay crossed her face. "You're still legally married?"

I was almost tempted to say yes just to see how she'd react, but I told the truth instead. "No."

Patiently, I waited for her to figure it out, her face tightened in concentration as she thought over everything I'd said, until it finally seemed to click and her eyes widened. "Oh. I'm sorry."

The genuine empathy in her voice took me by surprise. I hadn't been sure she'd be capable of it, and it affected me more than I expected it to. Though I nodded in acknowledgement, the lump in my throat made it difficult for me to reply.

I rarely got choked up about Shawna's death six years after it happened, but something in Nadiya's expression dug up all those old feelings again. Suddenly, she looked more open and interested than she had about anything we had talked about until then. It felt like, for the first time, I could see a glimpse of the woman behind the facade she'd created for herself.

"Can I ask what happened?" she followed up softly.

That was a perfectly reasonable question, and my fiancée ought to know the answer to it. "Cancer. She was sick before we got married, but she went into remission for a while. After our wedding, it came back."

Nadiya nodded, a gesture she did quite a lot, I had noticed already. I wondered if she even knew she did it so often. It just seemed to be her way of showing she was engaged and listening as she decided how to respond. I'd never met anyone who measured their words quite so carefully.

"You loved her." It wasn't a question, just a simple statement of fact, so I responded with one of mine, equally simple and equally true.

"I do."

I kept it in the present tense on purpose.

"I'm very sorry," she replied after a moment's pause, adding the 'very' to her earlier apology. "My mother died of cancer a few years ago as well. I know it's not the same, but..."

"It sucks either way." When a loved one died of cancer, everyone always brought up someone they knew who had lost their battle too. They did it to show sympathy, so I took it that way. "Cancer's a bitch."

She nodded once more. No one could argue with that. "Well, thank you for telling me. It's important that I know those kinds of things. Is that why you're not in a relationship now?"

That was surprisingly astute of her. "That's got a lot to do with it, yeah."

"And it doesn't bother you that people will think we're engaged?"

Once again, she surprised me. That had crossed my mind after she'd left that morning, wondering whether I'd be dishonouring Shawna's memory by agreeing to this farce of a relationship with Nadiya. However, when I thought back to my wife's mischievous streak and how she loved to pull off elaborate pranks, I thought that actually, if she was watching over me, she'd probably be getting a kick out of it.

She'd be happy to see me having some fun, anyway, and the most surprising thing of all that day had been the discovery that talking to Nadiya Varma could actually be kind of fun.

"I wouldn't have agreed if it would bother me," I told her truthfully.

Nadiya took a deep breath. "Okay. In that case, we should probably start making some plans. We've got a lot to learn about each other, Dex, and not a lot of time to do it."

~Nadiya~

As soon as I said we should start making plans, Dex glanced down at the watch on his wrist. He hadn't been wearing one earlier at his gallery, I remembered. It was a nice watch, so maybe he didn't want to get it dirty as he worked. I knew firsthand just how dirty his work could get.

"As fun as that sounds, Nadiya, I've got somewhere I need to be tonight. I wanted to make sure to come down and tell you about Shawna, but that's all I've got time for right now."

Shawna. He hadn't mentioned his wife's name before, but I didn't miss how his voice softened as he said it. In the way he spoke about her, the quiet certainty and the look in his eyes as she crossed his mind, I could see just how much he had loved her.

I didn't really know what that felt like.

I couldn't imagine loving someone so much that even six years later, he still wasn't ready for another relationship. I had literally broken up with Greg the night before and I would have had no problem dating someone new if the right person came along.

Or at least, I would if I didn't already have a fake fiancé.

Normally, other people's emotions made me a bit uncomfortable, but Dex's grief felt different. He wasn't showy about it or asking for any kind of response from me. He just stated things as they were: he loved her.

Loves her.

I could handle that.

And in a way, it actually made our arrangement even clearer. He had no interest in dating anyone else so pretending to be engaged to me wouldn't interfere with his social life, and it made the chance of any kind of complicating emotions between us even less likely. Not that I had thought it would happen, but the extra reassurance was good to have anyway.

The whole deal would be strictly business for both of us, the way it should be.

So, although I did wonder about what kind of plans he might have for the evening, I didn't ask. That was his personal business, it had nothing to do with me, and I stuck to my agenda instead.

"That's fine, but just so you know, my assistant has arranged for us to have supper with my father on Thursday so I can introduce you to him then."

Dex's eyebrows shot up. His handsome face was really quite expressive, letting me know how he felt about nearly every word that came out of my mouth. "Thursday? As in two days from now?"

"Is that a problem? Do you already have plans?" Maybe I should have checked if he would be free. I had never had to worry about that with Greg since he always worked around my schedule. He knew never to make plans without checking with me first.

Dex let out a big breath through his mouth. "It's not that, it just doesn't give us a lot of time is all. We still need to get our stories straight."

I had a plan for that too. "The way I see it, we don't actually have to know each other that well. This relationship is still new. Everyone knows I was dating someone until very recently..."

"Until yesterday, you mean," he pointed out with a smirk. "Let's call a spade a spade, Nadiya."

"Fine," I conceded. "Until yesterday, but that's exactly my point. I don't want anyone thinking I was cheating on him with you. Our cover story will be that we were working together on the gallery sale, we felt an attraction but didn't act on it because I was already in a relationship, then today, you found out that Greg and I broke up and you swooped in and proposed."

I thought it sounded perfectly plausible and even a little romantic, but the way Dex burst out laughing seemed to indicate he might have a different opinion.

"What's so funny?" I asked, feeling that familiar twinge of annoyance that usually accompanied the thought of Dexter Callahan, at least before we'd met.

"Oh, darlin', you do think a lot of yourself, don't ya?" He shook his head, still smiling broadly.

My eyes narrowed at both his tone and his words. "First, you promised you'd stop with the darlin', and second, I don't see the problem. It's believable. What's wrong with it?"

He continued to laugh softly. "Just the idea that I wouldn't even be able to wait a day is funny to me. That ain't really my style."

"People act a little crazy when they're in love," I pointed out. I didn't have any personal experience of it, but I'd always heard that, anyway. "And the people that you're going to have to convince don't know you anyway, so they wouldn't know whether it's your 'style' or not. Do you have a better idea?"

"I suggest we stick closer to the truth," he said, still chuckling. "You came down to my door first thing after your breakup and begged me to marry you."

And he said *I* thought highly of myself?

"That's not exactly what happened," I disagreed, even though I knew he wasn't miles off. "And besides, the whole point of this exercise is to make me seem a little softer, more demure. Going out and demanding a proposal isn't exactly soft."

Dex shook his head. "Nadiya, I don't know you very well, but I'm pretty sure 'soft' is not the word most people would use to describe you."

I opened my mouth to protest, but he held up a hand to stop me.

"I ain't saying it's a bad thing, but I don't get why you wanna be anything other than what you are. People can spot a fake, and being fake is worse than being a bit hard. Going after what you want can be a great quality, so just own it."

No one had ever said anything like that to me before. My whole life, people had told me I needed to be more delicate, more nurturing, more supportive. No one had ever just told me to be myself before.

He made it sound so easy, but unfortunately, I knew it wasn't. "Apparently, that isn't what my board wants right now, and the whole point of this is to appease the board. I don't plan to pretend to be something

I'm not for my whole life, just until I have the job."

"Right. You said that bit before, though I still don't really understand it. I'm going to need more information, but I'm afraid I don't have time to hear it all right now."

He glanced down at his watch again, making it clear that whatever his plans were that evening, they were important to him.

"Are you free tomorrow evening?" I asked. "You could come to my house so we can review things. I'll prepare a list of topics that are likely to come up over supper with my father."

His lips twitched. "Why am I not surprised you make lists?"

It felt like he was teasing me, but I wasn't sure why. "Lists are useful."

"Of course they are, dar... Nadiya." He caught himself that time, and I appreciated that he made the effort. "What time do you want me?"

"My assistant will send you the details, but let's say seven o'clock." I was usually in the office until at least six, and often later than that.

"Are you feeding me, or should I eat before?"

I didn't know what he had in mind, but I might as well set his expectations at the right level right from the start. "I don't cook."

He laughed again, looking genuinely amused. "Somehow, I never for a second thought you did, but you've gotta eat too, right?"

"I can order something," I conceded. I hadn't planned to make supper a part of it, but he was right: we did both need to eat. Eating together wouldn't be too intimate. It would be fine.

"Sounds good." He stood up, stretching out his firm legs. "See you tomorrow then, partner."

He held out his hand across the desk to me and I shook it firmly. "Thank you, Mr Callahan."

His eyes twinkled in amusement at me using his full name, but he didn't comment on it. He just gave me a nod before turning and letting himself out of his office. I could hear him saying goodbye to Luisa on his way out, his voice friendly and charming. Hopefully, he could be just the same way with the members of the board I needed to win over.

Luisa came into my office a minute later, ready to review the next day's schedule, but as she sat down across from me, she couldn't help glancing back over her shoulder. "So, that was Dexter Callahan?"

The surprise in her voice reminded me how shocked I had been that morning when I saw him for the first time. Luisa had listened to me grumble about him for months, she must have been confused about why we were suddenly being so friendly.

That gave me my first chance to try out my story and take it for a little test drive.

"That's Dex," I confirmed, dropping his nickname casually, like I said it all the time. "He's not exactly as I imagined."

"No kidding," she agreed enthusiastically before catching herself. Luisa was a great assistant, but she also liked to talk about things outside of work. It didn't take her long to figure out that wasn't how I operated, so she usually limited her conversation with me, though I still heard her chatting with others from time to time.

At that moment, though, her ability to share information around the office was just what I needed, so I tried to drop a few more hints.

"He's coming over to my house for supper tomorrow night. Could you send him the directions and make sure to order something suitable for us to eat?"

Luisa's eyes got so wide, I almost laughed. "At your house?" she repeated, squeaking a little on the last word.

I nodded as if it were a perfectly normal thing for me to say, though we both knew it wasn't. I never had people come to my house. Luisa herself had only ever seen my house once when I was sick and I asked her to come and drop off some files for me.

"We're going to be seeing quite a lot of him from now on," I told her, trying to sound vaguely mysterious about the whole thing.

From the look on her face, she clearly didn't find the prospect of seeing more of Dex an unpleasant thought, and I had to admit, I didn't entirely dread it either.

The whole day had been full of surprises.

Chapter Five

~Dex~

When I got back to my truck in the Varma Corp parking lot and glanced in the rear-view mirror, the smile on my face surprised me. I didn't usually go around smiling for no reason. In fact, my sisters liked to tease me that I tried to make myself look as unapproachable as possible, which wasn't true at all, or at least I didn't do it intentionally. I just rarely had a reason to smile unprovoked.

It must have been the relief of having the financial burden of the gallery off my back that caused the smile, I figured. When I got that phone call from the bank earlier telling me the mortgage had been paid off, I suddenly felt ten times lighter. Shawna's medical bills still weren't paid off yet, and the strain of that as well as trying to keep the business afloat had definitely taken its toll on me.

With that one call, everything felt a whole lot easier.

Although, as I hauled myself up into my truck, I realized that I still hadn't signed anything for the sale. Nadiya had mentioned getting the papers but then we got sidetracked by the rest of our conversation and it never came up again. For a moment, I wondered if I should head back up and take care of it right then, but I quickly reasoned that she'd probably have them waiting for me the next day when I went to her house. She didn't strike me as the type of businesswoman to leave any loose ends lying around.

And besides, I was already going to be late if I didn't high-tail it out of there. With the news I had to share, I'd have enough explaining to do that night without getting into trouble for being late too.

By the time I pulled up outside the ranch house in Glenbrook Valley, the smell of the charcoal grill already wafted through the air, accompanied by the shouts of kids playing and splashing in the pool in the backyard.

I let myself into the empty house and after a quick wash in the kitchen sink, a habit forced by countless repetitions over the years, I joined the chaos in the backyard.

"There he is!" My sister, Tonia, saw me first and shouted out to the rest of the family who were spread across the deck and yard. A chorus of greeting went up as Tonia came over to give me a hug. "I almost gave Cam grill duty. You made it just in time."

"God forbid," I replied in mock horror. "Unless y'all wanted your steak extra-crispy tonight?"

"Nothing wrong with a well-done steak," my brother-in-law retorted from next to the barbeque where he already had an apron on. "Some people prefer it done my way."

"Show of hands?" I requested. "Who wants Cam to cook tonight?"

As expected, not one hand went up, not even his wife's.

"Not a single one of you Callahans knows a good thing when you see it," Cam sighed as he untied the apron and handed it to me. "Beer?"

"Please." I would need something to help me through the announcement I planned to make later.

The rest of the family all came by to say hello as I started laying out the steaks on the grill. Since the Callahan family barbecue was a weekly occurrence, the menu was always the same and I always manned the grill, I knew how everyone wanted their steak done without needing to ask. A spread of salads and other fixings had been piled onto a table to the side along with an assortment of drinks to make any bar proud.

My other sisters, Laura and Billie, were chasing after their kids, making sure that no one got seriously injured, while their husbands, Jesse and Grey, sat chatting animatedly about something, probably sports. Meanwhile, my mother watched over it all like the proud matriarch that she was.

Shawna used to love our barbecue nights, even though they were quieter back then. There weren't any kids at that point, and Laura and Billie were still single. My Daddy was still there, and we all spent more nights than I could remember sitting out with a beer in the backyard as it got dark, shooting the breeze about anything and everything. I could almost feel her arm around me again as she perched on the arm of my Adirondack chair.

After Shawna died, it became hard for me to show up without feeling like my presence brought everyone down. Sometimes, I brought them down on purpose. Some days, I was so angry at the world I would take it out on anyone who came near. My family stuck by me through thick and thin, though, and when Daddy died, my mother and I understood each other better than ever. I got to be her comfort just like she'd been mine.

Six years on from Shawna's passing, I enjoyed every one of those nights again. They weren't the same as they used to be, but life never stood still. Things were constantly changing and I'd accepted that a long time ago.

"Dex, I've found the perfect woman for you," Laura announced as she leaned on the deck railing next to the barbeque while I flipped the steaks over.

"More perfect than the last twenty?" I asked sarcastically. I suspected that my sisters had a bet between them over who could successfully set me up with someone, since I couldn't think of any reason for how determined they seemed to be to see it happen. I didn't even want to imagine what the prize would be for the winner.

Laura ignored my comment and kept talking. "Mary-Beth met her at a beautician's event. Her name's Everly and she runs a hair salon downtown, so she's kind of an artist too. If you marry her, none of us will ever have to pay for a haircut again!"

She snickered into her beer as I gave her an incredulous look. "You're pimping me out for haircuts now?"

"Your new wife will have to bring *something* to the table. Look at the prize she'll be walking into."

She gestured to the whole of our family and I took a look around too, trying to see the scene through Nadiya's eyes. Cam and Jesse had been dragged over to the pool by Cam's son, Charlie, and Jesse's boys, Randy and Travis, to take part in their water gun war. The girls, Cam's daughter, Jenny, and Grey's daughter, Adele, were playing their own game in the shallow end, while Billie kept her 2-year-old, Teddy, away from the water. The best word to describe the whole scene would be chaos, but chaos of the very best kind.

What was Nadiya's family like? I had no idea other than what she'd told me that day about her mother passing away. But somehow, I suspected whatever it was like, it wouldn't be like mine. If she were to come to one of these barbecues with me, what would she make of it?

"I'm not sure if it's a prize or a trap," I pointed out to Laura. "Now make yourself useful and go round people up. Steaks are ready."

Those were the magic words and soon, we all sat around the outside tables, eating and laughing and talking under the big Texas sky. Between catching up with everyone's news and the chatter of the kids, there wasn't a quiet second while the food disappeared.

Not too long after the plates were clear, Laura brought up her hair-dressing friend-of-a-friend again. "She's free all weekend, Dex. Can I give her your number?"

Well, that set me up just about perfectly to share the news of my 'relationship'. *Here goes nothing.*

"Actually, I'm not available this weekend, or anytime at all, really. Truth is, I met someone."

A hush fell over the whole yard, as if I had just announced that I'd solved world hunger or had signed up for the next space rocket. Teddy started to whine about wanting to leave the table but his mother quickly shushed him.

My mother spoke first. "That's wonderful, Dexter."

Her eyes shone with such happiness that I immediately felt guilty for the lie. Deceiving my sisters was one thing, and a rather fun thing at that, but I didn't want to break my mama's heart. And yet, I'd given Nadiya my word, so I would have to tell my mother about it eventually.

"When do we get to meet her?" she asked.

"I'm not sure. I'm meeting her daddy in a couple days, so we'll see how that goes."

A chorus of 'oooooo's' circled round the yard, making me roll my eyes and everyone else laugh.

"Sounds serious, Dex," Billie piped up. "You're not usually the daddy-meeting type."

She wasn't wrong. Shawna's daddy had disliked me for a long time since I didn't have a 'proper' job. Eventually, he came around, but it had been uncomfortable for a long while. And since Shawna, well, there hadn't been any need for me to meet anyone's parents.

"This woman's a bit different," I replied as honestly as I could. "It's come on fast, but we *are* actually pretty serious."

I had them all eating out of the palm of my hand by that point. "How serious?" Tonia interjected, all eyes still fixed on me.

The time had come to let it out. If I were really going to go through with it, I'd have to tell them. Taking one last look around at all their eager, interested faces, I took a deep breath and said the words out loud: "We're engaged."

For a long moment, an eerie, unearthly silence descended over the whole group. My mom's backyard had never been so quiet.

And just as suddenly, everyone began talking at once.

"*Engaged?* Are you freaking kidding me?"

"How can you be engaged to someone we haven't met?"

"This is a joke, isn't it?"

"He's only saying that so we stop setting him up. Right, Dex?"

There were so many questions coming in from every direction that I couldn't tell who was asking what, so I decided to ignore them all and focus on my mother instead. She hadn't said anything yet as I stood up and walked over to her, taking a seat next to her at the table, ignoring my sisters, who were all arguing with each other about whether I was lying, and their husbands, who were trying to calm them down.

"Are you angry with me?" I asked her straight out. If anyone had a right to be hurt at the idea that I'd hidden a relationship from them, it would be her.

Her eyes were slightly watery as she looked up at me, and my heart sank as I braced for her disappointment, but when they came, her words weren't at all what I expected. "Of course not, Dex. I'm so happy for you. I thought there was something different about you when you came in here tonight, but I didn't want to get my hopes up."

Really? How did I seem different? It must have just been because of the relief I felt over the gallery, and she'd mistaken that for excitement over a new relationship.

"Come on, Dex, who is she?" Laura called out as everyone turned their attention back to me. "You can't leave us hanging like that!"

I glanced back over at my mother who just shrugged as if to say she couldn't protect me from their queries. "You know what they're like," she whispered to me conspiratorially. "A dog with a bone until they get answers. If you don't want them nipping at your heels, you might as well come clean."

The metaphor was a bit mixed, but I couldn't disagree.

Looking back over at my eager sisters, I put on my sternest expression. "Okay, listen: you get three questions, so choose wisely."

A lot of groaning greeted my pronouncement, followed by frantic whispering between them as they decided on the questions they wanted to ask. The other men all shot me sympathetic looks but none of them offered to help me out, I noticed. I was completely on my own.

Tonia fired the first shot. As the next oldest child in the family after me, she often claimed precedence over the younger two. "What's her name?"

I'd been expecting that question and could answer it easily. "Nadiya

Varma."

As I watched their mouths drop open, I had to struggle not to burst out laughing. Everyone in Houston knew the name Varma, and even if they hadn't known her from her business, my sisters had heard me ranting about her more than a few times in the last month.

"It must be someone else with the same name," Laura asserted to the other two before turning back to me. "Right, Dex? I thought you hated her."

"I don't think I ever used the word 'hate'," I argued.

Technically, that was true, but I *had* called her a few names as I vented my frustration over her determination and tactics to try to get me to sell the gallery. Hopefully, my sisters wouldn't feel the need to share any of those names with her if and when they met her, but knowing them, it would be the first thing out of their mouths.

"How long have you been seeing each other?" Billie piped up from the back.

That question was a little trickier and I gritted my teeth as I stuck to the story Nadiya had laid out. "Well, we were never really 'seeing each other'. We were in touch about the gallery. I found her annoying and frustrating, that's true, but I couldn't help noticing she's an attractive woman too."

Again, I didn't lie, exactly. I really had been surprised by her that morning at the gallery. She hadn't been at all what I had imagined.

Billie nodded in agreement. "I've seen pictures of her, she's very glamorous. Power is sexy too."

I couldn't say I'd ever really thought so before, but as I thought back to Nadiya sitting behind her desk in her expensive suit, completely in control, I actually felt a little stirring of... desire?

Where the hell did that come from? Damn Billie, putting ideas in my head. That was the last thing I needed to be thinking about when the whole thing was meant to be strictly professional.

"How did it happen?" Laura asked with her last question. "How did you go from arguing over the gallery to being engaged?"

That was the biggest question of all, and the one I really needed to convince them of if they were going to buy the whole story. Sticking as close to the truth as possible would be my best option.

"Like I said: I noticed her. When she's not trying to take over the world, she's not actually that bad." The flashes of vulnerability I'd seen in her and the rather empathetic way she took the news of Shawna's death flashed across my memory, backing up my words. "I guess she noticed me too. When she came to the gallery this morning and told me that she and her boyfriend broke up, a lightbulb clicked. Next thing I knew, we were engaged."

Technically, I hadn't lied, though I'd hardly told the whole story either, and I didn't know if that would be enough to satisfy my nosy family. However, to my surprise, they didn't really question it. If anything, they celebrated instead.

"I knew it!" Tonia told the others smugly. "You heard me saying it, didn't you? All that bickering, all his complaining about her, it was just sexual tension the whole time."

What? Where did they get that idea? Had Tonia really said that?

"She's just his type," Billie agreed. "Someone with strong ideas of her own, won't take no for an answer, it's perfect. If I knew her, I would have set them up myself!"

What the hell? The turn the conversation had taken completely confused me. I guess I did find those things attractive in a woman, but I didn't know my sisters knew that. I'd barely been aware of it myself, and Nadiya Varma was definitely not my 'type'. She couldn't be further from Shawna's warm, friendly, supportive personality, and *that* was my type, assuming I had one.

Billie's words about not taking no for an answer reminded me I needed to tell them about the gallery too. That might be an even bigger shock for them than the engagement.

"I agreed to sell the gallery to her as well," I blurted out. "A Work of Art is temporarily out of business."

In yet another surprise to me, no one looked shocked about that at all. "Well, of course you did, Dex," Tonia said. "It was always the smart move, you were just too stubborn to see it."

Did they all think that? Sure enough, as I looked around the yard, a bunch of heads nodded in agreement.

"Thanks for your support," I muttered sarcastically, and they all laughed.

Laura came over to throw an arm around my shoulders, squeezing me tightly. "Come on, Dex. You know you're not a businessman. You're way too sentimental and she did you a big favour by convincing you to sell. You could have lost it to the bank the way you were going."

When she put it that way, I certainly wasn't going to tell them how close that had come to happening, so I focused on the good news instead. "Nadiya's offered to make space for the gallery in the new building going up on the block, so I'll be able to reopen in the same location in a couple of years. In the meantime, I'll find a temporary spot to set up."

That news delighted everyone even more, and the conversation drifted between my new gallery and my engagement, requiring very little input from me. My sisters were happy to plan out my life between them, as they'd always been.

By the time I begged off, citing a busy day the next day, they were all in good spirits. Cam, Jesse, and Grey, who had all kept quiet while their wives interrogated me, took turns congratulating me and wishing me the best of luck. My mother gave me a long hug and told me again how happy she was for me, and once more, a wave of guilt ran through me. Hopefully, once she met Nadiya for herself, she would see that we weren't actually very well suited for each other at all, and therefore wouldn't be quite so heartbroken when we eventually called our engagement off.

This was going to be quite a balancing act, I thought as I headed back out to my truck and made my way home to my empty house. Hopefully, I could pull it off without letting anyone down.

~Nadiya~

The next day, I found myself glancing at the clock on my wall far more often than usual. Normally, once I got into my work, I lost track of everything else, but that day, my mind kept drifting to the evening ahead and what Dex and I needed to talk about.

I had spent the evening before making a list of the things I thought he should know about me. He said we could simply talk about them, but that seemed unnecessarily complicated. I hoped he had made a list for me that I could study after he was gone. I had never been good with remembering all the minutiae of other peoples' lives. Real estate facts and figures, I could recite off the top of my head, but who in the office had dated who, or which of my employees had gone to which Caribbean island on their vacation? I could never keep it straight and I didn't understand why anyone would want to.

"Ms Varma?" Luisa's voice cut through my thoughts and reminded me that I was, once again, staring off into space.

"Yes?" I quickly grabbed my computer mouse to make it look like I had been doing something productive even though, as the one in charge, I couldn't really get in trouble for slacking off.

"Here are the papers you wanted for your meeting with Mr Callahan tonight." She had a hard time hiding her smile when she said his name as she walked in and set the file folder on the edge of my desk.

"Thank you." I realized after he left my office the day before that we still hadn't signed the agreement, and I didn't know what was wrong with me. I never let anyone out the door after making a deal without getting their signature. It had been one of my most basic rules for as long as I could remember. Why had Dexter Callahan thrown me off my game?

"Mr Davison also left a message for you," she added, watching curiously for my reaction. "He asked you to call him when you get a chance."

'Mr Davison' was Greg, and I couldn't imagine what he'd be calling me about. As far as I was concerned, we had nothing left to say to each other after he walked out on me. "Thank you," I repeated, keeping my expression neutral so she didn't misinterpret it. "Anything else?"

"Just that you should probably leave soon if you want to be home before the catering arrives."

To my surprise, a little flutter of anticipation bubbled up in my stomach... or maybe it was just hunger. In either case, I ignored it, thanked Luisa once more and wished her a good night as I tucked the folder she'd given me into my Louis Vuitton tote bag along with the other work I was taking home for the evening. Supper wouldn't take too long, I imagined, so I should have time to get some other things done to make up for my distraction during the day.

Luisa's warning proved prescient as my driver pulled up outside my house just as the delivery van arrived with the food for the evening. Letting myself in, I directed the delivery person to the kitchen to set everything up while I went to my room and freshened up. The measures I took to get ready were no different than any other business meeting, I told myself as I sprayed on some fresh perfume and touched up my makeup, checking carefully in the mirror for any flaws. Aiming for a more casual look, I removed my suit jacket but kept my short-sleeved jade-green silk blouse and black suit pants on.

When I got back out to the kitchen, the driver had left and the smell of the food made my stomach growl loudly. Had I eaten lunch? Suddenly, I couldn't remember, and the last thing I wanted was to have Dex hear my body making those kinds of noises so I grabbed a bit of avocado that had fallen out of one of the tacos and tossed it daintily into my mouth.

"Couldn't even wait for me to get started, huh?"

Dex's voice nearly made me jump out of my skin as I spun around guiltily.

"How did you get in here?" I asked, my voice unnaturally squeaky as I put my hand to my chest, trying to slow my racing heart.

He stood in the doorway from the front hall, dressed once again in jeans and a t-shirt which was a little less tight than the one he had on the day before. Not that I noticed, I quickly admonished myself. The tattoos on his arms were on full display again, and I would need to remind him to cover those up for the meeting with my father tomorrow.

"Sorry," he apologized, looking genuinely sorry to have startled me. "I walked up just as the fella with the food was leaving, so he let me in. Must have thought I lived here or something."

"Do you usually just walk into someone's house without knocking?" My heart rate had begun to slow, but I still felt off balance. How did he keep doing that to me?

"Honestly? Yeah." He grinned before looking around my kitchen. "But most folks I know don't live in a place like this."

I followed his gaze around the room, just like I had in my office the day before, trying to guess what he was thinking. "It's a Mary Flynn design," I informed him before he could criticize my style again. The best interior designer in Houston and one of the best in the country would have to impress anyone.

He did actually look rather impressed as his eyebrows raised. "Not bad."

"Do you know who that is?" From his response, I couldn't tell.

A smirk crossed his face. "Just because I'm broke doesn't mean I live under a rock. Shawna used to dream about her coming into the gallery and falling in love with my work so that she'd commission pieces for all her projects."

That was a clever idea, actually. It sounded like his wife had some business sense, even if he didn't. I wondered why it had never happened.

"But that *does* explain why it doesn't feel like you," Dex continued, still looking around.

"She designed it especially for me," I countered. I had even had several awkward in-person meetings with her where she tried to understand my 'style personality,' though I didn't think we ever found it. In the end, I told her to do whatever she liked.

Dex's laugh was just as warm as I remembered it. "I'm sure she did, but what I mean is there's nothing 'Nadiya' about it. Like this piece over here: what does that say to you?"

He pointed to an abstract painting on the wall by the breakfast table and I looked at it curiously, really seeing it for the first time in… well, ever, maybe. I'd never paid all that much attention to any of the things on the walls, they were just there to complete the look. "It brightens up the space. Gives it some colour. Weren't you complaining about the lack of colour in my office?"

"Colour's great, but if it doesn't mean anything to you, it might as well be black and white."

This was not the conversation I wanted to be having with him, so I tried to steer it in a different direction. "Are you hungry? Come and grab some food and we can eat outside."

I didn't have to ask him twice. Dex took the plate I offered him and examined the food laid out on the island with great interest. "What do we have here?"

"Avocado tacos, fish tacos and artichoke enchiladas." As I pointed at the various items, I realized that I hadn't asked him what he liked to eat. With Greg, I had never bothered. He simply adjusted to what I ate, so it hadn't even crossed my mind to ask Dex.

To my relief, he smiled. "Sounds interesting," he said as he began to heap things onto his plate. "And it smells great."

It really did. My stomach growled again at the reminder and that time, he definitely heard it. With a laugh, he stepped to the side.

"Sounds like you need it more than me."

I rolled my eyes to hide my embarrassment and we both filled our plates before heading out to my backyard. Large and landscaped with trees, flowers, a winding path and a small pond, it made a lovely change from the modern interior, and Dex looked suitably impressed.

"I'm guessing you don't do all this yourself," he said as he took a seat at the patio table.

The assumption didn't offend me. "No. I've got gardeners who take care of it. What would you like to drink?"

"Beer would be great."

I set my plate down and returned to the kitchen to grab one of Greg's beers out of the fridge. It had been one of the few things he had left at my place, and as I wasn't a beer drinker myself, I was glad enough for Dex to get rid of it for me. Grabbing a glass of crisp white wine for myself, I returned to the backyard where Dex had already begun eating.

"This is really good," he exclaimed with his mouth full as I set the beer down in front of him.

His enthusiasm was actually a bit sweet, but I couldn't help wincing at the thought of him doing that in front of my father. "Rule number one for tomorrow night: take small enough bites that you can answer a question at any time without delay."

He laughed good-naturedly, but when I didn't laugh with him, his eyes widened in disbelief. "Wait, you're serious?"

Of course I was serious. "I learned that as a child. My father would put me to the test, asking me questions as soon as I put something in my mouth to make sure I wouldn't embarrass him."

His disbelieving look melted into something that looked a lot like sympathy. "That doesn't sound like much fun. You never just stuffed a whole hot dog in your face?"

That time, I was the one who laughed, the thought of doing that in front of my father being completely ludicrous. "No. I can honestly say I've never done that."

"You're missing out," he replied, his eyes twinkling in amusement. "But sure, if it means that much to ya, I'll be a perfect gentleman tomorrow."

"It's not me you have to worry about," I warned him. "My father doesn't hold back."

Dex shoved the remainder of his taco in his mouth before giving me a cheeky grin, his mouth full once again. "Alright, lay it on me then, Nadiya. What do I need to know about your daddy?"

Chapter Six

~Dex~

The change in Nadiya's body language when she talked about her father fascinated me. She looked prim and proper at the best of times, but when he came up in conversation, her back straightened even further as she pushed her shoulders back, as if he might suddenly appear and reprimand her for slacking off.

All that despite the fact that she was a grown woman who I would have sworn had never slacked off a day in her whole damn life.

It obviously meant a lot to her that I make a good impression on her father, so, despite my teasing, I intended to do my best. I wouldn't appreciate her showing up in front of my family and behaving in a way that would make me look bad, so I wasn't about to do the same to her, even if the definitions of 'appropriate behaviour' might differ wildly between our two families.

Therefore, when I asked her to explain what I needed to know about having dinner with her father, I was being completely sincere, even though Nadiya gave me a suspicious look that suggested she didn't quite believe it.

She answered my question anyway. "The less you say, the better. I can get him started on one of his favourite topics and we won't have to say much. Just nod and call him 'sir', and whatever you do, don't go quoting city regulations about zoning laws."

A smile spread across my face before I could stop it. That had been one of my favourite emails I sent her when we were arguing about the gallery sale. Every time she sent me a new message encouraging me to think about the benefits of selling, I tried to come up with the most irritating responses I could think of. For that one, I had a friend who worked for the city council give me all kinds of obscure facts to bolster my case about why my little gallery was better suited to the area than her massive development.

Apparently, she appreciated it about as much as I hoped she would, which was not at all.

Returning to what she said about how to behave around her father, her response only heightened my curiosity. "Is that what your last boyfriend did? Nodded and called him 'sir'?"

I didn't mean it as a compliment but Nadiya nodded anyway, looking almost proud. "He knew just how to boost Daddy's ego without making it obvious. It's a skill."

It didn't sound like a skill I was particularly interested in having, nor did it sound like Mr Varma's ego was in any need of inflating. "I can tell you right now, I ain't blowing smoke up anyone's ass. I can be polite and I can be quiet, if that's what you want, but I'm not going to compliment him unless he's done something worth complimenting."

She took a deep breath. "Fine. Polite and quiet will work. What are you planning to wear?"

Her message came through loud and clear: what I had on that evening wouldn't be appropriate, apparently. Nadiya didn't waste any time on subtlety, so I put the question back to her: "What do you want me to wear?"

Her eyes quickly scanned me, lingering just a moment longer than necessary on my chest before returning to my face. "No jeans. Dress pants and a long-sleeved shirt. He doesn't like tattoos so please cover those up. If you don't have anything appropriate to wear, I can have something sent to you."

Exactly how much of a neanderthal did she think I was? "I own dress clothes, Nadiya. I'll be fine."

Again, she gave me that slightly suspicious look as if I couldn't be trusted, but she didn't argue. "Good. Then the only other things you really need to know are to be on time, don't speak with your mouth full, and don't say anything negative about cricket."

"Cricket?" I repeated curiously. "The sport?"

She nodded again. Her neck muscles must have been very strong with all the nodding she did. "Daddy's one of the men behind the Houston Cricket League, and he loves it. It's the only thing other than work he's ever cared about."

Well, that was something to go on at least. Maybe I could brush up a little on the game before supper the next day. I didn't know anything about it, but I followed enough other sports that I should be able to pick it up. How difficult could it be?

It took a moment longer for her last words to sink in: she said cricket was the only thing he cared about other than work, but surely she meant other than his family too?

"Do you have brothers or sisters?" I asked, figuring that was also something I should know.

Rather than her usual nod, Nadiya shook her head. "No, it's just me. My mother... well, I won't go into the details, but my delivery did not go well and she wasn't able to have any more children. It devastated my father since he'd always wanted a son to carry on the family business."

"But you're doing that," I pointed out. Plainly, a son hadn't been necessary.

"Yes. I was the next best thing." She smiled as she said it, but I got the feeling she didn't mean it entirely as a joke. Either way, she quickly changed the subject before I could ask her any more about it. "What about you? Do you have siblings?"

The memory of the family barbecue the night before made me smile. "Three sisters," I told her, my smile growing as her eyes widened in surprise. "They're dying to meet you, by the way."

"You already told them about me?"

"I had supper with them last night, so I figured I might as well get it out of the way. They all know we're engaged and so does my mother."

She continued to stare at me, unblinking, and I gave her a curious look in response.

"We were meant to tell people, weren't we? I thought that's the whole point of this."

"Of course." She quickly pasted on a smile that looked a little too practiced. "I'm sorry. It just suddenly seems more real now that there are other people involved."

I knew exactly what she meant. Seeing the response from my mother in particular had made it all seem like less of a game.

"Why don't you explain to me exactly why we're doing this?" She'd told me a few things, but not enough that it really made sense to me.

We finished eating while Nadiya explained the situation with the Varma Corporation board. I leaned back with my beer as she got to the conversation she'd had with her director at the office the day before and how he already knew about her breakup.

"Definitely sounds like you need to watch your back with that guy, but I still think the whole thing is messed up. Nobody's got any right to tell you how to live your life that way."

"It is messed up," she agreed readily, the words sounding a little funny in her posh accent. "But at least it's only temporary. Once I'm CEO, it will be much harder for them to remove me without a valid business reason."

"And when's this vote supposed to be happening?" She had been pretty vague on the timeline so far.

"In about four weeks. We just have to fool everyone until then, and maybe a little longer so that it's not completely obvious it was a scam."

That was a good point. If we broke up the day after she got promoted, people could get rightfully suspicious. "What would happen if we were found out?"

Nadiya's grimace looked out of place on her pretty face. "Well, if they found out before the vote, I could kiss the promotion goodbye, not to mention the embarrassment of having everyone know I had to pretend to have a man."

With every bit of tension in her body, I could see how much this all meant to her. The stakes were high and she certainly had a lot to lose, so she had every reason to take it seriously. I understand that, but I still felt a little less clear on what it would mean for me.

"What about our deal? Is it contingent on you getting the job?"

She looked surprised that I would ask. "Of course not. I asked you to pretend to be engaged to me. As long as you don't deliberately sabotage it, I won't hold you responsible if it fails."

To be quite honest, that was more scrupulous than I had expected her to be. She continued to surprise me.

"Alright." I gave her what I hoped felt like a supportive smile. "In that case, I guess we better get to work."

~Nadiya~

The next evening, the perfectly styled and naturally beautiful hostess at Ristorante Cavour greeted me with a smile. "Ms Varma, it's a pleasure to see you again. Your father is already seated."

All the top restaurants in the city knew me and my father. We regularly dined with clients, together or separately, and we spared no expense. That was another of my father's business rules: people feel more comfortable making deals with someone who looks like they don't need your business at all.

"Has the other party arrived yet?" I asked as she stepped out from behind the desk to show me to the table. "Mr Callahan?"

"No, ma'am, not yet, but I'll show him in just as soon as he gets here."

Glancing down at my watch, I could see we still had five minutes to go, but I also knew that to my father, a second late was the same as ten minutes late. It showed a lack of respect for the other person's time, and if Dex arrived late, I didn't know how we were going to...

"Right behind you," a voice whispered in my ear, making me jump.

"Stop doing that!" I squeaked, my heart racing just as fast as it had when he surprised me in my kitchen the night before. Maybe he'd only agreed to this whole arrangement with me so he could give me a heart attack.

"Sorry," Dex apologized, but the amusement in his voice told me he didn't really mean it. "You're a little tightly wound, darlin'. We better get in there and get you a drink."

Ready to give him a reminder about not calling me darlin', I turned around, but the words died in my throat as I got a full look at him.

He had obviously made an effort. He actually wore a suit, for one thing, black with a deep blue shirt and perfectly-matched tie. He'd shaved recently, the five o'clock shadow I'd seen on him the previous two days nowhere in evidence, and his hair had been slicked back rather than being slightly tousled like the other times I'd seen him.

He looked damn good, I had to admit, though to my surprise, I actually kind of preferred the scruffier version.

The night before, after dinner, I gave him my list that I'd prepared, and once he stopped laughing about the fact that I *had* made a list, we went through it together. He was now armed with at least a basic list of my most pertinent likes, dislikes and facts about my life. He had *not* made a list, which didn't surprise me, but I asked him some questions and wrote down his answers so I could study them later, which I had done before bed and again on my lunch break at work so that I felt confident I could recite them from memory if needed.

We were going to be fine, I told myself. I had never lied to my father before, so he had no reason to suspect I would. We could do this.

"Do I pass inspection?" Dex asked me, pulling me out of my thoughts and drawing my attention back to his appearance again.

"You'll do," I replied, unwilling to admit just how good he actually looked. I hardly needed to though, not with the way the hostess eyed him up at the same time. When I raised my eyebrows at her, she instantly blushed as she realized I'd caught her checking out my date. "We're ready now."

"Of course, Ms Varma," she said, immediately snapping back to her professional demeanour. "This way."

As I began to follow her, Dex placed his hand on the small of my back and I immediately stiffened in surprise.

"Relax," he whispered in my ear, his breath hot against my skin. "Remember, we're supposed to like each other."

Right. My fiancé was allowed to touch me. Greg had made that same gesture a thousand times before.

Why did it feel so different when Dex did it?

The hostess led us through the restaurant where multiple pairs of eyes tracked our progress. I smiled and nodded at a few people I recognized, and I could see the curiosity in their acknowledgements, wondering who the man with me might be.

They would all know soon enough, but first, we had to tell my father.

"Hello, Daddy," I greeted him as we arrived at the table and the hostess excused herself. He was reading a newspaper, one of many he read during the day, keeping up on the day's business around the world. Retirement was a concept he hadn't quite grasped yet.

"Nadiya." He gave me his 'client smile' as he set the paper back on the table and stood up to kiss my cheek. That was for show too. He never did it when we were alone. "And this is Mr Callahan?"

When Luisa had arranged the supper for me, I'd asked her to tell my father that we were dining with Dex because of the deal we'd agreed, a way to celebrate finally reaching a solution on our impasse over the gallery. The other, far more personal, reason, had been left out, since I figured it would be better left to the in-person conversation.

"Daddy, this is Dexter Callahan. Dex, my father, Samesh Varma."

"Mr Varma." Dex stepped forward confidently, giving my father a firm handshake that I could tell impressed him.

That was a good start.

My father gestured to the other chairs, and Dex quickly moved over to pull my chair out for me, another gesture I hadn't expected from him. When I gave him a grateful smile, he winked at me, and my stomach almost seemed to flutter.

How strange. It must have been nerves over the upcoming conversation, nothing more.

When we were all seated, my father addressed Dex. "I must say, I was a bit surprised to learn that you had finally agreed to sell, Mr Callahan."

The rebuke in his words couldn't be clearer to me: it had taken far too long to come to an agreement and the fault for that lay at my feet. Before I could offer any kind of defense, though, Dex surprised me by speaking up first. "I was mighty attached to my gallery, Mr Varma, but Nadiya was very persuasive. She made me an offer I couldn't refuse."

He couldn't have phrased it any better, and my father looked suitably impressed. A tiny bit of tension left my shoulders.

"I made her an offer too, and I was delighted when she agreed," Dex continued, and immediately, my shoulders tightened again.

Now? *Already?* We hadn't even gotten our drinks yet, and I could definitely use one. The whole thing had been my idea, but at that moment, sitting there across from my father, it suddenly seemed impossible that we could actually pull it off.

My daddy looked over at me curiously, not having a clue what Dex was referring to. "What kind of offer?"

When I glanced at Dex, he gave me an encouraging smile, and when I hesitated, he reached out and took my hand beneath the table, his fingers squeezing mine supportively. "Do you want to tell him, or should I?"

How could he be so calm, and so good at this?

"No, I should." I gave his hand a gentle squeeze in return to show I appreciated the offer, noting how warm his hand felt against mine, and the roughness of the calluses on his fingers. He did say he worked with his hands, I remembered, and my cheeks grew redder at the reminder.

Focus, Nadiya.

"Daddy, there have been some big changes since the last time we talked," I offered as an opening.

My father's curious look turned slightly confused. "Since two days ago?"

I nodded. "Yes. I didn't get a chance to tell you then, but Greg and I broke up. We aren't seeing each other anymore."

A look of genuine dismay crossed his face, and I knew it had far less to do with him regretting Greg's absence in our lives than it did with what we had discussed in my office the last time we'd seen each other. His first thought was about how my breakup would affect the board's vote.

He clearly had a lot of things he wanted to say, but he held himself back because of Dex's presence, his eyes darting to the man beside me. Even so, his lips pursed in disapproval. "Nadiya, this isn't really the appropriate time for this conversation. We can discuss it later."

"Actually, it's the perfect time," I countered, lifting my hand that held Dex's onto the table, and my father's jaw nearly dropped as he took in the sight of our entwined hands. I had rarely seen him caught so off guard, so I pressed ahead while I had his full attention. "Dex asked me to marry him, and I said yes. We're engaged."

Dex beamed at me, looking every inch the proud fiancé, and I couldn't help marvelling at how naturally this all came to him. Maybe he'd taken acting classes at some point in his past? He was truly full of surprises.

I did my best to smile back and match his expression before turning to my father to focus on his reaction.

He was shocked, there could be no doubt of it, but he quickly covered it up, his years of practice at keeping a poker face coming in handy. "Well, this is certainly a surprise. We'll have to get some champagne."

He motioned to the waiter who came over immediately and took the drink order. Dex and I both stayed silent, waiting for the inevitable questions that would follow. I knew my daddy: this was a stalling tactic to give him time to think. The onslaught would still be coming.

I'd rehearsed my lines already, I reminded myself. Anything he might ask, I'd have an answer for it.

Or so I thought, but in all my preparation for the evening, I had forgotten one very basic thing.

"So," my father said, turning back to both of us. "It appears we have a lot to discuss. But first, beta, show me the ring."

~Dex~

Nadiya's face paled as her father asked to see her ring, and I had to press my lips together to keep from teasing her about it, trying not to laugh. I'd expected her to be a far better liar than she'd turned out to be.

As a hard-nosed businesswoman, she must have had experience of bending the truth to get what she wanted, but ever since we'd sat down with her father, she'd looked like she was only a few seconds away from being sick. I supposed it must be different when she had to lie to her own father, and after my experience with my own family, I could understand that.

When I reached out to hold her hand to try to keep her calm, it surprised me how neatly and comfortably her hand fit into mine. I'd tried holding hands with a few other women since Shawna – not many, but a few – and it had always felt awkward. With Nadiya, it must have been different because we weren't trying to be romantic. The gesture simply showed support between friends.

The idea that I could call Nadiya Varma a friend of mine still struck me as very odd, but what else could I call us? Business acquaintances? Co-conspirators? Friend had a nicer ring to it.

So, when she turned to me with a look of panic in her eyes, I simply gave her a teasing smile back before turning to her father.

"You've kind of stolen my thunder, Mr Varma. Nadiya hasn't actually seen the ring yet. I was going to give it to her later tonight."

She exhaled in relief, thinking I'd said that as an excuse for why she didn't have the ring on her, and it would have been a decent lie on its own too, except for the fact that I actually meant it.

Letting go of her hand, I reached into my pocket and pulled out the ring I'd had made earlier that day. One of the perks of being an artist in a city the size of Houston was that we all got to know the other artists and artisans pretty well. We weren't that big of a community, and one of the good friends I'd made at various trade fairs was a goldsmith named Max. When I let him know I needed a ring urgently, he'd been kind enough to drop everything and spend a few hours making it for me. I'd done him a few favours over the years, including painting a wedding portrait for him and his wife, and he insisted on making me the ring free of charge.

It didn't have a flashy diamond or anything, but I'd designed it with her in mind and I hoped it would be okay.

Nadiya's eyes widened in genuine surprise as she got sight of the ring in my hand. "Dex, I wasn't expecting…"

I couldn't guess for certain what the next words out of her mouth would be, but in her surprise, she might have forgotten that her father could hear every word, so I quickly cut her off. "… it to be ready so quickly? I know, but I put a rush on it. I couldn't wait any longer."

I held my hand out for her left hand, and she gently placed it on top of mine as I slid the ring onto her finger. I'd had to guess at her size, but it fit almost perfectly, to my relief.

"Is that a lotus flower?" she asked, leaning down to take a closer look at the delicate symbol etched into the top of the ring.

"Exactly," I confirmed, pleased that she recognized it right away. "It's a symbol of strength. The lotus has to push through the muddy waters where it grows until it reaches the surface and blooms. Just like how you always push through any obstacles to rise to the top."

When she looked up at me, her eyes were full of confusion. "You really had this made for me?"

"Of course," I replied, flashing her father a smile before looking back at her. "You deserve something as unique as you are."

Still looking a little unsure, she lifted her hand from mine and held it up, examining the ring under the light. A soft smile crossed her face for just a second, but almost as quickly, her eyes darted around the room and her hand quickly dropped back to the table. When I turned to see what had caught her attention, I found several people looking in our direction, all of whom had clearly just seen me put the ring on her finger.

Well, she wanted our engagement to be public. Looked like we were making a start on that right away.

"Let me see it, beta," her father instructed, and Nadiya obediently held out her hand to him. He took hold of her fingers and pulled her slightly closer, making her shift awkwardly forward in her seat. I reached out a hand to steady her as her father squinted down at the ring to see the etching. "It is different, certainly. If you want a diamond added, I'm sure that could be arranged."

Apparently, he didn't think it showy enough to be suitable for his daughter. Nadiya had warned me he wouldn't hesitate to voice his disapproval, but she surprised me by immediately declining the offer. "A diamond would ruin it, Daddy. It's perfect just as it is."

I happened to agree.

"14 karat gold?" Mr Varma asked, looking over at me critically.

Who honestly asked that, especially in front of the ring's recipient? Besides which, he didn't know what he was talking about anyway, and I did my best to keep my smile polite. "20, sir."

Since he had no rebuttal for that, he turned to his daughter once again. "As long as you're happy with it, Nadiya, I suppose it will do."

"I am," she assured him before turning and giving me a warm, grateful smile. She really was rather stunning when she smiled, I couldn't help noticing. "Thank you, Dex."

"You're very welcome. Now, is it alright if we order? I'm starving."

After running around to sort out the ring and my work packing up the gallery, I really was hungry and I'd been looking forward to this meal. I'd never eaten there before but the people I knew who had all raved about it.

Menus were distributed and I forced myself not to pay any attention to the prices. Between the champagne and meal for the three of us, this meal was going to cost more than I made in a week, and a good week at that. Not wanting to put a foot wrong, I simply copied Nadiya's order: roasted salmon with asparagus and sautéed garlic spinach, while Mr Varma ordered the lobster tails.

"Tell me about yourself, Mr Callahan," Nadiya's father invited once the orders had been taken. "You run a gallery."

"He doesn't just run it," Nadiya interjected before I could reply. "He creates the work they sell. Dex is a very talented artist, Daddy."

Very talented? I couldn't guess what she was basing that on since I hadn't seen her look at anything in my gallery other than the paint that had ended up on her suit.

"A painter?" Mr Varma asked, his tone clearly indicating he didn't see it as a positive thing.

"And sculptor, and potter," I answered calmly. My work might not earn me much, but it brought colour and beauty to people's lives, and that was way more important to me. No one was going to make me feel bad about it.

Nadiya turned to me curiously. "That reminds me: I wanted to ask you about the sculpture in the gallery window. It's beautiful. Is there any chance I could buy it?"

I hadn't realized she'd noticed it, and she was the second person that week to make an offer on it. However, my answer remained the same. "I'm sorry, that one's not for sale. It's mine."

"Surely, it belongs to you both, then," Mr Varma pointed out. "Nadiya doesn't need to buy it."

He had a point: if we were getting married, everything mine would be hers. Neither of us could contradict that.

"When will you be moving into Nadiya's?" Mr Varma asked next, just assuming I would move into her place. Even though her house *was* a significant step up from mine, he didn't know that and the presumption irked me.

"We're not rushing, Daddy," Nadiya answered for me again. "We'll wait until after the wedding to move in together."

That should be safe enough. Since there would never be a wedding, the move would never happen.

"That was my next question," her father replied, his eyes sharp as he looked between the two of us. "When exactly is the big day?"

~**Nadiya**~

Something in my father's expression when he asked for the date of the wedding had me worried.

He was getting suspicious, but I wasn't sure why. I thought we had done a pretty good job so far. Well, to be fair, I had done an okay job and Dex had done an amazing job; together, it averaged out as pretty good.

I still couldn't believe he actually had a ring for me. And not just any ring, but an absolutely stunning one made specifically with me in mind. When he explained the meaning of the lotus flower, I felt... well, I couldn't even explain how I felt. I'd never felt anything exactly like it before, like someone truly saw me and appreciated me simply for who I was.

My strength, that ability to push through obstacles that he'd described, was seen by most men as unfeminine, undesirable in a woman, and therefore something I needed to hide. Greg had certainly never celebrated my tenacity. If anything, he told me to tone it down, especially in front of others.

But Dex not only seemed to see it as a positive thing, he had it engraved right there on the ring for the whole world to see.

My throat grew tighter as I looked at it, and if he'd given it to me as part of a real proposal, I might have actually cried, which was saying something. I couldn't remember the last time I cried about anything.

I would have to find a way to thank him for it, but first, I needed to focus on my father's questions, putting on my best reassuring smile, the one I used for clients when I wanted to convince them that everything I suggested was in their best interests.

"We're still working out all the details, Daddy. This is all very new."

"I assumed so," he replied, still looking at me critically. "Is this why you and Greg ended things?"

I recognized the danger that people would jump to that conclusion, so I tried to nip that idea in the bud. "No, not at all. Greg decided to end our relationship, and I'm sure he'll make that perfectly clear to anyone who asks. After I told Dex what happened, he admitted he had been interested in me the whole time. I had noticed him too but hadn't done anything about it because I was already with Greg. Once Greg and I were no longer together, things just kind of happened from there."

I glanced over at Dex to see if he had any problem with me going with that version of events, and he gave me a slightly mischievous smile. "That's right. No matter how hard I tried, Nadiya kept pushing her way into my thoughts."

Obviously, he meant our exchanged emails, but hopefully, my father wouldn't pick up on that.

Luckily, he didn't leave it there. "When she suddenly became available, I knew I couldn't waste my chance. It wouldn't be long before someone else saw just how amazing she is, so I decided to go all out and propose to her right then and there. Happily for me, she said yes."

That answer couldn't have been more perfect as far as I was concerned, and I thanked my lucky stars again that I had picked someone to do this with me who was so quick on his feet. I wouldn't have made it sound half as good.

My father, however, still needed some convincing. "If you're that anxious to tie her down, you'll want to get married as soon as possible."

Why was he being like that? For the first time, Dex looked a bit flummoxed, and I didn't blame him. Something lay behind my father's line of questioning and I needed to find out what it was.

"Dex, would you mind giving my father and I a moment alone?"

A flash of relief crossed his face. "Of course. I'll be back soon."

He stood up and wandered off as I turned to my father, lowering my voice. "Obviously, you have something to say to me, so just say it."

"This is a ridiculous idea," he hissed at me, keeping his voice low as well so we wouldn't be overheard. "A fake engagement, Nadiya? Everyone will see right through it. You couldn't be more unsuited for each other."

My heart sank at the word 'fake' and kept going lower with every subsequent word. How had he figured us out? Was he going to pull the plug on the whole idea? And what did he mean that Dex and I were unsuited to each other? It seemed awfully quick to have jumped to that conclusion.

Whatever the reason, there didn't seem much point in lying any further. "Alright, Daddy, it's true. It's not real, but you're the one who told me I needed to be engaged! And Greg did leave me, that's not a lie. What else am I supposed to do?"

Triumph flashed in his eyes as I admitted he was right, accompanied by a bit of pride. "It's not a terrible idea, Nadiya. Honestly, I'm impressed with your creativity, but if you want it to work, you should pick someone more believable. Nobody will buy that a woman like you would be satisfied with a man like that, or a ring like that."

His lips curled into a sneer as he gestured to the beautiful gold band on my finger, and anger bubbled up inside me.

Had my father always been such a snob and I'd just never noticed it before?

"I love the ring," I told him honestly. "And there's nothing unbelievable about the idea that Dex and I would be together. He's a very handsome man, he's talented, and he's kind. He's everything any woman would want in a partner."

I hadn't realized I thought that until I said it out loud, but once I had, I couldn't deny the truth of it. Other than his stubbornness and his insistence on calling me darlin', I hadn't really found any serious flaws in him yet.

"His business is failing," my father pointed out. "Is that why he's doing this? So you'll bail him out?"

He was far too perceptive, and when I didn't immediately reply, he knew he'd hit the nail on the head.

"You can do better, beta. Let me help you. I can find you a nice, professional man who will do this charade with you, if that's what you want. As I said, it's not a bad idea, it just needs some fine-tuning."

"No, Daddy." I couldn't say who was more surprised at my outright refusal: him or me. "I've already chosen Dex and he's already told his family that we're engaged. What would he say to them if I changed my mind now?"

"That's not really your problem. He shouldn't have done that until you knew if it would work."

Did he really think I was so selfish that I wouldn't consider Dex's announcement to his family as my problem? I didn't like the picture my father was painting of me.

"It *will* work," I insisted. "If we have your backing, no one will question it."

He groaned in disapproval, but I pushed ahead anyway.

"People might be suspicious if it comes from me, but if you make it clear that you were aware of it and that you approve, no one will dare to disagree."

"It's dangerous, beta," he warned me. "If Brad Sherwood finds out…"

"He won't. We'll be careful. Dex is committed to making this work, as you can see."

I flashed the ring on my finger at him and my father sighed, looking away from me as he turned things over in his head. My stomach twisted anxiously as I waited for his verdict, but finally, he turned back to me and inclined his head slightly. "Alright, fine. If you are determined to go down this path, then I will support you."

Satisfaction and relief flowed through me until he opened his mouth once more.

"To avoid all suspicion, though, an engagement won't be enough, Nadiya. With Greg, that was one thing; everyone has seen you together for years. But turning up with a new man out of the blue, especially one so unlike your previous partner? There will be questions."

I knew he had a point, but I didn't know what solution he had in mind. "What do you suggest?"

He smiled as if he'd just been waiting for me to ask. "If you really want this to work, you're going to have to get married."

~Dex~

As I walked back to the table where Nadiya and Mr Varma were still talking, I did my best to gauge the mood. There had been a definite shift in the atmosphere earlier. At first, our announcement surprised Nadiya's father, but that surprise had turned to suspicion and I couldn't exactly say why. Hopefully, Nadiya had been able to smooth over whatever had gone wrong.

The food arrived at the table at almost exactly the same time I did, so I waited until everyone had been served before diving into the conversation I'd prepared for earlier. If nothing else got Mr Varma to warm up to me, hopefully this would.

"Have you been following the action from Lord's, Mr Varma?"

As I hoped, he looked over at me in surprise, and so did Nadiya.

"Dex…" she began, sounding like she wanted to warn me off, but I gave her a reassuring wink. She must have been worried I would say something wrong about her father's favourite sport, but I had actually done my homework. All day while I packed up the gallery, I listened to podcasts on my phone that explained how cricket worked, including a detailed rundown of the current ongoing test match between India and England taking place at Lord's Cricket Ground in London.

I could pull this off.

"Yes, of course," Mr Varma replied, looking at me curiously. "Have you?"

"A little bit." I figured asking him to explain things to me would be a good way to go. He seemed the type of man who liked to show off his knowledge. "I'm fairly new to the game, so I'm sure you know more than I do. Is England's batting always that unreliable?"

For the first time, he actually smiled at me. We traded observations about the match for a couple of minutes, and I could mostly follow everything he said and managed to hold my own pretty well, but for some reason, Nadiya grew more and more agitated beside me with each passing second. She hadn't even touched her meal yet even though her father and I were both nearly halfway through.

"Daddy," she finally burst out as her father launched into a lecture on the virtues of India's bowlers. "Don't you think we have more important things to talk about right now?"

He gave her a bemused look as he cracked open one of his lobster tails. "Just because you never understood cricket doesn't make it unimportant, beta. Besides, I'm sure you and your fiancé can work out the details between you and send me the date. I don't need to be involved in the planning."

The way he said the word 'fiancé' had me a bit concerned. I could practically see the quotes around the word as it came out of his mouth. What exactly had I missed? "Nadiya?"

She put both her hands in her lap, but from where I sat, I could see her squeezing the top of her right index finger with her left hand. She had done that before, I remembered, the first morning she came to my gallery, when she suggested this whole engagement idea to me in the first place. It must be a sign of nerves, but I didn't know what she had to be nervous about at that exact moment.

"He knows, Dex," she murmured quietly, glancing up at me anxiously from beneath her pretty eyelashes. "He knows about our agreement."

What? I'd only been gone for five minutes, how did things fall apart that quickly? I glanced over at Mr Varma, expecting him to be angry about being lied to, but instead, he still had the same slightly amused look on his face.

"I'm happy to go along with it, for Nadiya's sake, but as I just explained to her, an engagement is not going to be sufficient. For this to really be believable, you'll need to actually get married."

My gaze returned to Nadiya, expecting her to tell me that was a joke, but she just tightened her lips in discomfort, not meeting my eye.

"That's not exactly what we discussed, darlin'," I couldn't help pointing out.

"I know," she agreed, her eyes finally connecting with mine, with a pleading look. "But it doesn't really change that much, does it? It would still all be just for show. We could have a simple ceremony at City Hall. You could move in with me for a little while, for the sake of appearances, but you don't have to sell your house or anything. My house is big enough for the both of us. Your time would still be your own other than when I need you for events, and when it's over, we could get an annulment if you wanted to."

She rambled as she tried to justify her request, the words tumbling over each other out of her mouth in their rush to get out, so I reached over and put my hand on top of hers to calm her down. "Nadiya. Do you really want to do this?"

The physical contact seemed to ground her and she took a deep breath. "I want the job," she answered simply but with determination, her face taking on the steely look I'd come to associate with her most of all. "I'll do whatever it takes."

I knew that much about her already, and though I didn't understand her business, I had no doubt she was completely qualified for the job. It still seemed ludicrous to me that her relationship status should be part of the equation at all.

With Nadiya's feelings made clear, I looked back over at her father who watched the two of us carefully. "And you really think this is necessary?"

"It will limit any unnecessary rumours or speculation," he said with a shrug. "Perhaps it won't eliminate them entirely, but it will be less pressure for you both in the long run."

"I know it's a lot to ask," Nadiya added. "But I think he has a point. What do you think?"

What *did* I think? I had never imagined getting married again. Images of my wedding day with Shawna flitted across my mind: the picture-perfect day under the Texas sky on her parents' ranch, seeing her in her dress for the first time, exchanging our vows, dancing beneath the stars as evening faded into night.

Nothing could ever compare to that so I'd never expected to try.

But we weren't really talking about anything like that. This was no fairy tale love story. We'd go to City Hall, say a few words, sign a piece of paper, and that would be it.

Seen that way, that bit didn't really bother me. What *did* worry me was how my family would react. Getting engaged was one thing, but actually letting them believe we'd gotten married would be something else. My parents had always been big believers in not giving up on something once you'd committed to it. A lot of my stubbornness came from my mom, so how would I explain it to her when I called it quits on my marriage just a few months into it?

I supposed I could always claim temporary insanity. Everyone knew I was a bit of a romantic at heart, so I could probably convince them that I got so caught up in the moment, I let myself get carried away. We'd already set the stage for that with our whirlwind engagement. Then, in a few months, once reality set in, I could explain how it had all been a mistake.

It just might work, but to completely sell it, we'd have to move fast. If it seemed like we'd put *any* thought into it at all, that would work against me.

"Alright, I'm in," I told her, seeing the relief wash over Nadiya's face as I said the words. "On one condition."

She nodded before I even named it. "What is it?"

"We get married tomorrow."

~Nadiya~

My father had to pull a few strings to get the usual 72-hour waiting period waived, but luckily for us, money talked. My father's considerable social capital played a role as well, and the next afternoon found the two of us in a car, pulling up to City Hall where a Justice of the Peace waited to make the whole thing official.

Officially fake, I supposed.

Luisa couldn't hide her curiosity when I asked her to cancel my meetings for the afternoon, especially when I emerged from my private bathroom wearing the off-white Versace dress I had chosen for the occasion. I didn't want to go with anything that screamed 'wedding', but I also didn't want to turn up in my regular work clothes either. A wedding was a special day, even if it wasn't for real.

The whiteness of the dress made the gold ring on my finger shine even brighter and Luisa couldn't take her eyes off it as I made sure she had all the instructions she needed for the afternoon. "Is that a new ring, Ms Varma? It's beautiful."

It really was gorgeous. I had caught myself admiring it a few times already that day. Every time I looked at it, I thought of Dex and what he'd said when he gave it to me, and it made me smile. My lips started to curl again as Luisa brought it up, but I caught myself just in time. "It is. I have to go now, but I promise I'll tell you about it on Monday."

Dex and I had agreed not to say anything about the wedding ahead of time. He insisted it would be better if it seemed like a spur-of-the-moment thing, and I happily agreed to any stipulations he requested since he was making such a huge concession by agreeing to the wedding in the first place. Besides, I knew that Luisa would spread the word of my new ring around the office anyway, so by the time our wedding announcement came, everyone would be primed for it already.

My father already waited in the car outside when I got downstairs. Dex and I were each supposed to bring one witness along, and my father was my obvious choice. I asked if Dex would be bringing someone from his family, but he said that 'wouldn't work', whatever that meant. He planned to bring a friend, while I brought my father since he already knew about the whole thing anyway.

After I settled into the back of the car and gave the driver instructions to take us downtown, I turned to my father. "It's been bugging me since last night, Daddy. What gave us away? How did you know Dex and I weren't really together?"

I didn't ask simply out of curiosity. If I had done something wrong, I wanted to know so that I didn't make the same mistake in front of other people. For this to work, it had to be as convincing as possible.

My father smiled at me in the slightly patronizing way he did whenever he knew more than I did. "The way you looked at him when he gave you that ring, beta. It was too much. I've watched you with other men for years and you never looked at them like that. Next time you want to pretend to be impressed by something he does, just tone it down a little."

I hadn't expected that answer, mostly because I hadn't been pretending at all. As far as I could remember, I hadn't been thinking about trying to fool anyone at that moment. All I had felt was sincere gratitude for Dex's thoughtful gift.

Was I normally so closed off that when I showed some genuine emotion, it looked fake to those who knew me best?

When we got to City Hall, Dex already stood outside, wearing the same suit from the night before but with a white shirt and an understated cornflower blue tie that drew attention to his blue eyes. He really was a very attractive man, and I couldn't quite stop my smile as I caught sight of him. I could think of a few women in my social circle who were going to be green with envy when they found out about us, not knowing that there was nothing romantic between us at all.

Another man stood next to him, and as we got out of the car, Dex introduced him to me as Max. "He's the one who made your ring and the accompanying wedding band."

My heart immediately sank into my Manolo Blahnik shoes. I had completely forgotten we would be exchanging rings as part of the ceremony. How many times had I looked down at the ring on my finger and never once thought about what I would give Dex? What was wrong with me?

"Don't worry, darlin'," Dex laughed, giving me a wink. "He gave me one you could give me too."

My cheeks flushed red as I mumbled my thanks, burning with embarrassment over how easily he could read me, not to mention my shame over having forgotten the ring in the first place. Normally, organization was my strong suit, but around Dex, it seemed to disappear.

With the rings settled, the four of us made our way inside together where we were greeted by a clerk who had obviously been waiting for us. "Mr Varma," he greeted my father first. "It's such a pleasure to have you here today."

My father liked to make donations to politicians on both sides of the fence so that whichever side won, he would have some influence, and clearly, his strategy had paid off. We were quickly ushered into a small waiting room and told that it would only be a few minutes' wait. My father took a seat, pulling out his phone to check on the markets while Max excused himself to find the restroom.

"You still feeling okay about this?" Dex asked me quietly once we were alone.

"Yes," I answered truthfully. I certainly didn't want to back out now. "Are you?"

"It's not how I thought I'd be ending my week back on Monday," he pointed out with a laugh. "But I can't say it's not an adventure."

That was one word for it, anyway.

"Is everything packed up at the gallery?" He had told me the night before that he had almost finished and would be arranging movers soon. I had offered him my garage to convert into a makeshift studio while he stayed with me. I didn't own a car anyway since I never drove myself anywhere.

As I asked, I realized yet again that I still hadn't had him sign the papers for the gallery sale. Honestly, what was wrong with my head? The whole fake engagement and wedding business had really thrown me off my game. Soon, though, Dex would be at my house full time anyway, so there would be plenty of opportunities to take care of all the paperwork. Having forgotten until now was an annoyance but not a real problem.

"It's ready to go," he confirmed. "You really sure you're up for me invading your space?"

I had no easy answer for that. I'd never lived with anyone, not since I moved out of my father's house, and even when I lived there, we rarely saw each other. The house was so big and he was so busy, I saw the staff far more than I saw him.

I had never lived with any of my boyfriends simply because the idea of having them around constantly had never appealed to me.

However, Dex and I wouldn't be sharing a room or meals, or even any real time together. We would simply be two people living under the same roof who would say hello to each other if we happened to run into each other, and who would sometimes go out in public together. There was nothing more to it than that, so it would be okay. I'd managed to convince myself of that.

"It will be fine. I'm sure we can survive a few months without wanting to kill each other."

"That sounds like a challenge, Nadiya," he replied with a teasing gleam in his eye. "Don't tempt me."

Before I could reply, the door opened and we were called into the office, Max returning just in time to join us.

The ceremony was all very formal and unromantic, just as it should have been. No need to complicate things with emotions. The Justice of the Peace asked me if I took Dex as my lawfully wedded husband, with no unnecessary flowery language to accompany it, and I gave my assent. Dex did the same. We exchanged the rings that Max provided, mine a lovely delicate gold circle that nestled perfectly next to my engagement ring, and Dex's a wide, plain gold band.

As I held his hand in mine to slip the ring on, feeling his calloused fingers again, an odd fluttering sensation took hold in my stomach, almost like I'd felt the night before at the restaurant. Like nerves, but different too, and it only seemed to happen around him. How very strange.

With the rings on, we were officially pronounced husband and wife, and we signed the contract. There was no kiss and no photographs, nothing to prove it had happened other than the signed paper in my hand.

My go-to business rule: getting it in writing.

That piece of paper confirmed that, at least for the next few months, I was officially Mrs Dexter Callahan.

~Dex~

The whole thing still didn't feel entirely real. There had been no poetic vows, no music, no talk of love. Not even a kiss. Just our two signatures on a piece of paper to show that we were now husband and wife.

There had been one moment when Nadiya got out of the car in front of City Hall that it almost felt like something. She looked truly beautiful. For the first time, I saw her in anything other than a suit, and her ivory dress made her smooth brown skin glow. The smile on her face when she saw me made my stomach do strange things, and when the sun reflected off my ring on her finger, for a second, I could almost imagine that we actually meant something to each other.

It came as close to the feeling of falling for someone as I had felt for a very long time, but I quickly shook it off, reminding myself that all of it was only for show. I would need to be careful to remind myself of it if I started to feel that way again.

When Nadiya told me I needed to bring a witness to the wedding, I knew immediately that it couldn't be any of my family. First, I would never hear the end of it if I chose one of them and didn't tell the others, and second, it went against my whole cover story that we were so carried away that we didn't have time to think. In the end, I called Max first thing in the morning, told him I was being crazy and getting married that day and begged him not only to come as my witness but to scrounge up two additional rings from any cast-offs that he had lying around. To my relief, he agreed to both requests.

After Nadiya and I signed the marriage contract, he shook my hand. "Congratulations, Dex. We've all been waiting a long time to see you happy again. You deserve this."

The sweet sentiment only made me feel guilty. I had thought everyone would be shocked and maybe even appalled to find out about me and Nadiya, but instead, people were delighted for me. Knowing that I would have to disappoint them all in a few months' time when we announced our separation made it a bit hard to stomach.

Max stepped away to congratulate Nadiya, and Mr Varma came over to shake my hand too. "There are some photographers outside waiting for the two of you," he murmured to me. "They've been tipped off that there might be something to see."

"Does Nadiya know?" It didn't shock me that the Varmas would want to make our marriage public right away, but it *did* surprise me that Nadiya wouldn't have mentioned it to me.

Mr Varma shook his head. "No, I figured she should look surprised. After supper last night, I know she's not much of an actor."

He moved away to give his daughter a kiss on the cheek before I could ask what he meant by that.

Getting my picture snapped by the local paparazzi was hardly a typical occurrence for me and suddenly, things started to seem a lot more concrete. By the next morning, everyone in the city would know I had married Nadiya Varma, one of the richest and most powerful women in Houston. I'd never been subject to that kind of public scrutiny before, not to mention what all my family and friends were going to have to say about it. Now that everything was signed and sealed, reality was quickly sinking in.

"Are you ready to go?" Nadiya had snuck up beside me and looked up at me with a slightly curious smile. "Everything okay?"

Some of my concern must have been showing on my face so I did my best to relax. "Ready. What's the plan now?"

I suddenly realized I didn't even know if we were going out to celebrate, or whether she expected me to stay at her house that night or not. Everything had happened so fast, there were a lot of things we hadn't discussed yet.

"I thought we'd just have a quiet night in and do some strategizing. We'll need to make a bit of a splash over the next week, and things should quiet down after that."

"Just the two of us?"

"If that's okay with you." She sounded unsure whether it would be, but actually, I could use some time alone to wrap my head around what had just happened with the one other person who truly got how strange it all was.

"That sounds great." I offered her my arm and she gave me a slightly incredulous look, making me laugh. "Come on, darlin'. Let me be a gentleman just this once. I promise it won't be a regular thing."

Fighting a smile of her own, she acquiesced and took my arm as we walked together out the door and onto the steps, where we were quickly greeted by the clicking of cameras.

"Ms Varma!" one of the reporters called out. "Did you really just get married?"

Nadiya looked up at me in surprise, and I had to admit, her father might have been onto something. She certainly didn't look like she was acting.

"Go ahead," I whispered to her. "You wanted people to know, right?"

She nodded and swallowed before turning to the journalists with her polite smile, the one I'd seen her give her father and the people in City Hall. Her 'real estate' smile, I called it in my head. It didn't look the same as her real one, that sweeter version that I had spotted a handful of times so far.

"Thank you, everyone. We weren't expecting this, it was supposed to be a secret." She turned to me and gave me just a hint of that real smile, the one I'd just been thinking about, and I couldn't help smiling back at her.

"Who's your new husband?" someone else called.

"I think he can answer that himself," she replied, making everyone laugh before they all turned to me expectantly.

"Dex Callahan, folks," I introduced myself, feeling a little self-conscious but trying not to let it show. "The luckiest man alive."

There was a murmured 'awww', especially among the women in the crowd, and Nadiya bit her lip to hide her amusement. "Don't go overboard," she whispered to me, but I could tell by the amused twinkle in her eyes that she really didn't mind.

We answered a few more questions as we made our way down to the waiting car, and after saying goodbye and thank you to Max and Mr Varma, we were finally alone together for the first time since our supper at her house two nights earlier.

"I guess that's it," she exclaimed as we pulled away from City Hall, the reporters and photographers disappearing into the distance behind us. "No going back now."

"Nope. So, is now a good time to tell you about my pet snakes that are coming to live with us?"

Her eyes widened in alarm, and I couldn't keep a straight face, cracking up in genuine amusement.

"Oh, darlin', you are too easy to tease."

Shawna had always seen straight through me, rolling her eyes at me whenever I tried to pull anything over on her like that. Having someone who took me at face value was actually kind of fun.

Relief flashed across Nadiya's face before her eyes narrowed. "You might want to keep in mind that I am technically your landlord for the next little while. You'll want to stay on my good side."

"Trust me, I know. I've seen your bad side, remember?"

She gave a little snort, so unlike her usual prim, professional demeanour that I had to admit I actually found it kind of endearing,

Soon, we pulled back up in front of her house – or *our* house for now, I supposed – and as we got out of the car, she seemed to realize for the first time that I didn't have anything with me. "Where are your clothes?"

"I wasn't sure what we were doing tonight," I told her honestly. "Guess I didn't fully think it through. I could run over and pick up a few things now."

Nadiya bit her lip in uncertainty. "It's possible some of the tabloid papers might come and try to get some shots of us once word gets out. It might look a little strange if you were seen leaving here on our wedding night."

She had a point, and I didn't really care either way. "Well, I can go over in the morning then. I usually sleep in the buff anyway, so as long as you've got an extra toothbrush I can use, it shouldn't be a problem."

Her cheeks turned slightly pink as she turned away from me to open the front door, and once again, I found myself smiling. Flustering her was quickly becoming one of my favourite pastimes.

She used her thumbprint to open the door before turning back to me. "I guess I need to get you added to the security for the house. There are probably other things I'm forgetting too. I'm usually more organized than this, maybe we can make a list tonight."

"You and your lists," I teased her with a laugh. "Let's worry about all that tomorrow, okay?"

"Then what do you want to do tonight?" she asked as she pushed the door open and I followed her into her beautiful but slightly sterile home.

Kicking off my shoes, I pulled off my suit jacket too, already feeling a lot more comfortable. "Honestly? After the week we've just had, I think this is a perfect time for us both to get a little drunk."

Chapter Eight

~**Nadiya**~

My attention had strayed to Dex's discarded shoes, wondering how I could politely let him know that he couldn't just leave them at the door like that without sounding too uptight during his first minute in the house, when he suddenly suggested that we get drunk.

"Drunk?" I repeated cautiously, hoping he said it as a joke. "I've never been drunk in my life."

"You're kidding me," he scoffed, heading towards the kitchen like he had been there a million times before instead of once, leaving me trailing after him. "Never?"

"I had three glasses of champagne at my cousin's wedding once," I recalled. "I was a bit light-headed, but I wouldn't call it drunk."

"Oh, sweetheart, that's just pathetic." He laughed as he started to open up my kitchen cupboards one at a time. "Where do you keep your booze?"

"There's wine in the wine cupboard," I told him, pointing to the long, thin cupboard next to the pantry. "I don't have anything else."

Dex went to the cupboard and opened it, pulling out one bottle and looking it over. "How expensive is this stuff?"

"A couple hundred dollars a bottle?" I guessed. I wasn't entirely sure.

He whistled before putting it back. "Okay, let's save that for another time then. You ain't got anything else?"

I didn't think so. There was still one extra beer Greg had left in the fridge, but that certainly wasn't going to be enough for the two of us, and I wasn't a beer drinker anyway. Just before I shook my head, though, I remembered something I'd shoved in the back of a cupboard a few months earlier.

"Actually, Greg's sister gave me something last Christmas, but I don't remember what it is. It's in that cupboard there."

I pointed to the one just behind him and Dex opened it up, pulling out the glasses until he found the bottle, and the same impressed whistle as before came out of his mouth.

"Don Julio tequila? She must have really liked you."

I gave a snort of derision. "Hardly. She knew perfectly well that I wouldn't drink it. She just wanted to see me squirm, and she probably planned to drink it herself the next time she came over. That's the only reason I didn't just get rid of it: I figured she'd bring it up again."

As much as Greg's parents had liked me, his sister had never approved of me dating her brother. I heard the two of them talking about me once when they thought I was out of earshot. She made it clear she thought of me as stuck up and no fun, and suddenly, I got worried that Dex's sisters would feel the same way.

Making friends with other women didn't come easily to me. My father had raised me to feel at home in the world of business, so the things that most other women enjoyed were things I didn't have much experience of or interest in. We couldn't even bond over shopping. Although I wore expensive designer clothes, I didn't enjoy the process of picking them out so I had a personal shopper who took care of all of that for me.

At least Dex's sisters would only be in my life temporarily, so I didn't have to worry too much about winning them over. If they hated me, they hated me. It really didn't matter in the long run.

"Well, it looks like she gave us the perfect wedding gift, then." Dex grinned again as he started pulling open some of the other cupboard doors.

"What are you looking for now?"

"Shot glasses."

Although I had never used them, I did own some since they were included in the glassware set the designer had bought when I moved into the house. After pointing out where they were, I looked down at my dress. "I should probably change into something else."

Dex grabbed the glasses out of the cupboard and turned back to face me, his eyes travelling up and down my dress, perhaps a little slower than absolutely necessary. "Good idea. You can be a bit clumsy at the best of times, and that is definitely not a dress you want to ruin."

I narrowed my eyes at the reminder of our first encounter and he just winked back cheekily.

"Put on your comfy clothes, if you have any. Go on ahead, I'll get us set up."

I didn't know what he meant by getting set up and I wasn't sure I wanted to ask. Leaving him with free rein of my kitchen, I headed to my room and pulled off my dress. He wanted comfy clothes, huh? Most of my wardrobe was for work, but I did have a few old pairs of jeans tucked away in the back of a drawer, so I pulled one of those out along with an old sweatshirt from my time at Cambridge. Taking a look at myself in the mirror, I had to smile. It didn't look much like me at all, but I did feel rather comfortable. Hesitating just a second, I pulled my hair out of its twist too, letting it fall down onto my shoulders and ran my hands through it a couple of times.

There. He wanted comfy? I could do comfy.

When I got back to the kitchen, Dex had already poured out a few shots of tequila from the bottle. He'd found a container of sea salt from the pantry and was cutting limes into wedges on a chopping board. The top buttons of his shirt had been undone, presumably to make himself a bit more comfortable too since he didn't have any other clothes to change into.

Something about the sight of him standing there, the knife in his hand, the measured movements and the tiny bit of exposed chest I could see, struck me as rather sexy. An unfamiliar zing shot through my lower abdomen; unfamiliar only because it had been such a long time since I felt it.

Calm down, Nadiya. The last thing I needed was to be attracted to my temporary husband. Neither of us wanted that complication.

My entrance got his attention and he looked up, his mouth open to say something, but the words died off as he got a look at me. Once again, his eyes moved over me, and he blinked a few times in surprise before looking back down at the chopping board. That must have been the first time I'd seen him almost speechless.

"I hardly recognized you, darlin'," he finally said, his voice oddly tight. "Glad to see you do dress like the rest of us sometimes."

"If I have to," I teased, walking over and taking a seat at the island next to him. It felt good to finally be the one in control, for a change. "How does this work?"

"You've never done tequila shots before?"

Why did he keep sounding so surprised? "I told you, I'm not a drinker."

"In that case, I'm happy to teach you," he said with a laugh, setting the knife down and looking up at me. He seemed more like himself again, recovered from his earlier surprise. "First, lick your hand."

"What?"

The look of disbelief on my face made him laugh again. "Trust me. Just here, between your thumb and your fingers."

He ran his index finger down the spot he meant on my hand, and a little shiver ran down my spine. Feeling rather self-conscious, I did as he said, swiping my tongue across the top of my hand.

Dex's eyes lingered on my hand for a second before he cleared his throat. "Right. Now, I'm going to put some salt on it, you're going to lick the salt off, take the shot, and suck on one of these limes."

"Is that really necessary?" I asked, blanching at the idea of the sour lime.

"You're going to want it, I promise. Ready?"

I supposed so, though this was hardly how I had ever pictured my wedding night whenever the idea of it had crossed my mind.

He shook out some salt onto my hand, the crystals clinging to the moistened skin, and I quickly licked them away. Wincing from the sharpness of it, I took the shot and poured it down my throat as quickly as possible.

Not quickly enough. The alcohol burned the back of my throat, making me cough.

"Lime," Dex reminded me, handing one to me, and I took one, biting down on it gratefully in relief.

"That is awful," I winced as I pulled the lime out. "Why would people do this to themselves?"

"It gets easier," he promised, gesturing to the other shots already ready to go. "You'll see. Go on and try again, whenever you're ready."

~Dex~

I couldn't help but be impressed as Nadiya downed her second shot with determination. For someone who had sounded unsure about the whole thing, she sure wasn't backing down.

As soon as she'd swallowed the second, she reached for a third one, but I caught her hand to stop her. "Hold on. Are you planning to leave any for me?"

A blush spread across her cheeks, and I couldn't be entirely sure if it was from embarrassment or from the alcohol already. "I thought you wanted me to do all of them."

"I think we better give those two a chance to kick in." She must not realize how hard they were going to hit her in just a minute. "We'll see how we go from there."

I took my own first shot, licking the salt and downing it before sucking on the bitter lime. The warmth of the tequila quickly spread from my stomach through my body. I wasn't about to admit it to her, but it had been a long time since I'd done shots too. I often had a beer in the evening, with my family, with friends, or sometimes just on my own, but the last time I had tequila was probably at the bachelor party before my wedding.

My *first* wedding, many years earlier.

"Do you always have to excel at everything?" I asked as I grabbed another of the pre-poured shots. I'd set her the challenge of doing the shots and she took it so seriously, I had to guess she approached any given situation the same.

"I don't *have* to," she retorted. "I just do."

That was the Nadiya I felt more familiar with, and it made me smile as I took my second shot, which went down smoother than the first. The tequila was excellent quality, not the kind meant for shots at all, but I had been serious about wanting to get drunk, and shots would be the fastest way to do it. At that point in time, I simply wanted to turn my brain off.

Especially since all it wanted to think about was how good Nadiya looked.

First, there had been the sight of her in her wedding attire, which had been bad enough, but when she came back to the kitchen after changing, desire shot through me in a way I honestly hadn't even thought it could anymore.

I'd never seen her in regular clothes before, or with her hair down. Suddenly, she looked a lot less like Nadiya Varma, future CEO, and a lot more like the girl next door, someone that I could picture hanging out around a campfire with or cuddling up to under a blanket while we watched old Westerns on Netflix.

That was not the way I needed to be thinking about my new wife.

So, I hoped a little alcohol would mellow things out, get us loose and a bit silly with each other, and ease some of the tension in my body which seemed determined to follow its own agenda rather than what my brain tried to tell it.

I took a third shot, the last of the ones I'd poured out in advance, which should get me going, at least.

"Is this how you pictured your wedding night?" I asked her, trying to focus on the ridiculousness of the whole situation, and remind us both that the whole thing was fake. That should help to dampen the very real attraction that threatened to distract me.

At least I'd already done all this properly before. For her, this was her first wedding, and I couldn't help feeling a bit sorry that she'd had such a poor excuse for one.

Nadiya shrugged. "Honestly, I've never spent a lot of time thinking about it. I know a lot of women are planning their wedding when they're six years old, but that's not me."

I sat down on the stool next to her, curious to know more. "What was six-year-old Nadiya like?"

She laughed at the question, maybe a little longer than usual. The alcohol must have been starting to kick in. "She used to have boardroom meetings with all her stuffed animals."

"Seriously?" That was really cute and a little sad all at the same time.

"I wanted to be just like my father. I think most kids want to do what their parents do when they're little, since it's what they see as a normal thing to do. Kids with firefighter dads want to be firefighters. Mine was a CEO, so that's what I wanted to be too."

I supposed she had a point there. Billie often told me that kids in her school class wanted to be like their parents, and Laura had grown up to run the family ranch just like our daddy. Most kids, though, grew out of it eventually and came up with their own dreams, but it seemed that Nadiya never did.

"What does your daddy do?" Nadiya leaned over to rest her chin on her hand after asking the question, but somehow missed and nearly ended up smacking her face on the hard countertop instead. I reached out a hand to steady her.

"Maybe we oughta move this someplace with fewer sharp edges," I suggested as she giggled at her near miss. We both got to our feet, the blood rushing to my head as I stood up, and I followed her down the hall to a large living room, decorated in monochromes much like her office. "Seriously, darlin'? Did this come out of some blueprint from a Disney villain lair?"

Nadiya narrowed her eyes at me. "It's modern."

"It's boring," I replied bluntly as we both took a seat on the couch. She looked out of place among her 'modern' decor in her sweatshirt and jeans, and I caught myself staring again for just a second before focusing back on her face. "Anyway, you were asking about my daddy? He was a rancher, but he died a couple of years ago."

"Oh, I'm sorry." Her face showed genuine sympathy for a moment, but it didn't last long before her eyes lit up. "Is your mom still alive?"

"Yes," I answered hesitantly, not sure why she might be asking.

Her reply confirmed I'd been right to be suspicious. The tequila had definitely started to make an appearance as Nadiya giggled again. "We should set her up with my dad! Wouldn't it be funny if a real marriage came out of all this?"

Having met both the people in question, I couldn't quite picture it, but I found her enthusiasm charming anyway. "You wanna play matchmaker?"

"My dad needs to chill out," she declared, turning sideways on the couch to face me and crossing her legs in front of her. "He's supposed to be retied... retried... ret..."

Her struggle over the word proved just what a lightweight she really was. I had a pleasant buzz going, but Nadiya had gone well past that. "Retired?"

"Yes!" She pointed at me in triumph like I'd just solved a particularly difficult problem. "Retried."

It still came out wrong, and that time, we both laughed. "I get it. What's your point?"

"My point is..." she began before trailing off. "I don't remember. What are we talking about?"

"My mom and your dad." My grin grew even wider as I got to see a side of Nadiya Varma I suspected very few people had ever seen before.

With a sudden gasp, Nadiya leaned forward to grab my arm. "Your mom! She wasn't at the wedding."

"Did you just realize that, sweetheart?"

Nadiya's eyes were wide with alarm. "She's gonna be so mad at you."

I was definitely in for an earful from my whole family when they got wind of what I'd done. "Probably."

"We should call her before she reads about it in the paper in the morning," Nadiya suggested.

Shoot. I hadn't even really thought about that. I'd planned on going over to see her the next day to tell her in person, but by then, it would probably be too late. My mom always read the Saturday paper, and I suspected the story about me and Nadiya would be hard to miss.

"Maybe you're right," I agreed, pulling my phone out. "Give me just a second."

I hit the call button, but before I could raise the phone to my ear, Nadiya had grabbed it out of my hand.

"What are you...?"

I didn't get to finish the question before my mom picked up and I could hear her on the other end. "Dex, honey? What's up?"

"Mrs Callahan?" Nadiya asked, trying to put on her professional voice and managing to overcompensate so that she actually sounded more British than ever. "This is Nadiya Varma."

Part of me thought I should take the phone back, but the other part, the part curious to see how this might play out, decided to let her keep it.

"Nadiya?" my mom repeated in surprise. "It's lovely to hear from you. I was hoping we'd get a chance to meet soon."

"Yes, me too." Nadiya tried to keep a stern face on, but as she looked over at me, she started to giggle again. "But I have some news that can't wait."

I could almost feel my mom's confusion through the phone. "News?"

"Uh huh. Dexton and I... I mean, Dexter... you know, Dex, your son..."

My head fell into my hands as I tried not to laugh, and luckily, my mom sounded amused too. She must have guessed Nadiya was drunk; from the way she was talking, it didn't take a genius to figure it out. "I know who he is."

"Right. Well, we got married today, so now, he's my son too. I mean, my wife. Wait, no! My husband."

"Okay, that's about enough of that." The time had definitely come to intervene, and after taking the phone from her, I tried to smooth things over. "Sorry about that, Mom. We've been celebrating a little too hard and Nadiya ain't got much practice at it."

"Celebrating?" My mom's earlier amusement had vanished, leaving her sounding shell-shocked. "Did you really get married, Dex?"

I could hardly lie to her about it after that. "We really did. I'm coming over in the morning and I'll tell you all about it, okay? I love you."

"I..."

I didn't even wait for the reply, hitting the end call button and tossing my phone to one of the other chairs in the room, well out of Nadiya's reach. "What was that?"

"I said it wrong, didn't I?" Her eyes were wide with concern, making her look much more like a child who'd been caught with their hand in the cookie jar than the soon-to-be CEO of a major corporation, and the ridiculousness of the whole thing hit me all at once.

When I started to laugh, it set her off, and soon, both of us were nearly bent over double on the couch. Obviously, the alcohol had started to hit me too since it really shouldn't be as funny as I found it. My mom was going to kill me.

Eventually, the hilarity wore off, and when we finally got a hold of ourselves again, Nadiya looked over at me curiously. "What about you?"

"What about me what?" She could literally have been talking about anything. I had no idea.

"Is this how you pictured your wedding night?"

Ah, that. I'd almost forgotten I asked her that question back in the kitchen. "I already had a wedding night," I reminded her. "I know how it's supposed to go."

"How's it supposed to go?" She asked it entirely innocently, but the question immediately had me thinking of carrying her to bed, and that desire I'd been working so hard to control came raging back stronger than ever.

"I meant if this were real," I explained, trying to remind myself yet again that it wasn't.

"I'm real," she said proudly, making me laugh again.

"You sure are, darlin'."

"And you are too." She reached out to touch my face, and the moment her fingers made contact with my cheek, a current of pure energy passed between us.

Suddenly, all of it felt very, very real.

"Dex." Her fingers ran down my face as she said my name softly, the look on her face open and far more vulnerable than I'd ever seen her looking before. "We never kissed at the end of the wedding."

I swallowed hard, trying to fight against my body's reaction and the persuasion of the alcohol, and keep myself under control. "No, we didn't."

"Maybe we should. Just to make it official."

That was a bad idea.

A really, really bad idea.

But sometimes, tequila and bad ideas were made for each other.

~Nadiya~

I had never felt that way before.

I assumed it must be what being drunk felt like, though I was more aware of everything than I thought I would be. My thoughts were still my own, but the messages seemed to be getting scrambled on the way from my brain to my mouth, and everything seemed a lot funnier than it usually did. After my phone call with Dex's mom, Dex's laughter made me laugh too, so hard I couldn't stop, and I honestly couldn't remember the last time I had ever laughed like that.

Maybe I never had.

And somehow, we ended up close to each other with my hand on his face. He said something about us not being real, which also struck me as funny because I knew that I was real and I was pretty sure he was too, but I thought maybe I should touch him just to be sure.

When I did, everything got a lot less funny. Suddenly, it seemed electric instead, like the air had been primed for a detonation, just waiting for a spark to ignite it.

And then... Dex kissed me.

I might have asked him to, though I couldn't entirely remember. I had been thinking about our wedding and how we hadn't kissed, and I thought we should make up for it, but did I actually say that out loud? I couldn't be sure.

Either way, I had only really meant a little peck, just something to seal the deal, but he seemed to have a different idea.

He'd asked me the day we met if I had ever kissed a man before, when he was trying to get under my skin, and of course I had. I'd kissed quite a few men, actually. Maybe not as many as other women had, but some all the same.

None of them felt like this.

Dex's lips were warm and soft as they pressed against mine. A slightly earthy smell pierced my senses, like wet clay, making me wonder what he'd been working on in his gallery that day. Out of nowhere, an image filled my mind of his hands slipping through the wet clay, moulding it into whatever shape he chose, his fingers firm and controlled. As those same fingers reached up to gently stroke my cheek, a shot of pure desire rushed through me, stronger than anything I had felt in a long time, and I whimpered into the warmth of his kiss.

The sound only seemed to spur him on, and the pressure on my lips grew harder as my head continued to spin. Growing dizzier by the second, my body felt like it was on fire.

Did the tequila do that, or did it just come from Dex, all on his own?

Whichever was responsible, it felt amazing and I didn't want it to stop. My tongue pressed against his lips, wanting to taste him more fully, and he let me in with no hesitation at all. The taste of the tequila still lingered on his tongue as it tangled with mine, and every brush of it sent pulses of need through me.

As satisfying as his kiss was, it wasn't enough. I wanted more.

My arms wrapped around his strong shoulders, pulling him closer to me and he groaned deep in his throat as his arms circled my waist. His strong hands splayed across my back, making me feel just as pliable as the clay I'd imagined him working with earlier.

At that point, I'd let him shape me into whatever he wanted to.

Unfortunately, to my frustration, he pulled back, panting from the intensity of the kiss. His blue eyes looked darker than usual, clouded with an emotion I hadn't seen in them before.

"Just how drunk are you?"

What did that matter? "Enough not to overthink this."

I tried to pull him closer again, but he resisted me easily, like I hadn't even tried, and leaned further away. "Not overthinking is good, but doing something you might regret later isn't. We still gotta live with each other for a few months, darlin', and I don't want it to be awkward."

For some reason, him calling me darlin' at that moment worked as a turn-on too. Maybe I *was* more drunk than I thought.

I still didn't want to stop.

"It's not awkward," I argued, letting my hand rest against his chest.

His hard, firm, solid chest.

I let myself be distracted by the feel of it for just a moment before looking back up at his face. "We're married and it's our wedding night. It would be more awkward if we *didn't* do something about it. What are you afraid of?"

The muscles in Dex's jaw tightened. "I'm afraid of taking advantage of you, sweetheart."

"Do you *want* to take advantage of me?" I gave him my best seductive smile and his eyes somehow got even darker.

"Yes, and no," he replied through gritted teeth.

Trust me to end up with a husband with an overactive conscience. "What if I don't give you any choice?"

I got up on my knees, leaning over him, and Dex tightened his grip on my waist to keep me steady. "What are you doing, Nadiya?"

"Seducing you."

Amusement flashed in his eyes, along with something darker and more desperate.

"I ain't sleeping with you while you're drunk, darlin'." His words were tight and just barely controlled.

"I didn't say anything about sleeping," I teased, letting my full weight fall on him, taking him off guard so he had no choice but to land on his back, flat on the couch, with me on top of him.

"You're stronger than you look," he laughed, making me giggle too.

"Don't you forget it."

I leaned down over him, but as our eyes met again, just inches apart, his smile faded. "Nadiya, I mean it, I can't..."

I cut him off, kissing him hard, and any resistance he had seemed to melt away. As our mouths moved against each other, his hands roamed down my back and lower, following the curve of my ass in my jeans and pulling me closer towards him, letting me feel that, despite his protests, the situation turned on just as much as it did for me.

And after feeling him, I wanted a taste of that too.

That time, I was the one who pulled back, sliding myself down his body, pressing firmly against it the whole time, and he groaned at the friction my movement created. "Fuck," he muttered, his self-control clearly close to breaking.

I just had to push a little harder.

When I got back to my knees with Dex still laid out on the couch before me, I could finally see the bulge in his pants that I had just felt, and the size of it, even through the fabric, had my mouth watering.

Reaching out, I pressed the flat of my palm firmly against his hard length and he inhaled sharply. "Jesus Christ."

For a Texan man like him, I knew that meant more than any 'fuck'.

"I got to change into my comfy clothes," I reminded him, running my hand up and down the straining material. "But you must still be a little uncomfortable."

"Nadiya…"

The word sounded half like a warning and half like a plea, and I ignored it completely.

Instead, I reached for the button of his pants, undoing it and pulling down the zipper. He immediately seemed to grow even bigger, expanding to fill the increased space. "You don't want to take advantage of me, I heard you, but you never said anything about me taking advantage of you. Let me help you out here."

Grabbing the waist of his underwear, I lifted it up and over the top of his stiff cock.

Dex breathed out, his eyes closed as I lowered my head and ran the tip of my tongue along the ridge of his head. His cock jumped towards me, just as eager as its owner was hesitant.

I tugged down on his pants, wanting him fully free, and Dex's hips raised to help me out. Clearly, he'd given up complaining, and as I got a proper look at him, I had no complaints either. I hadn't seen all that many cocks that close up, but his was easily the most impressive: thick and long and straining with need.

He did have a few further words of warning though, sounding a bit sheepish. "Nobody's done… this… for a long time. It's not going to take much."

I could see how hard he was already. He didn't need to tell me.

Grasping his base firmly in my hand, I licked him straight from the bottom to the top, like a very large ice cream cone. It tasted just about as good too, a little salty but still sweet, and the quick taste only left me wanting more. After swirling my tongue around the top, I moved back down, flicking my tongue back and forth across the hard ridge that ran straight down his shaft.

Dex's groans and exhaled mutterings were music to my ears as I ran my lips across him next, back up to the top, where I then opened them up and took him deep into my mouth.

"God-damn fucking hell," came the curses from above me, making me giggle. The vibration against his cock which was still in my mouth only seemed to make him harder, and once I started sucking on him, moving my mouth up and down while my hand rubbed along his base, his prediction came true. It really didn't take long at all, not more than a few minutes until he couldn't hold back any more, releasing into my mouth as his muscles quivered beneath me.

I swallowed the lot and slowly sucked my way back up until I released him with a soft pop. Laying his wet cock back down on his stomach, I looked up to see him staring at me through half-closed eyelids, his lips parted as he breathed heavily.

Just as I opened my mouth to ask him if he enjoyed it as much as his reaction seemed to indicate, the alcohol I'd drank suddenly made a very unwelcome reappearance.

Clapping a hand over my mouth, I jumped to my feet.

"Nadiya?" Dex's voice echoed with concern as he quickly sat up too, watching me closely.

"It wasn't you," I promised from behind my hand. "But... I think I'm going to be sick."

Chapter Nine

~Dex~

Well, *shit.*

I really hadn't meant to let things go that far. Kissing Nadiya was one thing, and even that pushed the edge a bit, especially since the kiss was just as electric as I could have imagined. Despite all the things about her that drove me a little bit crazy, a definite attraction existed between us, and there were plenty of things I found appealing about her too. After that night, I would have to add kissing her to that list.

Her take-charge mentality didn't disappear during the kiss, and I had to admit it turned me on. She went for what she wanted with no apology, and apparently, for that moment at least, she wanted me.

But was it only because the tequila had stripped away all her common sense, like it seemed to be doing with me? I couldn't let her do something she'd regret, no matter how much she insisted she wanted it. At least, I thought I couldn't, but when she sat up and eyed my pants with that expression of pure lust, I suddenly lost the will to fight.

As she said, we *were* married, and my body begged me to give in. The way Nadiya looked at me and touched me made it obvious she knew what she was doing. Nothing about her expression could be called innocent; she wanted it as much as I did.

And, well, it had been a really, really long time since any woman had touched me like that. I hadn't been a total celibate since Shawna died, but not far off either. A few times, especially when anger still had a hold of me all the time I hung out at bars to drown my feelings, I found a woman looking for a release too. Those encounters involved very little talking, before or after, and usually left me feeling worse than I had before. Eventually, I stopped doing it.

But actually getting to know a woman and getting intimate with her? That hadn't happened since Shawna, and as Nadiya's pretty pink lips wrapped around the tip of my cock, I remembered exactly why not.

It felt a million times better than any of my random bar encounters, and desire and need and relief and guilt and a dozen other emotions all ran through me at the same time. I didn't want anyone else besides the love of my life to make me feel that way, I tried to remind myself, even as my throbbing cock proved me a liar.

When Nadiya finished – or when I finished, I supposed –she looked pretty damned pleased with herself, until her face suddenly went a bit green.

As she ran away from me down the hall, I quickly got to my feet, zipped my pants back up, and followed after her. By the time I got to the hallway, there was no sign of her, and I didn't know my way around the house well enough yet to know where she'd gone.

"You okay, darlin'?" I called out.

I wasn't taking it personally. Obviously, the tequila had acted up, rather than it being a reflection on what we'd just done. The satisfied smile she'd given me made it clear enough she hadn't had any complaints at the time.

"Don't come in here!"

The voice came from further down the hall, so I followed the sound of it, ignoring what she'd actually said.

An open door led into a large bedroom which must have been hers, decorated in the neutral white, black and grey I was quickly coming to think of as Nadiya-style. Did she actually like all this monochrome, or was it just easier than picking a colour scheme?

Another open door further inside the room led into an ensuite bathroom, and I found her there, on her knees in front of the toilet.

"Have you actually thrown up yet?"

Her startled eyes looked up at me as I asked the question. "I said not to come in."

Taking a few steps inside, I leaned back against the vanity. "I'm not going to leave you to suffer alone. This is partly my fault."

"Partly?" She raised her eyebrows in challenge.

"Okay, entirely," I conceded, giving her an apologetic smile since I *was* the one who'd suggested it and poured the shots. "You didn't answer me: anything come up yet?"

"No," she admitted, still gripping the toilet firmly. "I'm just queasy."

"Why don't you come and lie down then?" I gestured towards her huge bed that looked like it could fit ten Nadiyas in it. It surprised me that she didn't get lost in there. "I'll bring you a bucket just in case."

Although she narrowed her eyes at my teasing, she held out her hand just the same, so I pulled her to her feet and put an arm around waist to walk her over to the bed.

"Are you going to be okay to fall asleep in this, or do you want to change into some pajamas?" I glanced down at her sweatshirt and jeans as I asked the question, and quickly wished I hadn't. She looked far too enticing.

"Are you trying to get me naked now, Dex?" Although she tried to smile at me seductively, another wave of nausea hit her and the smile quickly turned to a grimace.

"Not tonight," I assured her with a laugh. "Come on, lightweight."

After pulling back the covers and getting her tucked in, I went and got a glass of water from the kitchen as well as an empty wastebasket that she could use if she did get sick in the night. I also found some aspirin in the bathroom that she might want for the morning and left it along with the water on her bedside table. Nadiya's eyes were already drifting closed by the time I finished.

"Sleep it off, sweetheart," I teased her, and before I could second guess myself, I leaned down and gave her a light kiss on her forehead.

A smile crossed her lips even though her eyes were shut, and I flipped the light off on my way out the door.

Well, that was a wedding night I'd never forget. It didn't take more than a few minutes to tidy up the kitchen from our shots, but as soon as I was alone with my thoughts, they started drifting back to the feel and the sight of Nadiya going down on me, and before I knew it, my cock had begun to get hard again.

With a sigh of frustration, I turned off the lights in the kitchen and went to try to figure out where I should sleep. I'd sidetracked Nadiya with the drinking idea as soon as we arrived back at her house, so I hadn't had a chance to ask her where she wanted me. There were at least three bedrooms besides her own, all of which seemed to be unused, so finally, I just picked one. It didn't take long to shed my clothes, and I climbed into the bed naked, trying to ignore my not-insignificant erection. I'd just gotten off half an hour ago and I wasn't a horny 20-year-old anymore. As a grown man, already on my second marriage, I should be capable of controlling myself. A few unsexy thoughts and I could go to sleep.

My mind, however, refused to cooperate, returning over and over again to the sight of my cock disappearing into Nadiya's mouth and the colour of her perfectly manicured nails as she held my shaft in her hand. The more I thought about it, the harder I got, until finally I had to accept defeat, throwing back the covers and heading for the bathroom. Luckily, there was an attached one in the room I'd chosen, so I didn't need to go out into the hall.

It hardly took more than a minute when I really started trying before I came again, pleasure and frustration and guilt flooding my body at the same time.

That was the first time in years that I'd thought of anyone other than Shawna while taking care of myself. It felt like cheating on her somehow, even though I knew how ridiculous that sounded.

Of course it felt good, but it also felt dangerous. Nothing about me and Nadiya was real, and I had to remember that or things were all going to get really complicated, really fast.

~Nadiya~

My room felt a lot brighter than usual when the morning sun came shining through the window. As I tried to open my eyes, a flash of pain spread across my forehead, making me wince.

Finally, I forced my eyes open, groaning all the while, and realized I still wore my clothes from the night before. When I saw the wastebasket sitting on the floor by the bed, suddenly, the whole evening came back to me.

"Oh, God." Grabbing an extra pillow from beside me, I covered my face with it, trying to hide from the memories. Unfortunately, I was pretty sure I remembered everything, even though I wished I didn't. I remembered taking the shots, going to the living room, talking to Dex's mom on the phone, kissing him, and then...

Another low groan came out of me, muffled by the pillow, but that one had nothing to do with the pain in my head. It was purely embarrassment.

What had I done? I promised Dex the whole arrangement would be strictly business and the first chance I got, literally the first night he spent at my house, I forced my way into his pants.

Not that he seemed to mind too much, I had to admit, based on the speed of his orgasm. But still, it could hardly be considered professional, and the idea of going out and facing him that morning made my cheeks burn with humiliation. What was it about that man that made me behave so completely out of character?

The tequila probably had something to do with it, I grumbled to myself as I lifted the pillow with a sigh. But I couldn't entirely blame the alcohol. There were other ways he made me behave differently too:

forgetting obvious things like a wedding ring for our wedding, or to have him sign the paperwork for the gallery sale, which I still hadn't done. He distracted me in ways I couldn't begin to understand, much less explain.

Hauling myself up to a sitting position, I finally noticed the glass of water and bottle of aspirin on the bedside table, and my embarrassment eased a little as I smiled. Dex really was thoughtful. The ring he got made for me already proved that, but the little gesture of making sure I had what I needed meant almost as much.

He truly was a nice guy. A lot of men wouldn't have been nearly as gentlemanly as he'd been the night before, refusing to sleep with me despite me literally throwing myself on him. And again, from the state of his cock when I got my hands on it, I could pretty confidently say he hadn't pushed me away because he didn't want me. He'd just been trying to be honourable, and that was surprisingly refreshing.

Thank goodness one of us had kept their head. With a grimace, I grabbed two pills from the bottle and swallowed them down with a swig of the water, not even wanting to think about how awkward it would have been waking up in bed with him that morning and still having to live together for the next few months. Facing him after what I did was already going to be bad enough, but hopefully, I could apologize for my behaviour and we could move on.

By the time I got dressed for the day and headed out to the kitchen, Dex had already made himself at home there, sitting at the breakfast table with a cup of coffee and some toast and the morning paper that had been delivered to the house. He still wore the suit from the day before, since he hadn't brought anything else with him.

As I walked in, he looked up and gave me a rather ungentlemanly smirk. "How're you feeling this morning, darlin'?"

"It's Nadiya," I reminded him. Obviously, I had let his little term of endearment go too many times yesterday, but I didn't want him making a habit of it. "And I'll be fine once I get some coffee."

"Left some for you over there," he said, gesturing towards the moka pot. "Took me half an hour to figure out how to work the damn thing."

"But it's worth it," I assured him, heading towards the Italian press and almost salivating at the smell. As I poured myself a cup, I looked over at him from the corner of my eye, but he was engaged in the paper again, munching on his toast.

It looked like he wasn't going to bring up anything about the previous night unless I did, which I appreciated, but it left me unsure about whether to mention it or not. Would it be better to clear the air or just pretend it never happened?

"You need to get some food in this place," he said before I had a chance to decide. "I woulda made you bacon and sausage this morning, lots of grease for a perfect hangover cure, but I couldn't find any."

Just the thought of it nauseated me as I grimaced into my coffee. "You definitely won't find anything like that. I'm a vegetarian."

He looked up at me with such a look of dismay that I almost laughed. It looked like I had just told him his dog had been run over. "For real? That wasn't on your list of things I oughta know about you."

I supposed not, but I hadn't thought it was that important, and definitely not worth the look he was giving me. "We had meat-free tacos the other night," I reminded him. "And fish at the restaurant. I do eat fish, so technically, I'm a pescatarian, but most people don't know what that means so I just say vegetarian instead. I don't eat any other meat."

He still looked shell-shocked. "I thought that was just some kind of health kick. Well, this is going to make things interesting."

"What things?" I didn't see how it impacted his life at all. I had no plans to force him to convert and we didn't even have to eat together if he didn't want to.

"Well, lunch with my mom, for one. She's already got a roast in the oven. I'm going to have to warn her."

"Lunch? Today?" I'd missed something, apparently, since I didn't know anything about any lunch.

"After last night's phone call, she's a little anxious to meet you," he explained, grinning over at me, and my cheeks flushed red at the reminder of how much of an idiot I had made of myself on that call. "I already checked your calendar and you didn't have any plans."

He pointed over at my wall planner where I kept track of important events. The day was, in fact, completely empty.

"Not to mention she already saw this," he added, turning the newspaper in his hands to show me what he'd been reading, and splashed across the front page of the lifestyle section was a picture of me and Dex on the steps of City Hall.

'Houston's most eligible CEO off the market' read the headline.

"I'm not even CEO," I exclaimed as I walked over and grabbed the paper from him.

Dex laughed into his coffee. "Seriously? That's your first reaction? Most women I know would be checking the picture to see if it got their good side."

"Being CEO is kind of the point of this whole thing," I reminded him, sinking into the seat next to him. I wouldn't admit it to him, but I did glance at the photo after he mentioned it, and the picture was actually quite a nice one of both of us. We looked good together. In it, Dex smiled at me while I had a slight blush to my cheeks beyond my usual makeup: the stereotypical blushing bride.

People might actually think we liked each other.

It did clarify further down in the story that I was COO, not CEO, but that those in the know expected me to be named CEO soon. The reporter had obviously done her research about Dex as well, including information about his gallery and about his first marriage too.

"Are you okay with all this?" I asked, looking back up at him. From our earlier conversation on the subject, I knew that he still had strong feelings for his former wife and I wasn't sure how he'd feel about seeing her name in print next to mine.

He shrugged. "It's no worse than I expected. At least they didn't find out about my cocaine habit."

My eyes widened for just a second before I realized he was teasing me again, and they narrowed instead, making him laugh.

"Ah, you're catching on to me already," he said in mock disappointment. "That's a shame."

Ignoring that, I laid the paper down on the table. "What time are we supposed to see your mom?"

"Lunch is at noon, but whenever we want to go is fine. I've still gotta stop at my house and pick up some things so we can do that first and head over afterwards. My mom'll be happy to chat with you all day if you want to."

That sounded a little daunting. My father had seen right through me, and now I had to convince Dex's mom that I was so madly in love with her son that I couldn't even wait to invite her to the wedding? "Maybe we should have a couple more shots before we go," I suggested, only half-joking.

Dex just laughed again. "Come on, she's not that bad. You can always try to set her up with your dad while we're there."

I groaned as that part of the conversation came back to me. "I forgot about that. What else did I forget?"

The smile fell away from Dex's face as a more serious look took its place. When he spoke again, there was a new huskiness in his voice. "I'm not really sure. What do you remember?"

There it was: the topic I'd been avoiding. He obviously wanted to know if I remembered just how inappropriate I'd been with him.

Of course I did. I remembered the feel of his cock in my hands, the warmth of his skin, that slight scent of clay that clung to him, and most of all, I remembered the taste of him. I remembered every second of it.

But maybe... maybe he didn't need to know that. Maybe it would all be a little less awkward if he thought I didn't. Weighing the pros and cons quickly, I made my choice.

"Honestly, not much," I lied. "I remember talking to your mom, but nothing really after that. I'm not even sure how I ended up in bed, so if you had something to do with that, thank you."

Dex nodded slowly and swallowed even slower. "You're welcome, darlin'. No harm done."

I almost thought he sounded a little disappointed, but only for a second before he smiled over at me again.

"Well, let's finish our coffee and head out. This is going to be an interesting day."

~Dex~

As we pulled up in front of my house, I watched Nadiya's face curiously. Only two bedrooms and built over forty years earlier, it had little in common with her house, but it was the house Shawna and I had bought together and it meant a lot to me because of that.

Had Nadiya ever spent much time with regular, working-class people like me? Though I wouldn't admit it to her, I had gone online and looked up some stuff about her ex-boyfriend, just to find out a bit about his background, and from what I'd read, I could guess he'd been pretty well-off too. He'd gone to a fancy school and worked for his family's company. A picture of him on the company's website showed his straight white teeth in a slightly too-bright smile and his hair perfectly styled.

He seemed a lot like her in a lot of ways. Way more polished than me, at least.

Though I was curious why things hadn't worked out between them, she hadn't volunteered any information, so I didn't ask. We were trying to keep things professional between us, and she hadn't asked anything about Shawna besides the bare minimum that she ought to know.

The night before hadn't been very professional, though. When she told me that morning that she didn't remember what we did, it truly surprised me. I really didn't think she'd been that drunk, and I felt even worse that I had let things go as far as they did. She had seemed fully in control, just with fewer inhibitions than usual, much the same as me.

But with no reason to think she would lie to me, I supposed it must be true, and I also supposed that was probably a good thing in the end. Things did get out of hand, and it would be easier for us to move forward in a business-like way if we didn't have the memory of being that intimate with each other.

Well, at least *she* wouldn't have the memory. It had imprinted itself pretty firmly on my brain, but for her sake, I would pretend it hadn't.

I refused to admit that even a little part of me might be disappointed she didn't remember. That only made sense if I wanted it to happen again, and I knew exactly what a bad idea that would be.

"How long have you lived here?" Nadiya asked as we got out of the car. Her driver had brought us there since I left my truck at home the day before, but she sent him away once we were at the house. I could drive her around the rest of the day.

"Almost ten years," I answered as we walked up to the front door. "We bought it not long before the wedding. My first wedding, that is."

Understanding crossed her face. "You and your wife lived here?"

I simply nodded, unlocking the door to let us in. Nadiya followed in behind me, hovering by the door as I picked up my mail from the day before and shuffled through it before putting it all down on the kitchen table. "Make yourself at home, darlin'. I'll just go pack a bag, it'll only take a few minutes."

Leaving her there, I headed to my bedroom and found a suitcase under the bed, covered in dust. It had been a long time since I'd been on a trip. I couldn't even really remember the last time, before the previous night, that I spent the night away from the house. Being there in that room where Shawna and I had spent so much time together helped me stay connected to her. Going to sleep in the same bed we had shared, waking up and seeing her photo on my bedside table, that was the closest I could come to feeling that a part of her remained with me.

Living with Nadiya was going to be a big change.

When the suitcase had no room left, I zipped it up and headed back down the hall to the living room, where I found Nadiya standing in front of a painting on the wall.

My heart constricted at the sight, though I couldn't really explain why. Something about seeing Nadiya looking at Shawna's portrait made me feel very strange in a way I didn't fully understand.

"This is beautiful," she murmured as she saw me come in. "Did you paint it?"

"Yeah." I tried to answer casually and not give away anything about the odd way my body had reacted. "Oil's not my best medium, I think my sculptures are my better work. That was just meant to be a rough sketch for one of my plaster pieces but Shawna liked it so much, she asked me to finish it up."

Nadiya continued to look at it carefully. "Was it a sketch for the statue that's in your gallery window?"

It really surprised me that she picked up on that. She had mentioned the other night over dinner with her father that she liked that piece, but I didn't know how much of that was just lip service. Apparently, she really had paid attention to it though. Not a lot of people made that connection.

"That's right."

"And it's your wife?" The question sounded a bit odd coming from her mouth, since technically, at that moment in time, *she* was my wife, but I referred to Shawna that way too. I never called her my ex-wife, since that implied that we had chosen to end things, which we definitely hadn't.

I was going to have to figure out what to call Shawna going forward so people didn't get confused.

"Yes. I made it during her first round of chemo, before we got married. The sculpture is about her struggle with her illness and how it didn't define her."

I had captured the frailty of her body as well as I could. The chemo had made her weak and far too skinny, but it hadn't done a thing to dampen the fire inside her, and I hoped that shone through in her face, both in the portrait and in the sculpture itself.

"I see," Nadiya said softly, her eyes still on the picture a moment longer before looking back over at me. For a second, I almost thought I could see a bit of moisture in the corners of her eyes. "Well, it's really beautiful."

"It's easy when you've got the right subject."

For a split second, I got a flash of how I might sculpt Nadiya. I could almost see the finished work in my head, but I quickly shook it aside.

We definitely didn't have that kind of relationship.

"You ready to go?"

She raised her eyebrows at me in a teasing way. "You're the one who had to pack. Are *you* ready to go?"

When I nodded, we headed out to my truck as I locked up my house. It felt strange to not be sure when I would be back again.

As we headed through the city over to my mom's place, I tried to give Nadiya an idea what to expect. "My mom's pretty laid back. It's my sisters you have to worry about, but luckily, they're not going to be there today."

"Worry about how?" Nadiya asked, sounding quite worried already.

"Oh, they'll just have a million questions for you. They'll want to know everything about you and they'll tell you everything about themselves too, even if you absolutely did not ask and never wanted to know."

"And you really think they're all going to buy this? That we're really together?"

"Apparently they want to believe it," I told her honestly. "I expected a lot more resistance when I broke the initial news to them, but once they got over the surprise, they were actually really pleased about it."

"They want you to be happy," she guessed, which was probably true. "And when we break up, they're going to hate me."

"That's not really your problem," I pointed out. "Once this is all over, you never have to see them, or me, again."

"Right." It sounded like that idea didn't fully agree with her, and to be honest, it didn't entirely sit well with me either. But that was the plan: a few months of pretending, and back to normal afterwards.

We pulled up outside my mom's and I left my suitcase in the truck as

Nadiya and I headed inside. "We're here," I announced as we walked in through the unlocked front door. Uncharacteristically, there was no immediate reply. In fact, the whole house felt unusually quiet. "Mom?"

Still nothing, so with a shrug, I led Nadiya towards the living room, and we both immediately froze in the doorway at the sight that greeted us.

Not just my mom, but my sisters, their husbands and kids, and a whole bunch of my friends as well.

"Surprise!"

Chapter Ten

~Nadiya~

For a brief, terrible moment, I thought that Dex had set me up. The thought flashed across my mind that he must have known about the surprise party but kept it to himself, to tease me or to test me, I wasn't sure which, and the idea of being blindsided that way on purpose made me question everything I'd concluded about him being a nice guy.

However, when I turned to him, the shocked look on his face quickly assured me that the gathering came as just as much of a surprise to him as it did to me, and that made me feel much better. We might have been ambushed, but we were ambushed together.

There were so many people. Since I'd never even seen a picture of Dex's family before, I had no idea who anyone was as they all started coming up to us, crowding us, offering congratulations and best wishes.

The situation clearly overwhelmed Dex, perhaps even more than it did me, so once my initial shock faded, I decided to take control. Working a room was one of my best business skills. I was born to win people over, to make the sale, and I'd always done better with large crowds than I did one-on-one, especially when none of them knew me personally. Give me a room of investors to pitch to and I'd have them eating out of the palm of my hand every time. This was no different, except instead of a real estate development, I had to sell the idea of me and Dex as a newlywed couple, madly in love.

I could handle that. How hard could it be?

"Thank you all so much," I started, speaking loudly and clearly so everyone could hear me. The room immediately quieted as everyone waited to hear what I had to say. "We weren't expecting this at all, were we, Dex?"

Leaning into him, I took hold of his hand, and he stared down at me in confusion. He might have done well acting in front of my father the other night, but with *his* family and friends, he looked a bit lost. That meant I got the chance to step up, just as he had done for me.

So, I gave him my best smile and looked back over the room. "I'm so sorry we weren't able to have you all at the wedding. We really didn't even plan to do it until yesterday morning. It's impulsive, I know, but we just couldn't wait. I couldn't let this one get away. I'm sure you understand."

There were a lot of smiles on people's faces as I made eye contact with as many of them as possible. As it became clear they all wanted to believe we were happy, some of the tension seemed to ease from Dex's posture and he squeezed my hand in thanks.

"Let's see the ring," a blonde woman called out from the back of the room, and everyone's eyes immediately went down to my hands. Luckily, I could comply, since Dex had given me something to work with.

"It's beautiful, isn't it?" I gushed, holding my hand up so everyone could see. "Dex had it made just for me."

A chorus of 'awww's circled the room, a reaction that he seemed to inspire in people quite often. I could see why: he was genuinely thoughtful and surely, that applied to everyone, not just me. He obviously had a lot of people who loved him. If someone tried to organize a party for me on such short notice, the turnout would have been a lot less impressive.

I couldn't help wondering if anyone would have come at all.

Dex finally seemed to find his voice. "Okay, folks, let's back it up a bit. As I'm sure you're aware, we didn't know y'all'd be here, so let's give my wife some space before she hightails it out of here."

His wife. The words sounded so natural coming out of his mouth that I couldn't help blushing, which only seemed to please the crowd more.

They did take a step back, as requested, but as soon as the pressure eased, a woman pushed her way to the front of the crowd and I knew without being told that she must be Dex's mom. The same blue eyes as her son, with the same kind expression in them, looked up at us as her beaming smile warmed the whole room.

"Sorry, Dex," she said, her eyes twinkling as she took her son by the hands. "Tonia called me and I told her you were coming over and one thing led to another..."

"I should have known," Dex muttered good-naturedly, casting a smirk over at the blonde in the back who had called out the earlier question. "Mom, this is Nadiya, as I'm sure you figured out by now."

The strength of her embrace took me by surprise as she pulled me in close. "I'm so pleased to meet you, sweetheart," she whispered against my ear where Dex couldn't hear. "I was beginning to think he was never going to open himself up to love again."

Guilt raced through my veins at her words and the depth of emotion in them. Every word sounded utterly sincere. Dex had told me he still loved his wife, and apparently, everyone else knew it too. Now, they thought he loved me as well, which simply wasn't true, and I hated that his mother in particular was being fooled.

"You're not angry about the wedding?" I asked tentatively, trying to steer the conversation away from talk of love.

"I've done the whole mother-of-the-groom thing before," she replied, brushing my concerns away as she let me go. "It's far more important that you're both happy."

Before Dex or I could say anything about that, she turned back to the room, her voice growing sharper with the ingrained authority only a mother had.

"Okay, everyone outside! It's time to eat."

The crowd began to disperse, apparently content to wait to speak to us until after they'd all had some food. All except the three women who cornered Dex as soon as the crowd began to thin.

"Where's our introduction?" one of them demanded, her arms crossed.

Dex rolled his eyes before turning to me. "Nadiya, my sisters: Tonia, Laura and Billie. Ladies, this is Nadiya. Be nice."

I quickly employed my usual trick for remembering people's names when I got introduced to a lot of people all at once, making a personal association with their name that I could remember if I got stuck. Tonia had blonde hair with some darker highlights so I could remember that as two-tone Tonia. Laura's brown hair had a shorter cut, like Laura Bush, a well-known Texan I'd met a few times through my father. And Billie looked like a bit of a tomboy despite wearing a dress, her arm muscles almost as defined as her brother's were, so I could remember she had a boy's name.

Keeping them straight wouldn't be too hard.

"We're always nice, Dex," Laura insisted before the three of them surrounded me, pushing their brother entirely out of the way. "I love this skirt, Nadiya! On the ranch, I never get to wear nice things. Is it a fancy name brand?"

"I still want to see the ring," Tonia insisted, reaching for my hand.

Billie had a different request. "Tell us about how Mr Romantic proposed. He wouldn't go into details."

I looked to Dex for help, but his mom had already roped him into helping her with something, leading him out of the room, so it looked like I was on my own.

"The skirt's Versace," I explained, trying to answer the questions in the order they'd been received. "I love the ring, but Dex didn't have it with him when he proposed. It was completely out of the blue, he didn't have anything prepared."

"Where did he do it?" Billie pressed. "His proposal to Shawna was so romantic, when he..."

Laura nudged her hard in the ribs before she could finish that story, giving her sister a look that was clearly meant to shut her up, even though I actually kind of wanted to hear about it. Considering how sweet he could be with me when he didn't even like me, I couldn't imagine what he'd done for the woman he loved.

In any case, I didn't want them to feel awkward around me, so I answered Billie's question more fully. "It was at his gallery, right after he spilled paint all over my favourite Alexander McQueen suit."

Laura's eyes widened in horror. From her immediate focus on my clothes, I had guessed she would appreciate the significance of that. "He didn't! And you still said yes?!"

"The suit can be replaced," I said with a shrug, as if it hadn't really bothered me. "There's only one Dex."

Laura shook her head in disbelief. "He must have some serious skills in the bedroom. That would have been a dealbreaker for me."

That time, Billie gave her sister a poke. "I don't want to think about Dex in the bedroom!"

"What, you'd rather think of him as a Ken doll with no junk?" Tonia laughed. "It hasn't got much use in a while, but I'm sure Nadiya can whip him back into shape."

By that time, my cheeks were flaming red. I didn't have any friends who talked so openly about their partners, and definitely not when they were related to the man in question. Not to mention that the discussion of Dex's 'junk' had me vividly remembering having it in my hands and mouth the night before.

My blushes didn't go unnoticed and all three of them burst out laughing. "You see?" Laura giggled. "I knew it had to be good."

"Are you guys behaving?" Dex called out from the kitchen door. "Stop hogging my wife and come on outside."

To my great relief, they agreed and we all headed towards the door, though they were still flanking me as if I might try to escape at any minute.

If that was the conversation we had in the first five minutes of me knowing them, I couldn't imagine how the rest of the day with his sisters was going to go.

~Dex~

The blush on Nadiya's cheeks as she walked into the backyard with my sisters had me a little worried. What exactly had they been saying to her? Knowing my sisters, it could honestly be anything. I started to head over to save her from whatever interrogation they were subjecting her to, but my mom cut off my path before I could get there.

"Stop staring at your new bride," she teased me. "No matter how pretty she is, she won't disappear if you look away for two seconds."

We must have been pulling off the act better than I realized because she really seemed to think I was besotted with Nadiya. When we first walked in and were confronted with the whole surprise party, I completely blanked and I thought for sure we were screwed. But Nadiya stepped up, taking charge of the situation in a way that truly impressed me. When she cuddled into me, taking my hand, she almost even had me convinced that she actually liked me.

"Besides, you need to get her something to eat," my mom continued. "You know she's not going to be able to get away with those three on her case."

I couldn't argue with that, so I headed over to the long table where an incredible spread had been laid out, as usual for my mom's house, but my heart sank as I realized that with everything else going on that morning, I'd forgotten to tell my mom one important thing.

"Did you use the pork drippings on those roast potatoes and vegetables?" I asked, even though I was pretty sure I already knew the answer.

"Of course," she replied, giving me a funny look. "As always."

As always. "Yeah... the thing is, Mom, Nadiya's kind of a vegetarian. She eats fish, but no other meat."

An adorably confused look crossed my mom's face, quickly followed by horror. "Dexter Mitchell Callahan! How could you not tell me that before I invited her over here?"

Oh, boy. She hadn't used my full name on me in quite a while. Since I didn't think admitting to her that I only found out myself that morning would be a good idea, I would just have to take the blame. "I'm sorry, it just slipped my mind."

"Slipped your mind!" Her hands were on her hips as she shook her head, surveying the table of food, none of which was going to be appropriate. "I guess I can whip up a salad, but it's not going to be very exciting. She probably has a chef who makes her gourmet food all the time! What kind of hostess is she going to think I am?"

She looked so genuinely distressed that I had to give her a hug. "It's all right, Mom. She came here to meet you, not for a five-star meal. I'll go make something for her, and you go and make sure those three aren't giving her too much grief."

I gestured over to the table where Nadiya sat with Tonia and Laura on either side of her and Billie across the table. They all appeared to be talking at once while Nadiya looked on, looking bemused and possibly a little scared.

"I guess I can get her a drink at least," my mom reasoned. "What kind of beer does she like?"

At least I sort of knew the answer to that. "I think she'd rather have wine, if you've got any."

Another glare was my reward for that suggestion. Of course my mom didn't have any wine, so I hastened to add some other options.

"Some iced tea would be fine too, or just some soda. She's not picky, I promise."

At least, I hoped she wasn't. I realized I didn't entirely know, but somehow, I had the feeling that despite all her fancy upbringing, she wouldn't kick up a fuss. She wasn't a snob like her father, even with all her expensive clothes and Mary Flynn-designed house. The Nadiya I'd seen the night before, in her sweatshirt and jeans, doing tequila shots in the kitchen, that was closer to the heart of her than all the rest of it, I felt certain of that. She just usually kept that side hidden, since I suspected she didn't want people to know how nice she could actually be.

It might ruin her reputation.

I made my way back to the kitchen, accepting more well wishes from friends along the way. Tonia's husband Cam was already at the counter, cutting up some food for his kids, and he gave me a sympathetic smile when I walked in.

"You surviving?"

"Just barely," I replied, joking right back with him. "You couldn't have held Tonia off another day or two?"

His eyebrows raised in challenge. "Have you ever been able to stop her from doing something she wants to do?"

Fair point. The Callahan women were strong and determined, and there wasn't much could be done to stop 'em if they got an idea in their heads.

Shawna had loved my sisters and they loved her too, which made me a bit surprised that they seemed so eager to welcome Nadiya in her place. Didn't they feel like they were replacing Shawna somehow? Or was that just me?

Cam pulled me out of my wonderings, asking about our living arrangements while I rummaged in the fridge to find something for Nadiya to eat. "Are you selling your house then?" he asked after I told him I was moving in with Nadiya. "I know a few people who might be interested."

I hadn't really considered how to answer that question yet, so I tried my best to come up with a deflection. "There's no rush. It's not like I need the money right now, so I'm going to hang onto it for a little while longer."

Thankfully, Cam nodded like that made sense. "I suppose you won't be hurting for money again at all, huh?"

For some reason, that irked me a bit. I knew he didn't mean anything by it, he was just genuinely happy for my good fortune, but I didn't like people thinking I only married Nadiya for her money.

Even though, to be completely honest, that had been a big part of the reason I'd agreed to the charade in the first place. Not for the money, exactly, but for the gallery... which really came down to the same thing in the end. That thought left me feeling slightly uneasy.

With a plate of salad in hand, I made my way back out to the table where my sisters and mother still had Nadiya engaged in conversation, and she looked up at me with some relief as I approached.

"I hope this is okay for lunch," I said, placing the plate down in front of her. "I'm just going to grab something for myself and I'll be right back."

Dismay flickered across her face at the idea of being left alone again, but she covered it quickly. "Sure, that's fine. Thank you, Dex."

I turned to head back to the food, but not before I heard Laura not-so-quietly whisper to my new wife: "Does he always make sure you get taken care of first then?"

Oh, sweet Lord. They all giggled as I walked away, pretending I hadn't just heard that. If that was any indication of the way their conversation had been going, I was going to have my work cut out for me to make it up to Nadiya later.

~Nadiya~

I'd hardly been able to get a word in edgewise since I sat down at the table with Dex's sisters. They didn't seem to need any response or any encouragement from me to keep going, chatting away about anything and everything. Laura asked about the shoes I'd been wearing in the wedding picture that appeared in the paper, and I managed to get the brand name out of my mouth, but that sent her off on a tangent about shoes that Tonia had borrowed from her and never returned and they started arguing about that until Dex's mom came over and offered me a drink as she sat down with us.

I took it gratefully, expecting that the sisters would adjust their conversation accordingly, but the fact that their mother was listening didn't seem to hinder them any more than the fact that they'd never met me before. They continued to speculate about my wedding night with Dex, which sent my mind drifting into dangerous territory even as I did my best to keep smiling serenely.

Only when they began guessing at the real reason that we couldn't wait to get married, casting not-so-subtle looks at my mid-section, did Mrs Callahan finally speak up, her tone impressively stern.

"Girls, hush up about that now. You don't want Dex to hear you."

For some reason, that actually seemed to chasten them. They almost looked embarrassed as they cast side-eyed glances at each other, which only confused me. Why would they be embarrassed about that but not about anything else they'd said?

"Doesn't he want kids?" I asked curiously. Their eyes immediately returned to my stomach, so I hastened to add a disclaimer. "Not that we're expecting. We're definitely not."

That would be impossible, but obviously, I couldn't tell them that.

Mrs Callahan gave me a slightly sad smile. "Of course he wants kids. He'd be the best daddy in the world too, but with all of Shawna's chemo, they never got a chance to really try. I'm not surprised you haven't talked about it, it's a bit of a touchy subject for him, and he doesn't need to be reminded of it."

That last bit was directed at her daughters, not at me, but I felt a strong pang of sympathy towards him all the same. He *would* be a great father, actually: thoughtful and easygoing, at least when he wasn't fighting me about his gallery sale. But even then, he only got stubborn defending something he cared about, which would be another really good quality for a father to have.

I could picture him playing with his kids, teaching them how to draw or paint, taking them horseback riding, and just spending time with them. He wouldn't be the type of daddy who always stayed late at the office, not getting home until after his daughter was already in bed, waiting for a goodnight kiss that never came.

The memories of my own childhood hit me hard out of nowhere, and I shook my head at how emotional and involved I had gotten. Whether Dex wanted kids or not made no difference. It had nothing to do with me.

And speaking of the devil, he walked over to us with a plate that he put down in front of me rather apologetically. The colourful salad didn't look like what anyone else had on their plates. Did he make it just for me?

As he walked away, Laura made another innuendo about his performance in the bedroom, which I had to hope he hadn't heard. When she asked if he always took care of me first, the thought of him doing just that made my whole body flush with heat. Of course, that hadn't been how things had gone the night before, and there was no point in imagining it.

Luckily, Dex's mom stepped in again. "Honestly, Laura, that's my son you're talking about. How'd you like it if Randy's sister talked about his sex life in front of you once they're all grown?"

I could only assume from context that Randy was one of the children I had noticed running around earlier.

Laura shrugged, not put off in the least. "At this point, I just hope Randy makes it to adulthood with his penis intact. He seems determined to wave it around as much as possible and it's gonna get caught in something sooner or later, and then what use is he gonna be to any woman? Lord knows no one's gonna marry him for his brains."

Keeping a straight face was a struggle, especially when no one disagreed with her.

"Besides," she carried on, "Nadiya knows I'm just teasing, right?"

Everyone turned to look at me so I nodded while taking a big bite of my salad so they wouldn't expect me to actually answer. The conversation was so far outside of my comfort zone, I wasn't sure I could even form a proper sentence.

The sight of me eating seemed to remind everyone that we were actually there for lunch, and Dex's sisters finally dispersed to go get their own food and check on their families. A minute later, Dex settled into the seat just vacated by Laura, with a plate piled high with food.

"Was that as bad as it sounded?" he asked me under his breath.

"That depends," I murmured back, trying to keep the smile out of my voice. "What did you hear?"

"Enough." His clipped reply made me laugh, and he smiled too, a little sheepishly. "Sorry about that. I should have given you more warning. Inappropriate is too mild a word for them sometimes."

"It's okay," I assured him, and surprisingly, it actually was. Now that the intense glare of their spotlight on me had faded, I actually found it rather funny. I couldn't imagine having that kind of conversation with anyone else, which made it refreshing. Being around Dex's family certainly wasn't going to be boring.

I did, however, feel I should give him a head's up. "They were hinting I might be pregnant. They thought maybe that's why we got married so fast."

The muscles in his jaw tightened and a flicker of sadness passed through his eyes. "I suppose I shoulda seen that coming."

It hadn't really crossed my mind either, but I could also see why people would make that leap. "Well, they'll quickly realize they're wrong," I pointed out. That didn't seem to make him feel any better, so I tried to think of what might make him laugh instead. "I'm far more concerned about your nephew Randy at this point anyway."

That got his attention, and he turned to look at me fully. "What's wrong with Randy?"

I repeated what Laura had said, more or less, and Dex's lips twitched in amusement. "I'm guessing family dinners at the Varma house don't usually involve that kind of conversation."

The idea made me giggle. If the word 'penis' had ever been used in our house, I couldn't even imagine my parents' reactions. "Not exactly. You're showing me a whole new world, Dex."

He fully grinned at that, his sadness forgotten at least temporarily, and soon, we were joined by other people wanting to wish us well and hear about our impromptu wedding. By the time we'd finished eating, had some amazing homemade pie and spoken to everyone who wanted to congratulate Dex, hours had passed. I realized as we said our final goodbyes that somewhere along the line, I had stopped worrying about slipping up and just enjoyed being with Dex and facing the world as a couple. A few times, his hand covered mine on the table or his leg brushed up against mine beneath it, and although I knew it was all part of the facade, it felt nice at the same time.

It almost felt natural.

We rode back to my house in his truck in comfortable silence, and only when we pulled into the drive did Dex turn to look at me. "I never mentioned to you that I go over there for supper every other week. They'll expect you to come too, but if you want me to say you're working and can't make it, that's fine. You don't have to see them again if you don't want to."

I had certainly done that often enough with Greg, sending him off to things on his own because my work took priority, but the idea of making Dex face his family alone, and the inevitable questions that would come with it, didn't appeal to me at all. "Of course I can go. Just send Luisa the times and she'll make sure it's in my calendar."

Dex gave an amused huff. "I gotta ask your assistant to make plans with my wife?"

Something about the way he said 'my wife' made my stomach flutter, with a possessiveness in it that I wouldn't have expected to find attractive. And yet, for some reason, I did, at least when it came from him.

"She's always had free rein over my whole calendar, day and night," I explained as we got out of the truck and headed for the front door, Dex carrying the suitcase he'd packed earlier. "She needs to know if there are times that are off-limits so she doesn't book me in for anything else."

"Maybe you need to take a look at your work-life balance, darlin'," Dex suggested as he followed me into the house, kicking off his shoes at the door again and leaving them where they landed. Strangely, it didn't bother me quite as much that time as it had the night before.

"I haven't worked at all today," I pointed out in my defense as we walked into the living room and took a seat next to each other on the couch while I tried not to look at the spot where he'd been laid out the night before, his pants around his knees.

Dex laughed. "It's Saturday, sweetheart. That's not an accomplishment."

If he only knew what my Saturdays were usually like. "Well, I do have to go into the office tomorrow, so you'll be on your own here. Try not to spill paint on anything while I'm gone."

He rolled his eyes at me, but I could see his lips twitching again. He liked me teasing him, maybe as much as I liked him teasing me. "Actually, my supplies from the gallery will be delivered tomorrow, so I was going to get my workshop set up. You're sure you don't mind me taking over your garage?"

"It's all yours," I promised him. "I never go out there."

"Well, that's tomorrow sorted then," he summed up before looking down at me with an expression I couldn't quite recognize. "Now, what's the plan for tonight?"

Chapter Eleven

~Dex~

Nadiya's eyes widened at my question. "Tonight?" she repeated. "What do you mean?"

That was a bit of an odd reaction to such an innocent query. "I mean the part of the day that follows the afternoon," I told her wryly, which earned me a dirty look. "You got any plans?"

Her eyes dipped from my face for just a second before coming back up. "No, I don't have any plans. Do you? You don't have to stay in, you know. If you want to go out with friends or do whatever you'd normally do on a Saturday night, you're free to go."

"Nadiya, we just got married yesterday," I reminded her. "People might think it's a bit strange if I go out on my own the next night."

"Oh. Right."

She swallowed nervously and my brow furrowed. Why did she look like the idea of staying in with me all night would be something unpleasant? I thought we had a pretty good day together. She seemed comfortable at my house and at my mom's, so what changed? "You're not afraid to spend time with me, are you?"

A hint of pink crept up her cheeks. "Of course not. I'm just... busy, and I thought you might be bored on your own."

"You just said you have no plans," I pointed out. Her blush grew stronger, and suddenly, I thought I understood. "Did you lie to me this morning, darlin'?"

Her eyes widened again, that time in alarm, though she quickly tried to cover it up. "What do you mean?"

That just made me even more sure I was on the right track. "When you said you didn't remember what happened last night, was that a lie?"

Her eyes dropped once more, and that time, I felt certain she was looking at my lap, and my cock twitched in response. *Damn it.* I didn't need that, and I tried to convince my body of it. Nothing else was going to happen between us; I simply wanted to know why she felt like she needed to hide the fact that she remembered it from me.

To her credit, she came clean when I called her out, giving me an awkward shrug. "I just didn't want things to be weird. I thought it would be better to pretend it never happened, but that's not fair to you. What I really should have done is apologize."

"Apologize?" I repeated curiously. "For what?"

That blow job was pretty firmly imprinted on my mind, and I couldn't think of a damn thing she'd done wrong.

"For being inappropriate. We agreed to keep things professional and I crossed the line. Even if I was drunk, it doesn't make it right."

Had she really been feeling guilty about that? What she'd done had been entirely for my benefit. Once again, I didn't see that she had done anything wrong. If anyone felt guilty, it should have been me.

"I coulda stopped you if I really wanted to, and I didn't. It takes two to tango. We both got a little carried away."

She nodded, exhaling deeply, with relief written clearly across her face. "Thank you for understanding."

"We're both adults here," I added with a shrug of my own. "You put any man and woman together like this and there's bound to be some friction. It's natural. We just gotta find our balance."

She muttered something under her breath, but I didn't quite catch it.

"What was that?"

Again, Nadiya's eyes widened, like she hadn't meant for me to hear her at all, which only made me more curious. I raised my eyebrows, waiting for her to repeat it.

She pursed her lips for a moment, trying to resist, but finally, she answered me. "I said 'not any man'. I hope you don't think I just go around doing that for anyone off the street."

I couldn't help it: I laughed out loud. "Trust me, Nadiya, that thought never crossed my mind."

Not very many were lucky enough to have received that particular honour, I had to guess. I did have some questions though, and it seemed as good a time as any to get them answered.

"I assume you were sleeping with Greg?"

Her lips pursed again, that time in disapproval. "We were together for years, so yes. That hardly makes me a slut."

"Whoa, hold on, I never said that." Where had that come from? Clearly, I'd hit a sore spot, though I had no idea why. "First off, I hate that word, and second, there's nothing wrong with a woman owning her sexuality. That has nothing to do with why I asked."

Nadiya seemed mollified, but also a bit confused. "Then why did you ask?"

"It's just... been a while for me," I replied, though that still didn't explain exactly why I'd asked. I wasn't sure I entirely knew the answer to that myself. "I guess I wondered if you were in the same boat, or if you'd been happy in that department in your relationship before it ended."

Knowing whether her level of sexual frustration matched mine might not have been a good idea, but I couldn't stop myself from asking anyway.

"Oh." She took a moment to think it over once I'd explained my reasoning. "Well, sex was frequent enough, I guess, but not particularly good."

Frequent *enough?* That definitely didn't sound good, and based on the brief taster I'd gotten the night before, I would have been willing to bet the problem hadn't been her.

"So, maybe we both had some pent-up frustration," I suggested. "And the alcohol loosened us up a bit. That's all. No need for either of us to be guilty or embarrassed, right?"

Finally, she gave me a genuine smile, the one that made her look far too beautiful for her own good. "Right. The tequila's to blame, and we won't make that mistake again."

"Definitely not."

With that agreed, the tension should have disappeared. Instead, it only seemed to get worse. For a heated moment, we both simply looked at each, the air seeming to grow thicker with each passing second.

"Although..." I started, hardly knowing what I intended to say even as the word came out of me.

"Yes?" Her eyes were fixed on me, flicking back and forth between my eyes and my mouth as she waited for the next words to come out.

"If we wanted to..."

"Yes?" She licked her lips, and I knew why. The air in the room suddenly seemed very dry, and also like there wasn't quite enough of it.

"There's no reason we couldn't..."

I couldn't quite bring myself to say the words, but I didn't have to. She knew exactly what I meant, and when she leaned in to kiss me, that time, I had no intention of stopping.

~Nadiya~

Somehow, Dex's kiss felt even better sober, and that was saying something since it had been pretty damn good drunk.

His hands cupped my face gently and his lips were warm and firm as his scent filled my nose, that special clay smell that I already associated so strongly with him. His mouth moved against mine with enough hunger to set my stomach fluttering again, the same way it had earlier when he called me his.

I could remind myself all I wanted that our relationship wasn't real, but it hardly seemed to matter. For at least that moment, it *was* real, and that kiss was really happening..

For that moment, I would happily be his.

I hadn't grown up in an environment where anyone talked about sex. Not like Dex's family did, naturally, since they were on the extreme end of the spectrum, but it really hadn't ever been discussed at all. My mom had been raised in a traditional household, and her mother in a far more traditional one still, back in India. Though we hardly spoke about it, on the rare occasions we did, I got the clear message that sex was something to be endured, not enjoyed, and that no respectable man wanted to marry a woman with a chequered past. My father never would have married a woman who'd slept with any other man.

But once I left home and went to university in England, my new friends there had very different ideas on the subject. My roommate was the epitome of what my mom would have called a 'loose' woman, but she certainly didn't seem to be suffering for it. In fact, she seemed to be having a lot more fun than I was.

I could never fully embrace her carefree lifestyle, but I did manage to loosen up over my four years there, and I lost my virginity at the age of 22 to a very handsome and very drunk posh British boy whose accent made me melt. We dated for a couple of weeks afterwards, but the attraction quickly cooled, and though I supposed I could have regretted it, I never did. At the very least, I was glad to finally know what all the fuss was about.

Since then, I'd slept with three other men, all of them serious boyfriends, and in all three cases, the sex was exciting at first, then okay, and finally, it became a bit of a chore. I began to wonder if my mother had been onto something, at least when it came to sex in a relationship. Maybe it really was a matter of bearing with it after a point.

And no matter how hard I tried over the years, I could never completely silence her voice in my head, telling me that men would judge me for how many men I'd had before them. So when Dex asked if Greg and I had been sleeping together, it put my back up and I snapped at him, obviously taking him by surprise. When he clarified what he meant and when he asked about how satisfying my sex life with Greg had been, my anger cooled, and I had to be honest with him: it hadn't been great.

I *was* a little frustrated. And if he was too, then, as he said, there was no reason we couldn't do something about it.

We were married. For the first time in my life, I could actually have sex without any guilt at all, and if I were being even more honest with myself, I hadn't been able to stop thinking about Dex's cock all day, not since I'd had it in my mouth the night before.

As soon as it crossed my mind again, I reached down to his lap and ran my fingers across the rapidly growing bulge in the front of his pants, and he groaned into my mouth.

"You sure about this, darlin'?" he asked, pulling back just enough so that he could look into my eyes, looking for the proof of my agreement. "It doesn't have to change anything if we don't let it. Tomorrow, we go back to business. Tonight, we're just two people helping each other out."

He knew exactly what I wanted to hear. "Just tonight," I agreed, pressing my lips against his again, already missing their warmth.

Dex chuckled deep in his chest. "In that case, your room or mine?"

Since he gave me the choice, I got to my feet and grabbed his hand, pulling him up with me. Without a word, I led him down the hall and into the room where he'd spent the night before, my heart racing and a deep, aching pulse growing in my abdomen and between my legs. I hadn't been this excited to be with a man since... well, I wasn't entirely sure I ever had. Before, there had always been some nerves mixed into the anticipation.

That night, I simply wanted him. With no expectations beyond that, I wasn't afraid at all.

As we got to the middle of the room, I turned back to him and my fingers grabbed the bottom of his shirt, pulling it up and over his head. His chest looked just as good as I had imagined it from what I'd seen beneath his tight t-shirt the day we met, and along with the tattoos on his arms, he had another one on the left side of his chest.

I ran my fingers across it, trying to get a better look at it, but Dex swooped in to kiss me again, distracting me. As soon as our lips connected, I couldn't think of anything else.

His fingers worked clumsily on the buttons of my blouse until he got it open, and his warm hands palmed my stomach, sending shivers of anticipation through my body. Those slightly calloused fingers felt good when he held my hand, but against my stomach, they felt even better, and I couldn't wait to feel them in other places too.

His lips never leaving mine, he pulled my shirt off entirely and expertly undid my bra, sliding the straps down my arms, his fingers leaving trails of goosebumps behind. Once he pulled it completely off, he leaned back for a moment to look down at me. When his eyes met mine again, they were full of heat.

"Beautiful," he murmured before kissing me again, his hands wrapping around my back as he pulled me close to him. The feel of his hard, firm chest against my stiff nipples made me moan, and Dex responded by dropping his hands to my hips and pulling me tighter against him there too. His cock felt like steel against me, letting me know he was just as turned on as I was.

Suddenly, I couldn't be naked fast enough. Without waiting for him, I unzipped my skirt, letting it drop to the floor, and Dex's hands moved lower, rubbing my ass through the lacy fabric of my panties. With a groan of his own, he dropped down to his knees and pulled the edges of my underwear down. They stuck between my legs for a second, the dampness there holding them in place, and when he gave them a harder tug to release them, he inhaled deeply. The smell of my arousal was hard to miss, and he didn't seem to mind. I was beyond wet for him.

I expected him to get back up once he had my panties off, but instead, his hands gripped my ass once more, tilting my hips just slightly as he brought his lips right to where I needed his touch most. His mouth slid across my clit, making my whole body jolt in response.

"Oh, fuck, Dex," I gasped, grabbing onto his hair to keep my balance.

For a second, my mind flashed back to the last time I'd had a man between my legs, not all that long ago really, and how I had been thinking of Dex at the time. Then, it had been in terms of getting him to sell his gallery to me, but there in his room, he'd laid claim to my thoughts in a completely different way, and nothing would be able to distract me from what he was doing down there.

His tongue drew lazy circles around my clit a few times before he took hold of my right leg, hooking my thigh over his shoulder to give him better access. I'd never had a man go down on me while standing up before, and my legs trembled as he dipped his tongue deep into my core.

"You taste so good," he mumbled before burying his face even deeper.

His words and the actions of his talented mouth were too much to take. My release built quickly, the aching growing stronger and stronger, and when he added his fingers, pressing them deep inside me, all the pressure inside me burst, leaving me with only the wave of pleasure that followed.

Dex's sister's words from earlier today floated across my mind: *Does he always make sure you get taken care of first then?*

It seemed like she might have been onto something.

My one remaining knee that still supposed my weight buckled beneath me as I came, but luckily, Dex was right there to catch me. Lifting me up, he took me over to the bed where he laid me down gently, giving me a soft kiss. My own taste was still on his lips and it immediately made me want more. In spite of the amazing orgasm he'd just given me, I ached for him again already.

"Dex," I pleaded, looking up at him through half-closed eyelids. "I need you inside me now."

~Dex~

Nadiya's taste lingered on my tongue as I pulled back from kissing her. She looked absolutely stunning laid out naked on the bed like that, her dark hair pulling loose from its usual twist and her light brown skin contrasting enticingly with the crisp white bedspread.

When she said she needed me inside her, I damn near lost control. Her demanding what she wanted was such a turn-on. Just like the night before, she took the lead, and where she led, I would be happy to follow.

There was one slight problem though. "I don't have any condoms with me," I told her a little sheepishly. "Based on our arrangement, I didn't think I would need any."

I didn't add that I couldn't remember the last time I even bought any. It hadn't been on my radar for a while.

Her eyes dropped to the now very noticeable straining at the front of my jeans. "I don't have any either," she said, and I groaned in frustration. "But…"

"But?"

Was she going to suggest a repeat of the night before? That would be good, but not exactly what I wanted.

"I'm on the pill, I've only been with one man in the last three years, and he always wore a condom. It's safe for me, if it's okay for you."

I didn't really want to tell her it had been more than three years for me, and besides, I was more curious about what she'd just said. "You were together three years, you're on the pill, and you still used a condom?" That seemed like overkill to me.

Nadiya raised her eyebrows at me. "Is that really what you want to talk about right now?"

Her hands slid across her stomach, close to the trim little triangle of hair below, and I immediately lost my train of thought. "Talk about what?"

She laughed, the sound deep and throaty. "That's what I thought. Now, take your pants off and get over here." She spread her legs invitingly, and only the thick denim of my jeans kept me from breaking loose right then and there.

As quickly as I could, I stripped off my remaining clothes and joined her on the bed, covering her body with mine as our mouths drew together again, unable to stay apart. Her kiss felt needier than before, more demanding, but that was fine with me. I needed it too.

As I'd already told her, it had been a long time since I'd done anything like this. Those few anonymous hook-ups I'd had since Shawna's death hadn't been about desire, not really. They were about trying to forget, trying to lose myself in a moment's pleasure, but that night with Nadiya, I didn't want to forget. That night, I was with a woman who I respected and found attractive, sometimes infuriatingly so, and I wanted to make her feel good as much as I wanted my own pleasure too. That was why I'd just gone down on her, something I definitely hadn't done with anyone since Shawna.

In the past, I'd been worried about replacing my memories of my first wife with someone new, but perhaps I needn't have worried. Being with Nadiya didn't feel the same as being with Shawna, but it felt good all the same, good in a different way, and I could keep the memories of both separately.

There was room in my head for both, at least, if not my heart.

Nadiya's hands slid up my arms, over my shoulders, her fingers curling around the hair at the base of my neck as we continued to kiss. Our hips were moving almost of their own accord, drawing me to her, leaving me powerless to resist.

I gave her one more chance to change her mind. "You're really sure?"

She groaned with impatience. "Stop teasing me, Dex. Don't I feel sure?"

Her hips thrust against me again, and I couldn't wait any longer. Reaching down between us, I took hold of my hard, aching cock and ran it along her entrance, coating the tip in her wetness as she let out a whimpered sigh, and, at last, I pushed into her.

"Oh, God." Nadiya's back arched, her head falling back as she took me in.

"You took the words out of my mouth, darlin'." I tried to laugh, but it felt too damn good. I'd almost forgotten how amazing it could feel. Was it just that we weren't using a condom? I'd always used one with every other woman since Shawna.

Or maybe... maybe it was just Nadiya?

Whatever the case, I would have to take things slow if I didn't want it to be over as quickly as the previous night's fun had been, and I definitely didn't want to rush. We'd agreed to just that one night together. Might as well make it count.

Nadiya's legs wrapped around my waist as I pulled out, all the way to the tip of my cock before slowly pushing back in again. "Fuck," she moaned with her eyes closed. "Just how big are you?"

That time, I did laugh. "I've never actually checked, sweetheart. You want to stop and find a measuring tape?"

"God, no." She laughed too, and somehow, the laughter made it even better. This wasn't just about need, as much as we both obviously needed it. I'd genuinely started to like her as a person, and I was pretty sure she liked me too, even if she wouldn't admit it yet. We could have a good time and still come out friends on the other side.

I thrust slowly into her a few more times, delighting in the feel of her tight, warm wetness, before another thought occurred to me. "Is this the position you want? We can do whatever you like."

Since we were supposed to be easing our mutual frustration, we might as well get the most satisfaction out of it that we could, and if she preferred something else, I would be happy to go with that.

She looked up at me in surprise, like she hadn't expected to be asked the question, bu she answered me honestly. "Well, actually, I usually prefer to be on top."

Of course she did. That didn't surprise me in the least. "Sounds good to me, darlin'."

Still buried inside her, I rolled us over until my back hit the bed with her on top of me. Nadiya pushed herself up onto her knees, giving me a perfect view of her incredible body and my hands moved to her breasts before I was even aware I meant to do it. She bit her lip as my fingers lightly pinched the puckered nipples, and she reached back to release her hair fully, letting it fall down over her shoulders.

"Goddamn it, Nadiya, you're beautiful."

She really was. I could hardly believe the woman on top of me was the same woman I'd spent months despising, or even the one I'd gone to see in her office earlier that week, the picture of cool professionalism. Riding me, she looked just as powerful but in a completely different way.

I couldn't help thinking she could tell me what to do anytime she wanted.

As she began to move, raising her hips and lowering herself back onto me, my hands continued to explore her body. She placed her own hands on top of them, following along with me as I traced the curve of her waist, the swells of her breasts and the dip of her collarbone. It wasn't long before I felt close, the combination of touching her and the exquisite friction on my pulsing cock so good I could hardly stand it.

As if she sensed the end nearing, Nadiya leaned forward without warning, pinning my hands to the bed beside me as she fully took control. Her hips moved faster, rising and sinking on my cock, grinding at the base to give herself the friction she needed too.

"Fuck," I muttered as she stroked me faster and faster, the buildup of pleasure so intense it was almost painful, but I sure as hell didn't want it to stop.

"Dex," she cried out as she hit her peak, and feeling her contract around me was more than I could take. I came too, sighing her name under my breath as I emptied myself deep within her. As her movements slowed, her head fell onto my chest and I reached up to stroke her hair, both of us breathing heavily as we let the full experience sink in.

I supposed an annulment would be out of the question after that, I thought sarcastically. We were definitely husband and wife.

Eventually, Nadiya raised her head and looked down at me with a smile that mirrored my own satisfaction perfectly. "Well, that was something."

It certainly was. Something unexpected, something amazing, and something I was afraid I would definitely want to do again.

Chapter Twelve

~Nadiya~

Dex looked just as pleased as I felt with how that had gone. From my perch on top of him, his cock still inside me, I had no doubt that he enjoyed it and so had I, far more than I would have expected.

In fact, it might have just been the best sex of my life.

It didn't all come down to the size of him, although that certainly didn't hurt matters. It felt like he reached me in places no one ever had before, and not just physically. Attentive and giving but still confident, he had me completely in the moment. I'd never come across a man who, the very first time out the gate, asked me what I wanted and let me take control.

He was secure enough in himself not to be threatened by giving me power, and I found that incredibly sexy.

Sliding off of him, I lay down on the bed next to Dex, still catching my breath. I'd also never let a man come inside me without a condom before. Greg had asked, more than once, why he couldn't since I was so fastidious about taking my birth control every day. The chances of an accidental pregnancy were very, very small, and I'd never really had an answer that satisfied him. I couldn't even explain it to myself, other than that I just didn't want him to. It felt intimate in a way I didn't feel ready for, and yet with Dex, it hadn't felt unnatural at all. In fact, it felt really damn good to have his bare cock in me, feeling every ridge as it worked against my inner walls.

Just the thought of it started to make me hot again. I needed a distraction, quickly.

Rolling over onto my side, I saw the tattoo on Dex's chest that I'd noticed earlier, and leaned closer to take a look at it. It looked like a cowgirl, all curves and hat, holding a branding iron, but I couldn't quite make out what it said.

"What does this mean?" I asked, running my fingers across it.

Dex shivered a little beneath my touch, but his face got uncharacteristically tight. "It's Shawna. It's her laying claim to my heart."

Oh. Once I looked closer, I could see the brand did, in fact, spell out her name. I already knew how much Dex loved her, he'd told me that openly and unreservedly, but seeing her physically marked on his chest made it even more real somehow. It couldn't be clearer that he was spoken for, at least when it came to his heart.

Not that it mattered to me. Our relationship was a business one, that night aside, and now that we'd had our fun, we should get back to that arrangement as soon as possible.

To that end, I sat up fully and swung my legs over the edge of the bed. "Well, I'll let you get on with the rest of your evening. I've got some work I should take a look at before tomorrow, so I'll go to my room. You can use the living room if you'd like."

"Nadiya." Dex propped himself up on his elbows to look over at me, his eyebrows drawn over his blue eyes in concern. "Are we okay? You don't regret this, do you?"

How could I regret it? I was pretty sure I'd remember that night for the rest of my life. "Of course not. We're fine, but we said just tonight, right?"

"Right," he agreed, sounding less certain of that than I expected. "But the night's not over."

That was just about the most tempting thing I'd ever heard, but looking down at the tattoo on his chest, I knew it would be a bad idea. I'd been curious about what it would be like to give in to our attraction and now I knew: it had been absolutely amazing. Repeating it wouldn't change that, but it could complicate things even further, and we'd already blurred the lines enough for one night.

"I think it's better that we stop there," I told him truthfully, and such strong disappointment flashed across his face that it almost made me change my mind. At the very least, it made me want to reassure him that I wasn't leaving because I felt awkward or guilty over what had just happened. "But I mean it: I don't regret it at all. That was just what I needed. I hope it was okay for you too."

Heat settled in his eyes as they scanned my still-naked body. "A little more than okay, darlin'."

The just-quenched desire for him started up again, unhelpfully, and I got to my feet before it became too strong to resist. Gathering my clothes, I headed for the door. "Have a good night, Dex."

Before he could say anything else, I fled down the hall to my own room.

~**Dex**~

Well, that didn't go the way I wanted it to. Nadiya told me she didn't regret what we did, and I had no reason to think she was lying. From the way her body had reacted, I felt pretty sure she got as much out of it as I did.

So why did she run away from me afterwards like the house was on fire?

Did it have to do with my tattoo? That was really the only thing we'd talked about between our mutual orgasm and her sudden departure, and I could see how it didn't make for the best pillow talk. I felt no shame about it, since I had never kept anything back from her about Shawna. Even so, I did feel a little awkward explaining its meaning to the woman I'd just slept with. Looking at it from her point of view, I could see that it might make her feel uncomfortable. I couldn't say I would have particularly liked seeing another man's name written across her body, even though objectively I knew it would have had nothing to do with me.

It had never bothered me to show it to any of the other women I'd been with since Shawna, so why did it feel a bit strange when Nadiya asked me about it?

Nothing about the evening had gone the way I expected it to when I woke up that morning, but all things considered, in the end, I didn't regret it at all either. The memory we'd make together would be one I was glad to have, and if it never became more than that one time, I could be satisfied with that.

I could almost convince myself I believed that.

The next morning, Nadiya had already left by the time I got up. She left a note for me in the kitchen, saying she'd be at her office but I could text her if I needed anything, giving no indication of how long she'd be gone for.

I sent her a quick text to let her know I'd got the note, and after some breakfast, I headed out to the garage to get ready for the delivery from the gallery.

Nadiya's garage had been built for three cars so it had plenty of space, even more than the workroom in my gallery had. It also didn't look like it had ever been used. I didn't have to do much more than give it a quick wipe down to get it ready to go. The moving van arrived shortly afterwards, and once they'd unloaded and gone, I got to work on setting things up the way I wanted them. It was hard, physical work, and by the time I finished, I'd completely lost track of time but my growling stomach suggested that lunchtime had passed me by.

Taking one last satisfied look around my new workspace, I locked everything up and headed back into the house, intending to grab a quick bite before taking a shower and cleaning up.

But when I walked back into the kitchen, Nadiya was already sitting at the island, a stack of documents in front of her and a small plate of vegetables beside her. Halfway through nibbling on a carrot, she glanced up upon my entrance, and her mouth immediately fell open.

In confusion, I glanced down at myself too, unsure what had caused that reaction. I supposed I had gotten a bit sweatier than I realized. Moisture soaked clean through my t-shirt, making it stick to me, and I probably didn't smell that great either. She probably wasn't used to dirty men in her pristine living space.

Greg didn't seem like the kind of guy to break a sweat.

I offered her a shrug of apology as I stepped into the room. "I'm on my way to the shower. Just wanted to grab a bite first. I didn't know you were back."

"Of-of course," she stuttered, blinking a couple of times before looking back down at her papers. "It's your house too, remember. You can do whatever you want."

A bowl of fruit next to her, so I went over and grabbed an orange, noticing the way Nadiya's eyes slid over to watch me peel it, her gaze fixed on my hands. "Did you want some?" I offered.

She glanced up at my face as if she'd been caught doing something wrong. "No, thanks. I'm fine." She quickly looked back at her papers again.

Hmmm. I was starting to get an idea what was causing her reaction, and it had nothing to do with me being dirty after all. Or at least, not in the way I originally thought.

As soon as the thought crossed my mind, all I could think about was the night before, the feel of her skin beneath my hands and the feel of her enveloping my eager cock, which was ready to jump right back into action at any moment if given the slightest encouragement.

We'd said only one time, but what difference did it really make if it became twice? None, as far as I could see.

So, I took a shot: heading out of the room, I turned back from the doorway to see if her eyes had followed me, and sure enough, she was watching me go. Her gaze dropped back to her papers once again, trying to pretend she hadn't been checking me out.

If she wanted it too, maybe she just needed a little nudge to admit it, and I had a good idea how to give it to her.

"There are a lot of dials and levers in that fancy shower of yours," I said truthfully. It looked more complicated than my truck. "I'm not sure I understand all of them. Do you want to come and show me how it works?"

~Nadiya~

I swallowed hard as Dex asked me to show him how to work the shower. He must not have meant that the way it sounded. Just because my mind had been in the gutter ever since he walked into the kitchen, his hair damp and his shirt clinging to him like a thirsty sponge, it didn't mean his mind was on the same train of thought as mine. We'd clearly agreed that the night before would be a one-time thing... though why, exactly, we'd agreed on that, I couldn't really remember.

Most Sundays, I spent at the office. With no one else there, it gave me the chance to get a lot of work done without any distractions, letting me be ready for the week ahead. But that day, even with no one else around, my mind kept wandering anyway. The words on the papers in front of me swam and rearranged themselves until they formed an image of Dex's naked body the night before, how he'd looked beneath me, calling out my name, and desire rushed through me yet again, making it impossible to concentrate.

Perhaps I shouldn't have left the house before breakfast. Seeing him in a more professional situation, clothes on, would have helped to refocus my mind, so I came home and set myself up in the kitchen with the contract for the gallery that still required his signature, along with a few other things I had to work on. I figured that Dex would find me sooner or later and we could talk and have a normal, business-like conversation and everything could go back to the way it had been.

That *had* been my plan, until he walked into the kitchen looking like a literal wet dream.

With his invitation to join him back in his room, or at least his bathroom, it felt like the universe testing me in some way, and I was determined to prove to both Dex and myself that I could keep myself under control.

"Sure, I can show you," I heard myself saying as I slid off my chair and headed towards him. I had dressed casually that morning in a pale yellow dress, trying to beat the summer heat, and my feet were bare as I walked along the hardwood floors of the hallway towards Dex's room. He followed behind me in his sweat-soaked t-shirt, jeans and socks, his clay scent even stronger than usual.

His ensuite bathroom wasn't quite as big as mine, but still a good size with a large, walk-in shower. I'd never used that particular shower before, but it had the same controls as mine. A large rainfall showerhead hung directly overhead and wall jets sprayed from the side wall, all of which had separate controls, so I figured that must have been where he'd run into trouble. Dex leaned his head in to watch as I stepped into the shower stall and stood in front of the control panel.

"These dials are for the overhead shower," I explained, running my fingers across the knobs. "This one is for strength, this one is temperature and this one can change the rhythm of it. These ones here are for the wall jets: again, strength, temperature and rhythm."

"Rhythm?" he repeated curiously.

"If you want it steady or... pulsing."

My breath caught slightly on the last word as I tried to ignore the increasingly insistent pulsing inside my own body. All I could picture at that moment was him standing in the shower once I left, water trickling down his muscular chest and stomach and even lower.

In my distraction, my hand slipped, making me lose my balance entirely. As I scrambled to regain my equilibrium, my hand pressed one of the buttons on the wall and instantly, a jet of water shot out, hitting me square in the chest.

"Damn it!" I sputtered, trying to hold back the water with one hand as I pressed wildly at the buttons with my other until the spray finally stopped.

How did I turn into a complete klutz every time he was around? Dex was going to have a field day with that, I had no doubt, and sure enough, his teasing grin greeted me as I turned to face him.

"Wait, I'm not quite sure I got it," he said, taking a step into the stall with me, forcing me to move backwards. "Was it this one?"

He pressed a different button on the wall and the overhead shower-head turned on, drenching both of us for just a second before he turned it back off.

"Dex!" I shrieked, not sure whether to laugh or scowl at him. "You did that on purpose."

"Maybe I did."

The smile on his face faded as his eyes drifted lower, taking in the soaked fabric of my dress that had turned almost see-through. He took another step forwards and my back hit the wall, his large frame boxing me in, and a little thrill of excitement ran through me. Maybe we were on the same train of thought after all.

"Since we're both already wet, how about you help me with the rest of the shower too?"

He leaned closer until our faces were just inches apart, waiting for me to make the call, and my mind raced with the possibilities. I knew all the reasons it wouldn't be a good idea. I should insist that we stick to just the one night, as we'd agreed, and I should leave his room to make my point.

There was just one problem.

I didn't want to.

Instead, my arms wrapped around his neck, pulling him closer to me until our lips connected.

A slight saltiness lingered in his kiss, his sweat mixed with the water that had just rained down on us from above, but I didn't care. Whenever Greg tried to kiss me after working out, I always insisted that he clean up first, but something about Dex being a little dirty was actually a turn-on. I didn't understand it, but I found myself licking his lips, my tongue tracing the whole circle of them as he pressed his body firmly against mine, showing me just how turned on he was too.

Dex hit the power for the overhead showerhead and water dropped onto us, soaking through our clothes, but yet again, I didn't care. He unzipped my dress, pulling it down over my shoulders, and it hit the shower floor hard, weighted down with water.

Taking a step back, his eyes travelled over my body, my white bra and panties already wet too, and he quickly pulled off his own clothes, making a pile in the corner, as I peeled off my last remaining items too.

The water dripping down his body looked just as good in reality as it had in my imagination, or possibly even better. Unable to stop myself, I leaned forward and licked some of the drops away, tracing them up to his neck and giving it a gentle suck as he moaned in pleasure.

Our hands slid across each other's bodies, the water making everything slippery, and when his hand found its way between my legs, the water from the shower joined with the wetness already there.

"One more time?" he asked, his eyes burning into mine with a heated desire that made my stomach flip over.

"One more time," I agreed, and as soon as the words were out of my mouth, he had my leg hitched up around his waist. With one single, perfect thrust, he was inside me, and I called out his name in ecstasy. "Oh my God, Dex!"

One of his hands stayed on my leg to hold me steady while the other went to the wall to balance himself as he took full possession of my body. The night before, he let me do things my way, but that afternoon was all him. With my back against the wall, pinned between him and the cold tile, his hard cock filling me completely, I was completely at his mercy.

And I loved it.

"You feel so good," he groaned as he sank into me, over and over, faster and faster, with growing need and growing anticipation.

He took the words out of my mouth. It had never felt so good for me, so desperate and yet so fulfilling.

His hand left the wall and he grabbed my other leg, hoisting me up so that the only thing keeping me upright was the wall behind me and his firm grip beneath my thighs. It changed the angle just enough that he hit my g-spot perfectly, and I cried out in pleasure.

"Right there, fuck!"

My orgasm hit me intensely, light flashing behind my closed eyes as my body surrendered to it, and only a few seconds later, Dex muttered my name once more.

"Good God, Nadiya."

I could feel him contracting inside me even as I pulsed around him, our bodies in complete sync as we clung to each other beneath the falling water.

I thought the night before had been as good as it could get, but apparently, I was wrong. What we just did felt even better, and I couldn't help wondering if it might be possible that there were more levels I hadn't even discovered yet.

Chapter Thirteen

Water trickled through my hair and down my back as I caught my breath, Nadiya's legs still wrapped around my waist, her back against the shower wall.

As she said the night before, that was... something.

Part of me thought that sex with her the previous night felt so good because it had been such a long time for me, but it hadn't even been 24 hours since then and somehow, what we just did felt even better.

It seemed I had to face facts: the attraction between us was stronger than I'd expected, and we had better set some new ground rules if we didn't want this to keep happening. Perhaps even more so if we did.

Most of all, we needed to figure out where we both stood.

Speaking of standing, I slid out of her and gently lowered her feet to the ground, keeping hold of her waist until she was secure and stable.

"I really do still need to have a wash," I told her with a smile. "Do you want to stay and help?"

The idea of having Nadiya run her hands over me, lathering me up, appealed to me far more than it should have, but to my disappointment, she took a step back. "I should go," she said, a little too quickly. "I was actually in the middle of something."

That stung a little bit, for reasons I couldn't quite explain. Our agreement had been to keep things professional, other than these couple of brief forays into tending to each other's needs. We'd certainly never said anything about spending time together in a more intimate way outside of that, so why did it disappoint me that she wasn't interested?

Nadiya slipped out of the still-running shower and grabbed one of the large, fluffy white towels off the rack. My eyes followed her movements as she dried herself off and wrapped the towel around herself. "I'll come back for my dress later," she said, keeping her eyes on the clothes on the floor rather than on me before she headed out the door and closed it behind her, leaving me alone with my thoughts in the steamy shower.

As I grabbed my body wash, I tried to figure out what caused my disappointment. Maybe it upset me how she ran away as soon as we'd finished, both the night before and this time too, because I didn't like the feeling of being used for sex? But we'd agreed that anything we did would simply be about scratching the itch, so why should it bother me if she treated it that way? I couldn't think of any good reason... unless I actually wanted something more.

Obviously, I found her attractive, that couldn't be denied, but I owed it to the both of us to figure out what else I felt before things got out of hand.

And there was only one place I could think of to do that properly.

After I showered and got dressed in some fresh clothes, having wrung out the soaked ones from the bathroom floor and hung them over the top of the shower rails to dry out, I headed back to the kitchen where I found Nadiya still looking over her papers.

She had put on a different dress, another light summer dress, pink in colour, and I couldn't help noticing the way it brought out the pink in her cheeks.

Yeah, the time had definitely come for me to take a breather.

She looked up at me with her business smile, that slightly impersonal one. "I was just going to order something in for supper. Would you like to take a look and see what you want?"

So, we weren't going to talk about what had just happened, apparently, but that was okay. I still wanted to sort out my own head before I talked things over with her anyway.

"No, you go ahead, darlin'. I'm going to head out for a little while if that's okay."

Surprise crossed her face, but her expression quickly settled back into her practiced smile. "Of course. I'll see you later."

With a nod of goodbye, I headed out to my truck. Only when I pulled out of the driveway and down the street did the papers in front of Nadiya cross my mind. Did they have anything to do with my gallery? I still hadn't signed anything, which seemed a bit strange. Surely, we still needed to make our whole agreement official.

Rather than turning around, though, I decided to ask her about it later, and kept going to my usual destination when I needed to really think about something. There was just one person I could talk to about something as important as this.

The beautiful early summer afternoon had just a bit of a breeze as I drove through the gates of Glenwood Cemetery. Shawna had never splurged on a damn thing in her life, but when it came to her burial site, I'd insisted on it being here, even though we didn't really have the money to spare. One of the city's oldest cemeteries and easily the most beautiful, Glenwood had elaborate statues and grave markers amidst well cared for trees and paths. The whole place felt like a beautiful park that just happened to have people buried in it, and we had often visited it together, looking at the different works of art that adorned the most elaborate burial sites and the more modest ones too.

I'd wanted to be able to visit her there, where I could remember those times and feel her presence, rather than at some modern, boxy cemetery, and when she saw how much it meant to me, she didn't argue.

Her memorial sat next to a longleaf pine tree. We'd only been able to afford a small plot, but she'd wanted to be cremated anyway, so it only needed to fit the urn. Marking the spot stood the sculpture I'd made for her, the one I had poured all my emotions of those last few months into. Whenever I wasn't at her bedside, I'd worked on it, and the sight of it always brought me right back to those days, connecting me with her in a visceral way.

The sculpture was the sister piece to the one in my gallery window. That one showed her in her struggle, fighting against the illness that restrained her, while the one in the cemetery showed her after the struggle's end, free of her chains at last as she leapt into the unknown.

Several times, I'd arrived to find people taking photos of it or just stopping to look at it, and it made me glad. I hoped that, if nothing else, they would read her name and the inscription on the statue's base, and just for a moment, she'd live again in the thoughts of the people reading it.

That day, there was no one around, so I went and sat down on the grass next to the sculpture, just like I usually did.

"Hey, baby." It wasn't the most inspired nickname, but we'd been young when we got together, and it had stuck through the years. I always called her that and I never used it for anyone else. "So, a few things have changed since the last time I came to visit."

Although I talked to her a lot no matter where I was, when I visited her at the cemetery, I always went over everything that had happened since the last time. That day, I filled her in on everything with Nadiya, how we'd gone from foes to fake fiancés to married all in the span of a week. I told her about taking Nadiya to my mom's and about everything intimate we'd done together. Lying to Shawna about it would be pointless; I figured she already knew it all, but she deserved to hear it from me anyway.

"It's a little bit complicated," I summed up, trying to find the words to explain how I felt. "I feel something for her, ain't no point lying about that. It's not like it was with us, but I know you told me nothing ever would be."

She'd made me promise her, when we found out the cancer was back, that if the worst happened, I wouldn't spend the rest of my life pining after her. I could still hear her voice in my head, clear as day: *You can't wait around for another me, Dex, 'cause I'm one of a kind. But something can be different and still good. Don't use the fact that it's not the same as an excuse not to be happy.*

She'd promised to haunt me if I ended up old and alone, but so far, she hadn't kept her word. Six years had passed without a glimpse of her.

Having laid out the situation, I got to the crux of my dilemma: "No matter what I'm feeling, she wants to keep it professional, and I don't want to make things uncomfortable. So, I really don't know what to do. I feel like there could be something more there, but maybe I should stick to business, like she says, and just forget about the whole thing."

A gust of wind swirled around me, the breeze picking up, and suddenly, something smacked me in the back of the head, just like Shawna used to when I said something she found particularly stupid. I quickly spun around, my heart beating faster, but there was no one there. On the ground, though, sat a large pinecone from the tree beside me. The wind must have blown it loose and knocked it into me.

A skeptic would think that, but I knew better.

It couldn't be much clearer to me that the pinecone was Shawna's way of telling me she didn't want me using her as a reason not to live my life, just like she'd made me promise not to. Maybe, the time had finally come to stop doing that.

"Message received," I told her, glancing skywards as I rubbed the back of my head. "Thanks, baby."

Pressing my lips to the statue's head, just as we'd both done on the day I showed it to her, I said goodbye and got back in my truck, heading back to my new home and the enigmatic woman waiting for me there.

~**Nadiya**~

My stomach sank as Dex walked out the door. It seemed I'd offended him by not staying to shower with him, but I still thought it had been the right thing to do. We'd already crossed the line between business and pleasure too many times, and nothing about scrubbing down his body in the steamy shower could be called professional, no matter how appealing it might be.

The situation between us was getting out of hand very quickly, and one of us needed to hit the brakes. If he wouldn't do it, then it would have to be me.

But if I felt that way, then why did it disappoint me that he wanted to go out rather than having dinner with me? When he moved in, I told him that we didn't have to spend time together in the house, so he hadn't done anything other than take me at my word, while I sat there wondering where he was going and why it appealed to him more than spending time with me. My thoughts frustrated me so much that I slapped the countertop to get the tension out, leaving my hand stinging.

That frustration was exactly what we needed to avoid, and once the week started and I got back into my work routine, things would be better. I just needed to get through that night without seeing him again, so with that in mind, I packed up all my work and took it into my bedroom instead. When my food arrived, I took it back to my room too.

Hiding away might be considered childish, but since I couldn't seem to behave like a responsible adult around him, I didn't seem to have many other options.

A couple of hours after he left, I heard the front door open again, signalling Dex's return. I could picture him kicking off his shoes at the front door and heading into the kitchen. Would he be disappointed not to find me there?

Honestly, Nadiya? I shook my head at myself, trying to focus back on the paperwork in front of me. I was worse than a teenager obsessing over her crush.

A few minutes later, a gentle knock sounded on my door. "Nadiya? You in there?"

I hadn't expected him to actually come looking for me, and I panicked. "Just having an early night," I lied. "I've got a busy week coming up."

"Oh, sorry," he apologized, which immediately made me feel worse for lying in the first place. "I'll see you later, then. Good night."

"Good night, Dex."

The next morning, I got up and out of the house before Dex made an appearance, which didn't really surprise me. With his gallery closed, he had no particular schedule to stick to. Demolition of the building was scheduled for that day, and the breaking ground ceremony for my development would take place later that week. It would be the first event I wanted Dex to attend with me, since the media would be there and they would almost certainly be interested in getting a glimpse of my new husband.

Since that day marked my first day back in the office after the wedding, I expected to have to deal with some reaction to the news, and sure enough, as soon as Luisa arrived for the day, she appeared at my office door with a big grin on her face.

"Come in," I told her, trying to hide my own smile at how giddy she looked. We always met first thing in the morning to review my calendar for the day, but I knew that wouldn't be the first thing on her mind that particular morning.

As soon as she'd taken a seat across from me, she leaned forward in excitement. "That was an engagement ring!" she exclaimed gleefully, reminding me that she had spotted my ring just before I left for City Hall on Friday. "I can't believe you kept it a secret. I would have been so excited, I'd have told everybody."

I held my hand out so she could get a better look at the ring. "We didn't want to make a big deal out of it. Dex isn't really one for showy displays."

We had that in common, I realized. Although my job forced me to live parts of my life in public, it had never been my natural inclination.

"He is so handsome," she gushed, making me smile again. "And nice. And talented too. I went on his website after I saw the news, his work is amazing!"

The fact that she looked up his work took me by surprise, and I immediately wondered how many other people might have. That would be an unexpected side effect of our wedding going public, but if it brought some extra attention to Dex's art, it could only be a good thing. He deserved it. He was definitely underappreciated as an artist.

"He's pretty wonderful," I agreed, feeling the familiar flush of heat to my cheeks as I started to think of the *other* wonderful things about him, and I quickly pushed those feelings back down. "Let's get to work, shall we? It's a busy day."

Luisa nodded, though I could see she still had more she would have liked to say. We spent the next twenty minutes going over everything until we were both crystal clear on the plan for the day, and just as we were wrapping up, her phone buzzed. "Mr Sherwood has just called a quick meeting in the boardroom for the whole executive floor. Should we go over together?"

Immediately, my defenses went up. I couldn't imagine what he was up to, but with no pressing reason not to go, I reluctantly stood up and followed Luisa down the hall to the boardroom.

"Congratulations!"

The loud call rang out from dozens of people, everyone gathered with glasses that they raised to me as I entered.

"What is all this?" I stuttered, completely thrown off by the unexpected gesture.

With his usual fake smile, Brad walked over and handed me a glass. "It's sparkling juice, not champagne, since it's Monday morning, but we couldn't let the occasion pass without a little celebration."

It would have been a thoughtful thing to do if anyone else had done it, but coming from Brad, I had my suspicions about how sincerely he meant it.

As if to prove my point, after I took the glass from him, he stepped back. "Why don't you tell us how this all came about, Nadiya? Last we heard, you were dating someone else."

There it was. He wanted to embarrass me, but luckily, I'd prepared for that question. "Greg and I were together for a long time, but as you already know, Brad, he decided to end things between us."

I gave him my sweetest smile, making sure no one missed my meaning: Greg dumped me and Brad already knew it, which made him the jerk for bringing it up.

Having made my point, I turned my attention to the rest of the room. "The next day, I had a business meeting with Dex. We'd been corresponding by email for quite a while, but we'd never met in person before, and I guess you could say it was love at first sight. When you know, you know, and we knew."

To punctuate the story, I held up my hand with the ring to gasps of adoration from the women and indulgent smiles from most of the men other than Brad, whose eyes had turned colder.

"Well, we're all delighted for you," he said with his insincere tone that had never fooled me, even though it seemed to take everyone else in. "To Nadiya and Dex."

Everyone echoed his toast and we all drank from our glasses before I placed mine down on the table. "Thank you all very much, but it is still a business day, and I have work to attend to. Just because I'm married doesn't mean anything will change around here."

A good-natured groan circled the room as people began to break up and head back to their own desks. I turned to go too, but before I could get out the door, Brad stopped me.

"This is all very convenient," he muttered quietly, keeping his plastic smile on his face in case anyone looked our way. "After months of holding out on the sale, Callahan agreed to sell and offered to marry you all in the same day, right after you and Greg split up? Sounds awfully coincidental to me. What exactly did you give him?"

My heart beat slightly faster at the implied threat in his words. He had decided my marriage was all for show, and he was, of course, completely correct. However, there was no way he could know that for certain, so I did my best to bluff my way through.

"You sound a little paranoid, Brad. I'm afraid it's all far less boring than that: just two people who fell in love, nothing more."

"I'm sure you're right," he replied, though his tone implied the exact opposite. "In which case, you've got nothing to worry about."

He walked away to make small talk with someone else and I left the room and headed back to my office with his words still ringing in my head. He might have suspicions, but he couldn't prove anything. He was just trying to rattle me with his empty threats.

Why was it working anyway?

~Dex~

My ringing phone woke me up, and I opened my eyes to look around the room in confusion, taking a minute to remember where I was and why. I had tossed and turned half the night, my mind refusing to rest, but apparently, I must have fallen asleep at some point because daylight streamed through the window of Nadiya's guest room and my ringtone – Lee Brice's *A Woman Like You* – was halfway through the chorus.

"Hello?" I mumbled into the phone when I finally found it. I didn't recognize the number, but I thought it might be Nadiya calling from the office or something. She must have been at work for a little while already.

"Mr Callahan?" an unfamiliar woman's voice asked on the other end.

"Yes?"

"My name is Catherine Sweetman. I'm calling from Mary Flynn's office."

It took me a second to wrap my head around that. Mary Flynn, the interior designer? The one who had designed the house I was currently living in? Why on earth would her office be calling me?

"Good morning, ma'am, what can I do for you?" I managed to ask, clearing my throat to sound a little more awake.

"Ms Flynn has been looking at some of your work and would be interested in meeting with you. Could we set up a time for her to come and visit your gallery?"

Could I still be dreaming? Shawna and I used to imagine this exact thing happening, the phone call out of the blue, and just three days after moving in with Nadiya, it happened for real?

Did Nadiya do this? I had a million questions, but I couldn't let them show, so I did my best to act like this kind of thing happened to me all the time.

"Well, my gallery's actually just closed down temporarily, but I'd be happy to meet with her at her office. I can bring photos of my work."

The brief pause on the other end made it feel like my heart stopped beating. Had that been the wrong thing to say? "She generally prefers to see the work in person. Is that not possible?"

Quickly, I offered an alternative, my heart still in my throat. "Well, she could come to my new workshop if she prefers. It's not much, but some of my pieces are there."

"That should be fine," she agreed, and I breathed a sigh of relief.

We set a date for the next week and I gave her the address details. That gave me a bit of time to get things looking a bit better out in the garage and bring a few of my other works out of storage. Hopefully, I could create some new ones too, ones that would be sure to impress her. I'd been a bit short of inspiration and time lately, but that morning, I felt positive. That kind of huge opportunity didn't come around every day.

"You heard that, right, baby?" I asked the empty room once I'd hung up, but of course, Shawna didn't reply. That had never bothered me before, but that morning, it crossed my mind that I had someone else I could tell now, someone who might actually respond, and I sent Nadiya a quick text.

Just got off the phone with Mary Flynn's office, she wants to see my work. Did you do something?

Her reply came back as I pulled my clothes on for the day. *That's amazing, Dex! I wish I could take credit, but I had nothing to do with it. People at the office told me they looked you up online after reading about you in the paper. Maybe Mary did too? If there's anything I can do to help, let me know.*

Her enthusiasm made me smile, and my fingers itched to call her so I could hear it in her voice, but she was probably busy. I'd have to wait and talk it over with her once she got home, but just knowing I had that to look forward to put an extra spring in my step.

The day passed quickly. My phone kept ringing with other people who had read about me in the paper, and my email was filled with enquiries from the website. I had to let most of them go unanswered if I wanted to have any time to work at all, and I wondered if it was too early to think about hiring myself a PA again. It had been a long time since I'd had any staff. I would have the money for it once the remainder of the cash from the gallery sale came through, but I supposed I still needed to sign the paperwork before that would happen. I would have to ask Nadiya about it that evening.

In the mood to celebrate, I went out in the afternoon to the grocery store and picked up a few things to stock up Nadiya's bare kitchen. Google helped me find some vegetarian dishes that I thought she might like, and when I got back to the house, I got straight to cooking, putting some music on in the background and singing along, badly, as I chopped and prepped everything for our meal. I couldn't remember the last time I'd been in such a good mood.

I must have been so caught up in it that I didn't hear the front door open, and only when Nadiya's red suit appeared in the corner of my eye did I realize that she'd arrived. When I looked over at her, she stood in the kitchen doorway, watching me with a rather amused smile on her face.

"I picked up some champagne," she said, holding up the bottle in her hand. "I was going to order a special meal too, but it looks like you've got supper under control."

"I like to cook when I'm happy," I explained, leaning over to switch my music off. "It's been an amazing day."

"I'm so glad." The sincerity in her eyes backed up her words. "Give me just a minute to clean up and I'll be right back out to join you."

She put the champagne on the counter and headed down the hall to her room while I dished up our meals. My former cattle rancher daddy would have been rolling in his grave at the sight of cauliflower steaks, but I actually thought they smelled pretty good.

It felt like the occasion called for more than sitting at the kitchen island, so I took everything into the dining room and poured some of the champagne. Nadiya joined me a few minutes later, still wearing her red suit pants but she'd lost the jacket. Beneath it, she had on a silky-looking white-and-black sleeveless top, and she'd let her hair down. She looked incredible.

"Dex, this looks incredible," she said appreciatively, unconsciously echoing my thoughts as she sat down. "We're supposed to be celebrating you though, not making you do all the work!"

I took a seat next to her rather than on the other side of the table. "I told you, cooking is fun for me. Although, this is a new recipe, so I hope it's okay. The no-meat thing is going to take some getting used to."

"You don't need to follow my diet," she insisted. "If you'd prefer to eat meat, that's fine."

"And cook two meals? I thought you didn't want to make extra work for me."

Nadiya smiled, but something else lurked in her eyes. "Dex, you don't need to cook for me. That wasn't part of our agreement. I appreciate this, I really do, but you don't need to worry about me."

"It's not about any agreement," I told her, taking a bite of the herb-crusted cauliflower. It actually tasted pretty damn good, if I did say so myself. "It's just a matter of common courtesy, Nadiya. Trust me, if I don't want to do something, I won't. If I do it, it's because I want to."

She didn't have any response to that, taking a drink of her champagne instead. "Well, speaking of things you do, tell me exactly what Mary's office said."

We chatted about the call and my other offers as we ate, and Nadiya was full of ideas about how I could expand and take advantage of the new interest in my work.

"You shouldn't be spending your time on admin," she pointed out, which I'd already figured out myself. "I can have someone here in the morning who can take that on for you so you can focus entirely on your art."

"In the morning?" I repeated in surprise. How could she possibly hire someone that quickly?

She laughed at my confusion. "Varma Corp has a pool of admin temps we can call on when extra work comes up. They've all been vetted already, and I'm sure they'd jump at the chance to get you organized."

She obviously operated at a whole different level of business than I did. "I don't want to put you out."

"They aren't working for me at the moment. They're just on standby, so it's not inconveniencing me at all. Let me arrange it for you, Dex. As a thank you for supper, if nothing else."

The two things hardly seemed comparable in my mind, but if she insisted, I'd be a fool to pass it up. "That would be great. Thanks, Nadiya."

Her pleased smile when I gave in sent a wave of warmth through my body, and when our eyes connected across the table, a new kind of hunger stirred in me. I knew she felt it too, if only because she quickly looked away. "Let me help you take these dishes back to the kitchen," she offered, getting to her feet.

I followed behind her, trying to figure out how to bring up the other thing I'd been wanting to talk about: namely, the attraction between us. It couldn't be more obvious to me that she was fighting it, but I didn't know exactly why.

"Just leave them here in the sink," she instructed, placing her own dishes down. "The housekeeper will take care of them in the morning."

That temporarily distracted me. "Seriously, darlin'? You don't even wash your own dishes? Do you know how?"

She looked as offended by that as I'd expected. "It's not that I can't, it's just not the best use of my time. Time is money, Dex. That's why you should be spending yours creating art and not answering phone calls."

The deflection was a good effort, but not good enough. "Or maybe you're just a little spoiled," I teased her. "Maybe you need to get your hands dirty a little more often."

As soon as the word 'dirty' came out of my mouth, the air between us seemed to shift. All I could think of was all the places I'd like her hands to be, and she looked up at me with such open desire that I couldn't help but reach for her. In an instant, I had her perched up on the island countertop, her knees spread open around my hips and our faces inches apart.

"We can't keep doing this, Dex," she whispered, though her eyes were telling me the exact opposite.

I honestly couldn't see why not. "Are we hurting anyone, darlin'?"

"No," she admitted, shaking her head just a little as her eyes stayed locked on mine.

"Do you *want* to do it again?"

She didn't answer out loud, but her nod was all I needed before I kissed her, hard and deep.

Chapter Fourteen

~Nadiya~

I had never been someone who gave in to temptation. I had no vices. I never smoked, rarely drank, ate a balanced diet and got eight hours of sleep a night. Discipline and self-control had been drilled into me from an early age by my father, reinforced by demanding teachers and tutors, and solidified by the cut-throat world I worked in. Emotional reactions were flawed and logic and business sense should take precedence at all times.

Since I'd grown up with that philosophy, I stuck to the same rules in my relationships too. Decisions about who to date and when to move the relationship to the next level were analyzed, the pros and cons weighed out before I made any decision.

But for some reason, whenever Dex was involved, everything I'd ever learned and lived by flew right out the window, and I couldn't even bring myself to be sorry to watch them go. With his lips on me, his hands roaming my body, logic was the last thing on my mind.

On the way home from work, I'd been in the back of the car, flipping through things on my phone when I reread his text about his good news and had a sudden desire not to turn up empty-handed. Again, that didn't usually come into play. When Greg had good news, or my other boyfriends before him, I congratulated them sincerely, but if they wanted to celebrate, I left it to them to arrange. Why it should have been any different with Dex, I didn't know, but I found myself instructing my driver to make a stop so I could buy some champagne. I had wine at the house but it felt like the occasion called for something a little more special.

And when I got home and found him in the kitchen, bopping his head goofily as he chopped up vegetables, a strange warmth spread through my chest at the sight of him. It only grew stronger when I sat down for supper and realized he had cooked us both a vegetarian meal, and a very good one at that.

In the grand scheme of things, it didn't mean anything more than me stopping for champagne did, but still, no one had ever gone to so much effort for me before. Greg had certainly never cooked for me. He said I was too picky so he preferred to order out, and logically I couldn't argue. It hadn't bothered me at all at the time, and yet, Dex going to the trouble, even if he claimed he enjoyed it, meant more to me than I thought it would.

So, when a chance came up to help him by providing him with a temp, it made me feel good to be able to make the offer, and even better when he accepted my help. Greg hated when I made suggestions for his business. He claimed I was trying to take over, that I always needed to be in control. Eventually, we stopped talking much about his work.

Eventually, we stopped talking much about anything important at all.

Each second spent with Dex showed me how staid and unfulfilling my relationship with Greg had really been, and I could hardly believe that I would have been ready to accept Greg's proposal if he had actually gone ahead and proposed. How sad it would have been to live the rest of my life not knowing what I was missing.

And yet, my relationship with Dex was an illusion. No matter how thoughtful he could be, no matter how good the sex, it still wasn't a real relationship, and it confused and frustrated me that I couldn't stop myself from falling for it just as the rest of the world had.

So, when he lifted me up onto the counter, his strong arms not straining in the slightest, and leaned in close to me, letting me feel the heat of his body as well as the heat in his eyes, I tried to resist. I really did. But when he asked me flat out if I wanted him, I couldn't lie. My whole body tingled in anticipation, aching for his touch, and when his lips found mine, the feeling that ran through me was pure bliss, nothing less.

All sense of caution or restraint was thrown to the wind as we clawed at each other's clothes, me pulling his shirt off and him quickly doing the same to me. His fingers skimmed along the edge of my bra as he kissed me again, his tongue laying claim to my mouth, tasting and exploring every inch. I tried to push back, to take control as I usually did, but he was too hungry, too insistent, and in the end, I couldn't fight it.

I didn't really want to.

My legs went around his waist, pulling his hips in closer and letting me feel his solid hardness beneath his jeans. Dex snapped open the clasps of my bra and pulled it off, then lowered his mouth to my breasts as I leaned back, my hands on the countertop, to give him better access. My head fell back as he took one nipple in his mouth and sucked on it, letting his tongue flick across the tip. His hands held me firmly, splayed across my back as he took his sweet time teasing and tasting me, and it took me a moment to realize the sighs and moans echoing around the kitchen were coming out of my mouth.

Eventually, he reached down and undid my pants and, with my hands still on the countertop, I raised my hips to let him pull them down. They were quickly discarded on the kitchen floor, leaving me naked and wet and filled with need, on top of the counter.

I had never done anything like this in my kitchen before. Sex was reserved for the bedroom, or very occasionally, the bathroom, but Dex didn't seem to have any intention of moving us. He quickly pulled off his own pants, and the sight of him, naked and hard and his eyes filled with the same desire that pulsed through me, sent a pang of need through me so strong that I almost came right then.

"You look good enough to eat, darlin'," he said, his voice thick with longing but with that sexy, teasing twinkle in his eyes. "Good thing I saved room for dessert."

He lowered his head between my legs and my whole body jolted, anticipation and pleasure and satisfaction racing through me all at once. "Oh, fuck, Dex," I moaned, falling back onto my elbows as my wrists refused to support me any longer. His mouth felt magical as he licked and sucked and kissed me in ways I never knew I wanted or needed, but damn it, I needed them then. From my vantage point, I watched as he added his fingers to the mix, pumping two of them, rough and skilled, into me as he latched onto my clit with his mouth, and the combination of sights and sensations became too much. I came hard, the orgasm lingering and reverberating through me as I collapsed even further onto the cool marble of the countertop.

"So beautiful, sweetheart," Dex muttered, still between my legs, and I managed to raise my head weakly to look at him. His lips glistened with my wetness and before I even knew I meant to do it, I sat back up and kissed him, tasting myself on him as he groaned in appreciation.

His hands gripped my hips, pulling me right to the edge of the counter and lining up his cock with my entrance. As he pushed into me, slowly and deliberately, I cried out again into his kiss. "Oh, yes, fuck!"

I should have been used to the feel of it by then, but somehow, it kept getting better. Maybe the angle made a difference, or maybe it was the thrill of doing something so brazen in my kitchen with the sun streaming in the window. If anyone happened to walk up to the window at that moment, they would certainly get an eyeful, and yet, I couldn't bring myself to care. All I knew in that moment was the perfect way he filled me and the anticipation of the pleasure yet to come. He wouldn't stop until I came again, and knowing him, I had no doubt that I would.

My hands wrapped around him, helping to support myself as he held my hips tightly, keeping the angle just right. "You fit me just right," he groaned as he thrust into me again. "Like a glove, darlin'."

I couldn't argue with that. It felt so right for me too, but I wanted more. I'd had him sweetly and I'd had him at my mercy, and that night, I wanted something new. He made me greedy that way. "Fuck me hard,

Dex," I begged. "Show me what these muscles can really do."

His eyes darkened as a low groan echoed in his chest. "Hold on then, Nadiya."

My grip tightened on him as his fingers dug deeper into my skin, and in the next moment, he began to pound into me so hard it made my teeth rattle. Our skin slapped together, my legs spread wide around him, and I had never felt so wild, so dirty, so... free.

"Oh God, yes," I cried out as my orgasm began to build again. Somehow, he moved even faster with my encouragement, his hips rolling into me, his cock hitting places I didn't even know I had, and when my pleasure peaked, I simply melted in his arms, unable to hold myself upright a second longer. Luckily, he didn't need me to since he came too, his cock buried to the hilt as he pumped deep into me.

That was truly amazing. I had never had sex like that, never felt comfortable enough with anyone to let myself fully go in the moment that way, and I had to guess by his reaction that he enjoyed it too. For whatever reason, we simply worked well together, at least when it came to our bodies.

It wasn't until the room began to take shape around me again that I realized my head was on his shoulder and I raised my head to look at him a little sheepishly. "Thanks," I managed to stutter, which made him laugh.

"Anytime, sweetheart," he said, giving my forehead a gentle kiss before he pulled out of me and helped me back down onto the floor.

Those words quickly brought me back to my senses. That was the problem, wasn't it? Our sexual encounter was supposed to be a one-time thing, but it kept happening, and as soon as the lust cleared from my head, my stomach sank again. How did I keep losing control that way?

"Well, I'm going to go get ready for bed," I started to say, bending over to pick up my clothes, but when I stood back up, Dex was right in my path, his arms crossed across his broad chest.

"Not this time," he disagreed. "First, Nadiya, you and me need to have a little talk."

~Dex~

Nadiya looked up at me like a deer caught in the headlights. "Talk?" she repeated, clutching her clothes to her chest as she stood naked in the middle of the kitchen. "About what?"

"About this." I gestured down at our naked bodies and to the countertop where she'd just been laid out in front of me like the most tempting damn thing I'd ever seen. "And why you keep running away from me afterwards."

"I'm not running away," she tried to protest, but I simply raised my eyebrows at her in response and she sighed. "Okay, maybe I am. A little."

"So let's talk about it," I persisted. "It ain't that you're leaving here unsatisfied. I know you felt that the same as me, darlin'. I wasn't coming on my own over here, so why are you acting like it's something to be ashamed of?"

Like *I'm* something to be ashamed of, I couldn't help adding in my head. Was that the problem? Was I good enough for a roll in the hay but nothing else?

The way she treated me outside of our sexual encounters didn't suggest that was the case. Over supper, she treated me like an equal, engaged and interested in our conversation. It was only after sex that she withdrew, and I really didn't get it.

Nadiya pursed her lips, obviously not sure what to say. At least she didn't deny that she enjoyed it, even though I would have known she was lying if she tried. She definitely wasn't faking her reaction to me, and when she asked me to fuck her hard, she must have been just as caught up in the moment as I had. Hearing that order from her was damn near the sexiest thing I'd ever heard. I loved that she knew what she wanted and didn't hesitate to ask for it, and I was more than happy to give it to her.

If only she didn't act like it had all been a big mistake as soon as we finished.

"Can we put some clothes on before we talk?" she asked, glancing down at my nakedness, her cheeks a little flushed.

"You weren't shy with me a minute ago, and rushing to put our clothes back on is just the kind of thing I'm talking about. If anything, we should be cuddling for a little while right now and enjoying what just happened."

Nadiya's eyes widened in surprise. "You want to cuddle with me?"

She said it like a foreign word, unfamiliar to her.

"Is that really so strange? Didn't you and Greg cuddle?"

Maybe bringing up her ex at that moment wasn't the best move, but I needed to understand where this reaction of hers came from. Did it stem from something about me, or did it have roots in her history?

"I don't think so," she replied, and I stared at her in consternation. How could she not know the answer to such a simple question? My confusion must have been clear on my face because she tried again. "I mean, I don't know exactly what you mean by cuddling."

Well, I could fix that easily enough. "Come with me."

I reached out my hand and she looked at it for a moment, clearly debating in her head whether or not to take it, but finally, and to my great relief, she gave in. The clothes in her arms dropped back to the floor as she placed her hand in mine and I led her down the hall to my room. Pulling the covers back, I climbed into the bed and laid on my back, my head and upper back propped up on the pillows, and held my arms open to her.

"Get on in here, sweetheart."

The look of hesitation on her face damn near killed me. Why was this so strange to her? What kind of relationships had she been in before? Whatever the reason for her hesitation, at least she seemed to be fighting against it, and she eventually crawled in after me, lying down beside me on her side. I pulled her closer so our bodies were aligned and covered us both up with the blankets.

That felt really good. I hoped she thought so too.

"So let's talk about what's going on, Nadiya," I tried again. "We said one time, but obviously, that ain't sticking. Tell me why you think that is."

I had some thoughts about why myself, but I wanted to hear what she had to say first.

Her hand trailed lightly across my chest as her head rested on my shoulder. "Well, as you said, the sex is good. Really good, I mean."

She hadn't said so out loud before, and it made me happy to hear her admit it. It was really good for me too, I couldn't deny that. "What else?"

"You also said that there's no reason that we can't. We're technically married and we're not hurting anyone."

I already knew the reasons I'd given her. I didn't need a recap, I wanted to hear what *she* was thinking. "What does your gut say, Nadiya? Why do we keep ending up naked together?"

She hesitated a moment longer, and I pushed a little bit more.

"Come on, darlin'. You can make million-dollar deals without batting an eye, but you can't tell me what's going on in that head of yours? Where's the fearless CEO now?"

Her eyes sparked with defiance against my challenge as she looked up at me, her eyes sparking, and I had to smile. *That* was the fire I wanted, the same fire I saw in her when she told me what to do to her.

The same fire that threatened to make me hard again as her body shifted against mine.

At last, she spoke her mind. "I'm attracted to you, Dex. You have to know that. You're a very good-looking man, you're great with your body, and I feel very comfortable with you. And that's fine, on its own. But then we take into account everything else going on between us, our quid pro quo with this marriage and your gallery, plus the whole situation with your family and your first wife, and it starts to feel like a bad idea. It feels like one of us could get hurt, or both of us, and that's not what I want. I want us both to come out of this as winners, and I think we're putting that in jeopardy if we keep falling into bed with each other. This was supposed to be just business, but it's turning into something else, something that I don't understand, and I have to admit... it scares me."

She continued to impress me. That was a lot further than I'd expected her to go, especially when it came to bringing up my family or Shawna, which must have been bothering her more than I realized.

At the same time, her admission of fear made me want to wrap her up and reassure her and protect her. Behind the public persona she'd so carefully built for herself was a woman, just a regular woman as lost as the rest of us when it came to relationships. Being vulnerable wasn't something that came natural to her, so I appreciated it more than I could say that she opened up to me that way.

Naturally, I owed her the same courtesy. "I'm a little bit scared too, Nadiya. That morning you came to my gallery, I was attracted to you straight away too, and that doesn't really happen to me. Of course, when I found out who you were, obviously that cooled me right off."

She gave me a bit of a dirty look, and I winked back at her, loving the chance to tease her.

"But then I got to know you even just a little bit, and I found there's a real person behind the name and the reputation, and she's someone I actually like. Now, don't get me wrong, you can still drive me crazy, but there's more to it than that. There's more to this than just our contract and more even than just our physical compatibility. And yeah, that scares me too. I wasn't looking for more. I thought that more wasn't ever going to happen for me again. But I also know that life is short, Nadiya, and if you find someone who makes you happy, it's stupid to spend time fighting it. We don't gotta put a label on it if you don't want to. We don't gotta make any decisions right now about what happens after you get your promotion. But right here and right now, I want to be with you, *really* be with you, and if you want that too, then I don't see any good reason why we can't just do it and figure the rest out later."

Her pretty brown eyes blinked up at me. "So... you want to date me?" she asked tentatively, and I had to laugh.

"If that's what you want to call spending time with my wife, then sure, I want to date ya. I want to give this a shot and see where it goes. If it doesn't work out, it doesn't work out, but at least we'll have tried and we won't have to regret not giving it a chance."

Her fingers returned to my chest and to the tattoo above my heart. "What about Shawna?" she asked softly, her eyes flicking up to mine for just a second before returning to the image beneath her fingers. "You still love her."

"I do. That ain't ever gonna change. But I had a talk with her, and she told me to stop being an idiot. Just because I love her doesn't mean I can't lo..."

I stopped myself before the word came out as Nadiya's eyes widened, her flight mode kicking in. That was a bit too far, too fast, so I quickly backtracked.

"... doesn't mean I can't see what's here too. She'll always have a place in my heart, ain't no changing that, but I've got a pretty big heart, Nadiya. There might be room for you too, if you want it."

In the silence that followed as she thought things over, I tried not to hold my breath as I waited for her response. Six years I'd waited to find anyone I could even consider being with again, and if she said no, who knew how long I'd have to wait for the next one to come along? Not to mention the fact that I thought I could be good for her too. She was different with me, different than she'd been even a week earlier, whether she realized it or not. Each day, she became a little less uptight, a little less controlled, and that could only be a good thing as far as I was concerned.

But what did Nadiya think? Would she agree to take a chance? Would she decide it was worth the risk? I'd said what I had to say, so I could do nothing but leave it in her hands and hope for the best.

~Nadiya~

Both my mind and my heart raced as I thought over everything Dex had just said.

He wanted more. This sexy, talented, thoughtful man actually wanted to be in a real relationship with me, not just a business one, and not just a sexual one either. He wanted to give it a shot, and I honestly didn't even know what that would mean.

I was pretty sure that Dex's idea of giving something a shot was very different from any relationship I'd ever had before.

When he asked if Greg and I cuddled, I honestly didn't know how to answer. *Did* we cuddle? We sat close enough to each other sometimes that we were touching. Occasionally, he put his arm around me, but usually only in front of other people. Was that what he meant?

Since I couldn't be sure, I asked him to clarify it, and when he took me to his bed and pulled me close to him, my naked body nestling against his warm, welcoming strength, with his unique clay scent even stronger than usual since he'd been out in his workshop most of the day, I knew the answer.

I had never done this before, never just lay in someone's arms for no reason other than to be close to each other. When Greg spent the night, we would have sex, and afterwards, we would go about our usual routine, getting up to brush our teeth and put our pajamas on, me checking my work emails, him doing whatever he did on his phone. When I got tired, we would give each other a quick peck on the lips before going to sleep on our separate sides of the bed.

That was enough intimacy for me. Or so I'd thought, anyway.

Being there in Dex's arms made me feel somehow stronger and more vulnerable at the same time. Strong enough to tell him the truth, and vulnerable enough to admit what that truth was: that the feelings growing between us scared me. It made me feel out of control and I wasn't accustomed to it.

When he told me he felt scared too, that should have been it. If we were both feeling scared, it should mean that something was wrong, but somehow, it made me feel the opposite instead. Knowing that we were both as lost and confused as each other made me feel like we were in this together, and that only by working together could we figure it out.

On the one hand, we were already married. Would it be such a big deal if we dated each other too?

But on the other hand, it *was* a big deal. In just over a week, Dex had already become a bigger part of my life than any other man had before. I'd never lived with someone, never had someone waiting for me to come home and cooking me meals and talking about our days. What if it did go wrong? We still had to live together for a few more months. If it blew up spectacularly and we ended up hating each other, it would make the whole thing painfully awkward, not to mention simply painful.

I already had a feeling that losing Dex's affection would hurt a lot more than my breakup with Greg ever did.

I honestly didn't know what to do, and Dex obviously sensed it. He reached down to cup my cheek, his rough fingers gentle against my skin as he tilted my face up so I had no choice but to look him in the eye.

"Don't leave me hanging, darlin', and don't overthink it either. Just listen to your heart. Do you want to give this a try, yes or no? That's all we gotta decide right now."

Listen to my heart. That definitely wasn't something I usually did, but when I tried, all I could hear was 'more'. I wanted more of being with him just like we were at that moment, being open with him and talking things through, being intimate with him in more ways than just sex.

Just because it might be new and scary that didn't mean I had to run away. I was Nadiya Varma, damn it, and when I really wanted something, I got it.

All I had to do was try.

"Okay. Let's give it a shot."

Dex's face broke into the sweetest smile I'd ever seen, making him look somehow even more handsome than before, which I wouldn't have thought possible, before he leaned down and kissed me. It wasn't the hard, demanding kiss of the kitchen, or even of the shower the day before. It felt soft and gentle, like a continuation of the conversation we'd just had.

It felt like a promise that we were in this together, that he was going to give it an honest try as long as I did, and I took him at his word.

He hadn't let me down so far.

Our kiss gradually grew deeper as our hands began to wander across our still-naked bodies, but still with no real urgency. Now that it wasn't just 'one more time' anymore, we had no reason to rush. I took my time exploring his body, trailing kisses across his firm stomach and his muscular thighs before taking his rapidly hardening cock in my mouth. Last time I did that, I'd been drunk, but that night, the only thing I felt high on was a new sense of hopefulness, a feeling of being exactly where I was meant to be.

Dex exhaled as I took him in deeply, but a moment later, his strong hands took hold of me and pulled me up before flipping me over onto my back. "As good as that feels, that's not what I need right now," he told me, his eyes filled with desire. "I want to make love to you, Nadiya."

A shiver of anticipation went through me, the words sounding important. I didn't exactly know the difference between that and what we'd been doing already, but it looked like I would soon find out.

His strong body covered mine, his fingers intertwining with mine as his ready cock found its way home with no help at all. My sigh of pleasure filled the room as he filled me, slowly and sensually.

"You feel amazing," he murmured against my ear.

"So do you," I told him sincerely. That couldn't have been much more of an understatement, but I didn't have the words for how good he felt inside me, or how right.

Dex took his time, taking the lead the whole way. With my legs wrapped around his waist, his hips moved steadily and surely, pumping in and out of me with exactly the right strength and speed. His hands never left mine and he kissed my lips, my face, my neck, leaving no inch of me untouched. When he leaned down to my neck and inhaled, telling me how good I smelled, my body reacted as strongly as if he'd done something physical. I never knew hearing something like that could be so sexy.

As amazing as it all felt, it couldn't last forever though. My need began to build and his obviously did too. He finally let go of one of my hands so he could reach down between us and rub my tender clit as his pace increased.

"This could never be just one time," he teased me as his cock drove into me again, harder and faster. "Not when it feels like this."

He had a point, but how could we have known that first time just how good it would be?

My back arched against him as my orgasm grew closer, and I opened my mouth to call out his name, but Dex kissed me instead, swallowing the words and claiming them for his own. He came right behind me, buried deep inside me with our bodies fully entwined.

So. *That* was making love. As I floated weightlessly on the wave of my pleasure, I knew that I had definitely never done that before.

And I also knew that I couldn't wait to do it again.

Chapter Fifteen

Nadiya's alarm woke me early the next morning. After we finished making love the night before and lay in each other's arms a while longer, she asked me where she should sleep.

"It's your house, darlin'," I pointed out with a laugh. "You can sleep anywhere you like, but wherever it is, that's where I'll be too."

After the talk we had and the intimate moments we just shared, I wasn't going to give her a chance to get cold feet, or give myself that chance either. I hadn't spent the whole night in bed with a woman since Shawna, but I felt ready, and I knew Nadiya did too as long as she didn't overthink it.

After a moment's deliberation, she decided to stay in my bed with me, so she went and got her phone so she'd have an alarm for the morning. In her absence, I got ready for the night and got back in the bed, and a few minutes later she returned, having brushed out her hair and scrubbed her face, and wearing a peach silk nightie that went just right with her warm brown skin.

"You really don't wear any pajamas?" she asked as she set her alarm and placed it on the nightstand next to the bed.

"I told you I don't." I'd mentioned it the first night I spent there.

"I remember," she admitted, and from the smile on her face, I believed she did, and that she had been thinking about me naked ever since.

We fell asleep cuddled up together, and when her alarm went off, I held onto her tightly for a moment.

"Dex," she whispered softly. "I have to get up."

"I know." I just didn't want the night to end. The whole thing had been amazing, just me and her in that room, and I wanted to hold onto it just a moment longer before the rest of the world intruded.

But eventually, I had to let her go, so I gave her forehead a kiss and told her to have a good day.

"I've got a meeting with some investors this evening," she told me. "I won't be home until quite late."

"That's fine." I hardly expected her to drop everything for me. "I've got some friends I should catch up with, so maybe I'll do that tonight."

My best friend Sawyer hadn't been at the party at my mom's on the weekend, and it had crossed my mind the day before that I hadn't heard from him at all since the news of my wedding came out. It wouldn't hurt to reach out to him and see if things were okay.

"Your new temp will be here at nine," Nadiya added as she headed out of the room. I'd almost forgotten she'd promised to arrange that for me, but apparently, she hadn't. "Try to put some clothes on before then, okay?"

She gave me a teasing wink, which made me laugh. "Don't pretend you don't love it, sweetheart!" I called out after her as she went down the hall to her room to get ready for the day.

There didn't seem much point in going back to sleep, so I got up and showered before heading out to my workshop to get started. For the first time in a long time, I felt truly inspired, and I sat down to make some sketches for a new sculpture that had come into my mind sometime during the night. I got so caught up in it that I almost missed the knock on the garage door, and when I glanced at my watch, I was shocked to see nine o'clock had already arrived.

"Come in," I called out, putting my pencil down and pushing the papers to one side, trying to make things a bit tidier.

I wasn't sure what I expected, but I supposed it would have been something like Luisa or the other women I'd seen in Nadiya's office, very professional-looking in a suit that rivalled Nadiya's. The woman who entered my new workshop, however, wore a pretty sundress and cowboy boots, with curly blonde hair trailing over her shoulders, the very picture of Texas sunshine.

At first glance, she could have been Shawna's sister.

My mouth went dry, the unexpected resemblance taking me completely by surprise as she walked over to me with a bright smile on her face. "Mr Callahan? I'm Daisy. Varma Corp sent me over to help you with some admin?"

I managed to nod, grabbing the bottle of water on my table to take a drink and give myself a minute to collect my thoughts. What was I supposed to make of this? I had been so sure Shawna gave me a sign to move on in the cemetery the other day, but now the universe sent me this woman? Others might call it a coincidence, but I'd never been much of a believer in coincidence.

In any case, this woman could hardly be faulted for looking like my dead wife, so I needed to try to act normally.

"Nice to meet you, Daisy. I'm afraid I need a lot of help."

I showed her through my system, such as it was, with my website and emails, and when she assured me she understood, I handed her control of my phone. She also asked for my diary so she could book things in for me if necessary, and I could only stare at her blankly. I'd never had to keep a real diary before. I'd never been that important.

"It's, uh, pretty open. Maybe just check with my wife's assistant for any engagements that she needs me for." Nadiya and Luisa would be on top of things, at least.

She promised me she had it under control and went to the desk I'd set up in the corner of the garage to get to work, leaving me with my art and my supplies, and the feeling that a great weight had been lifted from my shoulders. With nothing to do but create, I quickly fell back into it as the ideas came fast and free.

At the end of the day, Daisy ran through everything that she'd done with me, and I could hardly believe how much she'd accomplished. I definitely owed Nadiya my thanks for arranging someone so efficient to help me, though her appearance still managed to startle me every time I caught sight of her out of the corner of my eye.

She also said I'd received a reply from Sawyer, so she'd gone ahead and set up dinner with him at one of our favourite bars. Having someone manage my personal life as well as my work would take some getting used to, but I thanked her for going the extra mile, and once she headed home, I set out to meet up with my friend.

Sawyer was one of the few people in my life who had never known Shawna. He and I met at the grief support group I'd joined when my anger over Shawna's death reached its peak. He had lost his wife too, without warning in a car accident, and he felt just as bitter and resentful about it as I did about Shawna's cancer. Maybe even more so. Over the years, we helped each other a lot, and he was the only one who knew just how bad things had been with the gallery. I'd told him the whole story the last time we saw each other after the bank had foreclosed on me. He didn't know anything that had happened since then, so I had a lot of explaining to do.

As I got to our usual table, Sawyer already had a beer in hand. "Hey," I greeted him a little sheepishly. "So, I've got some news."

"No shit," he laughed, and I breathed a sigh of relief that he didn't seem upset about being out of the loop. "Nadiya Varma, huh?"

He'd listened to me complain about her for months, just like my family had, and I took a seat while our usual waitress brought over my regular beer without needing me to order.

"She's not what I expected," I tried to explain to him as I took a drink. "I honestly never expected this at all. You know that better than anyone. I really didn't think there was anyone else out there who could make me feel this way again."

Sawyer's expression immediately turned cooler when I mentioned feelings. "I do know that, which is why I don't understand why you're trying to bullshit me now."

His new tone made me frown. "What do you mean?"

He leaned closer to me across the table. "I mean: obviously you ain't in love with her, so exactly how much did she pay you to marry her?"

~Nadiya~

"Is everything okay, Ms Varma?"

My driver gave me a funny look in the rear-view mirror as I caught his eye. We were almost at the office and he didn't usually talk to me on the drive unless I spoke to him first. "Of course," I assured him. "Why do you ask?"

"You keep looking out the window," he replied almost sheepishly. "Normally, I only see the top of your head while you're looking at your phone. I just thought maybe you had something on your mind."

I certainly did. Or some*one*, to be more precise, but I couldn't exactly share that with one of my employees. I assured him everything was fine before looking back down at my phone.

I needed to get my head back in the game. Nobody at the office had been any wiser after Greg broke up with me, so I didn't need to let them know when things were going well either. I'd never had any trouble leaving my relationships at home before, but that morning, it felt frustratingly difficult. Every time I tried to read something for work, Dex's deep and sexy voice echoed in my head, or visions of him standing naked in my kitchen flashed across my mind.

That would be a problem if it interfered with my work, so as we pulled up to the entrance of the Williams Tower, I pushed Dex to the back of my mind. Luckily, once the morning's meetings got underway, I got caught up in the usual frantic pace of running Houston's biggest and best real estate development company, and everything else fell to the wayside.

Only after I had my after-lunch catch-up with Luisa did I let myself bring Dex up. Luisa had arranged one of the Varma Corp temps to help Dex that day, at my request. I told her to take it out of my personal budget rather than the company's, but that I wanted the best temp we had, the one who usually filled in for Luisa herself when she was on vacation. Martha was a firm and seasoned executive assistant who would have Dex's business plans in shape in no time. He might not thank me for her brusqueness, but he wouldn't be able to argue with her results.

But when I asked Luisa if she'd heard anything about how things were going, she gave me a slight grimace. "Actually, Martha called me earlier, sounding rather upset. Apparently, Mr Callahan requested someone else to come in at the last minute. Martha was already on her way over when she got the call."

That made no sense. Dex wouldn't have requested someone else; he wouldn't even have known how to. There must have been some kind of miscommunication with the agency, but I couldn't imagine how that happened. "Someone else went instead, then?"

Luisa nodded. "I don't know her personally, but the agency checked in with her about an hour ago and she said everything was going well."

Well, I still didn't understand what went wrong, but at least he had someone helping him. That was the important part, I supposed. I could ask him later if he was satisfied with the person the agency had provided.

"Speaking of Mr Callahan..." Luisa continued, and I glanced up at her in surprise, wondering if she actually wanted to ask me about our relationship. "Do you have the signed contract for me to file for the lease in the new building?"

Oh, right. She was still thinking about business, as I should be too. Worse than that, I still hadn't got Dex to sign either contract, for the gallery sale or for the new lease. "No, but I will tonight," I told her, trying not to sound as guilty as I felt for letting it slide so long. "Which reminds me: can you bring me the most up-to-date plans to share with our investors tonight?"

We were having a late meeting with the key investors behind my new building, the one that we'd be breaking ground for the next day on the spot where Dex's gallery used to stand, and I wanted to be able to show off all the businesses I had lined up for the stores on the ground floor. As much as I wished I could include Dex's gallery, it wouldn't be good business practice to mention it without having the signed contract in hand.

By the time I finished my afternoon meetings, Luisa had gathered all the information I requested and said good night after leaving it with me. The investors weren't showing up until seven o'clock, so I would have time to eat in my office beforehand. When a quiet knock sounded on my door a short time later, I assumed that it must be the delivery person with my food, so I called for them to come in, my head still down as I reviewed the papers in front of me.

"Nadiya?"

The voice nearly made me jump, and I lifted my head in shock. "Greg? How did you get in here?"

I hadn't seen him since the night he walked out on me, so to say his appearance at my office door surprised me would have been an understatement.

He winced at my question and my sharp tone. "Security let me in. I guess you haven't told them not to anymore."

That was true. I hadn't spent enough time thinking about him to remember to do that.

"Can we talk?" he continued. "I know you're busy, as usual, but you didn't return my call and there's something I think you should know."

"I don't think we have much to say to each other," I couldn't help pointing out, though to be honest, I had completely forgotten that he had called me. I'd been a little preoccupied. "Not when you went running to Brad Sherwood to tell him you dumped me."

Again, Greg grimaced. "Listen, it's Brad I want to talk to you about." He looked over his shoulder, making sure no one could hear him. "Can

I please come in?"

With a sigh, I beckoned him inside and he stepped in and closed the door behind him. As he walked over to my desk, I watched him with a curious feeling of detachment. I didn't feel particularly angry with him, and I certainly didn't feel any kind of longing for what we'd had. This man I had spent three years with felt almost like a stranger to me. In just over a week, Dex was far more real and more vibrant to me than Greg had ever been.

"I guess congratulations are in order," he said as he sat down across from me. "On your wedding, I mean."

"I know what you mean." I had no intention of talking about Dex with him. Our relationship was none of his business, but I supposed it wouldn't hurt to clear one thing up. "As you know, I didn't meet him until the day after we broke up, and I certainly never expected to fall for him."

He gave a slightly bitter smile. "I never expected you to fall for anyone, Nadiya. But if you're really happy, then I'm happy for you."

He actually sounded sincere, which confused me, and I tried to get to the point. "Why are you here, Greg?"

He looked over his shoulder one more time, even though the office door was firmly closed. "I want to warn you about Brad."

"What about him?"

"You know he wants the CEO job." I nodded, since that had never been a secret. "Well, I don't think there's much he wouldn't do to get it. I got to know him a bit at my gym. At first I thought he started going there by coincidence, and when he started asking about you and our relationship, I thought he was just being friendly."

An uneasy feeling settled in my stomach as his words sank in. I knew Brad had shown some interest in my personal life, he'd proven that over the last week, but Greg made it sound more sinister than merely taking notice. "He asked about me?"

"It started with a few backhand comments, like he noticed how much time you spent in the office and that must be hard on me. Just being sympathetic, you know? Eventually, I started talking to him a bit more and he was always so receptive to it. I thought he was just being a good friend. Then he started asking questions about our future, about what kind of a family life we'd have with you as CEO, and it got me thinking about how important I really was to you."

My blood heated up more with every word, quickly reaching a boiling point as I reached the same conclusion Greg obviously had: Brad put him up to this. He actually encouraged Greg to break up with me. Maybe it wouldn't have worked if Greg didn't have doubts already, but even so, it was an incredibly sneaky and underhanded thing to do.

"What made you decide he wasn't just being a friend?" I asked.

"Well, I told him last week when I ended things. Based on what you said earlier, I guess he must have shared that with you. Since then, I haven't heard a thing from him. He stopped going to the gym, he hasn't returned any of my messages, and I can't help feeling I've been used. I think he just wanted to break us up the whole time, and I played right into it. I'm not trying to pass the blame, I totally own my part in it, but I wanted to let you know to watch your back. If he would stoop to that level, I can't even imagine what else he'd do."

"I understand."

Nothing more needed to be said, and Greg heard my words for the dismissal they were. He got to his feet and headed for the door, but turned back again before he reached it. "Listen, Nadiya, obviously I don't know exactly what's going on between you and Callahan. When I first heard about it, I assumed it must be a stunt, but then I saw the pictures of you at City Hall, the way you were looking at him, and I wasn't so sure. But either way, if there's anything Brad could use against you, be sure to cover it up really well, okay? I don't want to see you lose the job you deserve, and especially not to someone like him."

"Thank you." Once again, I felt pretty sure he was being sincere. He'd thought things out logically before coming there, just as he'd always done before, just as he and I always did.

I couldn't help imagining what Dex would have done in his place, and

I didn't think he'd be slinking around the corridors, hiding from Brad.

Greg let himself out and my food arrived just behind him, letting me finally settle in with the plans I was going to share with the investors that night. I'd just taken a bit of my eggplant parmigiana when something new in the plans caught my eye, something that definitely had not been there the last time I looked at it.

"Son of a bitch," I muttered under my breath, my appetite immediately gone, and I reached for my phone.

Brad answered on the second ring. I knew he'd be around since he would also be attending the meeting with me that night. "What can I do for you, Nadiya?"

The smugness in his voice made me want to reach through the phone and wring his neck, and I didn't waste any time on pleasantries. "My office. Now."

~Dex~

My stomach dropped as Sawyer asked me if Nadiya had paid me off to marry her. While he didn't have it quite right, he wasn't a million miles off either, and hearing it stated so plainly made me feel uneasy in the same way I did when my brother-in-law commented that I wouldn't have to worry about money anymore.

Yes, I married a wealthy woman, but not for the reasons people seemed to think. Why couldn't they see there was so much more to her than that?

It definitely wasn't the whole story.

Still, I could see why Sawyer would make that leap, based on everything I'd shared with him over the years. He had heard me say more times than I could count that I would never get married again, so my sudden change of heart must have taken him by surprise. Although I wanted to explain myself to him, I couldn't tell him the full truth either, so I would have to choose my words very carefully.

"It's not like that. I know Nadiya and I had our differences when it came to business. She could rile me up like nobody else, as you know, but once we met in person, it was..."

I trailed off, trying to find a way to describe the change in me since Nadiya and I met.

"It was kind of like a switch being flipped, one that I thought had grown so rusty it would never be turned on again. I got used to living in darkness, but suddenly, a bit of light ame in. I know it sounds corny, but does that make any sense to you?"

He gave me a critical look. "You sound like John."

That stung, as he knew it would. John was another guy who'd joined the support group not long after Sawyer and I did. Six weeks after his fiancée's passing, he was in a new relationship, and Sawyer and I were pretty harsh on him. We said, to each other and to his face, that he must not have loved his fiancée very much if he could move on that fast.

I hadn't thought about him in a while, and shame filled me as I remembered some of the things I'd said to him. I hadn't been in a good place at the time, but that didn't excuse it.

"It's been six years for me, not six weeks," I pointed out to Sawyer. "And we probably coulda been more understanding with John anyway."

That obviously wasn't the right thing to say, since Sawyer's expression hardened. "Do you even hear yourself? That sounds just like something he woulda said. There's no expiry date on real love."

"Of course not," I quickly agreed. "I just mean: there's more to it than I realized. I always thought it had to be either/or, but it doesn't. Caring about Nadiya doesn't mean I love Shawna any less. She ain't asking me to. It's not a replacement, it's just something different."

He still looked unconvinced, so I pulled out my big guns.

"Shawna always wanted me to get married again, you know that."

We'd had that conversation many times before, about how Shawna had encouraged me to keep living when she was gone. Sawyer had obviously never had that kind of talk with his wife since her death came out of the blue, but now that I was seeing things in a new light, I kind of felt she would have said the same thing if she'd had the chance. I couldn't imagine loving someone and wanting them to be miserable for the rest of their lives.

Why hadn't I ever seen that quite so clearly before?

"But why would you get so married so fast?" His tone still sounded far from understanding. "Dating her would be one thing, but married?"

That was tougher to answer, but I tried my best. "You know me. Why do something half-way when I can go all the way? The day we met, she had just broken up with somebody, and when we clicked, I asked and she said yes. I know it's a bit crazy, but sometimes you just gotta take a chance. So far, it's working out even better than I could have hoped."

That last bit was certainly true, and I hoped he would hear it in my voice.

"And it's got nothing to do with your gallery?"

My lips tightened as I weighed my response to that. I hated the idea of lying to someone who had always been so open and raw with me so I tried to stick to the truth as much as possible.

"Nadiya offered me a deal on the gallery, a different deal than the one she'd been making all along. If I sold it to her, then she'd give me space in the new development. So I get to keep the gallery after all, just in a different building, and it gives me some breathing room in the meantime. It was her offering that deal that made me realize that there was more to her than I thought before. She's not just about the bottom line."

"So you signed some kind of contract with her?"

The way he asked the question struck me as odd. Why would Sawyer care about whether or not I'd signed anything?

"We made an agreement," I replied, keeping things vague.

"And all this publicity probably ain't done you any harm either." He gave me another appraising look that I couldn't quite understand.

"I've had a lot of new people interested in my work," I had to admit before trying to change the subject. The whole conversation had started to make me a bit uncomfortable. "Listen, I've been talking about me and Nadiya all week and I'd love a break. Tell me what's going on with you."

We talked about Sawyer's work, and gradually, he loosened up to be more like his regular self. By the time we said goodbye, I put the whole thing down to his annoyance at me making such a big change without talking to him first. I told him I'd introduce him to Nadiya first chance I got, and hopefully he'd see for himself that there really was something between us. It might not have been true at first, but things had changed.

When I got back to Nadiya's house, she hadn't got home yet so I went back out to the workshop for a little while. Looking over the sketches I'd made that day, I saw a few small ways they could be improved and I spent a little while making some changes until I felt satisfied. By the time I was finished, it had started to get dark out, and when I headed back to the house, the lights were on inside.

Instantly, my heart beat a little faster at the thought of seeing Nadiya again. I'd missed her face all day, her voice, her smell. I was looking forward to hearing about her day, having her in my arms, and hopefully having her in my bed again that night, all those little things I hadn't had in my life for so long.

But when I got inside, I found her sitting in the living room with an apologetic and unhappy look on her face. "Come and sit down, Dex. There's something I need to tell you."

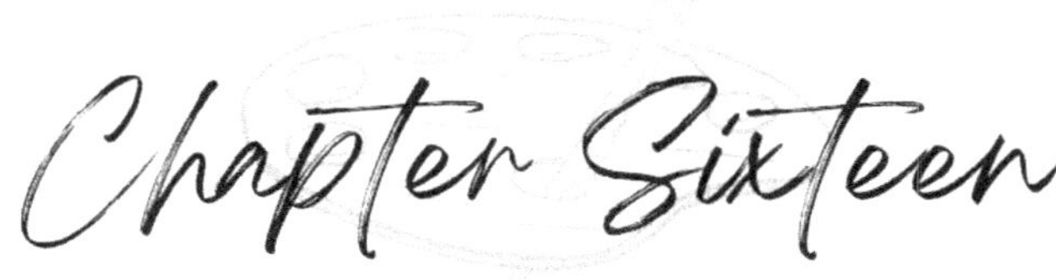

Chapter Sixteen

~**Nadiya**~

Dex looked uncertain as he sat down next to me on the couch and I couldn't blame him. If even a little of my nerves came across in my body language, he must have been confused.

When Brad arrived in my office earlier that night, I did my best to keep calm. Letting him see how rattled I was would only make him happy. He *wanted* to rattle me, so I needed to keep any advantage I had, though at that moment, I had a hard time seeing what advantages I had left.

"You summoned me?" he asked rather sarcastically from the door as he came in and closed it behind him.

"The Rice Art Gallery?" I asked, jabbing my finger down on the plans on my desk as he walked over. Right in the spot I had marked out for Dex's new gallery, a completely different art gallery had been written into the plans instead. "What is this? I have final approval on all leases, and I didn't approve that."

A fake look of surprise crossed his face. "You didn't? I wonder how that happened."

My eyes narrowed, waiting for his explanation, which came a moment later.

"Oh, that's right. That was all negotiated on Friday afternoon, but you weren't available. You must have been at your 'wedding'." I could hear the quotes around the word as clearly as if he'd drawn them in the air.

"We didn't want to miss the chance for such a perfect match for the new development, so I went ahead and signed it on your behalf."

"You had no right to do that. I'm already in negotiations on that space, and I..."

"You are?" He cut me off, still with that completely false appearance of confusion. "But there's nothing in the files about it."

"It's in my personal files," I told him through gritted teeth. "And it doesn't matter, because I didn't agree to this. You'll need to have the contract terminated."

"On what grounds?" he challenged me, still feigning surprise. "There are still other spaces available. You can move your negotiation to one of them, can't you? I don't see the problem."

He knew exactly what the problem was, but how he knew, I wasn't sure. As I'd just told him, the contract that I'd drawn up for Dex on that space was in my personal files. Only Luisa and I had access to those and I knew Luisa wouldn't have shared them with anyone.

The problem was that we had a policy in place that we could only have one business from each 'category' in the limited retail space in the new building. By signing an art gallery to that space specifically, he had ensured that I couldn't sign Dex, not just to that space, but to any of the remaining spaces available either.

How the hell did he know what I intended to do?

"The problem is that I didn't approve it," I repeated. "You're the one who signed it, so you can get it unsigned."

"And risk them taking us to court over breach of contract? That would be bad publicity for Varma Corp, and what would our defense be?"

"Our defense is that the negotiation had already begun. The space still showing as available was an internal error. I have time-stamped copies of the draft contract for a different business in the same category..."

Brad suddenly dropped all pretense of not knowing what I was talking about. "Which conveniently coincides with your shotgun wedding to the owner of said business. How is that going to look in the papers, Nadiya? Like nepotism, or something even worse? A quid pro quo, maybe?"

A lump filled my throat as I realized he was right. No matter the truth of it, if someone wanted to, they could certainly spin the whole thing to look like some kind of scam. He had my hands completely tied and he knew it.

Why hadn't I just got the papers signed right after I made the offer? That stung worst of all. I'd gotten myself into this mess, and thanks to Brad's backhanded dealings, I couldn't see a way out of it.

Brad must have known that would be the case, and his eyes glinted with triumph as he took a step back from the desk. "I'm sure Mr Callahan will understand. It's just business, right? It's not like any other kind of agreement exists between you?"

"Get out," I instructed, trying to cling to any semblance of control over the whole situation.

He went, but not without a parting shot. "I'm sure the investors in the meeting will be delighted about the new gallery addition."

Somehow, I made it through the meeting with the investors with no one noticing my inner turmoil, but I couldn't escape the sense of dread that filled me as I thought about telling Dex what happened. Would he be angry with me? Would he believe it had been an honest mistake on my part? Would he blame me for my carelessness, or would he suspect something even worse?

And now, the moment I dreaded had arrived, with Dex's blue eyes watching me curiously from the other side of the couch.

"What is it, darlin'? You look like you swallowed a lemon. If you pucker those lips any tighter, I might have to kiss that look right off your face."

His sweet teasing made me feel better and worse all at the same time, and I tried to stick to the words I had prepared. "Dex, I've got some news about your gallery."

"Oh, have you got the papers with you?" He glanced around the room as if I might be hiding them somewhere. "I've been meaning to ask about them, I just keep getting a little distracted whenever we're together."

The look in his eyes told me exactly what kind of distraction he meant, and I completely understood since I had exactly the same issue. Unfortunately, it still didn't excuse what I'd done.

"I've got the papers for the sale, but there's a problem with the ones for the lease in the new building."

His eyebrows drew together in confusion. "What kind of problem?"

I took a deep breath, steeling myself for the words I had to say. "I can't offer you the lease anymore, at least not in that building."

I winced as I waited for his response, but none came. He just stared at me, bewilderment written across his handsome face, and my stomach sank even further.

I rushed to fill the silence with the rest of what I'd been thinking all night. "But don't worry, we'll find you a new location, and you know, it might even work out better. You won't have to wait for the building to be complete for it to open, and now that you've got all this momentum going with Mary Flynn and everyone else interested in your work, the sooner you get back into a physical space, the better. I can put some of my team on it, I bet we could even have you up and running again in a few weeks. I know it's not what we agreed, but…"

"No, it's not." His words were quiet, but they stopped me in my tracks just as much as if he had shouted them. "It's not having *a* space that's important to me, Nadiya. I told you that. It's *that* space, that location."

I knew that. I knew he hadn't wanted to sell to me until I made him that particular offer. I had promised him he could have it and I was going back on my word, and I hated it. Though neither of us had moved, he felt further away from me with every word either of us uttered.

"I know, Dex. I remember what you said and I know what we agreed. Please believe me, this isn't my choice."

"How is it not your choice?" He sounded genuinely baffled. "It's your company, ain't it?"

"Yes, but…"

"Your building?"

"Yes, but…"

"Your handshake that we agreed on?"

I winced again as his words became more pointed. "Dex, I absolutely meant it when we agreed. I had every intention of going through with it, but we haven't signed the paperwork yet and another gallery has been offered the space instead. I swear, I have no idea..."

"No, you really don't." Once again, his words were soft, but the hurt behind them ripped into my skin. "I thought the hard businesswoman from the emails was the facade and the Nadiya I saw here was the real you, but maybe I've got it backwards. Maybe it's been the other way around all along."

~**Dex**~

The words coming out of Nadiya's mouth were unbelievable to me. I didn't think I could have been any clearer about the importance of the location for my gallery. I'd been willing to go bankrupt rather than sell to her in the first place, and yet Nadiya sat there talking about finding me a different location like it would be a good thing. Like she was doing me a favour. She couldn't really believe that, could she?

Added to how the rest of my day had gone — the temp that looked like Shawna and Sawyer's probing questions — it started to feel like the universe was trying to tell me something: namely, that this whole arrangement had been some kind of mistake.

Nadiya was obviously nervous about giving me the news, which she damn well should have been. I may not know much about running a successful business, but I did know one thing: if you gave someone your word, you kept it.

That went double for a personal relationship. How was I supposed to believe anything she said to me after that? Or even before it? How could I know if everything she'd ever told me had been a lie?

Had it been her plan all along to pull a bait and switch when I got too far in to do anything about it?

Did she even really care about me at all?

Confusion and hurt filled me, far more hurt than I wanted to admit even to myself. I really thought I had found something special, that she had let me see a part of her that no one had seen before, and now, I struggled to understand if any of it had even been true.

But when I told her that I didn't know which version of her was the real one, something shifted in her expression.

"You're right," she said, straightening her shoulders. Before my eyes, her nervousness seemed to fall away. "I *am* a hard-hearted business-woman. I don't know why I haven't been acting like it."

My brow furrowed even further at her unexpected response. Was she actually agreeing with me? Did that mean she really had been lying to me all along?

"Dex, I screwed up," she continued, looking me straight in the eye. "I should have had you sign those papers the first day. It's a mistake I wouldn't have made even on my first day on the job, let alone after years in the business."

"So, why didn't you?" If she felt so certain of that, then the only explanation I could think of was that she'd done it on purpose.

"I don't know. And I know that's no excuse, believe me. If I really had to guess, I would say maybe I didn't do it because my subconscious thought that it would have made everything between us more busi-ness-like, and even from the very beginning, that wasn't all I felt for you."

Every word out of her mouth made me more confused. What was she saying?

"I never made a conscious decision not to have you sign them, but I can't think of any other reason I wouldn't have insisted. Now that it's come back to bite us both, but you especially, I'm so sorry. That was never, ever my intention, and I'll do everything I can to make it right for you."

"The only thing I want is what we agreed on." I didn't care if I sounded stubborn. This was the hill I'd chosen to die on, and I needed her to respect that.

"I understand," she promised. "And if Brad thinks this is going to make me roll over and give up, or just let him take my job, he knows even less about me than everyone else does."

Absolutely none of that made sense to me and I put my fingers to my temples, trying to calm my thoughts enough to sort through it all. She had mentioned Brad to me before. He was the one in the running for the CEO position against her, and the whole reason she wanted to get engaged in the first place. "What does he have to do with this?"

Nadiya answered me grimly. "Everything. Somehow, he found out that I planned to offer you the space for your gallery, so he went over my head and signed another gallery into that exact same space. He did it when I was out of the office to marry you. He must have had it all planned in advance, it would have taken a few days to set it all up, but how he knew about it, I have no idea."

Things still didn't entirely make sense to me, but it sounded like this guy was trying to screw over the both of us now, so I tried to help her figure it out. "Who *did* know about it?"

"Hardly anyone. I called the bank myself to pay off the mortgage and buy your building. My assistant Luisa drafted the contracts and saved them to my personal drive on the company network. She and I are the only ones who have access to it."

"Could Luisa have told Brad?" I asked. It didn't seem to fit with the woman I'd met, but I had to admit, I didn't know her all that well.

Nadiya quickly shook her head. "I can't believe that. She's always been loyal to me, and she finds Brad just as slimy as I do."

"Could he have overheard something, then?" Focusing on the mystery helped to slow my pounding heart. Though I was still far from happy, at least it felt like something productive to do.

Again, Nadiya shook her head. "I don't see how. We usually talk in my office with the door closed."

"And nobody could get into your computer files?" I definitely didn't know much about computers beyond using one myself, but in the movies, people were always hacking into things.

Nadiya frowned as she thought that over. "I suppose it's possible. I'm sure he's charmed some of the people in IT. And that might explain..."

She trailed off, clearly trying to put something together in her head.

"You didn't request a new assistant today, did you?"

The sudden change in topic took me by surprise. It had nothing to do with anything that I could see, but she seemed very interested in my answer, so I rolled with it. "Of course not. Daisy isn't really what I expected, but she seems to know what she's doing."

"Daisy?" Nadiya raised her eyebrows suspiciously, as if the very name sounded problematic. "You were supposed to have Martha. I picked her specifically for you, but apparently, this morning she got a call saying you'd requested someone else."

What the hell? "Of course I didn't call anyone. I wouldn't even know who to call."

Nadiya nodded. "That's what I thought. And the only person who knew I had requested help for you was Luisa. I sent the request to her work phone..."

"... and the message could have been seen by someone with access to her login," I finished for her. It made sense to me, but that was about the only thing that did. "Why would Brad switch my temp?"

"I don't know," Nadiya admitted. "You said she was good? There weren't any problems?"

I couldn't entirely hide my grimace. "Workwise, she was great, but her appearance took me by surprise."

"What about it?" Nadiya's lips tightened as she asked the question.

Was that... jealousy? The thought made me a little happier than it should have, especially considering I still didn't know what to make of the whole situation. In any case, I answered her honestly. "She looks a lot like Shawna, right down to the way she dressed."

"That son of a..." Nadiya muttered under her breath, before giving me a look filled with sympathy. "I'm sorry if that upset you."

"It ain't your fault, but if Brad switched her on purpose, what did he want to achieve?"

Nadiya had a guess for that. "He wants to break us up, or expose us. Apparently, he talked Greg into breaking up with me in the first place."

"What?" This guy sounded unbelievable.

"I guess he really wants the job," she said with a shrug. "I can understand that, even if I would never use these kinds of tactics."

I must have been missing something about just how great being CEO of Varma Corp would be, because I had a hard time believing someone would go to all that trouble just for a job. It seemed to me like there must be something else behind it. "Usually when someone goes on the offense this hard, it's because they've got something to hide."

She frowned once again. "What would he be hiding?"

"I have no idea, but I think you better figure it out. I've already got enough people sniffing around, thinking I'm lying about us." My frown mirrored hers as my mind went back to the conversation with Sawyer.

"What do you mean?"

I told her a little about the things Sawyer asked me, and how he brought up whether we had signed a contract specifically. "That's not something he would normally be thinking about. It struck me as really odd."

"Do you think Brad got to him?"

That seemed like a stretch, but if Brad really had done all the other things we were talking about, who could say how far he'd be willing to go?

"I'm not sure, but it sounds like this guy's playing for keeps. I think you better figure out what he's trying to protect, Nadiya, and fast."

She nodded, her eyes darting back and forth as she thought things over. "I'll get started first thing tomorrow. He's not going to get away with this."

"So you can still get my gallery space back?" We had moved away from that, but it remained at the top of my mind.

She winced again. "I'm not sure, but I promise I'll try, Dex. I'll do everything I can. And I really appreciate you talking this through with me. You have every right to be furious with me."

I did, and yet, I didn't feel angry anymore, not really. Concerned, yes, and still a bit confused, but no longer furious. I believed she hadn't withheld the papers from me on purpose, at least. She might have been a bit careless, but it didn't seem to have been malicious.

Everyone made mistakes. Heaven knew I'd made enough of them.

"It's pretty late," she pointed out, and a quick glance at the clock up on the wall confirmed that assessment. When I looked back at her, she gave me a hesitant smile. "I'm going to head to bed."

The invitation in her words couldn't be much clearer: she wanted to know if I would join her, or if I wanted her to join me.

But even though my anger had come off the boil, I still needed a bit of time to think things over, on my own, so I turned her down as gently as I could. "Yeah, I think I will too. I'll see you in the morning, Nadiya."

Giving her a simple nod, I got to my feet and headed down the hall to my room.

~Nadiya~

My heart sank as Dex walked out of the room without a backward glance. Maybe he didn't get my hint that I wanted to spend the night with him again, or maybe he did and he was simply too disappointed with me to want to be close to me that way.

In either case, I wasn't sure what to do about it. Greg and I had never really argued, or at least not over anything that really mattered. That had been why his angry words on the night he left shocked me so much. With Dex, though, feelings ran deeper on both sides. My screw-up had truly hurt him, and I felt awful about it.

As I told him, he had every right to be angry with me. I expected him to be. But after the way he sat and talked things through with me, I thought we were making progress. I thought that maybe there was a chance he wouldn't hold it against me after all and we could work together to solve the problem.

After he walked away, I didn't know what to think.

Maybe I read too much into it, since we had only really spent one night together in our 'real' relationship. We didn't exactly have a usual routine yet, but him going to bed on his own felt like a rejection anyway, one that stung far more than I expected it to.

Still not sure exactly what I meant to do next, I got to my feet, but before I could decide, my phone buzzed in my pocket. Normally, no one contacted me so late in the evening unless there was a problem, so I quickly pulled it out to check.

It didn't seem to be an emergency, though; just a text from Dex's sister Tonia. She'd taken my number at the party at his mom's house but I hadn't heard from her since, and I'd almost forgotten I gave it to her.

Hey, new sister! It's ladies' night at the Armadillo Palace. You in?

Although I felt both flattered by the invitation and pleased that she actually wanted to spend time with me, I was normally already in bed for the night by that time, and the next day would be a busy one for me with the ground-breaking ceremony for the new building. The responsible thing to do would be to refuse, but as my fingers hovered above the keys, I paused.

Tonia knew Dex better than just about anyone, and she definitely had no trouble telling the truth. I had witnessed that first-hand. Maybe she would have some advice on how I could make it up to her brother for making such a huge mess of things. I couldn't tell her exactly what happened, since that would give away our initial deception, but perhaps I could get some general pointers. It might be worth the late night, especially since I wasn't sure I could go to sleep with my emotions all churned up anyway.

Making up my mind, I grabbed a light jacket and called a taxi.

I'd been to Goode's Armadillo Palace before, but only ever to the restaurant, with clients. I'd never even seen the dance hall, but Tonia took me straight there after greeting me at the door. Country music blared through the speakers dotted around the room as groups of tanned and toned young women in jeans and cowboy hats danced or drank, or both, beneath the coloured lights.

I still wore my suit from my day at the office, earning me several bemused looks as Tonia led me towards a slightly quieter corner of the large room. Billie and Laura were already seated at a high table, drinks in front of them and a few empty glasses too. I hadn't realized all of Dex's sisters would be there, and I greeted them a little sheepishly, feeling very much out of my element.

"What're you drinking, Nadiya?" Laura asked as I took a seat next to her on the tall bar stool. She fit right into the crowd in her cowboy hat and plaid shirt, which, since she lived on a ranch, were probably just her regular clothes.

Immediately, memories of my drunken wedding night with Dex flashed in front of my eyes, and just the thought of the tequila almost made me gag. "Nothing," I quickly declined. "I've got work in the morning, I really can't stay too long."

Thankfully, they accepted that with no argument. "Well, we're glad you came out anyway," Billie assured me. "It's always a spur of the moment thing when we can all get our husbands to agree to man the fort at the same time. I'm teaching in the morning, so I won't stay out too late either."

Her sisters' laughter made it clear they didn't believe that for a second.

"Do you guys do this often?" I asked.

"Not as often as we'd like," Tonia laughed. "But yeah, when we can. Us girls need to stick together, right?"

I'd never really been one of 'us girls' before, but that gave me a great opening for the reason I had decided to come. "Actually, while you're all here, I'd love to get your input on something, if you don't mind."

They all leaned forward together, as if they had choreographed it in advance. "What's going on?" Billie asked curiously. "Dex didn't screw up already, did he?"

She made it sound like he regularly did, which hadn't been my experience. "No, not at all. Actually, I did, and I'm not quite sure how to make it up to him."

They all groaned in disappointment, leaning back in unison as Laura rolled her eyes. "That's easy! Put on your sexiest thong and let him find you 'accidentally' bending over in it. He'll forget all about whatever's got his panties in a twist."

The other two nodded as if that was particularly sage advice instead of a completely inappropriate thing to say about their brother.

"It's not just a little thing though," I tried to explain. "I really screwed up. I'm afraid I've broken his trust in me." To my annoyance, my eyes started to get a little watery but I pushed ahead anyway. "We still don't really know each other all that well, and I don't want him to think this is who I am. He's the first person to really see me and I don't want to lose that. I don't want this to be over when it's only just started."

I didn't even realize until the words came out of my mouth just how afraid I was that I had messed things up beyond repair, but obviously, the fear in my voice came across ust as clear to them as it did to me, because they all immediately turned serious.

Tonia reached over to put her hand on mine, the warmth of it feeling strangely comforting. "Hey now, Nadiya, I'm sure it's not that bad. Dex is a pretty forgiving guy. He's stubborn as hell and he'll pout like a little boy who just lost his favourite Hot Wheels down the storm drain, but that's just because he's a Callahan. We're all the same. If we didn't care, we wouldn't get upset."

She looked at her sisters for confirmation, and they quickly nodded in agreement.

"One thing he doesn't do, though, is hold a grudge," Billie promised me. "If you show him you're sorry and you try to do better, he'll get over it. And trust me, that man is so head-over-heels for you that he is dying to forgive you. I bet it's eating him up inside that you're not there right now."

A lump filled my throat at her certainty about Dex's love for me when he'd never said those words. We must have fooled everyone at the party better than I thought.

Maybe if he really did love me, he would forgive me as easily as she claimed, but I couldn't rely on that when I didn't know for sure exactly how he felt.

Tonia jumped back in with more advice. "Whenever my Cam messes up, I always wait for him to come around begging. Unless I've completely dropped the ball, ain't ever going to be me to give in first, but by the time he owns up, I'm always just as eager to make up as he is. Just swallow your pride and tell him how you feel."

"How do I show him I'm sorry?" I asked, looking for some concrete tips. That kind of apology was completely foreign to me, let alone with someone whose feelings I cared about as much as I cared about Dex.

"Do something he wouldn't expect," Billie suggested.

Laura nodded eagerly. "Something that'll take him by surprise and knock him straight out of his funk."

Something that would take him by surprise, huh? As my eyes scanned the room, I started to get an idea. It would definitely surprise him, but if he didn't like it, I would feel like a complete idiot.

But maybe, making an idiot of myself was just the kind of chance I needed to take.

Chapter Seventeen

~Dex~

Lying in bed, I tossed over onto my other side, kicking the blankets away and trying to get comfortable. I'd already been in bed for a couple of hours but my mind refused to switch off. It kept cycling through a hundred different moments and conversations: starting up the gallery and the promise I'd made to Shawna when she got sick again not to give up on it, the day Nadiya and I met and the deal we'd made, and everything that had happened with her since then.

I believed her when she said she didn't intentionally try to screw me out of the gallery space, but I still didn't really understand why it had happened at all. My brain kept returning to what she'd said when I asked her why she didn't get the papers signed. It had been one of so many things in that conversation that I didn't fully absorb at the time, but lying there alone in my bed, I could almost hear her saying it again.

If I really had to guess, I would say maybe I didn't do it because my subconscious thought that it would have made everything between us more business-like, and even from the very beginning, that wasn't all I felt for you.

What exactly did she mean by that? What did she feel for me at the beginning besides our business deal?

I reviewed every interaction we'd had, trying to pinpoint the moment my own feelings for her changed from being simply business into something more, and I couldn't come up with an answer. Did it take place so gradually I didn't notice? Or, as she suggested, had there always been something more there, right from the very beginning?

Finally, I sat up, unable to contain my agitation any longer. If I wanted to get some sleep, I needed to talk things out with her first. Maybe she was just the same, driving herself crazy over the fact that left things unfinished. Or that *I* had, I supposed. I was the one who walked away, so the way I figured it, I needed to make the first move. Grabbing my jeans off the floor by the side of the bed, I pulled them back on, not bothering with any underwear. I didn't need to get fully dressed, I just didn't want to go in completely naked and give her the wrong idea about what I'd gone there for.

Once I was decent, I poked my head out into the hall. Nadiya's bedroom door was closed and the lights were off but that didn't necessarily mean anything. My light had been off but I hadn't been asleep, so I didn't let that stop me. My bare feet were silent on the hardwood floors as I made the short trip to her door and knocked quietly.

"Nadiya? Are you up?"

No response came, and a little flush of annoyance ran through me at the idea that she would be sleeping soundly while I stressed over our argument, but I tried to be rational about it. She had to work in the morning and I knew what kind of discipline she had. In all fairness, she was probably a lot better at compartmentalizing her emotions than I was. As an artist, emotions were encouraged, while for the sake of her business, she needed to control hers.

I knocked again, a little louder. "Nadiya?"

Once again, there was no reply, but going back to my own bed didn't seem to be an option if I wanted to get any rest that night, so I opened the door and slipped inside anyway. Although dark, I could make out the shape of her bed in the small amount of moonlight sneaking in past her curtains. Walking over towards it, I spoke again softly, trying not to startle her.

"Nadiya, it's just me, Dex. I'm sorry to wake you, but I need to talk to you."

Silence answered me and I frowned as I got to the bed. Apparently, she really did sleep deeply. Sitting down on the edge of the bed, I reached for her, but my hand found only the empty mattress. Frowning, I reached further, searching for her form but finding only blankets. Finally, I reached over and flipped on her bedside lamp.

The bed was completely empty and still made. It didn't look like she'd been in it at all that night.

My heart began to beat a little faster as the worst case scenarios began to run through my head. Where would she be, well after midnight? Moving quickly, I headed back out to the living room, followed by the kitchen. No lights shone anywhere, and I couldn't find any sign of Nadiya. Maybe our conversation upset her more than I realized. She wouldn't have done anything rash, would she? I had to admit I really didn't know. Since we'd never fought before, I had no idea how she normally dealt with it.

Just as I was about to head back to my room to grab my phone, something caught my eye out the window: light from beneath the garage door, meaning someone had to be in my workshop since I definitely hadn't left it on myself.

More confused than ever, I headed outside, the night air a little cool against my bare chest. It had to be Nadiya, I figured. The door had the same locks as the house which could be unlocked with her thumbprint or mine, but what in the world would she be doing out there?

Using my own thumb to unlock the door, I let myself in, but when I caught sight of her, I stopped dead in my tracks.

She had her back to me, apparently not having heard me come in. She must have been fully concentrating on whatever she was doing, but I couldn't even take it in.

All my attention immediately focused on the way she was dressed.

The suit she wore earlier was nowhere to be seen. Moving upwards from the ground, my eyes scanned across her cowboy boots, her bare legs that seemed to go on forever until they ended in a barely-there pair of jean shorts. No sign of a bra could be seen beneath her white tank top, and her dark hair tumbled down her shoulders, topped off with a white cowboy hat.

If it weren't for the colour of her skin and the deep ebony of her hair, I wouldn't have known her.

"Nadiya?"

My voice startled her and she spun around, causing the paintbrush she held to swipe across her top, leaving a streak of blue across the whiteness.

"Oh, for the love of..." she muttered, looking down at herself. "How does this keep happening?"

The reminder of our first encounter made me smile and she smiled too, looking a bit sheepish. Immediately, I felt lighter than I had since I left her hours ago.

"What in the world are you doing, darlin'?"

I could see that she had a small canvas set up behind her, but I couldn't quite make out what was on it. When I tried to peer around her to see it, she quickly blocked my view with her body. "Please, don't look, Dex. It's so bad!"

"What is?" I still didn't have a clue what she was doing out there in the first place.

She winced, closing her eyes in frustration. "Alright, you can see, but just... don't laugh, okay?"

Utterly confused, I watched as she stepped to the side, revealing...

Actually, I had no idea what I was looking at. The image on the canvas was vaguely person-shaped, in the same way as a Picasso. The dimensions and symmetry were all off, but the use of colour was impressive. I didn't even know that Nadiya knew there were that many colours in the world.

The blue on her paintbrush seemed to be for the figure's eyes. I took a step closer, biting my lip to keep from smiling as she watched me anxiously.

Finally, I had to ask: "What is it?"

She groaned. "It's supposed to be you."

Really? My lips pressed tighter together to hold back my grin as I examined the image. "And my stomach is all bumpy because...?"

"It's supposed to be muscles," she told me, her eyebrows drawn together in frustration.

"And why does it look like my arm's been burned?"

"That's your tattoo!" she exclaimed, running her hand down her own arm

As our eyes met, my lips twitched and hers did too. That was enough to break the dam and I couldn't hold it in any longer. Laughter burst out of me and Nadiya covered her eyes with her hand, laughing just as hard.

It had to be one of the funniest things I had ever seen in my life. I'd met two-year-olds who could draw a more convincing person. My nieces and nephews would paint circles around her.

"I tried," she protested as our laughter began to fade, throwing the brush down onto the work table.

"You did." That much, I could see, but nothing else about it made sense. I needed her to explain it to me. "Why?"

"I wanted to apologize. I talked to your sisters and they said I should do something surprising to get your attention, so I got this whole outfit and I was going to come to your room and... I don't know, really. Try to do something sexy, I guess."

With a shrug, she gestured down at the clothes she wore, making me more confused than ever. When did she talk to my sisters? Where did the outfit come from?

"But when I got home, I saw the workshop, and I thought maybe making something would be a better idea. I wanted to show you how I see you."

As I looked back at the image she'd created, a shudder ran through me. "If that's how you see me, darlin', you should be running away screaming."

Though she tried to give me a dirty look, she ended up laughing again. "I'm so bad at this, Dex."

I couldn't disagree with that. "The art needs a bit of work, sweetheart."

She shook her head as her smile faded. "No, I mean, *this*. Us. I've never done anything like this before, and I feel like I'm messing up at every turn."

She'd lost me again. "You were just in a relationship for three years."

"I was, but not like this. I never really had to say I'm sorry before. And I am, I really am. I just wanted you to know that."

She certainly had gone to some lengths to prove it to me, and I never would have predicted she'd do something like this. Finding her asleep in her bed, I would have believed, but this? This was something completely unexpected.

"You didn't need to go to all the trouble of the painting," I told her honestly, my eyes sweeping across her again. "The outfit would have been fine on its own."

I took one step closer to her and just like it had the first night we slept together, the air shifted around us, suddenly full of energy and possibility.

Hope flashed through her dark eyes. "You like it?"

I liked it far more than I would have anticipated. "I do, but I think I'd like it a whole lot better on the floor."

~Nadiya~

I really hadn't been sure dressing up would work. Dex's sisters seemed convinced that it would when I tentatively suggested it, sure enough to approach a total stranger in the bar and convince her to swap outfits with me. The slightly-confused blonde woman left with my thousand-dollar suit and I got her tiny shorts and tank top, along with her boots and hat. Despite having lived in Texas most of my life, I had never worn either cowboy boots or a cowboy hat before and I thought they would look ridiculous on me.

The look on Dex's face suggested that he thought otherwise.

His eyes wandered across my body, which reacted to his gaze almost as much as if he were touching me. My nipples hardened, puckering beneath the taut white fabric, and as he breathed in, his nostrils flaring, I felt sure he noticed it too. Tonia had insisted that I had to leave my bra off, and it appeared she'd been right about that as well.

It all sounded so easy as Dex's sisters encouraged me, but when I got home and actually faced the prospect of going into his room, I completely lost my nerve. What if he laughed at me? What if he threw me out? The prospect of that kind of rejection seemed too daunting, and for that reason, I went into the workshop instead. At least with the painting, I could leave it for him and I wouldn't have to see his reaction.

That had been the plan anyway, until he turned up, shirtless and shoeless, his hair a little tousled from being in bed, and his eyes burning not with anger, but with something else entirely.

Suddenly, I felt a whole lot bolder.

He took another step towards me, reaching for me, but I slipped out of his grasp, dropping to my knees on the concrete floor instead.

"Nadiya." My name sounded slightly strangled as it came out of him.

"I still owe you an apology," I reminded him, looking up at him from beneath the brim of the hat. "Let me say sorry."

His eyes closed, in resignation or anticipation, I couldn't be sure which, while my hands went to the button of his jeans. As I pulled the zipper down, I saw that he wore nothing beneath them, just as I'd left my bra off, and my thighs clenched together, the seam of my tiny shorts providing a little of the pressure I desperately wanted between my legs. Hopefully, he'd help me out later, but first, I needed to make things right by him, and I started by tugging his jeans down until his cock sprung loose from its confines. His excitement had obviously been building for a little while already, and when I gripped his base firmly in my hand and took his head into my mouth, Dex groaned happily above me.

The hat didn't last long. Dex pulled it off as I began to suck on him, reaching down to hold my hair out of the way for me.

"You're so beautiful," he muttered between sharp intakes of breath as I took him deeper and deeper. "Fuck, Nadiya."

Having him in my mouth and at my mercy felt even better than it had on our wedding night. For one thing, I was a lot more sober that time, but more than that, I knew him so much better than I had then. I knew what would turn him on, what his breathing and grunts meant, and I could tell when he got close. He'd been half-way there before I even started, so once I added my hand in, pumping him as my mouth and tongue continued their tantalizing work, it didn't take long at all before he came, his head falling back as he whispered my name into the air.

Once I'd swallowed and licked him clean, I stood back up and he immediately pulled me tight to his chest, his bare skin warm against mine as he gently kissed my forehead.

"I'm sorry," I told him one more time. "I'll make it right, somehow."

"I know you will." The certainty in his voice made my heart swell. "But first, let me give you some pointers on painting, darlin'."

"I was kind of hoping you'd forgotten about that," I admitted, and his chest shook with laughter beneath my head.

"It won't take long," he promised, letting me go and moving over to the work table where I had laid out the paints and brushes I wanted to use. He kicked off the jeans that were around his knees, leaving him completely naked. The sight momentarily distracted me until he picked up the brush I'd just been using, the blue I had chosen for his eyes, and walked back over to me with a teasing twinkle in his eyes. "Now, most people, they look pretty much the same on one side of their body as they do on the other."

I narrowed my eyes at him even as I tried not to smile, well aware of exactly how bad my painting had turned out. "You think you're that perfectly symmetrical, do you?"

"I think I look pretty good." His eyebrows raised, daring me to contradict him, which I couldn't do. "So, when you draw an eye on one side..."

He reached out and made a small circle with the paintbrush on my cheek, making me gasp in surprise.

"Then you should do one on the other side too."

His brush swirled against my other cheek as he bit his lip in amusement, obviously enjoying my shock. I couldn't believe he painted on me, but I never backed down from the challenge. Instead, I went to grab my own brush and dipped it in the brown paint I'd used for his hair before turning back to him with my sweetest smile.

"But what if they're not perfectly matched in reality? What if you shaved one side of your face…"

My brush drew a light line down his jawline on the right side of his face as he tried not to smile.

"But you missed a patch over here?"

I dabbed a large blob of paint on his left jaw, and he couldn't hold back his laugh.

"Then you're allowed a little artistic license," he agreed. "For instance, I've always thought that breasts should be multi-coloured."

Without any warning, he reached down and pulled my tank top up over my head. His eyes darkened as they travelled over the exposed skin, just before he reached out and painted one blue streak across my left breast. A small whimper escaped my lips as the brush crossed over the stiff nipple.

Dex turned around and dipped his brush in a different colour – pink, I think – and drew another line, forming an x over the peak of my breast. "What do you think, Nadiya?" he teased me. "Should we add a few more colours?"

I could only nod, craving any kind of touch from him. Red and yellow and brown followed, his brush swirling around my aching nipple, flicking across the tip of it, until I was ready to cry out in frustration. However, two could play at that game. When he turned back to me the next time, I ran my brush across his chest in return, making him laugh until he looked down at the brown line. Instantly, his smile faded and mine did too.

Without meaning to, I had painted straight across the brand with Shawna's name on it.

"I'm sorry, Dex," I quickly apologized, my heart sinking. "I didn't mean to..."

"I know." He cut me off, raising his eyes back to mine. An odd expression lingered in them, a mix of desire and wonder and something slightly bittersweet too. "No harm done. I thought it was perfect as is, but maybe adding something to it wouldn't hurt."

He said that as if he were talking about more than just the tattoo, but before I could question him, he pulled me to him and kissed me hard. Any other thoughts flew out of my head as his hands cupped my breasts, his thumbs sliding across the still-wet paint, blending all the colours together as he pinched and teased my tender nipples. My hips moved against him instinctively and I could feel him starting to harden again, obviously as aroused by all of this as I was.

Soon, he turned the tables from what I'd done earlier, dropping to his knees and yanking my little jean shorts down before burying his face between my legs. "Oh, God, Dex!"

That talented tongue of his kissed and licked and sucked my clit as his fingers pressed into me and it seemed like no time at all until I lost control, coming onto his hand and face. I had barely recovered before he got to his feet again, his eyes still heavy with lust.

"The table, darlin'," he instructed, and I happily followed his lead as he led me over and bent me over his workshop table, pushing all the paints and brushes to the side, not caring about the mess left behind.

His hand ran across the curve of my ass as he pressed his now-hard cock firmly against my entrance. "You got something to hold onto, sweetheart?" he asked, his voice rough with need, and I nodded as I gripped the edge of the table tightly.

As he pressed into me, his hard length splitting me open, I moaned in shameless and complete satisfaction. Nothing had ever felt as right as the feel of him inside me. He must have felt at least a little the same, based on the murmured words I could hear behind me.

"Goddamn, darlin'!"

He took me roughly, my breasts pinned against the table as I hung on for balance, but I knew that beneath the need and desire, there was affection too, and that only made it better. As I came again, Dex following close behind me, I had a moment of utter clarity.

I'd never felt anything like this before. Never before had anyone accepted me completely for who I was, and yet made me feel safe to try new things too, to step outside of my comfort zone and take risks. Never before had I wanted to please someone as much as they pleased me. Never before had I put myself on the line that way.

As far as I could see, it could only mean one thing.

I was falling in love with my husband.

~Dex~

My heart kept on pounding as I slid out of Nadiya, and not just from the physical exertion of what we'd just done. She got me worked up, no question. From her very first email, she'd been able to push my buttons like no one else. I'd been upset earlier, but the more I thought about it, the more I realized my unease wasn't just about the gallery space. It came from the fact that, for a moment, I'd been afraid that my perception of Nadiya hadn't been based on reality, and that thought devastated me. I wanted that woman to be real, more than anything.

Once again, her words from earlier came back to me: *Even from the very beginning, that wasn't all I felt for you.*

What did I feel for her? More than simply attraction, that was for damn sure. She made me laugh, she drove me crazy, and she made me so dizzy with need for her that I could barely keep my balance.

I might be stubborn, but even I had to admit it felt a whole lot like love.

I had sworn I would never love anyone else the way I loved Shawna, but somehow, this didn't feel the same. It still felt like love, yes, but it felt completely different too, and just like I'd said to her when she painted my chest, adding something to a work of art that I'd thought was finished didn't necessarily mean ruining it.

Sometimes, it even made it better.

Those were things I needed to talk to her about, but not right at that moment. Not with her standing there in her cowboy boots, her jean shorts around her ankles and both of us covered with paint in the middle of the night. That would be a conversation that needed a little preparation, a little thought ahead of time. So for the time being, I simply kissed her gently and grabbed our clothes off the workshop floor.

"Time for bed, Nadiya."

She nodded as she pulled her shorts back up and reached out her hand for her t-shirt.

I bit back a grin as I shook my head. "I dare you to make a run for it."

Her mouth dropped open in shock, just as I expected it to. "I can't go outside naked!"

"You're not naked. Just topless, and it's the middle of the night. Who's going to see you? Come on, darlin'; live a little."

The way she nervously bit her lip as she thought it over made it perfectly clear she'd never done anything like that in her whole life, which was really just a little bit sad. "What are you going to wear?"

I held my bunched-up jeans in front of my midsection. "Nothing. I'll cover up, just in case, but I ain't putting anything back on. I'd have to take it off in two seconds when we got back inside anyway. What do you say?"

I raised my eyebrows at her in challenge, a move I had begun to learn that she had a very hard time resisting, and once again, she did just as I expected. With determination, she walked over, flipped off the workshop light and opened the door, one hand across her chest to cover herself as she peeked outside.

"Anyone out there?" I teased her, and she threw me a dirty look.

"Come on," she urged, stepping out into the darkness.

We hurried across the driveway to the front door, the air cool against my bare ass, and Nadiya let us in the front door of the house, breathing a sigh of relief as she closed the door behind us.

A second later, she covered her face with her hands, laughing at herself. "I can't believe I just did that."

"I can. You're fearless, Nadiya."

Her eyes met mine as her hands dropped. "I'm not sure that's the word I would use. Sometimes, I'm afraid of a lot of things."

A new vulnerability in her eyes suggested she was talking about a whole lot more than a little streaking, but once again, we didn't have time to get into all of it that evening. "That's only because you haven't realized just how strong you really are. Now, let's go to bed. You must be exhausted, darlin'."

Taking her hand, I brought her to my room. In the bathroom, I removed her few remaining clothes before running a washcloth under some warm water and lathering it with soap to wash the paint off her body and she did the same to me. Once clean, we climbed beneath the covers together and finally fell asleep, wrapped up in each other's arms once again.

My pleasant slumber was brought to an abrupt end by the sound of Nadiya's doorbell. I'd never heard it before, and as I sat up, Nadiya jumped up too. "Oh my God," she gasped, her eyes wide with panic. "What time is it?"

I had no idea, but the brightness of the room suggested it must have been pretty late. She usually got up and out of the house before the sun was up, but in all the activity of the night before, both of us must have forgotten to set an alarm.

The doorbell rang again as I grabbed the phone off my bedside table and my stomach sank as I got a look at the time. "It's just after 9," I told her, and Nadiya's mouth dropped open in disbelief.

"Nine o'clock? Fucking hell," she swore as she ran out the door of my room towards her own room. I heard the door slam as I pulled myself out of bed and quickly threw on my same jeans from the day before and a clean t-shirt before heading to the front door.

Daisy stood on the other side, dressed much the same as the day before, in her cowboy boots with a different pretty dress on. "Mr Callahan? The workshop's locked, I didn't know if there was a problem?"

I told her the truth. "No, sorry, I just overslept. I'll open it up for you so you can get set up, then I'll just need a couple of minutes to get ready."

Without putting shoes on, I led her back across the driveway, unable to keep from picturing myself and Nadiya walking across it half-naked just a few hours earlier. When I walked into the workshop, it looked a little messier than I remembered. Nadiya's painting sat on the easel with open pots of paint and messy brushes on the work table, which had been splattered with paint. Her cowboy hat still lay on the floor where I'd tossed it as she was down on her knees, my cock in her mouth.

Fuck, I was going to get hard again if I didn't focus.

"What happened?" Daisy asked with wide eyes, looking around at all the mess before settling on the canvas. "Is that... one of yours?"

I had to stifle a laugh. "Um, no, that was just an experiment. I'll clean all this up, you don't have to worry about that. Go on and get settled and I'll be right back."

I almost made it to the door before Daisy called out again. "Mr Callahan? Is this your phone?"

She picked up a phone from the work table that I hadn't noticed. It didn't belong to me, so it must have been Nadiya's. "Thanks." As I took it from her, I glanced down at the display, where more than a dozen missed calls were showing, no doubt from people wondering where on earth she was.

I jogged back to the house and knocked on Nadiya's door. "Can I come in?"

A groan of acknowledgement came from inside, which I took as an okay, so I opened up the door and headed inside to find Nadiya already dressed and pulling her hair back in front of her mirror.

"What can I do to help?" I asked, feeling bad as I saw the distressed look on her face. For me, being late to work wasn't the end of the world, but obviously, it meant a lot more to her.

"I need to call the office, but I can't find..." she started to say, and immediately, I held up her phone.

"You left it in the workshop."

She let out a puff of air. "Right. Can you call Luisa for me? Let her know that..."

She didn't even get the words out before the phone in my hand rang and her assistant's name flashed across the screen. I answered it and put it on speakerphone before placing it down on the table in front of Nadiya.

The two of them immediately dove into rescheduling appointments and a bunch of other things that made little sense to me. "I'll head straight over to the development site," Nadiya said as she finished applying her mascara. "Dex will be with me."

My stomach sank again as I realized I had completely forgotten about the ground-breaking ceremony that day. She had told me about it, but with everything else going on, it had completely slipped my mind. I snuck out of the room as she kept talking to go and get dressed in something more appropriate for the occasion, and by the time I came back out, Nadiya was ready to go, looking professional and collected as always. Only the tightness of her mouth gave away the anxiety she had to be feeling.

"Are we going to be late?" I asked, trying to gauge her mood.

"No, if we leave now, we should be okay," she said, to my relief. "The driver will be here any minute."

Something tugged in the back of my brain as she mentioned her driver. Why didn't he wake us up that morning? As far as I understood, the same man picked her up each day. Wouldn't he have knocked on the door if she didn't show up?

Before I had a chance to ask her, she hurried me out the door.

"I should let Daisy know I'm going," I remembered.

Nadiya looked like she had forgotten all about my assistant. "Oh, right.

Since I'm here, I'd like to meet her."

Together, we went into the workshop where Daisy jumped up to introduce herself to Nadiya. She looked a little starstruck as she shook my wife's hand, which made me smile. She certainly didn't look at me that way.

Nadiya, however, looked significantly less impressed. "Is this how you usually dress for work?" she asked, her eyes scanning the younger woman's outfit with distaste.

Daisy's face immediately fell at the implied criticism. "I... uh... the agency said this is how Mr Callahan wanted me to dress?"

She looked over at me, pleading for confirmation, but I had no idea what she was talking about. "I never said anything like that," I assured Nadiya.

Her jaw clenched. "No, but I can guess who did." When she turned back to Daisy, who looked more chagrined by the second, her expression softened a little. "It seems to have been a miscommunication, so don't worry. Going forward, business casual will be fine."

"Of course, Ms Varma," Daisy agreed, nodding her head vigorously.

We said goodbye and headed out to the street where a car waited for us. As we climbed into the backseat, I tried to guess what she was thinking. "You think this Brad guy told her to dress like that?"

Nadiya nodded grimly. "I do. He's determined to cause trouble for me, but whatever he's trying to pull, it ends today. First, we get through this ceremony, and afterwards, Brad and I are going to have a little talk."

Chapter Eighteen

~Nadiya~

I had never been late for work a day in my life. I'd never missed any of my extra-curricular activities in university or been late for a single class in school. I'd even been born ten days early. My father used to joke, with no small amount of pride, that I wanted to get a head start right from the very beginning.

Therefore, it came as no surprise that poor Luisa thought something dreadful had happened to me when she arrived at work and found my office empty. When she tried to phone me and I didn't answer, she got even more worried. She called my driver and found out that he'd arrived to pick me up as usual, but almost immediately, his phone rang with someone from Varma Corp telling him he wouldn't be needed that day.

That last part made my blood run cold when she said it. Brad must have made that call; it wouldn't have been anyone else, but how could he have possibly known I would sleep in? Was he spying on me? It felt like he had invaded every corner of my life, and so when I met Dex's assistant and found out that she had been told to dress a specific way, it didn't take much to put together who was behind that request too. From the genuine look of dismay on her face when I asked her about it, I believed she hadn't done it deliberately.

"Give me your phone." I held out my hand to Dex as the driver Luisa arranged, not my usual driver, pulled out into the street to take us downtown for the ceremony.

He handed it over readily enough, but with a hint of confusion. "What's wrong with yours?"

"It might be hacked," I reminded him, even though he'd been the one to suggest it the night before. "If Brad is seeing private communication between me and my assistant, he must have access to her account or mine, or both."

Dex nodded in understanding. "Makes sense. Who are you phoning?"

"The only person who has more influence at Varma Corp than Brad does."

My father answered on the third ring, as always. Never appear too eager, never keep people waiting; yet another of his business rules.

"Beta, where are you? Shouldn't you be at the ceremony by now?" He had planned to be there too, and it sounded like he'd already arrived, waiting for me.

"I'm on my way, but I need your help, Daddy."

As succinctly as I could, I explained to him that I thought Brad was accessing my personal communication and files.

A short pause followed my words before he spoke. "That's a serious accusation, Nadiya."

"I know, and I wouldn't say it if I didn't think it was true. Can you talk to someone in IT and ask them to check if my accounts or Luisa's have been accessed from outside our own phones and computers? And make sure they keep the fact that they're looking into it confidential."

"Of course." The head of Varma Corp's IT department was one of my father's oldest friends, which was the main reason I'd gone through my father rather than doing it myself. The CIO would treat a request from my dad as a personal favour, not just business. "Don't let on to Brad that you suspect anything when you see him at the ceremony, and I'll let you know when I hear anything."

"At the ceremony?" I repeated in surprise. "Why would I see him at the ceremony?"

Brad had nothing to do with the project. The new development was my baby and everyone knew it.

I could almost hear my father's grimace through the phone. "He said he'd heard you might not make it, so he wanted to be on hand just in case."

Of course he did. My jaw clenched in frustration at how he always seemed to be a step ahead of me. "I'll be perfectly professional," I said, though at that moment, I felt anything but. "Thank you, Daddy."

As soon as I hung up, Dex took his phone back from me, immediately dialling someone and holding the phone up to his ear.

"Who are you calling?"

"My private investigator," he answered with a teasing smile.

A moment later, I heard a woman's voice answer on the other end. "Well, good morning, Dex," Tonia said, loud and clear. "I'm guessing you had a very good night last night."

I winced as Dex rolled his eyes. "None of your business, but I need a favour, and fast. Nadiya, what's this asshole's full name?"

There could only be one asshole he meant. "Brad Sherwood."

"You get that?" he asked into the phone. "Good. Now listen, this Sherwood guy's fixin' to screw Nadiya over, and me in the process. I need you to dig deep and find out anything you can about him and what he might be trying to hide. Call me back as soon as you've got anything. Thanks, Tonia. Yeah, yeah, I'll owe you one. Bye."

He hung up and slid the phone back into his pocket as I gave him a curious look. "Tonia's a private investigator?"

Dex laughed. "Not literally, darlin', but she's well-connected with all the other Houston work-from-home moms who know everything about everyone in this town. She'll tap into her grapevine and if Sherwood's got so much as an unpaid parking ticket, they'll have it flushed out in no time."

That sounded a little unlikely to me, but I had to admit I knew nothing about how gossip worked. It had never interested me before.

"So now we wait, I suppose?" I said, and Dex reached over to take my hand.

"Now you go and charm everyone at this ceremony," he contradicted me gently. "And when it's over, we take on Brad Sherwood, together."

Knowing he had my back made me feel a million times better. "Thank you, Dex."

"Anytime, darlin'."

We lapsed into silence for a moment, both of us lost in thought, until Dex turned to me again.

"I still haven't signed anything to sell the gallery to you."

I hardly needed to be reminded of that. "I know. The paperwork is back at the house, we'll take care of it tonight, and hopefully the lease as well."

"I get that. What I mean is: how is this whole ceremony happening when you don't even technically own my property yet?"

My carelessness made me wince again, but I told him the truth. "I okayed the whole thing based on our verbal agreement. If you pulled out now, it would be a big problem, both legally and from a public perception point of view. It's not how I usually do business, I promise. I just..." I trailed off, realizing I had no idea what I meant to say before shrugging. "I don't know. I have no excuse."

I expected him to look disappointed in me, but instead, the expression in his blue eyes softened as he looked down at me. "So, you put yourself on the line as much as I did here, going on faith alone."

I supposed that was one way to look at it. "I trust you, Dex."

"I trust you too, Nadiya."

My throat closed up a little as I nodded. Those words sounded far more significant than they should have. I couldn't remember the last time something had meant quite so much to me.

It only took a couple of more minutes before we arrived at the now-cleared city block which would host my new building. Dex swallowed hard as he looked out the window to the spot where his gallery used to stand.

"Is this okay?" I asked. Perhaps I should have prepared him for it somehow, but with everything else going on, it hadn't been at the top of my mind. Considering someone else's feelings would still take some getting used to.

Thankfully, Dex nodded. "It'll be fine. Come on, we don't want to be late."

A small crowd had already gathered: people from Varma Corp, the construction company running the project, some of our investors, some of the new tenants and of course, the media. My father nodded at me from the group he was speaking with, and when I caught sight of Brad chatting to some of the investors, his face tightened as we made eye contact and I shot him a sweet smile.

"That's him?" Dex asked, his voice low in my ear, having noticed my gaze.

"The one and only."

Speaking of the devil, Brad excused himself from his conversation and came over to me and Dex. "Nadiya. I was beginning to think we might not see you here today."

Remembering my father's warning, I bit back the sarcastic retort on the tip of my tongue and smiled at him instead. "Of course I'm here, and I'd like to introduce you to my husband, Dexter Callahan. Dex, this is Brad Sherwood, one of my directors."

Calling him merely a director was a slight to his position, and he didn't miss it. He took a quick glance around to make sure no one was within earshot before he leaned in closer. "I know this whole marriage is a farce and I can prove it. If you don't back out of this ceremony, I'm going to the press, and both you and Varma Corp will suffer a huge blow to your reputation. You're going to have to make up your mind real fast, Nadiya. What's it going to be? Are you going to keep playing this game, or are you going to step aside?"

~Dex~

I couldn't believe the nerve of this guy. After everything he'd done, or at least what we suspected him to have done, he actually gave Nadiya an ultimatum. What made him think he was the one in control?

"What exactly is the press going to say?" I asked, taking a step closer to him. It pleased me to see I was several inches taller than him and quite a lot wider. If he knew what was good for him, he should be intimidated.

Brad did take a small step back, but otherwise held his ground, pulling out his phone and holding it out to me. "This is the draft article. See for yourself."

Nadiya peered down curiously as I grabbed the phone from Brad's hand and held it out for her to see too. The screen was laid out like a newspaper article with an old picture of me on horseback in a cowboy hat and jeans, a picture I recognized from a fundraising event I did for Shawna's treatment years earlier. Where the hell had he dug that up from? Next to it sat a photo of Nadiya in a traditional sari, dripping with jewellery and looking, I had to admit, pretty damn gorgeous. Above both photos read the headline: *Cowboy and Indian*.

"Seriously?" I growled as I glared back up at him.

Brad just smirked. "You haven't got to the good stuff yet."

As I scrolled down, my stomach sank lower with every word. As I'd expected, the article asserted that Nadiya and I married for convenience. He actually had the details of that pretty damn close to the fact: that we had agreed to marry in order to fool the public so she could improve her image, offering me cash and incentives for my gallery in return. Put as starkly as that, even I had to admit it sounded pretty sleazy.

The article even had a quote from me: *We made an agreement. Nadiya offered me a deal on the gallery. I've had a lot of new people interested in my work.*

"I never said that," I protested. "I never talked to any damn reporter."

"But you did say it." Brad's eyes glinted triumphantly. "I've got it all on tape from your conversation with your friend at the bar the other night."

Nadiya looked up at me with hurt and confusion in her eyes and I had to clench my fist tightly to keep from clocking him across the face right in front of everyone gathered there. "I might have said all those words, but not in that order. I never meant it like that. And how the hell did you record my conversation anyway?"

I remembered how odd Sawyer had acted that night, asking me questions about a contract with Nadiya. Did that mean he was working with Brad?

"I just planted a few ideas in your friend's head over a friendly beer before you arrived," Brad told me, looking awfully proud of himself. "And planted a bug at the table while I was there."

So, Sawyer *didn't* know he was being used? That made me feel better and angrier all the same time.

"That's illegal," Nadiya pointed out. "You can't just record someone's private conversation."

"It doesn't really matter, does it? By the time you fight against any of the things in this article, the damage will already be done. Only a quarter of people who see the news ever see the retraction."

Any of the things in the article? What else was there?

Scrolling further, I could see it started talking about how much I was still in love with my first wife, as proof that I could never actually feel anything for Nadiya. There was a quote from Sawyer, unsurprisingly, presumably from that conversation he had with Brad where he didn't know he was being recorded, followed by a photo of me at Shawna's grave with the caption: 'Mr Callahan visiting his wife's grave two days after his wedding.'

Once again, Nadiya looked over at me in surprise, looking for confirmation, and I gritted my teeth as I replied. "That's true. I talk to her sometimes when I need to think about things, and I had a lot to think about that day."

Although she nodded in acceptance, concern still lingered in her eyes and I wished I could explain further what I had actually talked to Shawna about that day: that I'd actually gone there to talk about Nadiya. But that would have to wait, since I didn't plan to say a word in front of the slimy weasel who was still watching us, grinning gleefully.

"You haven't got to the best part yet."

Reluctantly, I returned to the article, afraid of exactly what else he might have engineered, and I couldn't even muster up much surprise when it started talking about Daisy. It said how I specifically requested an assistant who looked like my first wife, and as 'proof', it showed a photo of Daisy heading into my workshop the day before in her dress and cowboy boots, next to a photo of Shawna looking almost identical.

From there, it went on to suggest that I was sleeping with Daisy, backed up by two photos – one showing Nadiya at some kind of bar in her suit, sitting with my sisters, and the other showing my pixelated behind on the driveway between the workshop and the house, with a figure in shadow in front of me. All that could be seen of her was her cowboy boots and bare legs, the top half of her completely in the dark.

The implication couldn't be clearer: while Nadiya was out with friends, I was fooling around with my assistant in my workshop.

"That's Nadiya!" I nearly shouted as I jabbed my finger at the photo, attracting attention from a few people nearby and Nadiya quickly put her hand on my arm to calm me down. Trying to remember where we were, I took a deep breath and lowered my voice before speaking again. "This is ridiculous. It's lies and manipulation, all of it."

"It doesn't matter." Nadiya's voice was quiet next to me, and I looked down at her in surprise.

"What do you mean?"

"He's right, Dex," she said, looking up at me with a look of resignation in her eyes I'd never seen before. "It doesn't matter if it's true or not. It's how it looks that matters. By the time we clear this up, if we even can, the damage will be done."

Brad's smug, gloating smile turned my stomach. "I always knew you had some sense. Though you did surprise me with this whole scheme of yours. I honestly wouldn't have thought you had it in you. I thought Greg breaking up with you would be the end of it."

I'd almost forgotten about him getting Greg to break up with Nadiya in the first place. "You cowardly, pathetic little piece of shit…"

I moved towards him again, but once more, Nadiya reached out to stop me. "Dex, everyone's watching."

At that point, I really didn't care, but Brad's next words stopped me cold. "Go ahead and hit me. I've already got some testimony about your temper and the fights you got in after your wife died. I didn't add them because it didn't seem necessary, but if you attack me now, it'll be great backup to show just how unstable you are."

Fuck. How did he manage to be one step ahead of us at every turn? How much time and money had he put into having us followed and photographed?

What the hell was he trying to cover up?

"You win, Brad," Nadiya said from beside me, and I looked down at her in disbelief. She couldn't really mean that? "I'll go and you can tell everyone I had an emergency to attend to. You can do the ceremony. Just don't publish that article."

"It's not just the ceremony I want," he pointed out, which was obvious enough already. "I want you to step down from Varma Corp. Without you there, the CEO position is as good as mine."

"She's not going to quit her job for you," I snarled at him. "She's the best damn businesswoman in this city, she's been running that company for years…"

"I'll do it." Once again, Nadiya's voice was quiet, but the words held as much weight as if she'd screamed them.

"What?" The article was bad, that couldn't be denied, but not bad enough to give up everything she'd ever worked for. We had to fight, we couldn't just let this asshole win.

Brad grabbed his phone back from my hand. "When your resignation letter reaches the board, I'll kill the article. Not before."

She nodded and he smirked at both of us one more time.

"Pleasure doing business with you both."

As he walked away, I turned back to my wife with disappointment and confusion racing through my veins. "What the hell, Nadiya? You're just going to let him walk all over you like that?"

With Brad's back turned, the meek and humble look on her face instantly dropped away and she looked back up at me with determination, a smile playing on her lips. "Not a chance. But now that he thinks I am, that gives us a bit more time to figure out exactly how to take him down once and for all. Let's get over to Varma Corp and have a little look around Brad's office before he gets back, shall we?"

A relieved smile spread across my face as I realized she'd been faking it the whole time. "Are we playing dirty now, darlin'?"

"As dirty as it gets," she promised me. "Come with me, cowboy."

~Nadiya~

Sometimes, you needed to lose the battle to win the war. My father taught me that, and I'd never understood it as clearly as I did at that moment.

I would let Brad do the ground breaking ceremony, thinking he'd broken me. It disappointed me not to get the moment in the spotlight after all the work I'd put into the development, but compared to putting Dex through the public scrutiny that would follow the publication of that ridiculous article, or the threat of potentially losing my job, it hardly mattered.

Finally, Brad had shown his hand. Now that I knew what his ultimate goal was and how he planned to achieve it, all I had to do was stop him.

With each word Brad said, I became more convinced that Dex had it right when he suggested Brad must be hiding something. This went far beyond any kind of normal competition for a job. There must have been something that he didn't want anyone to know about, and I had to guess he specifically didn't want *me* to know about it if I became CEO. That would explain why he was so determined to stop me from getting the position: not just so that he could get the job, but so that I *didn't* get it.

My phone rang as the car wove through the downtown streets, heading towards the Williams Tower and the Varma Corp offices. The call display showed my father's name, but still afraid my phone had been compromised, I let it ring and called him back on Dex's phone instead.

"Nadiya, where are you?" His voice sounded nearly frantic, which was very unusual for him. "Why is Brad doing the ceremony? I saw you here but then you left."

"It's a long story, but I'm heading to Brad's office now and I need your help. I want the floor cleared and someone with admin access to Brad's computer to meet me in his office."

A pause followed as my father processed what I was asking for. "Nadiya, if you're wrong about this..."

"It will mean my job," I filled in. "I understand that, Daddy. Please, trust me."

With a sigh, he agreed, and we hung up so he could make the arrangements. Dex took his phone back and texted Tonia for an update. She said tidbits were starting to come in but no smoking gun yet. She promised to keep us updated.

"What are you thinking?" Dex asked me as he put his phone away.

"My gut says it's financial." It had come to me as I watched his reactions as we read through the article. He looked smug, yes, but nervous too. "The CEO is the only person besides the Chief Financial Officer who has oversight of all the company's accounts. My father has always been more about relationships than numbers. If there was something just slightly off, he wouldn't necessarily notice, especially if the CFO said it was fine. But *I* would notice, and I think that's what's got Brad worried."

Dex nodded slowly. "And your CFO wouldn't notice something was wrong?"

The abbreviation sounded a bit funny coming out of his mouth, like a word from a foreign language. "He should, but he and Brad have been friends for years. It's possible he's in on it too, or that Brad was able to get information out of him on where things might slip through the cracks. He seems to be good at manipulating people."

"You can say that again," Dex agreed with a scowl.

By the time we arrived at Varma Corp, my father had worked his magic. The executive floor had been emptied, so that if Brad did have any spies reporting back to him, they wouldn't know what was going on. The head of our IT department waited for us in Brad's office along with a younger man who I had to assume would be the one actually doing the work.

"Ms Varma," the IT director greeted me. "We've just accessed Mr Sherwood's network drives as well as his desktop folders. Do you know what you're looking for?"

"Not exactly," I admitted. "But it will be something he accesses a lot. It will definitely be on a private drive, and my guess would be that it's a spreadsheet, possibly one that's feeding from the company's live financial accounts."

Dex looked over at me in surprise. "How'd you work all that out?"

"If it's something he's so anxious about that he's going to all this trouble to cover up, he's going to check on it regularly to make sure nothing's going wrong," I explained. "He'd also want to be notified immediately if anything changed that would affect him, so having it feed off the live data makes most sense."

A rather proud-looking smile pulled at Dex's lips. "Makes sense to me, darlin'."

Two weeks earlier, the thought of someone calling me any kind of pet name in public would have been a nightmare, but as the IT director looked over at me in surprise after hearing Dex use the word, I simply jutted my chin out proudly. My husband could call me whatever he liked, as long as he said it in that affectionate, sexy tone.

"Did you find anything about Mr Sherwood accessing my own networks?" I asked the director as his subordinate got to work in searching Brad's computer.

"We can't tie it to Mr Sherwood directly," he told me. "But someone has definitely been accessing your assistant's login from outside her usual workstations. We couldn't find any evidence of yours being hacked. Perhaps they thought that would be too risky. They've covered their tracks well though, my team isn't able to determine where the access is coming from. You'll probably need someone specialized in that sort of tracking to be able to pin it down any further."

That would take too long. I needed evidence immediately, before Brad had a chance to wreak any further havoc.

"Is it worth us looking around in here?" Dex asked, peering around Brad's office.

"I don't think he'd be careless enough to leave anything physical lying around, but I guess we might as well, while we wait."

We left the other two men to the computer while Dex and I started going through Brad's filing cabinets. Everything looked pretty much as I expected to find it: organized and all relevant to his job. Nothing jumped out at me. As helpful as it would have been to come across a file labelled 'nefarious takeover plan', that didn't seem too likely.

"You won't even know if what you're looking at is appropriate or not," I pointed out to Dex as he got down on his knees to search through the desk drawers.

"Not in terms of files, maybe, but I can guess this is probably not appropriate for work."

From the back of the drawer, he gingerly pulled out a pair of lacy women's underwear.

That was interesting, certainly, but not really conclusive of anything. "They could just be his," I pointed out, making Dex laugh.

"I suppose that's possible," he agreed, but he kept them out just in case.

The IT director soon called us back. "Ms Varma? This might be what you wanted."

Dex got back to his feet as I walked over to the desk and we both leaned in to take a look at the screen.

As I'd expected, the file on the screen was a spreadsheet, with a live link to the company's account reports, updated hourly from the bank. Named with a random assortment of letters and numbers, nothing about it would stand out to anyone looking at filenames on the system.

"And he accesses this a lot?" I asked.

"Several times a day," the young man in front of the computer told me. "Including this morning."

"Move," I said in reply, pushing him gently out of the way so I could sit down in front of the computer myself. I recognized a lot of the information from my own reports, but there were additional accounts that I'd never seen before.

In particular, one account seemed to be feeding off the main company account. Scrolling through the pages it looked like money went into the account from just about every transaction the company made, a tiny fraction of a percent each time, not enough to raise any alarms, but no money ever returned.

That had to be it. I couldn't think of any good reason for an account like that to exist. I would need to double check with my father and with the bank, but it felt like I was very much on the right track.

"Copy this to my personal network," I instructed before getting to my feet again. "I'll review it in my own office."

"Yes, ma'am."

As Dex and I stepped out into the hall together, he let me know he was on the same train of thought I was. "He's been funneling money out?"

His phone buzzed and he pulled it out as we walked quickly to my office.

"That's my guess," I agreed. "I just need some hard proof. And a motive would be nice, something more concrete than simple greed."

Dex huffed as he read the text on his screen. "Looks like I might be able to help you there. According to Tonia, there's a very good reason he might be in need of a little cash."

~Dex~

Pride and admiration filled my chest as I watched Nadiya take control of the situation. Once I shared Tonia's findings with her, she got her father on the phone and reviewed the accounts with him. She spoke to some of the company accountants to confirm her suspicions, and then she got the company's lawyers involved.

"I think I have it," she told me as she hung up the phone in her office. "And even if it's not entirely right, it's enough to sink him anyway."

"What's your plan?" I asked.

"I'll wait for him to get back. He'll still be thinking he's won, so I'll call him in here and lay it all out for him."

"Do you want me to go?" With no official position at Varma Corp, I really had no reason to be there, but Nadiya looked surprised I would even suggest it..

"Of course not. He's been out for you as much as me. You should get to see the moment he realizes just how screwed he is."

That sounded pretty damn good to me.

As we waited, Nadiya had Luisa print off a new copy of the paperwork for the sale of my gallery and I *finally* officially signed it over to Varma Corp. The lease was another issue, but Nadiya promised me she would review the contract Brad had signed with the other gallery as soon as we'd dealt with the more immediate matter.

Nadiya also let her father know what was happening and soon, he joined us, telling us that he had left the ceremony as things were winding down, so Brad shouldn't be far behind.

"Is this what you imagined when you married my daughter, Mr Callahan?" my new father-in-law asked, giving me a wry look. "Corporate backstabbing and blackmail?"

I glanced over at Nadiya with a soft smile. "Nothing about our marriage has been exactly how I imagined it, sir."

Finally, we got the call we'd been waiting for: an alert from the building security that Brad had returned. They were on standby to escort him out later, once Nadiya was finished with him. She had all her bases covered.

Luisa let Brad know that Nadiya would like to see him in her office to discuss her resignation, so when he turned up at the door, a profound look of satisfaction hung on his face. That smug expression quickly melted away when he saw both me and Mr Varma there as well. Nadiya sat behind her desk while the two of us stood to the side.

Brad's eyes cycled between the three of us suspiciously. "What's going on?"

"Come in and close the door," Nadiya said in reply, her voice cool and calm.

He did as she said, shutting the door behind him and warily taking a few steps closer to her.

"Sit down," Nadiya instructed, in a tone that left no room for argument. As soon as he had complied, she dove straight in. "I've asked you here to go over the terms of your resignation."

Disbelief flashed across his face, with just a trace of fear that he quickly tried to cover up. "What are you talking about? You're the one who's resigning."

His eyes flicked to Mr Varma, clearly wondering just how much he knew about the whole situation, but he must have decided he had nothing to lose because he laid it all on the line.

"If you don't resign, every news outlet in Houston is going to be running that story in the morning. You'll be finished in this town. No one will take you seriously anymore."

"Not if I pitch them a better story," Nadiya countered, sounding completely in control.

"Perhaps one about a Varma Corp director who's been embezzling company funds to cover up his affairs?"

Brad's face drained of colour, leaving him looking a little sickly. "I... I don't know what you're talking about."

Nadiya raised her eyebrows. "Really? How about I refresh your memory then?"

She pressed a button on her phone, a pre-arranged signal between her and Luisa, and the door to Nadiya's office opened again, revealing a very pretty and nervous-looking woman in a tight white dress.

"Come in, Ms Whiting," Nadiya invited her as Luisa closed the door again behind the other woman. "We were just discussing your relationship with Mr Sherwood."

The woman's face turned almost as pale as Brad's had. "Ma'am?" she squeaked, looking frantically over at Brad, who refused to meet her eye.

Nadiya opened her drawer and pulled out the pair of panties we'd found earlier. "I think these are yours? At least, I hope they are, for your sake. If not, then he's been screwing someone other than you in his office as well. Or maybe they belong to one of his previous assistants. They all looked a lot like you, you know."

Luisa had provided that particular piece of information. Nadiya had never noticed, which didn't surprise me, but apparently, Brad had a type. Perhaps that explained why he thought he could tempt me with a Shawna look-alike.

"You could have gotten those from anywhere," Brad interjected, focusing only on the underwear in her hand and ignoring everything else she'd just said. "It doesn't prove anything."

"You're right, it doesn't," Nadiya agreed. "But it's interesting how your wife has recently got herself a new car, and a new ring, and is talking about a holiday as well. All paid for by 'guilt money', as she put it. My guess is that she found out about your little office romances and is milking it for all its worth. She must know how much the board wants to project a happy family image, so it'd be worth it to you to keep the family together. It's pretty manipulative, but then, she did marry you, so I suppose you have a few things in common."

Brad's face sagged a little lower. "She didn't tell you that."

"No, she didn't," Nadiya agreed again. "But she told her best friend when they were having a spa day, when they weren't entirely alone. Isn't it annoying when something you thought was private is overheard?"

She gave him a cold smile, making it clear she was referring to him recording my own conversation with Sawyer.

"You can't prove anything," he insisted, sticking to his denial rather pathetically.

"Not about your love life, no," Nadiya conceded. "But the embezzlement? That, I can prove."

She turned her computer monitor so that Brad could see the spreadsheet on it, the one she'd found on his drive.

"I haven't figured out if you started embezzling the money to keep your wife quiet, or if it was already underway before that and the two things happen to coincide, but in the end, it doesn't really matter. Unless you have a better explanation for this account, I think the press will believe the story I give them, don't you? By the time the real truth comes out, the damage will be done. The perception is what's important. Isn't that what you told me?"

"Brad? What's she talking about?" His assistant obviously didn't have a clue about the financial fraud, but Brad completely ignored her, his jaw clenching as he focused entirely on Nadiya.

"What are you going to do?"

"That depends on what you do. If you go quietly and repay every cent that you've stolen, I won't press charges. I couldn't care less about your personal life, but I want you to sever all ties with Varma Corp. Don't even list it on your résumé. As far as we're concerned, it will be like you were never here."

"Nobody will hire me without a reference," he protested. "I've worked here for twelve years. What am I supposed to say?"

"That's not my problem," she said, sounding not at all sympathetic. "That's the deal. If you refuse, the alternative is prison. And of course, it goes without saying, you will also get rid of all the ridiculous 'evidence' you've gathered about my own marriage."

He thought it over for a moment, looking for an angle he hadn't yet exploited, but in the end, he had to come to the obvious conclusion: he was completely and utterly screwed. "I'll take your deal."

"I thought you might." Nadiya opened the leather-bound folder on her desk in front of her. "This is the non-disclosure agreement you'll need to sign before leaving today, along with the amount you'll have to repay. Ms Whiting, there's an agreement for you too. Your services are no longer required at Varma Corp, but we'll provide you with a severance package so long as you don't say anything about what you've heard here today."

She placed the papers that the legal team had prepared on her desk and invited Brad's assistant to have a seat. Both she and Brad looked miserable as they reviewed the documents in front of them, and Nadiya came over to speak to her father and me, moving us out of earshot.

"Well done, Nadiya." Her father's eyes glinted with approval. "Though I think you're letting him off a little too easily."

Nadiya shook her head. "It's better this way. If we had him arrested, it would be all over the news that he had managed to take money from us for months with no one noticing. It would make the company look weak and unstructured, and no one would want to do business with us. I wouldn't want to. For the sake of Varma Corp's reputation, this is the best choice."

Her father looked as impressed with that reasoning as I was. Not many women could be so cool and rational when someone had made things as personal as Brad had. Not many men could be either, for that matter.

Mr Varma nodded as he looked between the two of us. "Well, with Brad out of the picture, the CEO position is yours, married or not, so I guess this little arrangement can be ended whenever you like. I assume you laid out all the terms for dissolving the union in your prenuptial agreement."

Nadiya's eyes met mine briefly before returning to her father. "Actually, we didn't sign a prenup."

Mr Varma's eyes widened in disbelief. "What?" He glanced at me briefly, as if wondering whether he should speak in front of me, before pushing ahead anyway. "Nadiya, how could you be so careless? He could claim half your assets. It could drag out in court for years. This isn't like you."

I bristled at the implication that I had ever been after her money, but Nadiya put a hand on my arm to calm me. "Daddy, there's not going to be a divorce. Dex and I are staying married, but you're right about one thing: I have done a few things lately that were careless."

She gave me a little smile, that special genuine smile of hers that was just for me.

"And you're right that it isn't like me, or at least not like the old me. I've changed in the last couple of weeks, but I think it's for the better."

"I don't understand what you're talking about." Her father looked completely confused, so much so that I almost felt sorry for him.

"I'll explain it to you later," she promised, glancing back over at the two people still sitting at her desk. "Maybe you can come to dinner at our house on Friday?"

He nodded, still looking uncertain, but I could only focus on one thing she'd said: *our* house.

It sounded perfect to me.

When Brad and the other woman had both signed their agreements, Nadiya called Luisa to check that security was ready to escort them both from the building.

"Your belongings will be sent to you at home," she told Brad, her professional voice back on. "And the finance team will send you the payment schedule to repay the debt. Any issues you have, you can deal with the financial coordinator directly. I don't want to hear from you again, but if you aren't complying with the terms of the agreement, then we reserve the right to press charges."

"I read the agreement," he muttered. "I understand."

He looked over at me, making eye contact with me for the first time since he'd entered the room, with an odd mix of resentment and jealousy in his expression.

"I hope she's paying you well for all of this."

I followed Nadiya's lead in giving him a calm, slightly patronizing smile. "Trust me, I'm getting more out of this than I ever dreamed. I owe you one."

The scowl on his face was hugely satisfying.

When they were gone, Nadiya went over a few more things with her father, and when he left, we were finally alone again, just the two of us in her office.

There were so many things I wanted to say to her, but first, I had to satisfy my curiosity on what her father had brought up. "You never even mentioned a prenup, darlin'."

It had never crossed my mind since it had never been something I'd worried about before, but for someone in her position, it did make a lot of sense. If I had less honourable intentions, I could certainly try to take advantage of her.

Nadiya shrugged her shoulders in a self-deprecating way. "I know. I don't know what's wrong with me. It's almost like I trust you or something."

The teasing tone in her voice was new, and I had to admit I liked it. "I trust you too, Nadiya. And more than that, I care for you. I think..." I swallowed hard in preparation for the words I never thought I'd say to another woman again. "I think I love you."

I winced at how uncertain that sounded, but even saying that much was a big deal for me. And I didn't have to worry for long as Nadiya stepped closer to me, close enough to put her hand on my cheek.

"I think I love you too, Dex."

Amusement and relief and happiness rushed through me all together and I couldn't stop my grin, or stop myself from picking her up and twirling her around right there in the middle of her office.

It was still early days, I knew. We hadn't known each other that long, and we certainly didn't have a conventional courtship, but looking ahead to my future, I couldn't imagine it without her in it. From the look in her eyes, I knew without her having to say it that she felt the same.

"I wish I could take you home right now and show you just how hard I'm thinking it," I murmured against her ear as I put her gently back on her feet.

"Who says we need to go home?" she asked, biting her lip in anticipation as she looked up at me.

My eyebrows shot up in surprise. "What exactly are you suggesting, Ms Varma?"

She grinned right back at me, unable to stop her smile. "I'm suggesting, Mr Callahan, that we seal the deal right here in my office. Unless you have any objections to that?"

Chapter Nineteen

~**Nadiya**~

Dex's gaze turned heated as I suggested we take a moment to celebrate our success right there in my office.

"Is this something you do often?" he asked, teasing me as usual.

Of course I didn't, and I knew he knew that. I had never so much as kissed anyone in my office, let alone what I envisioned doing with Dex. But I *was* imagining it, and my body already felt more than ready. Flush with the thrill of having defeated my enemy and almost certainly securing myself the long-coveted CEO position, I felt strong and powerful, and I wanted nothing more than to indulge that feeling with the one person who had respected those qualities in me from the very first time we met.

Giving him a wink, I went to the door and locked it before picking up the phone on my desk. "Luisa, there are still a couple of things Mr Callahan and I need to work out. Please make sure we're not disturbed."

As I placed the receiver back in its cradle, Dex chuckled softly. "What are we working out then, darlin'?"

I took a couple of steps towards him. "Well, we signed your contract, Mr Callahan, but there's still the matter of your bonus to settle."

Amusement flashed across his face, his eyes still filled with desire. "What kind of bonus is that?"

"A performance bonus. If you can satisfy me that you're the right man for the job..." My hand went to his chest before starting to trail lower. "Then you'll be entitled to some additional compensation."

Dex's breath grew shallower as his eyes stayed fixed on me. "Is that right? Well, I'm certainly willing to work for it, Ms Varma. Just tell me what you'd like me to do."

The previous couple of nights, in my kitchen and in his workshop especially, Dex had been the one to take the lead, but in my office where I had always been the one in charge, he gave me control, and I loved him even more for that.

I loved him. I still couldn't quite believe I'd said that to him, or that he'd said it to me either. I couldn't say it to Greg the night he left after years of being together, but after what really amounted to a handful of days with Dex, the words came out. Maybe not easily or gracefully, but they came out anyway, and I truly meant them. I had always thought maybe something about me didn't work that way, that I wasn't built to fall in love the way other people talked about, but now I knew that had never been true.

I just hadn't met the right man yet.

"I want you to take your pants off and have a seat in my chair," I told him, surprising myself with my boldness.

Dex hurried to comply, pulling the zipper of his pants down and letting them fall to the floor, followed quickly by his underwear too. His cock was already hard and ready, which only made me feel even more powerful. The way he reacted to me, like he just couldn't get enough, was something else entirely new for me.

Especially since I couldn't get enough of him either.

Following my instructions, he went over and sat down in my chair behind my desk while I quickly shimmied out of my pants too, growing wetter by the second as I anticipated the pleasure to come. Dex's eyes were slightly hooded as he watched me, his hands gripping the armrests of the chair.

"Now, Mr Callahan," I said as I sauntered over to him, still wearing my shirt and suit jacket but completely naked on the bottom, other than my high heels. "About that opening that needs to be filled…"

Dex groaned as his hold on the armrests tightened. "Fuck, Nadiya."

"Exactly," I teased him. "Let's see if you're the man I need for this job."

With his legs pressed tightly together, I climbed onto the chair on top of him, straddling him, my legs on either side of his. He reached between my legs, stroking my wetness, his fingers brushing my clit as I bit my lip, trying to hold in the moan that wanted so badly to come out. His lips brushed softly against my neck as he lifted his stiff cock, placing it firmly against my entrance.

"You want to see how I can fill it?" he whispered in my ear, teasing me just as I had teased him.

I nodded, desperate for the feel of him inside me. "That's right. Show me what you've got."

Thankfully, he didn't keep me waiting. His hands moved to my hips, pulling me down firmly onto his waiting cock and we both groaned in satisfaction as we fit together just as perfectly as always. His mouth found mine in a deep, searing kiss as my hips pressed against him.

Voices sounded outside my door and for a second, panic filled me at the reminder that only a thin wall separated us from the rest of the Varma Corp staff. But the voices faded as the people they belonged to walked past, and when I looked down at Dex, the rest of the world faded away too.

"Come on, darlin'," he murmured, his hands slipping beneath my remaining clothes to run across my bare skin. "Show me who's boss."

With an invitation like that, how could I refuse?

My hands on his shoulders, I began to lift my hips, feeling him stroke me from the inside as I pulled nearly all the way off him and sank back down again. I couldn't imagine how that feeling would ever get old, the perfect way he completed me, filling a need in me I had never known needed to be filled. My eyes darted up to the window behind us, the open expanse of glass that looked out onto the city below. I had always loved the view, having the city at my feet, but never had I felt quite as on top of the world as I did right then.

Dex sighed with pleasure as I rode him, harder and faster, my hips grinding against him with each pass. One of his hands strayed between us, his fingers playing with my clit as my peak began to build, and I ran my hand through his hair, loving the way he exhaled as I did it. How the hell did I get so lucky, I wondered, to find a man that could make me feel admired and desired and respected and dirty all at the same time?

"Oh, God," I moaned, trying to keep my voice low but unable to stop the words from escaping as his hands and cock worked together to give my body just what it needed. I almost didn't care who heard me, so long as he didn't stop what he was doing.

"You got that right," Dex groaned back, his fingers flying faster against me. "Fuck, Nadiya, I can't wait..."

That was all I needed. Knowing he was about to lose control pushed me over the edge too and my body surrendered, clamping down on him as his head fell back in his own bliss. He pumped into me as we both melted into the chair, our bodies suddenly turned to liquid.

"Damn, darlin'," he muttered as we both caught our breath.

"Yeah, pretty much," I agreed, making him laugh.

As I climbed off him, my legs still shaking, Dex grinned up at me. "So? Did I earn my bonus?"

My grin matched his in pure happiness. "I'm satisfied, yes. I think you'll do."

"And what kind of bonus do I get?" He leaned forward, his eyes meeting mine curiously.

"Did you actually have something in mind, or was that just part of the game?"

Actually, I had been thinking about something, but I didn't want to spoil the surprise. "I'll show you when I get home," I promised before sighing. "For now, I do actually need to get back to work. This whole day has been a bit of a write-off."

Dex laughed again as he got to his feet and went to pick up his discarded pants. "Perhaps, but I don't think I'd call any of it a waste of time."

"Definitely not," I agreed as I slipped my own pants back on. "Luisa can arrange for someone to take you home, and I'll see you later, okay?"

"I can't wait," he said sincerely, his eyes full of not just wanting but love too as he gave me one last kiss and a final wink from the door as he unlocked it and let himself out.

I really couldn't wait either. For just about the first time in my life, five o'clock really couldn't come soon enough.

~Dex~

I couldn't stop grinning on the way back to Nadiya's house. *Our* house, as she'd said, and I supposed it really was.

As I thought that over, though, I couldn't help wondering what happened next. She told her father we weren't getting divorced, and she told me that she loved me, which felt amazing, and we had that even more amazing encounter on her office chair, but we still hadn't fully talked about the future. I supposed I would have to move the rest of my things and sell my own house if we were really in this for the long term.

Getting married had been one thing. Saying 'I love you' was something else. What happened next, I couldn't be sure of.

Daisy was still at her desk in my workshop, but she immediately leapt to her feet when I walked in. "Mr Callahan, I'm so sorry about earlier. I had no idea you hadn't actually set the dress code, I didn't mean to..."

"Daisy, it's fine," I cut her off. After everything we'd learned about Brad that day, I knew she hadn't been involved any more than Sawyer or Luisa were. She was just another innocent person who got manipulated. "It's not your fault. Someone was trying to mess with Nadiya and he used you to do it."

"I don't really understand." She looked genuinely confused and I couldn't blame her.

"You don't need to, and you don't need to worry about it. In fact, take the rest of the day off. I'm not going to be getting much done anyway."

"Are you sure? You've had some new inquiries come in, and there are some things we should review before your meeting with Mary Flynn next week..."

"We can do it tomorrow. Honestly, Daisy, it's been a crazy day. I can't concentrate on business right now."

Thankfully, she accepted that answer and after packing up her things, she said goodbye and left. I finally set about cleaning up the mess that Nadiya and I had made the night before – well, Nadiya more than me – and the sight of the portrait she painted had me laughing all over again. After examining it a bit closer, I wrapped it up to take it into the house later. With the space tidy again, I spent a bit of time on my sketches, having had some new inspiration after the day's events. Finally, I went into the house and got started on dinner, getting ready to welcome Nadiya home.

When she arrived, at pretty much the earliest time she could have after leaving the office at the stroke of five, she seemed to be in just as good a mood as I was. A smile lit up her face as she entered the kitchen, her suit jacket draped across her arm.

"That smells amazing, Dex," she said, giving me a light kiss before peering curiously into the pot on the stove. "What are you making?"

"It's a veggie chilli. Just don't ever mention it to my mom, she'd kill me if she knew I used her recipe but left the beef out."

"My lips are sealed," she promised with a laugh. "Let me just go get settled and I'll be right back."

She disappeared for quite a while, but that worked out fine since the chilli needed a bit more time to simmer anyway. Once she got back, the food was ready, and we went to eat outside, just like we had the first night I came over. As we talked and laughed, reviewing everything that had happened in the last few days, it seemed hard to believe that not that long ago, we thought this would be a fake engagement and nothing more.

When I started to clean up in the kitchen after supper, Nadiya stopped me. "I pay people to do that, remember?"

"You're really not ever going to wash your own dishes?" I couldn't help teasing her.

"Not when there are better things I could be doing," she retorted. "Besides, I thought you wanted the bonus you earned earlier."

The reminder of our time in her office sent a rush of blood straight to my groin and I couldn't wait to find out what she had in mind. "You're going to tell me what it is now?"

She held out her hand and bit her lip in anticipation. "Come with me."

I followed her willingly out of the kitchen and down the hall, past the door to my room until we got to her room. She pulled me inside and I looked over at the bed with a growing sense of anticipation, but to my surprise, Nadiya didn't head that way. She took me over to the closet instead.

"I hope this is okay," she said, looking uncharacteristically nervous as she pulled the sliding door of the closet open.

For a second, I didn't know what I was supposed to be looking at. There were dozens of suits, different colours, all perfectly pressed and hanging neatly, along with dresses and blouses, exactly what I would expect to find in a high-powered businesswoman's closet.

But a moment later, I realized that hanging next to her things were my own clothes, the few items I had brought with me when I packed my bag at home after our wedding.

It shouldn't have really surprised me. We were already married and living together, but for some reason, the sight of those clothes, the his-and-her-ness of it all, suddenly made the whole thing seem a lot more real, and all those things we hadn't discussed yet rose again in my mind.

"I guess there are a few things we need to talk about."

Immediately, she seemed to deflate. "You don't have to move into my room if you don't want to, I just thought if we were sleeping together anyway..."

"Whoa there, darlin', hold on. I never said anything about not wanting to. It's just that we've done this whole thing so backwards, there's some stuff we never talked through that most couples would have dealt with before they got married."

"Like?" The question and her expression were so innocent and uncertain, it was all I could do not to wrap her up in my arms right then and there.

"Let's have a seat." I took her hand once more and led her over to the bed. Once we got settled, I kept hold of her hand, wanting her to feel connected to me. "So, we already agreed we're giving this a proper chance, right?"

Nadiya nodded at me. "Right. That's why I thought..."

She gestured towards the closet.

"You thought right," I assured her. "I definitely want to sleep next to you every night and wake up next to you in the morning, and it makes far more sense to do it in here than in your guest room."

She smiled in relief at both my words and my light-hearted tone. "Okay, good. What else?"

"Well, there's some pretty big stuff we never talked about in terms of the future. Like whether you want to have a family or not."

Nadiya swallowed, her eyes darting away from me. "That's a pretty big question."

"I know. And you don't need to answer it right now, but it's something we should be on the same page about if we want this to work."

Tentatively, her eyes returned to my face, searching for clues. "You *do* want a family though? With me, I mean?"

"Well, I definitely don't want one with anyone else," I teased her. "That would make things really complicated."

She tried not to smile, but didn't quite succeed. "You know what I mean."

"I do, and yeah, Nadiya, I'd like to have a family. With you, I mean. Doesn't have to be right away, but eventually, that's something I want."

I could almost picture a miniature little version of Nadiya in a suit of her own, strong and confident just like her mother. The image made me smile.

"It's something I always assumed I would do eventually too," she admitted. "But I could never really imagine it. I didn't entirely see how it would fit into my life. But now, I think... I think I can see it."

I bent down to give her a soft kiss. "That's perfect, darlin'. As long as you aren't opposed to the idea, we can figure the rest out later."

"There's something I've been meaning to talk to you about too," she added. "If this is going to be for real, people might expect me to take your name."

That honestly hadn't even really crossed my mind yet. "Do you want to take my name?"

"No, I don't think I should."

That was fine with me, but I was a bit confused why she had brought it up then. "It's your call, Nadiya, but do you mind telling me why not?"

"Well, for business purposes, I think it's better for me to stay as Nadiya Varma of Varma Corp. People already know the name."

That made sense to me. Her reputation was well-established.

"And privately... well, there was already a Mrs Dexter Callahan, and I know I'll never replace her."

Her eyes dropped to my chest, where my tattoo hid beneath my shirt, and I wasn't entirely sure how to answer that. Honestly, she never would replace Shawna, but that didn't mean I didn't love her too. Somehow, I needed to make her understand that.

My words came out slow and measured, wanting to make sure I didn't mess them up. "There was only one Shawna Callahan, just like there's only one Nadiya Varma. You're not really anything alike. Nobody could ever accuse me of having a type."

She smiled at that, but her eyes stayed down, still focused on my chest.

"But there's one big thing you've got in common, and that's the way you both made me feel like the luckiest man alive when you told me you loved me."

Finally, her eyes raised to meet mine again, and I could see both hope and caution within them. I wanted the hope to win out, so I laid it all out for her as plainly as I could.

"I really didn't think I would fall in love again, Nadiya. I told you that flat out the day we met, but it turns out: I was wrong. No, you ain't ever going to replace her, but you're just as important to me. There's a Nadiya-shaped part of my heart now, and that means I'm going to give you everything I can. If you want my name, it's yours. If you don't, that's fine too, but don't make your choice based on what you think I want, because all I want is for you to know that I'm in this for real."

That seemed to do the trick as the most beautiful, genuine smile spread across her face.

"I'm in it for real too," she promised, and when I kissed her that time, I couldn't stop. We made love in her bed for the first time and we fell asleep afterwards, both of us still naked.

Nadiya's alarm woke us up in the morning, and after turning it off, she grabbed her phone, as usual. I reached out in the darkness, wanting to steal just a few more minutes before she had to go to work, but Nadiya had suddenly gone rigid.

"You've got to be kidding me," she breathed in disbelief, and immediately, my eyes shot open.

"What's wrong, darlin'?"

The phone screen illuminated her tightly-drawn face, her eyebrows pulled together and her jaw clenched.

"It's that article that Brad showed us yesterday, the one about our marriage. The bastard actually went ahead and ran it."

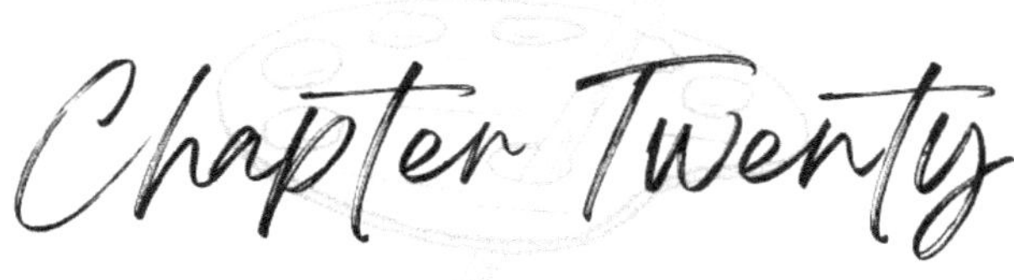

Chapter Twenty

~Nadiya~

I kept blinking, hoping the words on the screen would disappear. That whole stupid article that Brad put together, right down to the vaguely racist headline, had been posted overnight on some sleazy tabloid-style website.

It wasn't the front page of the Houston Chronicle, at least, but in the end, it hardly mattered. Either way, it had gotten out and people were posting about it on social media and tagging Varma Corp, so I would have to deal with it just the same.

"What are you going to do?" Dex asked, his blue eyes filled with concern as I flipped on the lamp on my bedside table and headed for the closet, completely nude. I never slept naked, but somehow, with Dex, it felt right.

With him, everything felt right.

"I'm going to go see Brad right now," I told him, making up my mind as I pulled out my clothes for the day. A black Givenchy suit with a red and black camisole underneath should leave no one in doubt that I meant business. "Since he broke his promise, the deal he signed is null and void. I'll be passing the evidence I have to the police, and I'm going to tell him so."

"And you have to go over in person to tell him that?" Dex got out of bed too, heading for the closet.

"I don't have to, but I want to ask him what on earth he was thinking. Does he really hate me so much that he'd go to prison just to embarrass me?"

I couldn't understand the logic behind it. As sneaky and underhanded as Brad had been throughout all of this, he'd always been logical. What changed? I wanted to know, and I also wanted to be sure there were no more surprises coming.

Dex pulled a shirt over his head before looking around. "Where'd you put my pants when you moved my clothes?"

I couldn't help smiling as I looked down at him, despite everything else going on. "I kind of prefer you without them."

He raised his eyebrows at me as a smile pulled at his lips. "I definitely prefer being without them when I'm around you too, but if there's any press over at Brad's house, they might not appreciate it."

I pointed him to the drawers in my dresser where I had put his underwear and pants. "What are you talking about?"

"I'm going with you," he explained as he pulled his pants on. "He should know that I'm on your side."

That wasn't necessary, but I didn't contradict him. Having someone have my back felt rather nice.

When we were both ready, we headed out to my waiting car, with my usual driver. He looked a little surprised to see Dex, and even more surprised when I directed him to Brad's house instead of the Varma Corp offices. Normally, I wouldn't have known Brad's home address, but Luisa had sent me a copy of the signed agreement from the day before, which had all his personal details on it.

As the car made its way through the quiet, early-morning residential streets, I scanned through the posts that were popping up while Dex read over my shoulder.

"How much of a problem is this for you?" he asked.

"It's not great," I admitted. "At least most of the comments seem to be aimed at me personally rather than the company, so that's a good thing."

If Varma Corp's reputation got dragged through the mud because of me, that really *would* be a reason to consider not giving me the CEO position, one that I couldn't argue with.

Dex scowled at my reply. "I wouldn't call that a good thing. What are they saying about you?"

"It's fine," I quickly assured him, turning the phone off and shoving it in my pocket before he could read any of the worst ones. "The usual garbage men like to say about women in power. It'll pass."

I'd long ago grown accustomed to people calling me a bitch simply because I dared to be good at my job. They would just use this as another excuse.

"I'm more worried about what your family's going to think," I told him.

From the look on Dex's face, I could tell that hadn't crossed his mind yet, and I could see the moment he realized exactly what it meant. "Oh, fu... I mean, crap. They're going to see that bit that tries to make it look like I'm cheating on you."

I grimaced. "Yeah, and they might start to wonder again about the whole sudden engagement and wedding."

Dex exhaled loudly. "Well, shoot. Guess I'm going to have some explaining to do."

"Are you going to tell them the truth?"

I hated the idea of Dex's family knowing that I had strong-armed him into our relationship, but I didn't like the idea of continuing to lie to them either. Maybe this was our chance to come clean and start over.

"I think I probably should," Dex said, clearly thinking along the same lines as me. "They'll rant and rave for a little bit, but I think they'll understand, especially when I tell 'em that we ended up falling in love for real anyway."

"That does make the whole thing a lot easier to take," I agreed, leaning over to kiss him softly right as the car pulled up outside what had to be Brad's house.

It looked like the picture of prosperity, and I gritted my teeth remembering that at least part of it had been paid for with stolen Varma Corp money. As we got to the front door we could hear yelling inside, a man's voice and a woman's, and Dex shot me a curious look. "You still want to do this?"

I nodded firmly. "I need to look him in the eye one more time."

When I rang the bell, the yelling immediately stopped. Thirty seconds later, the door opened, revealing an unshaven Brad, still in his pajamas.

"Nadiya." His face was pale as he took in Dex and me standing there. "It wasn't me."

That was what he was going with? He didn't honestly think that would work, did he? "Someone else just happened to write those exact same words and use the same photos you took?"

He winced at my tone. "The article was mine, yes, but I didn't share it. I'm not an idiot. I know what it said in the agreement I signed yesterday."

"Then who posted it?" Dex demanded.

"I don't know." Brad must have seen the look of disbelief on my face, because he quickly added more. "I swear, I don't. Why would I do it? I know I was lucky you didn't press charges right away. I can't go to prison, Nadiya."

Real fear bled into his voice as he looked back and forth between me and Dex.

"I'm not cut out for that. And my wife is freaking out about everyone knowing what I did and where our money came from. There's no upside for me in this. Why would I want to make things worse for myself?"

He did have a point, but I didn't understand who else it could be. "Who did you share the article with before we spoke yesterday?"

"No one," he said miserably. "Trust me, I've been trying to think who could have had it, but I used different private investigators to get the photos. Nobody knew the whole story except me. I don't understand how this could have happened."

"What happened to your phone?" Dex asked the question, and Brad looked over at him in confusion.

"What?"

"Your phone," Dex repeated. "The one you showed us the article on. Was that Varma Corp property?"

Brad nodded, his eyes lighting up as he realized why Dex was asking. "Yeah. Security took it from me when they kicked me out of the building yesterday. I thought they were just going to wipe it, but you're right: whoever took it could have accessed what was on it."

He looked over at me hopefully, and I had to admit Dex might be onto something. If somebody else had access to his phone, they could have been the one to share the story. As much as I didn't trust Brad, I really couldn't see what he had to gain from leaking it, and he looked completely shell-shocked by the whole thing.

"I'm going to the office," I announced to them both. "I'll find out where it went."

"Are... are you going to get the police involved?"

Brad looked so pathetic, standing there in his pajamas, that I could almost feel sorry for him.

Almost.

"It depends what I find out," was all I could promise. "Come on, Dex."

We returned to the car and I instructed the driver to take me to the office.

"What's our next move?" Dex asked.

"*Your* next move is to go back home," I told him. He opened his mouth to protest, but I quickly placed my finger over his lips. "You've still got work to do, remember? You need to smooth things over with your family, and I need to handle the board and the business on my own. It's my mess, I should clean it up."

"I think we got pretty messy together," he pointed out, and I had to smile at that, remembering our night covered with paint in his work-shop.

"True, but it was my idea in the first place. If anyone should take the blame, it should be me."

"Take the blame?" he repeated. "Does that mean you're going to tell the truth? To everyone?"

"In a way." I was still working out the details in my head, but all the misogynistic posts I'd read earlier had given me an idea. "We'll regroup at home later, okay?"

I could see he still wasn't thrilled about the idea of leaving me, but he gave in anyway, trusting my judgement, which meant a lot to me.

"Alright. I'll see you at home, darlin'," he said, giving me a sweet kiss. "Or at least I will if there's anything left once my sisters have had a go at me."

From his grimace, I could tell he had doubts about that, and I didn't envy him that conversation at all as we said goodbye.

~Dex~

I got on my phone as Nadiya's driver took me back to the house after dropping Nadiya off. First, I sent a message to our family group chat, calling an emergency lunch meeting at my mom's house. I figured I didn't need to tell them what it was about. Someone in Tonia's network would pick up on the story quickly enough and spread it around, and Tonia would filter it to the rest of them.

I might as well wait until we were together in person to offer my explanation.

I also called Daisy and told her to take the day off. I had too much to do to worry about the business side of things that day. I wanted to do some work later, but the artistic kind, not the admin side of things.

Lastly, I called Sawyer and asked if I could come in for an appointment that morning, a long one. It would give us a chance to talk, and to take care of one of the other things I wanted to do as well.

Soon, I settled into his chair, and as Sawyer worked, I told him what happened with Brad. He hadn't seen the article yet since he wasn't a social media kind of guy, but he grew livid when I explained how Brad had recorded both the conversation the two of them had and the conversation between me and Sawyer afterwards.

Sawyer scowled as he worked. "I hope you rearranged his face."

The old Dex might have done that, the one Sawyer first got to know, but ever since Nadiya came into my life, I hadn't felt that all-consuming anxiety or rage. I'd been angry, for sure – with Brad and with her at different times - but I hadn't felt out of control, and that made a really nice change. I hadn't even had to use my breathing exercises since that day I couldn't pay my mortgage, the day before Nadiya and I met face-to-face for the first time.

I told Sawyer the truth about Nadiya as well, or most of it, at least. He looked relieved when I explained that we married for convenience, but confused as I described how I'd fallen in love with her since.

"I just don't know how that could happen," he admitted, and I knew nothing I could say would make it make sense to him. I had felt the exact same way just a few short weeks earlier, that feeling that kind of love again would simply be impossible.

"I hope it happens for you too someday," I told him honestly. "It's pretty damn amazing. Part of me died along with Shawna, and finally, for the first time in years, it feels like I'm all the way alive again."

When we finished up there, I headed over to my mom's. There had been no reply from my family other than to say they'd be expecting me, so the onslaught that hit me as soon as I walked in the front door didn't surprise me at all.

"This isn't really a fake marriage, is it?"

"How could you lie to us?"

"If you're really cheating on her, I'm going to twist your balls off right now!"

I winced at all of it, but the last one in particular. "I'll tell you every-thing," I promised. "Just leave my genitals alone, okay?"

All three of them scowled at me. "No promises," Laura said.

As we sat down over the amazing lunch my mom had made, I told them everything. To my surprise, they mostly listened, only interrupting when they thought I left something important out. They were most concerned about the allegations that I was sleeping with my new PA, but when I told them that part had no basis in reality and that it had actually been Nadiya in the boots in that picture, they relaxed a bit. By the time I finally got to the present, to the fact that we were committed to making a proper go at our marriage, they were actually smiling.

"You really don't see it, do you?" Billie asked, sharing a knowing look with the others.

"See what?"

"You fell for her right at the start," Laura said, picking up the torch. "We could see if that first day you told us about her. If it had been complete bullshit, we would have known then."

"What could you see?" I honestly didn't know what they were talking about.

"That little light in your eyes when you talked about her," Tonia filled in. "The almost nervous way you said her name. Those are the signs of a guy who's got it bad, and you, my dear brother, were a classic case."

"But... I hated her," I reminded them all, looking to my mom for support. Surely she would believe me.

However, she took my sisters' side. "Maybe you thought you did, before you met, but I have to agree with the girls. I knew that very first day that this was something different, and when you brought her over here, it became even more clear. You never had a chance, Dex, and neither did she. Some things are just meant to be."

"So... you guys aren't mad at me for lying to you?" I couldn't have been more surprised at how calmly they were taking all of it.

"You weren't lying to us," my mom corrected me. "You were only lying to yourself, Dex."

By the time I got back to the house, it felt like I had run a marathon. *How're things going, darlin'?* I texted Nadiya.

Her reply came back quickly. *It could be worse. You're still alive?*

Surprisingly, yes. The part about how things could be worse didn't sound great, but I trusted her to ask for my help if she needed it. Until then, I'd leave her to handle things the way I knew she could. *I believe in you. Can't wait to see you later.*

Sliding my phone back into my pocket, I headed to my workshop.

The sketches I'd been working on for the past few days were finally coming together in my head, and I was ready to make a model for the project I had in mind. Rolling up my sleeves, I got out my clay and modelling tools and set about creating the rough miniature version that I would base the finished piece on.

As always when I really got into my work, I lost all track of time. I only realized how late it had gotten when the door to my workshop opened and Nadiya walked in.

"Hey. What are you working on?" she asked, trying to see around me, but I quickly blocked her view.

"Not yet, darlin'. I'll show you when it's ready, I promise." I stepped closer to give her a kiss, partly to distract her and partly because I simply wanted to. "I'm sorry, I didn't realize it was so late, and I ain't even started supper yet."

"That's fine, we can order in," she said, patting me on the chest. The friction stung, making me wince, and she frowned as her fingers ran over my shirt, feeling the padding underneath. "What's that?"

"That is something I'll show you later," I promised. "Come on, let's go get some food and you can tell me all about your day."

"Well, actually, I don't need to tell you," she said as we walked across the driveway to the house. "You can see it for yourself."

She refused to explain any further as we ordered some food and sat down in the living room where she turned the TV on. As the local news came on, I glanced over at her, desperate for at least some kind of clue.

"Did you find Brad's phone?"

Her pursed lips answered me even before she said a word. "Not yet. So far, all I've been able to find out is that someone took it from the IT department, so it does seem possible that someone else leaked the story. Security is going to review all the footage from the hallways and elevators and see what they can find out."

That seemed to rule out seeing Brad getting arrested on the six o'clock news, so what were we watching for?

I had to wait to find out until after the first commercial break, when the anchor announced that they were heading over to Varma Corp for an exclusive interview with Nadiya Varma.

I glanced over at her in surprise. "What did you do?"

"Shhhhh," she whispered. "Just listen."

Looking cool and confident in her office, Nadiya gave an intelligent and poised interview about the expectations placed on women in business. She didn't specifically talk about the Varma Corp board or any of the accusations in the article, she just spoke about the challenges women face in general and the double standards that existed. Articulate and well-spoken, making many valid points, she looked completely in control.

I couldn't be prouder of her. That was the fearless woman I'd fallen for.

Only at the very end did the interviewer ask her if she wanted to respond to the things that people were talking about, and Nadiya gave a soft smile - her real one, not the CEO version. "All anyone needs to know is that I love Dexter Callahan, and I'm planning to stay married to him for a very long time."

The camera switched back to the anchors and Nadiya muted the TV before looking over at me tentatively. "What do you think?"

Putting my feelings into words wasn't easy, but I did my best. "Nadiya, that was amazing. You didn't sink to their level but you made your point perfectly. Now, if anyone tries to come after you for anything in that article, they'll be making a fool of themselves, not you."

Her face broke into a relieved grin, and I could see how much it meant to her that I approved. "That's exactly what I was going for. I thought about speaking to the board directly. First thing this morning, that's what I planned to do, but then I thought: I shouldn't have to beg for their forgiveness. This whole thing only happened because of their ridiculous expectations in the first place. You called it bullshit on the day we met, and you were right. I don't want to play their game anymore, so I thought I would set some new rules."

It touched me that she remembered that, and it touched me even more what she'd said at the end of the interview. "About that last quote…" I said, leaning over closer to her. "How long is a very long time?"

She bit her lip, looking up at me from beneath those gorgeous lashes of hers. "How long have you got?"

I had to kiss her then, my mouth and my whole being hungry for her, and she kissed me back, just as hard. When her hand went to my chest again, she must have remembered about the padding there because she pulled back and looked up at me, her eyebrows raised in a clear repeat of her earlier question about what the padding was for.

"I'll let you have a peek. Just remember that food is still on the way, so I'll have to put my clothes back on eventually."

She laughed, watching curiously as I pulled my shirt off. Her eyes went wide as she saw the gauze across my chest and she looked up at me with genuine dismay. "You didn't have your tattoo removed, did you? Dex, I never would have asked you to do that. It doesn't bother me, honestly, I understand…"

That time, I put my finger on her lips, just as she'd done to me in the car that morning. "Just hold on there, darlin'. Wait and see what it is."

Gently, I pulled back the tape holding the dressing in place. Still a little raw and raised, it would need a few days to settle, but she could get the general idea at least. Shawna was still there in her cowgirl hat with her brand, hovering above my heart. But underneath it stood Nadiya, wearing a suit with splashes of paint on it, painting her name across my chest just as clearly as Shawna's brand.

I drew the image and Sawyer did it for me in his tattoo parlour that morning.

Nadiya stared at it for a long moment, her eyes taking in every detail before finally looking back up at me. "That's for real? It's permanent?"

"I sure as hell hope so for how much it hurt," I teased her. "You said you're in this for a long time, right? Well, so am I, and there's the proof."

Her eyes returned to my chest and her hand reached out to touch it, so I quickly covered it back up again.

"Hang on there, not yet. It needs to heal a bit first, but I'm looking forward to having you run your fingers over it later. Along with a few other places on my body."

We leaned towards each other, ready to get started right then, but the doorbell rang before our lips could connect.

"Supper," I groaned, and Nadiya laughed.

"We can eat quickly," she promised before giving me a wink. "Then straight to bed."

~Nadiya~

I had a hard time not smiling too much at work the next day. After an amazing evening in bed, Dex and I lay in each other's arms afterwards and he told me the things that his family had said about how they thought we had fallen for each other right away. Thinking back to the first time I saw him in his gallery, before I even knew who he was, I couldn't say they were entirely wrong. Perhaps they saw something that we hadn't been ready to admit to ourselves.

I suggested to him that he invite everyone over for supper the next night, along with my father who I'd already invited. My daddy would certainly be outnumbered by the Callahan crew, but the kids could run around our backyard and his family could all see our house for the first time. It would be a good chance for everyone to meet, and it actually sounded like fun to me.

Dex offered to cook but I reminded him that he'd already lost two days of work that week, so he needed to focus on that the next day. I would order food in. He smiled and told me I sounded like Shawna, and I took that as the compliment I knew he meant it as.

I could hardly believe he tattooed me on his chest next to her. When he fell asleep, I whispered a silent prayer to the sky, thanking her for loving him so well. She must have been an amazing woman to inspire such devotion in a man like Dex, and though I knew I would never take her place, I hoped I could make him happy too. He certainly seemed to have faith that I would, and I was determined to prove myself worthy of that trust.

As I sat in the back of the car the next morning on the way to the office, I caught up with all the news and social media reaction to my interview, which to my relief was overwhelmingly positive. There were even calls from people to boycott Varma Corp if I *wasn't* named the next CEO. The board could hardly ignore that.

As the day wore on, I was in such a good mood that I didn't think anything could bring me down. I just had to tempt fate, though, and soon, the head of the building's security knocked on my door. "Ms Varma? I think we've found the person who took the phone you were looking for."

I invited the man in and he loaded his flash drive into my computer. A video popped up of the hallway outside the IT department's storage room and after a few minutes, a figure appeared on the screen and let himself inside, and my stomach dropped.

My father.

"Nobody else went in there during that time frame?" I asked, trying to keep a poker face and not show just how shaken I was by the idea that my own father had been behind the leak.

"No, ma'am," he replied. "This was after-hours, the rest of the staff had gone home. We can't see the phone in the video, but it doesn't look like it could have been anyone else."

"Thank you."

After he left with the video, I sat at my desk, motionless, trying to figure out what to do next. Why would my daddy have done that? Although in the end, it hadn't done me any harm, it certainly could have. And it could have hurt Dex too; the accusations about him were actually worse than the ones about me. The article claimed that I had schemed to get the job I wanted, but Dex was accused of using me for financial gain and cheating on me all at the same time.

Did he *want* to create trouble for Dex? Did he have a problem with my husband? As I thought back to his disbelief when he found out I hadn't had Dex sign a prenuptial agreement, I realized maybe he really did think Dex was some kind of golddigger.

Whatever the reason, I needed to get to the bottom of it, so I sent him a text telling him we'd moved up the time for supper that night. Having him show up an hour earlier would give me a chance to talk to him before Dex's family arrived and, if necessary, time to send him away before they got there if he really did have a problem with us being together.

When I got home, Dex was still in his workshop, so I didn't disturb him. In my room, I changed into more casual clothes, jeans and a not-too-dressy blouse, something more in line with what I figured Dex's sisters would be wearing.

My father arrived right on time, as always, and as he followed me into the living room, I saw him looking around curiously. "Isn't your husband here?"

"Dex is still working," I told him, taking a seat on the couch while he sat down in one of the chairs opposite me. "I wanted to speak to you before everyone else gets here. I assume you saw my interview yesterday?"

He nodded as he relaxed back into the chair, his arms spread wide on the armrests. "It was very well done, Nadiya. The board will have no doubt that you are the right woman for the job."

He actually sounded proud, which I didn't expect. If he released the article, why would he be happy that I had shut it down so quickly?

"It wouldn't have been necessary if that article hadn't been published," I pointed out, watching his reaction carefully.

"We can't always control what people will say about us," he said with a shrug, repeating one of his favourite business mantras. "We can only control how we respond."

Each word confused me more, so I decided to come right out and ask him: "Are you the one who released it?"

His eyes widened in surprise, but a moment later, to *my* surprise, he smiled. "Yes, of course I did. I thought it might take you a little longer to figure it out though."

"Daddy!" I didn't know what to be most upset about first. "I almost called the police on Brad Sherwood. I thought he had broken his agreement."

"But you didn't," he pointed out. "You sought clarification first, as you always do. You are always fair, beta."

He still sounded so pleased about everything, which didn't make any sense to me at all. "The public reaction could have been much worse than it was, what if the board had decided..."

"Nadiya." He cut me off, leaning forward with his elbows on his knees, his hands folded together in front of him. "I knew you could handle it, and you did. You were brilliant, just as I expected."

I still didn't understand. "But why? I wouldn't have had to handle it at all if you didn't release it."

"Sherwood would always have that information, not to mention whoever took those photos may have kept backups. Leaving potential blackmail that could have been used against you later didn't make sense. It was far better to get it all out in the open and deal with the consequences up front."

I supposed there was some truth in that, but it still seemed cold to me. "Why didn't you warn me?"

He laughed, leaning back again. "You're a terrible liar, Nadiya. Don't you remember introducing me to Dex at the restaurant, trying to convince me that you simply fell in love when you didn't believe it yourself? If you knew this had been leaked on purpose, you would have overthought it and gotten nervous, and it would have shown. But because you saw it as an attack, you responded with the killer instinct I know you have."

"But Dex could have been hurt..."

"Why?" He sounded genuinely curious. "You obviously love and trust each other, so you had nothing to worry about."

"How do you know I love him?" He kept surprising me with every new thing he said.

"Nadiya, you had your prenup drafted for Greg before he even proposed, but you never asked Dex to sign one. I had my suspicions about how you felt before then, but that was when I knew for sure."

He really knew that Dex and I were in love, and he was okay with it? Happy about it, even? Everything about the conversation surprised me.

"It was still a risk."

"Perhaps," he agreed. "But sometimes, risks are worth taking. And I was right, wasn't I? Now, you have no more skeletons in the closet, nothing to come back to bite you once you get the CEO position that should have been yours all along. Your conscience is clear."

I shook my head at his strategizing, but in the end, I had to admit he *was* right. Dex had come clean with his family and I'd gotten the board on my side. We had nothing to hide. Everything had worked out for the best, no matter how unorthodox his methods.

"Now, when is supper?" He slapped his hands on his knees happily. "I'm starving."

The food arrived shortly afterwards, followed by the first of Dex's family: his sister Billie, her husband and their children. The older one, a sweet, dark-haired girl with Down Syndrome, marched right over to my father and gave him a hug, and he surprised me once again by taking the girls outside to play while I showed Billie and Grey the house.

"Grey's a plumber, so if you ever need some help, you can always give him a call," Billie offered on his behalf.

He gave his wife a bemused smile. "Should I be telling her you can teach her kids too?"

"They don't have any kids yet!" Billie admonished.

"They don't have any plumbing problems either."

Their light-hearted teasing made me smile, and as we finished our quick tour, Dex came rushing in from the workshop. "I'm so sorry, darlin'," he apologized, giving me a quick kiss on the forehead. He smelled strongly of clay, leading me to guess he must have been working on his new secret project that he wouldn't show me. "Give me two seconds to get changed, I'll be right with y'all."

He stepped into our bedroom to change his clothes and Mrs Callahan arrived a minute or two later, followed closely by Tonia and her family. Laura and Jesse and their boys weren't far behind either. My house had never been so full or so loud, but as Dex joined me, freshly washed but still with that lingering clay smell that I now found ridiculously sexy simply because it smelled like him, I found that the noise made a welcome change. I didn't mind having so many people in my space. It actually felt right.

Dex went to the backyard to call my father and the kids inside, and I quickly introduced him to all of Dex's family. When I got to Dex's mother, my father quickly ran a hand through his hair before taking her hand and kissing it, suddenly full of proper old-school manners.

As everyone filled their plates from the food I'd ordered and headed outside to eat, I leaned over to Dex and gestured towards our parents with my head. "Did you see that?"

"Don't look at me," he laughed. "You're the one who wanted to set them up in the first place."

The memory from our drunken wedding night made me laugh, and the rest of the evening was filled with a lot more laughter. My father only looked shocked by Dex's sisters a couple of times, which I counted as a win, and he barely left Mrs Callahan's side.

When the food had all been eaten, the kids had gone back to running around and the drink glasses were nearly empty, Dex got to his feet. "Can I have everyone's attention for a minute?"

I looked up at him in surprise along with everyone else. He hadn't told me he planned on saying anything and I had no idea what he might have on his mind.

"Now, everyone here knows that Nadiya and I didn't have a typical start to this relationship."

A murmur of agreement rippled through the others gathered around the table.

"But I also think you know that typical or not, this here's the real deal, and I'm happy to have the people I love most in the world here to recognize that. We didn't have you at our wedding, but this almost feels like the same thing."

Smiles beamed back at him from around the table.

"And since we're celebrating, I wanted to show y'all the next piece I'll be working on. It's the one I'm going to be showing Mary Flynn when she comes over to meet with me next week. Just wait here one second."

My excitement probably exceeded everyone else's, eager to see what he'd been working on in secret for the past couple of days. He ran over to the workshop and returned in just over a minute, carrying something beneath a white sheet. Setting it down in the centre of the table, he turned to me with his charming, inviting smile.

"You want to do the honours, Nadiya?"

Full of anticipation, I reached out and gently pulled the sheet back.

Though I was vaguely aware of the gasps of appreciation from Dex's family, all I could really focus on was the sculpture in front of me. Completely different from the one in his gallery window that I admired the day I went there, the work in front of me was equally stunning.

It obviously represented me, my features carved into the clay delicately and beautifully. The figure stood in a stormy sea, waves crashing around her so realistically, I could almost feel their spray. But despite the turmoil, the woman in the centre of it looked unaffected by any of it. Her chin was raised, a determined look on her face as her hand reached out, as if to pull herself up and out of harm's way, though no support could be seen.

She seemed to see something there that no one else could, and in my mind, I felt certain she was looking at Dex, just out of my sight.

"I call it Fearless," Dex told everyone before turning back to me, his eyes full of love.

"Just like you, darlin'."

Epilogue

Six months later

~Dex~

"Nadiya? We're going to be late, darlin', come on out of there."

The bathroom door opened and her head popped out, a pout on her pretty face. "I look ridiculous."

"Oh, I'm counting on it, sweetheart," I teased her with a grin. "Now, come on, let me get a look at ya."

With a sigh, she threw the door open and stepped all the way out. "How bad is it?"

That day was the annual Varma Corp staff BBQ and baseball tournament, and when I heard that Nadiya had never actually played ball before, I knew we had to change that. People would love to see the CEO out on the diamond, not to mention it would probably give me enough ammunition to tease her for days, if not weeks.

But as she turned from side to side to show me her uniform from different angles, ridiculous was the last word on my mind.

"I never found baseball players sexy before," I admitted. "But damn, darlin'. You make that look good."

She wrinkled her nose at me, clearly not buying it. "The pants are a bit tight," she said, biting her lip. "Do you think anyone will notice?"

Her stomach had only started to have a tiny little bump a few days earlier. We were nearly at the three-month mark of her pregnancy, nearly at the point where she felt comfortable telling people, and I knew she didn't want to give anything away just yet. Still, the sight of that small swelling made my heart swell too. I could hardly believe that in six months, just one year after our crazy wedding, we'd be having a baby.

We only found out a month ago, when Nadiya was already two months pregnant. She had surprised me, two months after our wedding, by saying she wanted to come off her birth control. She figured it would take a while for her cycle to get back to normal and it might take a while to conceive after that, so she thought it would be better to do it sooner rather than wait until we were really itching to get pregnant and might get disappointed if it didn't happen right away.

As thrilled as her decision made me, I tried not to get my hopes up too much. Like she said, it could take a while.

When she didn't get her period the next month, she didn't think much of it. She was busy with work, we both were, and as she said, her body was still adjusting to being off the pills. She said if nothing happened in another week or two, she'd take a test.

But between her taking on the CEO job, her 30th birthday party, and the excitement of my new contract with Mary Flynn, we both forgot all about it until we were lying in bed one night, both of us catching our breath after a particularly energetic lovemaking session, and it crossed my mind that she hadn't said anything else about it.

"Did you ever get your period, Nadiya?"

I didn't think so. We made love just about every night, so I felt pretty sure I would have noticed, but I thought I'd ask just in case.

Her eyes widened as she thought back. "No, I guess I haven't. I'll set a reminder for myself to pick up a test tomorrow."

She reached for her phone, but I grabbed hold of her arm. "Let me do it, darlin'. You're busy enough. I can handle picking out a pregnancy test."

I thought I could, anyway. When I found myself confronted with the rows upon rows of different tests in the pharmacy the next day, I felt completely over my head. Luckily, one of the store workers saw me staring at them all in confusion and came over to give me some advice. I ended up getting three different kinds, just in case, and Nadiya shook her head at me when I produced them all for her that evening.

After taking a quick look at all three boxes, she chose one decisively and headed into the bathroom. I waited on the bed, my heart beating faster until she came back out with the test in her hand. "It's going to be two minutes. What do you want to talk about while we wait?"

"Baby names?" I suggested, making her laugh.

"We don't even know if it's positive yet. Besides, I've got a feeling you're already got some in mind."

"I do," I admitted. "But I'm open to a compromise."

When she flipped the test over after the two minutes were up and we saw the positive reading, it had to have been one of the happiest moments of my life, but a little bittersweet too. After we kissed and celebrated together, chatting happily about all the things we'd teach our new son or daughter and all the places we'd go together, I couldn't help thinking of how badly Shawna had wanted a baby, how she used to cry at night after spending time with our niece and nephew, when she thought I didn't know. Tears came to my eyes against my will, and Nadiya immediately grabbed hold of my hands.

"Do you want to go talk to her?" she asked softly, and I could only nod, giving Nadiya a kiss before heading over to the cemetery.

Nadiya never minded that I still went to talk to Shawna. Sometimes, she even came with me, the two of us walking through the beautiful paths like Shawna and I used to do, but when we got to Shawna's sculpture, she always stepped back, giving me time and space to catch Shawna up on everything that was going on.

It meant the world to me that she wasn't threatened by the love I still had for Shawna and always would have. She understood that it didn't have anything to do with my love for her, which only grew stronger every day.

So when she asked me if I thought anyone would notice her growing belly in the baseball pants, I could only smile. "I sure hope so."

Nadiya gave me a dirty look. "Not when it's the whole company looking! I'm not ready for that just yet."

We were planning on telling our families in just a few days. We'd already had her 12-week scan just the other day, where they told us the sex of the baby. The doctor warned us it might not be completely accurate so not to go painting the nursery yet or anything, but I felt in my heart that we had it right.

It looked like we were going to have a girl. A little mini-Nadiya, just like I'd imagined, and we'd already agreed on a name too.

Karishma Shawna Varma-Callahan.

A bit of a mouthful, I had to admit, but when Nadiya told me that Karishma meant 'miracle', I knew we had to go with it. Our whole relationship felt like a miracle to me, every single day. We'd call her Risha for short.

When we got to the park where the BBQ was set up, Nadiya and I made our way through the crowd, making small talk with all the Varma Corp employees. They were all getting used to me by now, having seen me at a few of these events. They seemed to accept I wasn't going anywhere, and most of them seemed to like me pretty well. I liked them too.

Mr Varma was there as well. Although he had finally officially retired, he still liked to appear at public events, and more and more often lately, that included bringing my mom along. They wouldn't admit they were dating yet – they called it 'keeping each other company' – but it seemed pretty clear to the rest of us what was going on.

"Is everything finally settled for your new gallery space, Dex?" Mr Varma asked me as I stood chatting with him and my mom, Nadiya having been pulled away to speak to some other members of her team.

"It is," I confirmed. "It took Nadiya a while to find a fair way out of the contract Brad signed, but she did it."

Once Nadiya had determined that the other gallery wasn't to blame for Brad's manipulations, she didn't feel right about simply declaring the contract void, so she worked with their owner to help them locate a different space that would be equally appealing to them. It went above and beyond what she needed to do, but she did it anyway so that I could have the space she'd promised me.

I trusted she would keep her word, and she did. My gallery was due to reopen the following year, and I already had plans to bring in some other artists to join me, just to keep up with demand.

After chatting with our parents for a while longer, I went to find Nadiya again, but when I located her, she had a frown on her face. "What's the matter?"

"Kevin from accounts sprained his ankle," she explained. "We're a player short for our team in the tournament."

"It's not a regulation game," I pointed out. "Nobody's going to care."

That answer didn't please her, apparently, so I offered another.

"If you want, I could call Sawyer to come over, he loves a ball game."

She agreed, so I got my friend on the phone. With his tattoo parlour closed on Sundays, he didn't usually have much going on, and the promise of free beer sufficed to entice him out. When he arrived, Nadiya was already out with her team and I wasn't sure where he was needed, but I spied Nadiya's assistant Luisa who always knew what was going on.

"Hey, Luisa, Nadiya said you needed an extra man? This is my friend Sawyer, he can help you out."

She turned to look at him and to my great surprise, Sawyer's cheeks turned a bit pink as they made eye contact. "Howdy," he mumbled.

"Hi," she replied, also looking far more unsure than usual. "You, uh... you've done this before?"

He blinked at her in confusion, making *her* cheeks colour.

"I mean, you've played baseball before?" she clarified.

"Oh. Yeah. I've definitely done that before."

She led him away to join up with his team and I watched them go with no small degree of wonderment. Could there be something there? Only time would tell, I supposed. Not everyone got married four days after meeting someone. That one might take a little longer.

"Dex, come on!" My own teammates called out for me, and I jogged over to the field, ready to take on the world.

Nobody's life was perfect, but at that moment, mine felt pretty damn close.

At times, it might get a bit messy, but in the end, when I looked at the big picture, all I could see was one great big work of art.

~~THE END~~

The Callahans

You can read about the other Callahan siblings in their own books:

A Matter of Time - Tonia's story
A Piece of Land - Laura's story
A Change of Heart - Billie's story

More from the Author

<u>Contemporary Romance – New Adult/Clean</u>

It Figures duet
It Figures
Figuring It Out

<u>Historical Romance – 18+</u>

Lady in Waiting Series
Lady in Waiting
King in Training
Princess in Hiding

<u>Paranormal Romance – 18+</u>

Standalone
Out of My Depth

Cold Lake Pack Series
The Curse and the Prophecy
The Spell and the Legacy
The Dream and the Destiny

Mismatched Mates Series
Mismatched Mates
Misguided Motives
Mistaken Meanings

Serena's Story
The Alpha's Second Chance
The Returned Mate
The Vampire's Consort

Sacrifice Series
Blood Donor
Life Giver

<u>Paranormal Romance – New Adult/Clean</u>
The Alpha's Prey

Keep in touch

Daily updates from my works-in-progress, bonus chapters and more can be found on my Ream account, Chilli & Chocolate, along with Emma Lee-Johnson:
https://reamstories.com/chilliandchocolate

You can find and follow me on Facebook at:
facebook.com/melodytyden

Join the Facebook group Melody's Romance Corner for fun games, interaction with the author and exclusive news and excerpts.

You can also sign up to my newsletter at www.melodytyden.com for all the latest news.